Praise for *The Murder List*

"Put *The Murder List* at the top of your list of must-reads."

—Julia Spencer-Fleming

"Twisty, unpredictable, and utterly irresistible: suspense at its finest."

—Jessica Strawser

"In this riveting novel of suspense by the absolute master of the genre, Ryan conjures the consummate twisty thriller."

—Erica Ferencik

"Masterly plotted—with a twisted ending—a riveting, character-driven story. *The Murder List* is guilty of inciting shock and amazement at the author's skill. VERDICT: A must-read."

—*Library Journal* (starred review)

Praise for *Trust Me*

"Mesmerizing! Hank Phillippi Ryan has outdone herself in this taut thriller of damaged lives, uneasy alliances, and deadly cat and mouse. Who can you trust indeed?" —Lisa Gardner

"The tension mounts at a blistering pace, while Ryan dazzles on the page, weaving a sinister story that readers won't be able to put down. A must-read!" —Mary Kubica

"Chilling, suspenseful, and impossible to put down."

—Megan Miranda

BOOKS BY **HANK PHILLIPPI RYAN**

Trust Me

The Murder List

The First to Lie

The Jane Ryland Series

The Other Woman

The Wrong Girl

Truth Be Told

What You See

Say No More

The Charlotte McNally Series

Prime Time

Face Time

Air Time

Drive Time

THE
MURDER
LIST

HANK PHILLIPPI RYAN

A TOM DOHERTY ASSOCIATES BOOK / NEW YORK

THE MURDER LIST

Copyright © 2019 by Hank Phillippi Ryan

All rights reserved.

A Forge Book
Published by Tom Doherty Associates
120 Broadway
New York, NY 10271

www.tor-forge.com

Forge® is a registered trademark of Macmillan Publishing Group, LLC.

Library of Congress has cataloged the hardcover edition as follows:

Names: Ryan, Hank Phillippi, author.
Title: The murder list / Hank Phillippi Ryan.
Description: First Edition. | New York : Tor, 2019. | "A Tom Doherty
Associates Book."
Identifiers: LCCN 2018054459| ISBN 9781250197214 (hardcover) |
ISBN 9781250197238 (ebook)
Classification: LCC PS3618.Y333 M87 2019 | DDC 813/.6—dc23
LC record available at https://lccn.loc.gov/2018054459

ISBN 978-1-250-19722-1 (trade paperback)

Our books may be purchased in bulk for promotional, educational, or business use. Please contact your local bookseller or the Macmillan Corporate and Premium Sales Department at 1-800-221-7945, extension 5442, or by email at MacmillanSpecialMarkets@macmillan.com.

First Edition: August 2019
First Trade Paperback Edition: January 2020

Printed in the United States of America

10 9 8 7 6 5 4 3 2 1

As iron is eaten away by rust, so the envious are consumed by their own passion.

—ANTISTHENES

The knives of jealousy are honed on details.

—RUTH RENDELL

But I like not these great successes of yours; for I know how jealous are the gods.

—HERODOTUS

PART
ONE

CHAPTER ONE

NOW

We never fight. Not in the past six years, as long as we've been married. Not even in the months before that. It isn't that Jack is always right or I'm always right. Usually our disagreements are about things that don't matter, so it's easier and quicker for me to acquiesce. Jack's a lawyer, so he likes to win. It makes him happy. And that's good.

But now on a Saturday morning in May, sitting face-to-face across our breakfast table in sweats and ratty slippers, we're definitely on the verge of a real fight. This time, the fight matters. This time I have to win.

"I forbid it," Jack says.

I burst out laughing—all I can think to do—because "forbid" is such an odd word.

"Forbid?" I say the word, repeating it, diluting it, undermining it. "What're you gonna do, honey, lock me in the castle tower? You're not *that* much older than I am. Come on, sweetheart. Get real. Have some more coffee. Read your *Globe*."

He doesn't look up from the Metro section. "It's absurd, Rachel," he says into the paper. "That woman is evil. Plus, I can't understand why you'd want to fill your brain with that kind of . . ." He shakes his head as he snaps a page into place, the newsprint crackling with his impatience. "Absurd. An exceedingly unwise decision on Gardiner's part. And yours, too, Rach."

I take a sip of dark roast to defuse my annoyance and to clear the looming emotional thunderstorm. I know his problem isn't my summer internship in the Middlesex County District Attorney's Office. Jack's impatience with me is fueled by the headlines he's reading, news stories that feature his name. Jack hates to lose. Especially in court. And especially to Assistant District Attorney Martha Gardiner. My new boss.

Martha Gardiner. The woman Jack usually refers to as "Satan in pearls." He never laughs when he says it.

"Honey?" I soften my voice, knowing there are many ways to win. Law school is teaching me that. "It's only for three months. I'm required to do it. All the 2L students are, or we can't be 3Ls. And then we can't graduate. And there goes all that law-school tuition you've loaned me. Plus, we've planned the whole thing. We're gonna be partners. You'll get me on the murder list. And we're a *team*. Your very own word. Remember?"

"Team? Certainly doesn't feel like it. I thought you chose a side." He lowers the paper, one inch, looks at me with narrowed eyes. "And not that side. Not hers."

"But—" How do I handle this? He pays the bills, at this point at least. As a student—at thirty-six, the world's oldest law student—I have zero income. *You're my investment,* he told me. I took it as a compliment. "But—"

"There are no 'buts.' Gardiner's a predator. She maligns the law. Twists it. Corrupts it. Her every instinct is to destroy and defeat." The newspaper barrier goes back up.

I can't escalate this, so I'll ignore the fact that prosecutors are supposed to be the champions of law and order. Jack's oversensitive because Gardiner's the one prosecutor who can beat him. My dear husband is not the most reliable narrator, though, and he's probably exaggerating when he spins me stories about her disturbingly unfair and manipulative tactics. But Martha Leggett Gardiner is a touchy subject.

Jack's frown, hidden by newsprint again, chilled me. I've seen that same expression in the courtroom, and it's never a good sign for the witness he's about to interrogate. But I'm not his witness. I'm his wife.

"I know you're upset." I decide on instant capitulation and a subject pivot. "But even you have to lose a case once in a while. Especially since your client, you know, did it."

"That shouldn't matter. Or are your profs holding back that tidbit until your third year?" Jack flaps the newspaper to a new page. Hiding the DORN DID IT headline I know is there. "That jury of morons wanted someone to be punished. And Gardiner had the judge in her pocket."

"I know. It stinks. I know. It does." This morning hadn't been the optimum time to spring the Gardiner situation on him, but it's the only time. Harvard had emailed the final 2L internship assignments to us late last night, and our jobs start this coming Wednesday. I could hardly hide reality, and, besides, I'm excited. Nervous but excited. Still, life's a juggle when your husband is cranky.

Jack's old plaid Saturday shirt is buttoned wrong, his hair like windblown straw. He's bitter over every courtroom loss, so we've ridden out a few iterations of this before. The second newspaper headline reads JURY TO JACK KIRKLAND: DROP DEAD. I'd almost hidden the paper from him, a gesture in affectionate futility.

"But it was a *murder-list* case," I say. Maybe I can provide some comfort, or some logic. "Marcus Dorn was lucky to have the state appoint you as his attorney. You can't help it if your key witness decided to vanish. Plan the appeal, honey, you'll win. You're the best defense lawyer in Boston. Or anywhere."

"Appeals take *years*." Jack stands, tosses the paper to the floor, paces to the window. Our tiny garden's perennials are flourishing in this spring's incessant rain, but I figure he's not thinking about peonies or pink thyme. He's replaying that verdict. He truly cares about justice, defending his clients, even the ones he knows are guilty. It's one of the reasons I married him. And he almost always wins. Another reason.

"Martha Gardiner's doing this to screw with me," Jack says, turning back to me. "Like she tries to every damn day in court. She's using you, Rachel. Are you too naïve to see that? This is about *me*. Can you possibly have some misguided notion that this is about *you*?"

I take a deep breath. "I'll only be working with her for the summer. And then I'll be back with you. Against her. She can't win against both of us."

No answer.

Okay, then. In the silent tension, I'll tell him my plan. The truth. "Honey? I'm doing this for *us*. It's the perfect strategy. I'll work with her. I'll learn her methods and techniques. It's like opposition research, scoping out the competition from the inside. The more I understand her prosecution, the more I can structure our defense. See? It's brilliant."

No answer. It's risky, I know that. Such is life.

I sip my coffee, pretend to read the *Times* on my iPad, and let him sulk. Secretly, I feel fine that Marcus Simmons Dorn is behind bars forever. He'd been charged with the gruesome murder of a perfectly lovely couple after breaking into their high-priced—and supposedly high-security—suburban condominium called The Westmoreland. He stole their jewelry and a manila envelope of cash, then slit their throats. Turned out, Dorn himself was the security guard. So much for security.

And Jack, swearing me to marital secrecy, had shown me the graphic crime-scene photos, Manson-esque scrawls in the victims' own blood, which he'd managed to keep away from the jury. Jack had been proud he'd convinced the judge to suppress them. I love how he values the rule of law. Even when he knows his successful defense might result in a murderer walking free.

In the Dorn case, though, suppressing those photos was Jack's only victory. The jury voted guilty. But Jack doesn't lose often. I'm relying on that.

Especially since I'll eventually become my husband's law partner. I won't be on the state's special murder list, like Jack is, since I'll be a novice for a while, and not experienced enough for the state to appoint me to represent accused murderers who can't pay for their defense. But he's promised me we'll be Kirkland and North. Once I pass the bar exam.

I close my eyes briefly, almost swooning with the need for that to come true. Jack and I will be protecting our clients' rights. Together. As for Jack's one-sided philosophy, I truly love him for it, but hey, it's law school. I'm training to understand two sides. Defense *and* prosecution. The devil you know.

"So you're insisting on this travesty? Signing on with the devil woman?" Jack, as if reading my mind, comes back to the table, retrieves the paper, places it beside his coffee mug. Lays his left hand flat on top of it. His wedding-ring hand. "Even if it might end our marriage?"

My eyes well with tears at his tone. At his suggestion. At that possibility. At that disaster.

"What?" I hear my voice tremble as I try to read his face.

"Kidding, sweetheart," Jack says. He kisses me on the top of my head. "Only kidding."

CHAPTER **TWO**

You walk through the door, or you don't. Those are the only choices.

I put my hand on the brass knob of the wood-framed entrance to the Middlesex County First Assistant District Attorney's Office. Small gilt letters on the smoky, wire-reinforced glass announce that this is where Martha Gardiner holds the key to my future. If I open it and walk into her waiting room, I won't be the same person when I come out. If I turn around and walk away, I won't be the same person, either. No matter what happens, I'll be different. I suppose that's what I want.

We all have our reasons.

Jack left before I did this morning. I heard the crunch of gravel as his vintage Audi pulled out of the driveway, and I ran downstairs, barefoot, perplexed and annoyed. And frankly, hurt. His "might end our marriage" crack had been unnecessary, and I knew he regretted it. But Jack's not big on apologies.

We'd skirted the Gardiner topic since Saturday, Jack "working" and me "studying." We'd talked about the Red Sox game, whether Tito's vodka was worth the price, whether the lawn-mowing guy would come as promised, where to plant the geraniums. Shallow and infinitely polite, tacitly understanding that pursuing our disagreement would only lead to more disagreement. Even last night, the eve of my first day on the job, I'd avoided the topic. I couldn't risk making Jack unhappy.

How long does it take to ruin everything? One moment. One wrong decision. One mistake. One unfortunate assumption or ill-chosen word or even a misunderstood gift. The dominoes fall, never to be righted.

Still, when I'd arrived in the kitchen, wrapped in my white towel and damp from my shower, I found the note Jack left me on one of his yellow legal pads, saying "early meeting" and "good luck." I convinced myself it was his attempt to apologize. Jack's set in his ways. I've learned how to deal with them.

Now the gilt-lettered office door opens, as if on its own. A harried-looking man, glasses askew on his nose and clipboard in hand, more Jack's age than mine, looks me up and down. I pull my hand away from the doorknob and take a step backward into the fluorescent-lighted entryway. As if I've just arrived. As if I hadn't been hesitating.

"Rachel North? You're Rachel North. Correct?"

Behind him there's a beige couch, empty, two beige stuffed chairs, empty, and a file-strewn wooden desk.

I'd succumbed to the jitters of first-day-itis, so I know my black heels are unscuffed and my new black suit jacket is buttoned properly. New shorter haircut with new even-blonder highlights, ends tucked behind understated gold earrings. The cordovan leather of my not-new brief-case, a welcome-to-the-law present from Jack, is burnished enough to prove I use it. But this man's scrutiny makes me second-guess myself. Not auspicious if I'm to be a convincing prosecutor in training.

"Correct." I try to make my voice confident. "Are you—?"

"This way," he says, cutting me off, pointing his clipboard behind him. "I'm Leon Colacetti, Ms. Gardiner's assistant. The others are already inside."

I'm not late, I'm certain I'm not, so I suspect this is Leon trying to show me who's boss. Typical man. Plus, who "the others" will turn out to be is a more intriguing concern. We aren't provided advance intel on the list of our fellow interns, so I only know we're all law students and our stated goal is to spend the next three months trying to impress the hell out of the DA. It'll soon be clear who my competition is.

This whole role reversal is pure irony. Back in my statehouse days, a "career" that ended six years ago, I supervised ambitious interns of my own. Now I'm the newbie. At thirty-six, the newbie.

Three twenty-something faces look up at me as Leon—I decide that's what I'll call him—ushers me into a windowless conference room, a faux-mahogany paneled box with an oval table so oversize there's barely enough room for the high-back black swivel chairs around it. The whiteboard on the wall is blank. Three of the eight swivel chairs are occupied.

"She's here," Leon says, announcing me. The door closes behind him.

There's a moment, on the first day of school or a new job or new adventure, when you're presented with the cast of characters in whatever challenge you're about to face. There are no rule books. No biographies, no histories, no names or vices or motives. Are these three my teammates? Or adversaries?

I'm the only one standing. The three are all men—each with a legal pad on the table in front of him, each with a paper cup of what looks like coffee, each in a dark suit that mirrors mine. Two have fresh-looking preppy haircuts, and one must have graduated West Point or someplace. In unison, they wave me to the unoccupied chair at the end of the table. As if they'd agreed on my seat assignment.

"Elijah Lansberry," says the charcoal pinstripes. "Eli's fine. Howard undergrad, BU Law. My mother's in the Suffolk County DA's office."

"Nick Soderberg." The blond guy has a stud earring in place, and I see holes where several others must go. "BC undergrad, BC Law. Computer geek, right? I-T."

I try not to make snap judgments about those two, judgments as Darwinian and inevitable as friend or not-friend. Smart or not smart. Hiding something or not. Ulterior motive or not. They must be doing the same for me, thinking: *Woman*. She's older, she's married, she's the one who—but no. I'm as much a cipher to them as they are to me. Good.

"Welcome to boot camp." The third man stands, salutes. "Andrew DiPrado. *Semper fi*."

"Ignore him." Eli waves him off. "Listen, Martha Gardiner herself is apparently on the way. *With* our assignments. DiPrado's worried he'll have to go to the murder scene and see the dead body."

"Like *you'd* be up for that, Lansberry," DiPrado says.

"Big time," he insists. "Isn't that what we're here for? I know *I* am."

"Rachel North." I decide to avoid the territory-marking and the offering of bona fides. Also to be circumspect about adding my particular law-school details. Some people, mainly envious law students, hate Harvard. Besides, once these guys hear about Jack, they'll assume he's connected with the law school's Kirkland House, and that'll be that. I'll be branded the favored legacy. The advantaged insider. The manipulative opportunist.

I take my seat, pull out a yellow pad, stash my briefcase under the table. What the others don't know is—they may have their histories, but I have experience with power. With office politics. And, yeah. I have Jack. "Dead body? Did someone get killed?"

"Didn't you hear the news this morning?" Eli's eyes narrow behind his tortoiseshell glasses. He's almost sneering. "The Auburndale nurse?"

That's such a lawyer thing. Why not answer me? Why make everything a quiz or a cross-examination? Men. What would Jack do?

I act like I already know. "Oh, right," I say.

The doorknob clicks. As one, the four of us turn to see who's arriving. And then, as one, we jolt to our feet, our wheeled chairs padding against the walls.

Martha Gardiner stands framed in the open doorway. Doesn't even cross the threshold. Two blue-uniformed state cops lurk, men at the ready, behind her. The ADA hasn't changed from when I last saw her in her other job, six-ish years ago now, still a study in icy patrician neutral. Silver hair, pale blue eyes, white silk blouse. Dark taupe suit, precisely tailored. Discreet espresso-suede heels. Expensive, every stitch of it.

"Good morning." Her voice is welcoming, confident, as if she's greeting a new jury.

"Good—" Nick begins.

Gardiner silences him by ignoring him. "Andrew DiPrado," she acknowledges with a trace of a nod.

"Yes, I—"

"Elijah Lansberry? Nick Soderberg?" She semi-smiles at the two men, seeming to guess.

"Yes," they say. Then apparently they can't decide whether to laugh about their simultaneous response.

She ignores them.

"Rachel North."

She's turned to me, lingering a fraction of a second longer than she did with the other three. Or I could be wrong about that. Does she remember me? Or is it even about remembering? Maybe, as Jack predicted, she's chosen me on purpose.

"Come with us, Ms. North," she says.

I know I am not imagining a tone in her voice, a tone no one else would notice, a tone she could deny. But I know it's there. Or it could simply be that Jack's suspicions are coloring my perception.

"Should I bring my—" I begin. What does 'Come with us' mean? With who? Why? Where?

But the doorframe is empty.

CHAPTER **THREE**

The white front door of the triple-decker was closed when we arrived. Plastic ribbons of yellow crime-scene tape, crisscrossed over the front porch, formed a first line of defense, reinforced by the bulk of one uniformed police officer. Her dark hair was covered with a regulation billed cap, and she stood, hands behind her back and motionless as a palace guard, beside a terracotta pot of wilting white pansies.

I'd traveled in the prisoner seat of a blue-and-gray cruiser, chauffeured by Gardiner's pair of state police minders, a taciturn duo who apparently did not understand the concept of conversation. "Ms. Gardiner will meet you there," one of them told me. "Wear your seat belt, miss," the other said.

After my attempts at en route camaraderie, then teamwork, and finally mere civility were met with monosyllabic silence, I checked my phone for an atta-girl text from Jack—none—and wondered what the hell was going on. The staties had turned on the siren, possibly to shut me up, then careened onto the exit for the Mass Pike. Possibly to slam me into the door. Didn't take a detective to deduce we were headed to Auburndale, what they call a "village" in the bigger city of Newton.

I knew what awaited me there. The nurse. The victim Eli Lansberry talked about. The dead body Andrew DiPrado wanted to see. This was my first day on the job. But not my first death.

The siren stops as we brake at the curb, front wheels bumping the sidewalk. One cop hops out and opens the back door for me. Slams it closed as I climb out. The car's idling.

"Over there," he says, in one motion waving me toward the house and getting back in the car. "We're outta here. Good luck."

A scraggle of onlookers, each with a cell phone clamped to their ear or texting or taking photos, lines the opposite side of Gorham Street. They all turn to look at the departing police car, then they scrutinize me, pointing and whispering, probably wondering if I'm a big shot or a witness or a suspect. Houses stand shoulder-to-shoulder too, mostly copycat mirror-image duplexes with doors closed, windows shuttered, driveways empty. The medical examiner's black van—black windows, black tires, black everything—is parked at the curb. PHILLIP ONG, MD, the lettering says. If he's still here, the victim's still here. I straighten my shoulders and lift my chin, trying to look like I belong.

I'm up to speed now, and know from checking the news updates on my phone in the cop car that a nurse, as yet publicly unnamed, was murdered here sometime overnight. No suspects yet, so say the news articles. Martha Leggett Gardiner, silk blouse impeccable, stands, arms crossed, at the beginning of a fissured bluestone front walk. Her back is to the white clapboard house at the end of it. As if she's more interested in me than what's obviously the crime scene.

As I walk toward her, trying to look comfortable in my suddenly too-heavy suit jacket, I try to decide what I need to care about. What I'll need to remember. Jack's warned me Gardiner's "notoriously hands-on" in homicide investigations and that some detectives resent her for it. Some fear her. I know Gardiner made headlines at the Suffolk County District Attorney's Office for a chunk of years, then six years ago moved to what she spun to the newspapers as a more prestigious job in Middlesex County.

She's a Leggett, Jack had imitated her snipped Brahmin sneer. Old

New England family. Old New England money. She doesn't need the big bucks, he'd explained. She's a zealot. In it for the glory. For the power. For the win. Plus, she's got her eye on the attorney general's office.

"Female, approximately twenty-seven years of age," Gardiner says when I get close enough to hear. "No sign of a break-in."

"Did she live here?" I want to ask—Why are murder victims always women? *They aren't,* I mentally argue with myself. "Do we know who she is?"

"Was," Gardiner corrects me. "So, Ms. North. Do you know why we're here?"

I'd thought about this on the way here, trying to anticipate my role as apprentice. Fine, a pop quiz. Bring it on.

"The district attorney's office represents Massachusetts in the prosecution of criminal offenses and is the state's chief law-enforcement officer and top prosecutor." My response might have come from a fifth grader's civics book, and I try to indicate by inflection that I know I'm doing that. Unstoppably halfway through, I realized humor was not the best choice. Gardiner is not amused. I alter my expression and tone, all business. "We're also here in case the detectives need a search warrant."

"Correct." Her cell phone pings, one brief tone. "Wait here," she tells me. She turns her back, just enough to let me know I'm dismissed, and speaks into the phone. "Yes?"

What Gardiner thinks of me, how she assesses my skills, my instincts, and my actions—it could be life altering. It's a tightrope that I agreed to walk. Must walk. If all goes as I hope, if I learn everything I need, my future will be safely with Jack. As a partner in a successful law firm. As a partner in making sure people get a fair defense. He'll rely on me, and I on him. My life depends on it.

I stare past her back, past the crime-scene tape, into the home where late last night something terrible happened. A tragedy that's Gardiner's job, and now mine, to investigate. And I'll learn exactly how she does it.

Jack, though, would be thinking how he could defend the accused murderer. He'd be hoping the cops make a mistake. Hoping a detective breaks some rule. Hoping Gardiner blows it. Hoping he could argue the case, get an acquittal, and, as a result, set the man—or woman—free.

Two sides. And me in the middle.

But why did Gardiner bring me here? Why me, in particular, from her new crop of interns? The cop on the porch stares into the street, stolidly guarding the bright line between life and death. I imagine who's inside this house. Crime-scene techs, the ME, detectives. Hoping they can reconstruct the circumstances of this murder. I know that doesn't always happen. I know the police are not always right.

A row of TV vans, satellite dishes pointed skyward, idles a few doors away. One uniformed cop stands sentry between the vans—with the reporters who must be lurking inside—and the crime scene.

"Ms. North? Hello? You with us?" Gardiner shades her eyes with one hand.

I almost flinch as she speaks, her tone verging on derisive. But I'd simply been waiting, exactly as instructed. She'd been the one on the phone.

"So tell me." She stashes her cell, gestures toward the house. "Since you're correct that we're here in case the detectives need a warrant—why might that be?"

Fine, another quiz.

"If the resident refuses to give permission to search the premises," I say. "Or isn't home."

"What if someone is home, and not a suspect but a spouse?"

Gardiner's enjoying this sparring match, I can tell. I am, too. Law school is all about what-if. Just like my life.

"A spouse can give permission."

"Very good, Ms. North." Gardiner may have smiled, then allows half a nod. "Either you've been paying attention in class or watching too much *Law & Order*. Or, perhaps, getting tutored at home?"

She has a tone, an inflection, one that twists her words, tilts them sideways. As if she's amused by her power. She obviously knows who my husband is.

"Thank you," I say, taking the high road. Yes, because I get tutored at home, I also know Gardiner always oversees her own crime scenes. It's another thumb on the scales of justice that the prosecution gets there first.

By the time a suspect is arrested, the crime scene is cold. The longer the cops investigate, the colder it gets. And those who might be on the run are long gone. Or have cemented their alibis.

"The whole damn crime scene becomes hearsay," Jack complained to me as he investigated the grisly Marcus Dorn murders, poring through files of photos and spiral-bound transcripts stacked on our dining room table. "It's unfair from moment one. What if the cops miss something? Or ignore something? Or get it wrong? Or destroy something? It changes the truth of the case. Changes the reality. And the good guys will never know."

The good guys. Except the prosecutors think *they're* the good guys. Where does that leave *me*?

Half a block away, the door to one of the TV vans opens. Two black pumps emerge, followed by two tanned legs and then the short-skirted body and celebrated auburn hair of Clea Rourke, the "face" of Channel 3. The reporter pokes her head back into the van, comes out with a notebook and cell phone. Sets her sights on Gardiner. Strides toward us.

"Hell no," Gardiner mutters. She stabs out a number on her cell. Obviously gets an instant response. "Get her away from here," she orders.

Outside the van, the sentry cop in the street is on his phone, too. They're too far away to hear, but I watch, like seeing a silent movie, the pantomime between cop and reporter. Cop stashes his cell, steps toward reporter, shaking his head. Rourke stops and holds out both hands, entreating. The cop shakes his head. The reporter brandishes her cell phone. The cop slams his hands on his hips, blocking her way. The reporter points her phone at Gardiner, then demonstrates *Call me.* Then she points to her, makes a circle of her thumb and fingers, then points to her own chest. I eavesdrop on their silent exchange, trying to translate. Maybe she's saying *You owe me*? Gardiner ends the silent conversation with a shrug, shaking her head, miming "*What can I do?*"

The scene closes as the reporter whirls, clambers into the van, slams the door.

"Lesson one," Gardiner says. "Never. Ever. Talk to a reporter."

I keep silent. I know that.

"Who we have here is the former Tassie Lyle," Gardiner goes on, as if we hadn't been interrupted. "A second-shift nurse at Boston Medical who apparently made the mistake of ordering takeout from the wrong pizza place. We found the receipt, the open pizza box, and the large pepperoni with extra cheese. And, as a result of her demise, extra—well, we needn't go into that. Suffice it to say the detectives who found her will not be wanting pizza anytime in the foreseeable future."

I wince, imagining what might have spattered onto the pizza. "Is that DA humor?"

"It's reality," Gardiner says.

She pauses, looks at me with a trace of—whatever it is that I can't describe.

"It's a pity your husband won't get assigned to defend this case," she adds. "Seeing as how you'll now be privy to confidential information."

I can't read the look on her face, and I wonder if she can read mine. Surprise, she'd see. Or dismay. I hadn't thought about that. Every case I touch is irrevocably off-limits to Jack. *Oh.* I feel my eyes widen as another possibility emerges. Is that why she chose me? To blackball Jack from getting murder-list cases? I bite my lower lip, worrying. Jack would be so angry.

"Ms. Gardiner?" The front door of the crime scene has opened. A uniformed body is silhouetted in the frame. "Ready for you."

We step across the threshold and stand on the hardwood floor of a wallpapered entryway. I'm trying to be something I'm not, not yet, and it's difficult to keep track of who that is and how I'm supposed to think.

Especially now that Gardiner mentioned Jack. Brought him up, specifically. Unnecessarily. And with that tone again. I suppose it's not surprising that dealing with the devil has its pitfalls.

As Gardiner instructs, I slide the pale-blue paper booties over my black shoes, the top elastics tight against my bare ankles. We both snap on skin-tight lavender plastic gloves—nitriles, Gardiner calls them. The law-and-order accouterments, protection from errant footprints and fingerprints at this still-active murder scene, are not helping my first-day-with-Gardiner nerves.

The dark-paneled door to what must be the crime scene is open, but I can't see anything inside except the back of a tweed couch, the back of a blue police uniform, and a suggestion of rooms beyond. No crime-scene tape cordons it off. Low voices murmur, or maybe it's a neighbor's TV. The brass lantern light fixture above us is off, so there are no shadows, the dim light gray and even. Stairs in front of us go up, but none go down. A stack of unopened mail waits by a healthy-looking scarlet begonia on a slim marble-topped table. I catch a glimpse of myself in the mirror above it. I see Gardiner's reflection, too, behind me. Watching me. When I try to read her face, she looks away.

I know I'm too suspicious. Too edgy. But I've had the rug pulled out too many times to feel on solid ground. These days I'm a wife. Student. Intern. Apprentice. And now trying to be someone else. But the law is all about analysis. About knowing the rules and, more important, how to use them.

"Rachel?" Gardiner is infinitely polite.

I still get to make choices. I'll be better at it now. I have to be.

CHAPTER **FOUR**

I may never eat pizza again. Tassie Lyle's kitchen reeks of it, the tangy acidic tomato sauce and sickly sweet yeast and that sharp stab of oregano. A large-ish pepperoni-and-cheese in an open flat box, two slices missing, sits on top of a square kitchen table. Hadn't Gardiner indicated—DA humor—that there was something disgusting spattered on the pizza? I don't see anything like that, but I can't possibly look more closely, or even imagine. I try not to breathe, but too late. Pizza will forever smell like death.

All of our eyes now focus on the same place.

Underneath the table.

It feels wrong to stare at the dark curls on the white linoleum. The flowered tunic. Legs bent in white-trousered disarray. Her eyes are open and dark brown. It feels wrong, but I stare. This is who I am now. This is who I have to be. Like in my old job in the statehouse, once again my job is to make things work. Unlike my statehouse experience, this time I'll succeed. Why would someone kill this woman? I could imagine a million reasons.

A bespectacled man, wearing a too-big white lab coat and a draped stethoscope, crouches beside the motionless body.

Keeping to the background, I tuck myself behind Gardiner and in front of a spotless white enamel stove. A silver teapot with a tiny red ceramic bird perched on the spout sits on one gas burner. The oven door is hot against my leg. I understand my role. Watch, listen, think. And, as they instruct us every day in school, think like a lawyer: issue, rule, analysis, conclusion.

The issue here is murder. The rule is—that's illegal. The analysis is what's beginning right now.

"Anything, Dr. Ong?"

"No bullets, no stab wounds, no blunt trauma." Ong shrugs, unfolds to his feet. "We'll check for DNA, under fingernails, wherever."

Gardiner uses a pencil to close the cardboard top of the white pizza box.

"Oregano Brothers Pizza," she reads. She lets the top flop back onto the table. "O.B. have an order for this? Who delivered it? That's our man, seems to me. Where's the nearest one? And where's her phone? If she ordered this, how'd she do it? Too bad Ms. Lyle didn't cook her own dinner."

"Your staties can figure that out," Ong says. "They're bringing crime scene, I'm told. They're all en route, supposedly including CJ Malinoff. So they say."

Gardiner looks at her watch. "Let's hope so. And hope they bring CJ. He'll expedite the DNA."

Though the local police are first on the scene, in a town this size state police detectives attached to the DA's office will handle the murder investigation. That's the brotherhood—mostly men, still—of the prosecution. The state police and the DA's office work together, along with the state police crime-scene team. I know from Jack that what they discover and what they tell the defense are often two completely separate things.

"Meanwhile, Phil. Suffocation?" Gardiner asks. "Drugs?"

"We shall see." Dr. Ong stoops again, rolls his neck, not taking his eyes off the woman on the floor.

"Time of death?"

The medical examiner pushes his wire-rimmed glasses onto his forehead. I'm wondering exactly how they can tell. The kitchen is warmer than the entryway because she had the oven on. I wonder if that matters.

"I love how you always ask me about TOD, Martha," the ME says. "As if someday I'll reply, 'Oh, it's amazing, this time I know for absolutely sure.'"

"Estimate, Phil." Gardiner's voice seems to balance sarcasm and affection.

"My pleasure. I'm told Nurse Lyle apparently left Boston Med well after shift change. Say, four? A.M. Estimating, of course."

"Can you *never* tell exactly how long someone's been dead?" I'm hoping to ask a few more questions, too, but I stop after Gardiner's raised know-your-place eyebrow.

"Dr. Phillip Ong, meet Rachel North." Gardiner surprises me with this moment of courtesy. "Our newest intern. Harvard. Et cetera."

"Lucky you." Ong has pulled a tablet from his medical bag and taps on the glowing screen, maybe entering data. He looks up, a barely assessing glance, goes back to his screen.

I can't quite read him. Is there polite chitchat at a murder scene? Issue, rule, analysis, conclusion. I don't know the rules. Yet.

"Thanks," I begin, deciding, like in class, you might get points for participation. "And you know, I can feel the oven is hot. So when it comes to time of death, would that matter?"

"Yes." He nodded, twisting his stethoscope. "The in situ temperature of the—"

"Phil?" Gardiner interrupts. "Know who Rachel's husband is?"

Lovely. Is this how it's gonna go? But her nasty—*is it?*—comment makes me realize I'm seeing this murder scene through Jack's eyes. Exactly what I need to do. If I were defending an accused killer and not prosecuting, and someday I *will* be, I'd be looking for evidence of another truth. For ambiguity. And remnants of what happened before.

BEFORE
SIX YEARS EARLIER

"Hello?" I picked up the phone, heart racing, blinking in the pitch dark. I almost said "Office of the Senate President." It took me a beat to let go of my dream. Another to get my bearings. Home. Couch. "Hello?"

Midnight, the muted TV told me. Friday. Well, into Saturday now. What the hell? "Hello? Hello?"

Nothing. Stupid wrong numbers. I hung up, wrapping the fuzzy blanket around my shoulders. My thinning Depeche Mode T-shirt was no match for February in Boston. I'd lucked into this quirky ground-level apartment, three short blocks from my statehouse office where I'd snagged the almost-not-entry-level job as constituent services aide for Senate President Thomas Rafferty. Cheap enough for my taxpayer-dollar salary, because even though the living room faced a London-esque Beacon Hill side street, the bedroom and bath were on the ground floor. "Ground" meaning "below the ground." So, this time of year, it was not only freezing, but dark. *Buried alive* always crossed my mind. But now it was almost spring, if you convinced yourself to believe that.

I burrowed myself into the corner of the couch again. Then leaped to my feet.

Someone was buzzing my door. A mistake? A prank? Some sort of horrible news? About the senator?

"Shut *up*, Rach," I instructed myself. Unsettled and preliminarily anxious, I wrapped the couch throw tighter. Then, with one finger curling the pale linen, I pulled back the curtain over my front window to look out onto Lime Street.

Through a powder of languid snow and the flare of my streetlight—a black car. Idling at the snow-banked curb. I squinted but couldn't see anyone inside. No one in sight, not anywhere. And then I saw the footprints. Clear and precise outlines in newly fallen snow. Coming up my front walk.

Emily and Martine lived in the apartment above, but they were out of town. Unless this was some moron with a wrong address, this visitor wanted *me*.

At midnight? On a Friday?

The buzzer rang again. If I answered, that assured the villain-burglar-rapist that I was home. The blue TV light coming through the front window might already have given that away, as well as my silhouette against the window when I looked out. Were the buzz and the phone call connected?

If I answered the buzzer, I decided, it didn't mean I had to open the door. I pushed the button for the intercom.

"Yes?" It came out a dry-throated whisper.

"Rachel?"

I recognized that voice.

There was no time, no time to do anything, not to comb my hair or put on makeup or change to real clothes. The senator was here. Senate President Thomas Ames Rafferty. *Tom.* Here. At my apartment door. Unannounced, unscheduled, astonishing. I had imagined this moment. So many times. Not like this, certainly, but our lives are full of the unexpected. That's what dreams are about.

Rachel, he'd said. That one word he spoke through the intercom seemed to hang in the air. Even over the muffled fuzz of the old-fashioned speaker, that single word, my name, seemed filled with promise. *Prince Charming's not going to come knocking at your door*, Mom had insisted to little-girl me. Wrong.

"Yes?" I leaned in close to the speaker, feeling his presence, pretending I didn't know who it was. Pretended to do what anyone would do if they were surprised by the doorbell on a snowy Boston midnight. Pretended my knees were working. I drew the soft woolen blanket closer around my shoulders.

"Rachel? It's me," he said. "May I come in?"

It was ridiculous, something out of a Lifetime TV melodrama, but I felt like crying. With joy.

Because this visit was about *us,* my only-imagined *Rachel and Tom.* It had to be.

What should I do?

I pushed the door-release buzzer. Heard the front door unlatch, then close again. I picture him, walking down the corridor, walking toward me. Why was he here? I closed my eyes a fraction of a second, considered tossing my tawny shawl-blanket over the entryway chair. *No underwear,* my brain managed to remind me. I kept the shawl in place as I opened my door.

"Are you all right?" The words came out before I could filter them. "Senator? Is something wrong?"

My boss did not answer or cross the threshold of my apartment door. He stood, eyes locked with mine. His dark hair glistened with melted snowflakes, droplets of the powdery white spackling his navy overcoat. His dear face seemed red, maybe because I'd left him waiting in the cold on my front steps. No hat, no scarf, no gloves. He carried a manila envelope in one hand.

"You must be freezing." I stepped away from the door, allowing him to walk past. This had never happened before, and the way things were now, there was no conceivable reason why he'd show up here. This time of night, or ever. Unless something was truly wrong. Or, I dared think, truly right. But so much would have to change to make it so.

What should I do?

I closed the door as he entered my foyer. He'd initiated this, this unlikely visit at an impolitic time. The first move had to be his. Only then could I gauge mine. *Your wife,* I wanted to say. *Your career. Mine. Ours.*

Outside, the wind had picked up, and the snow. Icy flakes tapped on my front windows, rattling the aging glass panes in their weathered wooden frames.

"I'm probably making footprints on your oriental," he said.

I looked down. Two arms' length between us, but on the rug, our shadows overlapped.

"Do you want to—" I stopped. *Want to what? Take off your coat? Take off everything? Kiss me? Stay the night?* "It's okay," I said, waving away his concern. "It's seen worse. But Senator? Is everything okay?"

"So. Rachel. I know it's late. I came from the office."

I had never seen Tom—the name came easily now, for some reason—fidget or look uncomfortable. Here was a man who thundered his passion from the well of the Senate chamber, who fired articulate and informed answers to clueless reporters, savvy enough to negotiate the elements of laws that would change lives. Now here he stood, red-nosed and damp, awkward as a wet puppy.

"Okay, no problem," I began. I was an employee, after all, and possibly he had an urgent task for me. But the senator seemed uneasy. Why? If he was about to cross a line, that would be a move that, once made, check and mate, could not be undone. "What's up?"

"This is for you." He handed me the envelope, a blank eight-by-ten rectangle, its clasp closed, the flap sealed. "Can you hang on to it for me? I didn't want to wait until Monday."

I took it with one hand, clutched my blanket closer with the other. He kept his hand on the envelope, too, didn't let go of the paper connection between us. I felt a signal, somehow, a communication, pass between us. He was asking me a favor, and not from the black leather chair behind his hundred-year-old Senate desk. In my living room. At midnight.

Politics—like life—is driven by the balance of power. Working in the status-driven machine of the statehouse on Beacon Hill, it hadn't taken long for me to learn that. Tom Rafferty claimed Beacon Hill's top rung. Why would he jeopardize his leverage? What was in this envelope?

"Dare I ask? What's inside?" I kept my voice light, trying to decide how to play it. Wondering whether I was an obedient employee or trusted professional confidante or potential soul mate.

Or, it crossed my mind, dupe.

Handing a mid-level staffer a sealed envelope on a snowy midnight was almost preposterously the fodder of that Lifetime melodrama I'd imagined. Not to mention the stuff of blazing political headlines, and if I let my imagination run, reputation-ruining humiliation. Even prison. Handsome and charismatic leading man or not, romantic fantasies or not, I did not intend to play the hoodwinked heroine.

CHAPTER FIVE

"Hey you. So, Mrs. Kirkland, how was your first day on the job?" Jack opens our back door before I can get my house keys out. He's wearing a navy canvas apron over his Red Sox T-shirt. The apron, double-tied around his waist, has the state shield logo of the Committee for Public Counsel Services, the public defender agency of Massachusetts. CPCS oversees the murder list, the group of hotshot lawyers not only qualified to handle murder cases for indigent clients, but also benevolent enough to take them for a reduced fee. (Jack sometimes says those defendants are his own personal murder list—the list of accused killers whose cases, and lives, he's responsible for.) That's how Jack got assigned to represent now-convicted slasher Marcus Simmons Dorn. But most of his career involves handling high-paying cases. Including the one that brought us together. In flowery font that mimics the US Constitution, Jack's apron says TO SERVE MAN.

"Hey you," I say, our call and response. "Well, Mr. North, it was fine, thank you."

If Jack's going to be conciliatory, I'm all about that. Early on, he'd asked whether I'd change my name to Kirkland when we got married. I'd suggested he change his to North. We kept the status quo, but it stayed our private joke.

Jack's welcoming hug and promissory kiss on the neck almost evaporates the residual stress of my first day on the job. As I'd parked my Jetta in our driveway, I'll admit my first thoughts were of sweatpants. And wine. And Jack, of course. Driving home, I'd debated with myself about how much to tell him about today. How much I was *allowed* to tell, given the constraints of what's probably—clearly?—privileged information versus my leeway as a spouse. Issue, rules, analysis, conclusion.

Jack untangles us with a final peck on the cheek.

"First day of anything is always the worst," he says. "Can't wait to hear about it. What you're willing and able to reveal at least. No pressure."

From down the hall in the kitchen, I hear something beeping.

"Is the oven beeping?" I ask. "Are you cooking?" Jack's not much in the kitchen. Microwave popcorn for Red Sox games—that he can do. He makes a mean martini. But usually I'm the cook. I know it's old-school. But he pays the mortgage, so it's a balance.

"Run and change. Take a shower." He points toward upstairs. "Wash off the stink of the prosecution."

"Hey!" I drop my briefcase, slam my fists onto my hips. Honestly? He's going to do this?

"Kidding, sweetheart," he says. "I know it's good experience. But I loathe that woman." Whatever is beeping keeps beeping. "Meet you in what, fifteen? And I chilled our martini glasses in the freezer. To celebrate."

"Oh, honey." I stand there, looking at my Jack, my dear Jack, who's passionate about his work and can't let it go, but in the end, we're married and nothing can change that. Jack's a lawyer, and lawyers like to win. I should remember that even when the stakes turn personal, Jack's laser-beam approach is difficult for him to shake. Also to remember that a conversation between two reasonable people needn't escalate into a disaster. Or a guilty verdict.

"I'll hurry." I stash my briefcase by the hall table and trot up the stairs.

Only a few more than fifteen minutes later, my hair damp and dripping wet spots on my black T-shirt, I'm smiling with the anticipation of our rapprochement. Maybe I can tell Jack a *little* of what happened today. After all, he fills me in on his cases, knowing I understand how to keep a secret. I stop in the middle of our claret-and-navy carpeted hallway, laughing for a moment at myself. That's an understatement.

"I'm late, I know," I call out as I reach the end of the hall. I stop. Sniff. And then, although my every instinct is screaming at me not to, I take the final three steps into the kitchen.

Jack's got the oven door open, his face flushed in the heat. Both hands are encased in bright-blue oven mitts. "You're gonna be so proud of me," he says into the oven. "I got home early and got inspired. And I made this from scratch. Your favorite. For you. My darling little D-A."

I can smell it, sharp and pungent, before it comes out of the oven. And then I see it. It's square, not round like Oregano Brothers. But unmistakably, sickeningly, pizza. I stare, touch one hand to the kitchen wall. Become acutely aware of my knees. Something happens to my stomach. I see past the counter to our kitchen table. Ours has nobody—no body— underneath.

"I know, I know, it's not the prettiest," Jack says, setting the aluminum cookie sheet onto the stove top.

The fragrance of oregano is unbearable.

"Fine. It's damn wonky," Jack is saying. "I know I'm not the best in the kitchen. But you've got to give me points for effort. If you drink enough martini, you won't even notice."

"It looks—it smells—" I search for a word. A word he'd approve of. After all, he has no idea about today. "Perfect," I say. "But I forgot something. Upstairs. Be right back."

Down the hall, up the steps, into the bathroom. I lean on the counter, close my eyes. Splash cold water on my face. I refuse to get upset by pizza. I am not Tassie Lyle, and life goes on. This is one of those coincidences that—that's a coincidence. Jack's being loving and caring. Being a husband. I am being an idiot. A weak-stomached idiot. I puff out a breath, change the expression on my face. I almost pinch my cheeks to get the color back. Too bad no one could do that for Tassie Lyle. A dead girl's face almost replaces mine in the mirror. I close my eyes again and shake it off. When I open them, the mirror shows only me.

The martini is perfect. The bullet of lemony chilled vodka begins to erase my memories of murder, and I take my place at our kitchen table—trying not to look beneath it—and pretend Jack's pizza has nothing to do with Tassie Lyle's. I haven't had the courage to take a bite yet. Soon, Jack will notice.

I use my fork to cut off a tiny corner. Take another sip of my drink, the sleek gold-rimmed martini glass frosty from the freezer.

"You're quiet," Jack says. He's chewing at the same time, but we're married, so I know not to sweat the small stuff. It's not like I'm going to change him.

"Well, yeah." I put down my fork, stalling. Then give up. I grimace, telegraphing I'm about to confess. "It's the pizza, I'm afraid. Martha Gardiner took me with her to a murder scene this morning. Some first day, right? It was so—upsetting. And there was pizza. I mean, the victim had ordered pizza. She didn't have time to eat all of it. Or, I don't know, someone stopped her from eating it." I *suppose* someone stopped her. And I guess it won't matter that I told him that stuff. Clea Rourke's probably already put it on the news. Along with every other reporter. "So, you know. I've got a little PTSD, maybe. This beautiful martini is helping, though. Medicinal."

"Oh, crap, honey." Jack stands, whisks away my essentially untouched slice. He stops, plate midair. Frowning. "That bitch took you to a murder scene? For the love of—Where? Who's the victim? How'd they die?"

I reach out, take back the plate. "Of course you didn't know about the pizza," I say. "And I'll be fine. It'll be yummy. In a minute."

"I bet it was that nurse," Jack says. "It was on the TV news. That reporter. Rourke."

"Am I allowed to talk about it?" I look out the window beside me instead of looking at Jack or the pizza. I can see across the street to Crystal

Lake, this time of year, even now, after seven in the evening, the sun glints on the water, sugar maples and sycamores fully green. It's a pointillist painting in motion, with bicyclists and joggers and dogs pulling at almost-invisible leashes, a silhouetted family of mallards gliding soundlessly, left to right. I've watched those ducks, or ones like them, close-up, from one of the wood-slatted benches surrounding the lake, the place I go to sit when I need solitude or solutions. I study the V-shaped wakes left by their invisibly paddling webbed feet. The water gets disturbed, changed, diverted—but only temporarily. Then every trace of the ducks vanishes. Like they were never there.

"Talk about what?" Jack fishes a green olive out of his martini glass, then sucks it and the vodka from his fingers. "Rach? Where'd you go? Is something happening out on the lake? Talk about what?"

"You know, today. The murder."

"Why not? What would be secret?"

"Well, that's what I'm asking *you*. I mean, Gardiner didn't tell me not to say anything to you, but maybe she figures she doesn't need to tell me. I couldn't very well ask her, 'Hey, am I allowed to tell my husband about this?' And, Jack, you can't take this case anyway, because—" I stop. My shoulders drop. "I mean, this is okay, isn't it? It's not like I'm stealing a potential defendant from you."

"No?" Jack bites the corner off his slice.

I remember what Gardiner said outside Tassie Lyle's house. 'It's a pity your husband won't get assigned to defend this case.' I decide to leave that out of this conversation.

"I mean, because you were assigned the Dorn case, you can't be next up on the murder list. Right? And there's not even a suspect yet."

"No?"

"What do you mean, 'no'?" That's a strange thing for him to say. "Have you heard there *is*?"

"How could I hear there is, Rach?" Jack stands, plops his plaid cloth napkin on the table. "I'm getting more of this awesome pizza. Is that okay with you?"

He's about to drive me up the wall, answering questions with questions, but that's what he does. I understand why witnesses break down under his skepticism or doubt or suspicion or whatever combative attitude he's trying to convey. He's making me second-guess myself. I almost wonder if I'm not the only one hiding something.

"Jack? This is nuts." I look away as he transfers another cheesy-gooey slice to his plate, then steel myself and look at him. "Look. I know you hate Martha. But can you not take it out on me? I'm doing my best here to balance my need to stay professional in a difficult situation with my"—I flutter my eyelashes, dumb, but trying to change the mood—"my unending lust for you. And supreme respect, of course."

"I lust for you, too," he says. He takes two wineglasses from the cabinet by the sink, tucks a bottle of cabernet under his arm, brings it all to the table as he talks. "But since your 'Martha' has no suspect, as you say, and as a result no case, and moreover, even if there were, I couldn't, as you correctly recognize, take it, then as far as you and I are concerned, there's nothing privileged or confidential about what happened at the scene. Right?"

"Well . . ." I try to untangle his words. In law school, we're taught not to use compound questions, because it makes it difficult for the witness to give a clear answer. Seems like trial procedure doesn't count at the kitchen table.

"Right." He stabs a corkscrew into the wine bottle, yanks it out, sniffs the cork. Then he salutes me with it, punctuating his verdict. "Sustained. Tell me everything."

CHAPTER SIX

Apparently the job of an intern includes daily bafflement. Second day, another quandary.

Newly arrived at the reception desk, I put down my briefcase and hold up the envelope Leon Colacetti had given me the moment before. "I'm supposed to take this envelope? To Ms. Gardiner? Um, in her office?" I point down the empty corridor.

Leon leans over from behind his file-strewn desk, hands me a scrap of legal paper. "Nope. Here. And *she's* already there."

I see what he must mean to be a smile.

In block-printed black felt-tip pen, the paper shows an address in Newtonville, a once-blue-collar Boston suburb now feeling the march of gentrification from gig-economy millennials.

"Look for the maroon Crown Vic," Leon says, looking at his computer screen. His phone blinks green with an incoming call. "You're going to be even later if you don't leave now."

Why doesn't he simply tell me what's going on? He's cornering the market on passive-aggressive here, but I can play, too. And might as well see if I can elicit some information.

"Is Ms. Gardiner expecting me? Or am I the early bird?"

"She predicted you'd be first." The blinking green light disappears. He takes a sip of coffee.

I assume it's coffee, I remind myself.

"Great," I say. "Will I need to go inside at this address to find her? Or—"

Leon turns to me, scratches his cheek with one finger, impatient. I can tell it's all he can do not to roll his eyes. But how am I supposed to know what to do?

"You are holding the search warrant for the home of a person of interest in the case you are assigned to." He speaks with elaborate patience. "Ms. Gardiner, along with her state police investigators, are in their vehicles, three of them, at the address I gave you, waiting for said warrant. They are also waiting for *you*. That said, I am happy to take some time to elaborate on the search-warrant procedure, if you like, Ms. North."

"Got it." Maybe this is a test, or hazing, or the newbie gauntlet. Maybe he's just a jerk. Fine. I need to keep everyone happy. "And thank you so much. Next time I'll know."

I walk out of the building and into the parking lot as two car doors slam. Eli Lansberry and Andrew DiPrado converge on me, each carrying a briefcase in one hand and a lidded paper cup in the other.

"What's up?" Eli looks at the envelope I'm holding. He gestures at it with his coffee cup. "What's that?"

"Where're you going?" Andrew glances at the front door, then back at me. His red-striped tie is tight up to his neck, and his khaki suit almost looks starched.

Once again, I have no idea what to say or do. Are my fellow interns supposed to be in on what I'm doing?

"Apparently interns double as delivery service," I say, waving the envelope. "Early bird gets the scut work, right?"

I don't wait for a reply. And I wonder, as I head for my car, what Leon will tell them. *She's headed to deliver a search warrant in a murder case and then she'll be there when it's executed* will hardly sound like scut work. I have no idea whether Leon is an ally or is conspiring, for some reason, to make my life miserable.

I push the ignition. No politics like office politics. And no humiliation like office humiliation. Once the toxic buzz of speculation begins, there's nothing powerful enough to extinguish it. I back out of the parking space and sneak a glance at the front door as it closes Andrew and Eli in behind it. It's 8:20, and Nick Soderberg has not arrived. Again— that I know of. Maybe Gardiner, dividing and conquering, has sent him on a mission somewhere as well. Or maybe he's simply late.

Halfway to Newtonville, that white envelope is burning a hole in my passenger seat's upholstery. I let out a breath, imagining some poor guy—guy?—blissfully doing whatever he's doing this morning, coffee or whatever, when in reality the full force of law enforcement is about to steamroll his life.

Inside this envelope is their instrument of power. The search warrant includes the person of interest's name and address and a detailed list of exactly what the detectives will look for there. It's essentially Martha Gardiner's outline of her theory about who killed Tassie Lyle and how they did it. Maybe even why. It's the inside of this case. The rules.

To my right, a silver convertible, the Red Sox–capped driver impatient, blasts through the red light, making a left turn in front of me. No cops around to catch him, the driver probably figured. So he'll get away with breaking the law.

Unlike the poor sap who's named in this search warrant. Unlike the poor sap whose home—or wherever—is about to be searched within an inch of its life. And whichever of his possessions are listed on the warrant are about to be sorted, labeled, bagged, sealed, and removed. Bags that will seal not only the incriminatory items but his fate. What can link him to the crime? What do the cops look for? Little does this person know—I hum the *bum-bum* notes of *Law & Order*—the good guys are on to him. And we are after him.

What could be ahead for this now-suspect is handcuffs, a miserable stay in the Middlesex jail, a wrenching murder trial, and if all goes as Gardiner plans—life in prison without parole.

If they can prove he did it, I hear Jack's voice lecturing me. His defense attorney, whoever that turns out to be, will have other plans for this suspect.

Exactly why does Gardiner think this person is guilty? I need to think like a defense attorney now.

BEFORE

Showing up at midnight on a Friday, uninvited, at a subordinate's apartment? Manila envelope in hand, I paused, waiting for Tom to answer. Our eyes remained locked, but his expression stayed unreadable. As an employee, it was protocol for me to wait for instructions, and possibly impertinent for me to have asked what was in the envelope he was giving me. But he's the one who'd thrown protocol out the window.

"I wondered if you'd ask," he finally said.

"Well, yeah. Envelopes at midnight?" I proceeded carefully. Made my tone amused. He had to own this. "I feel like I'm in a bad movie, Senator. I'm not sure of my lines. How can I help you?"

Tom looked at the carpet, not at all the confident politico I was used to. He jammed his hands into his coat pockets, then looked down at me. He was five inches taller, and never was it more evident than at this moment. I had the power here. He must know that.

"Well," he finally said, "I said I needed to deliver an envelope to you. I didn't explain what was in it. I'm the boss." He smiled, maybe shy, maybe conspiratorial. "And there you have it. So if anyone asks, you can confirm it."

So the line in the sand appears. The decision looms. I'm not naïve, I know what men do and how they behave. The senator had obviously made some decisions. And was acting on them. *I couldn't wait until Monday,* he'd said.

He trusted me, on some level, to pretend what he was doing was aboveboard and acceptable. When, in truth, it was neither of the above. Not even in the old boy "go along to get along" playing field of Beacon Hill. My only play—because office politics are politics, too—was to pretend I believed what he was saying.

"Constituent complaints are a never-ending struggle," I said, placing the envelope on the narrow table under the entryway mirror. "Shall I look at it—now? This weekend?"

"Whenever you want," he said. "How are you, Rachel? You know how much I rely on you. How well you understand your job. And me."

I saw him glance toward the front window. Which is when I remembered. *Wait.* I'd seen his car at the curb. Idling. Was someone inside? And if so, that meant there was someone else who knew he was here.

"Is someone waiting for you?" I asked.

He frowned, as if that were a loaded question. "At home, you mean?"

Guilty conscience, I thought. He's got to be thinking of Nina Perini, his high school sweetheart, prom queen, corporate powerhouse, big-time fund-raiser. Wife of however many years. Not a day goes by when *I* don't think of her. Nina Perini. La la la. It's musical, almost rhymes, like an ingenue in a cheap romance novel. She only uses "Rafferty" when she's at political events. So very power-woman. Maybe he's sick of it.

"No, no," I said. As if we were having a normal conversation and not negotiating our futures. "In the car. Waiting for you in the car."

A look crossed his face again, unreadable. If someone had driven him here, that meant someone could know he'd visited me. A witness. Which meant it might actually be about some papers. Could that be true? The envelope sat there, taunting me from the side table. If he was working late, and had invaded my private space by bringing me some damn paperwork that would as easily have waited until Monday—talk about crossing the line. That was unacceptably imperious. And if there was someone in the car, waiting for him to leave, that was certainly the case. That meant it wasn't about "us." It was about *him.*

Maybe I had romanticized this whole encounter. Maybe I was a silly girl with a crush. Maybe he was a self-centered narcissist who thought I—and the rest of his staff, probably—had nothing better to do than bow to his every whim.

I thought about ripping the envelope open.

I thought about handing it back to him and saying—*bring it to my office on Monday.*

I thought about dropping the woolen blanket to the floor, as if I'd forgotten it was there. I would stand here, in my threadbare little T-shirt, and challenge him. *What do you want?* I could demand. Up in his Beacon Hill office, he wielded the power. He could change my life, certainly. For better or worse. With one word, one gesture, one phone call. But at 22 Lime Street? *My* territory. He was the visitor. The subordinate. The petitioner. I could do or be or say whatever I wanted. I could also ruin him.

But I would never do that. Not to him. Not to me. In the silence, I wrapped the heavy shawl even closer. He could help me. He could also ruin me.

"Is there?" I persisted. "Someone waiting for you?"

Outside a horn beeped. Twice, polite taps. Tom flinched, hearing them. Looked toward the window. Someone *was* out there. Waiting.

I took a step backward, away from him. As much as I longed for him, I also needed to keep my self-respect. And allow him his. Fantasy was one thing. But when it came to a late-night encounter with one's boss, very few happy endings could be written.

"I have to go, Rachel." He'd turned to me again. "But listen. There's nothing in that envelope. I only wanted an excuse to, well, there's one more thing. I can trust you, correct? To keep it between us? I know I can."

"That's my job, Senator." I kept my tone professional. Though this was weird as hell.

He reached into an inside coat pocket, pulled out a flat book-size box. Robin's egg blue, I could see through the taped bubble wrap. Turquoise blue. Tiffany blue.

"Hold on to this, Rachel," he said. "And soon we'll talk."

And there it was. The doors to two diverging futures opened before me. But being the easy catch was not my style. The horn beeped again, this time insistent.

"It's very late," I said. "And if there's someone out in the cold, waiting for you to 'deliver the envelope'"—I gestured toward the window—"you have accomplished that. And now? You should probably go."

He held out the box again. Like the horn, this time insistent. "Rachel?"

I took it.

CHAPTER **SEVEN**

"You're up to speed?" Gardiner, in the front passenger seat, points at the driver of our maroon sedan, a black-clad guy in a black baseball cap, obviously SWAT, who Gardiner introduced only as Ben. I'm in the back, naturally. Me, she ignores.

"Got it," Ben growls. He eases us around the corner.

Jeffrey Paul Baltrim, white male, five-ten, brown hair, age twenty-eight—as Gardiner just explained—lives two blocks away.

I touch my seat belt, running a hand down the gray protective webbing snapped across my navy court-worthy jacket. Our lives change so fast. When we least expect it—unless we always expect it—our freedom is snatched away. If he's poor enough, this guy may get assigned a murder-list lawyer. At this moment, though, our target is defenseless. Is he home? Is he oblivious? Is he worried? Or has he already headed for the hills?

"Baltrim's the guy who delivered that pizza to Tassie Lyle," Gardiner goes on. She's looking over the warrant as she talks, page two, the list of what they're allowed to search for. "Confirmed, no question. Lyle ordered it herself, so says the restaurant manager. Baltrim's a new hire. He never came back to the store after that delivery."

"Was she alone when he arrived?" I dare to ask. "Were there witnesses?"

Gardiner doesn't answer.

What might make a jury find him innocent? My brain concocts defense-worthy excuses. *It was a mistake. An accident. She made me do it. She deserved it because . . . whatever.* This warrant, a piece of paper signed by a judge, gives law enforcement—us—the right to break down Baltrim's door.

We creep toward the house, maybe ten miles an hour. Not a dog barking, not a bird singing, not a lawn mower droning across some needy lawn. I'm in an unmarked car with Ben the SWAT guy, an assistant district attorney, and a search warrant for a suspected murderer's house. Two black sedans accompany us. *How I spent my summer semester.*

"You'll stay back, Ms. North," Gardiner says. "Way the hell back. And then—"

My cell phone rings from my tote bag. Bing-bonging, interrupting Gardiner mid-instructions. It's Jack. I slam it off, my face burning. *Damn it, Jack.* But he probably figures I'm behind a desk, reviewing documents. There's no way he could know where I am. I should be grateful instead of annoyed.

Gardiner does a full turn, looks at me over the seat back. "If you're ready, Ms. North?"

She doesn't wait for my answer.

"Do it," she instructs Ben. "If we find probable cause," Gardiner goes on, unbuckling her seat belt, "then we'll—*damn.* Hang on." She points out the windshield. The front door of 36 Raeford is opening.

"Is that him?" I whisper. It must be. Framed in the doorway of the careworn vinyl-sided ranch and wearing a white T-shirt with the smiling pizza logo of Oregano Brothers and jeans is a white male. Brown hair, five ten. Who looks about age twenty-eight. But in front of him is a little boy, maybe five, wearing blue jeans and a Red Sox cap.

"Plan B," Gardiner says. "Plan B, Plan B."

I hear a radio crackle. Ahead of us and behind us, the two black cars pull away.

Baltrim, if that's who it is, has closed the front door, and he and the boy are walking toward the sidewalk. After a few steps, the boy points toward the sky, tripping over his colorful rubber-soled shoes. Baltrim looks up, and I do, too, curious at what's piqued the child's interest. Two airplanes' contrails have crossed above them, making a gigantic white X-marks-the-spot in the cloudless cobalt sky.

"Okay, Ms. North," Gardiner says. "The kid is a monkey wrench. But Baltrim's out of the house. Appears unarmed. Follow my lead. Got it?"

No, I want to say.

But Gardiner is opening her door. "*Now,* Rachel," she says. "Improvise. Somehow get his name. Confirm it. Then I'll take over. The good guys have arrived."

I get out of the car and approach our target, attempting to look pleasant. But Gardiner's improvisation scenario—which means lying—seems misguided. Am I allowed to dupe a person into identifying himself? Trick him? A judge might say no.

"Excuse me? Sir?" I attempt to sound needy. "We might be lost. We're looking for Raeford Street?"

Gardiner's so close behind me I can almost hear her heart beat. Are we facing a murderer?

"You found it," Baltrim eyes us, assessing. "This is Raeford."

"This is *his* house!" The boy, eager to help, points to it. "Number thirty-six. And we're going to the park. Uncle Jeff says—"

"That's enough, Jonah," Baltrim interrupts the boy. Maybe he didn't notice the two departing black cars. Maybe he's not seeing Ben behind the wheel of ours. "Anything else?"

"Yes," I say, staying pleasant. Now for the name. "Are you—"

I hear our car door click open. Ben's head, only marginally less intimidating without his black baseball cap, appears. And then the rest of him.

"Uncle Jeff?" The boy's eyes widen as Ben—a battleship in black boots and webbed straps—walks to the back of the car, then steps around it, toward us. If the child has seen *Star Wars,* he'll be terrified. "Who's that?"

If we're supposed to be nonthreatening, this is not how I would have handled it. But what do I know? If Baltrim's a killer, as they—we—suspect, this morning may be about to take a turn.

"Jeffrey Paul Baltrim?" Gardiner interrupts. "We're from the—"

"Are you a police?" The boy takes a step forward.

"Run home, Jonah," Baltrim says. "Your mom'll be home soon. We'll go to the park another time." The boy stays put. Baltrim reaches toward his own back pocket.

Ben's fingers poise, warningly, over his holstered weapon. The holster's snap tab is open. "State police. Let's see your hands."

"I was getting my cell phone," Baltrim says, but obeys, holding out both hands, palms up. "Because three strangers are on my sidewalk, in front of a kid, asking for—"

"I'm Assistant District Attorney Martha Gardiner. Middlesex County District Attorney's Office." Gardiner does not offer to shake Baltrim's hand. "This man is from the state police. We're here to—"

"Middlesex . . . the what? Well, why didn't you the hell say so?" Baltrim stands his ground but leaves his hands in front of him. "You've terrified a child, trespassed on my property, and lied about—"

"We have a warrant to search these premises," Gardiner interrupts, "and if you continue in this vein, we'll be forced to take you in for resisting."

"Hey. I'm not resisting anything." Baltrim puts his arms down, with a dare-you glare at Ben. He tucks a wide-eyed Jonah behind him. Crosses his arms over his chest. "Search? What are you talking about? Search for what?"

I've stepped back a foot or two, as instructed, staying out of this. Is this standard procedure? Scaring a kid and goading a suspect? If Baltrim ever complains about these tactics, if they *are* tactics, there'd be no outside witness to confirm what happened. Except a maybe-five-year-old child.

"We can do it with you or without you." Gardiner has pulled the envelope out of her blazer pocket. Hands it to Baltrim. "If you're willing to open the door, fine. If not . . ."

Our two black cars, probably summoned by Ben, are once again turning onto Raeford Street. Unlike our surreptitious arrival, they make no pretense of stealth.

Gardiner, almost smiling, gestures to the cars. "We have people, as you see, who will open the door anyway. You may not be pleased with how they do it. Your decision. You have, I'd estimate, thirty seconds."

Baltrim has opened the envelope. Pulls out the stapled pages, unfolds them. Scans the front, turns the page. I see the blood drain from his face.

"Run home now, Jonah," he says. "Tell your mom I'll call her later."

You shouldn't use up your phone call, I want to tell him. *You need a lawyer.* But I keep quiet.

BEFORE

As I tramped up the perilously snowy hill toward the statehouse, I replayed Tom's words.

"Soon we'll talk," he'd said. What did that mean? What did "Hold on to this" mean?

This time of the morning, even before the earliest Monday rush hour, Beacon Hill seemed like another world, with steep one-way streets and narrow sidewalks. Rows of brownstones, with their shared walls and ornate front doorways, windowpanes, some glowing with light, so delicate they were almost lavender. Trees edged with snow, gnarled bare-branched magnolias and dogwoods old enough that Samuel Adams might have seen them. Cars, most of them blanketed white in their coveted parking spots, would probably not move all day. Dark wrought-iron gates protected the shuttered enclaves of the superprivate superpowerful.

At the carelessly shoveled back steps of the statehouse, I stomped the snow from my boots, saw my breath in the air, felt off balance from the senator's midnight visit. What would happen inside this building today? It could not be the same for us, not ever. I paused, in longing and in uncertainty.

The parking lots, domain of the upper echelons, were newly plowed, though the line of old green dumpsters at the rear, lids down, were blanketed with snow, too, white bumps indicating the rocks holding each rusty top in place. Trash guys came Friday, and then not again until Monday evening. Tucking my thermal coffee mug under one arm, I dug out my employee ID card and showed it to the uniformed guard, who waved me by without looking at it. The statehouse, lofty, marble-floored, and walled with oil portraits of founding fathers, is public space, former governor Patrick had once declared, so security was pretty casual.

Once inside, I brushed the melting snow from my black coat and unwrapped my plaid wool scarf, spattering droplets on the yellowing marble floor. I pushed the silver button for the unreliable elevator, and as we arrived on the second floor, I looked, as I can't get over doing, at the glorious stained-glass windows of the senate president's Communications Office, circa turn of the last century, a rainbow mosaic with medallions and swords and two sailing ships, the *Arbella* and the *Mayflower,* sailing timelessly on a turquoise glass sea.

Calvin Coolidge once worked in these offices. I wonder if *he* hit on his staffers.

Senator Rafferty—as I was retraining myself to think of him now— certainly would not mention his visit to my apartment. And I certainly would not. Mutually assured destruction, I supposed it was. Although I hadn't done anything. Nothing at all. Except take the envelope. And the box. And what was inside. A necklace. Clasped around my neck now and tucked underneath my black sweater. Like a talisman. A promise.

I jammed my damp coat and scarf over the top rung of the curved rack by the door. I shouldn't keep the necklace, I'd decided. I couldn't let him think I was available that easily. But I could wear it secretly, this once, and then I'd put it all back, exactly how it was. And return it. Maybe I'd keep a picture of it, for . . . nostalgia.

"In *fact*," I said out loud.

"In fact *what*, Rachel?" Logan Concannon's oboe voice entered the room before she got through the doorway. Clipboard, glasses, cell phone in hand. Tom's—Senator Rafferty's—chief of staff has some kind of parabolic hearing. Or maybe she's simply proficient in being at the right place at the wrong time. I've heard her called Gollum, though I personally had never done so out loud. It was her job to keep all the political and administrative moving parts moving. And stop the ones that needed to be stopped. As a result, she'd managed to not only know everything her boss was doing, but also everything everyone else was doing.

My hand trembled a bit, thinking of that, as I dumped a spoon of sugar into my coffee mug.

"You're an early bird," she went on. "How was your weekend?"

I knew that's simply what one said on Monday. I knew she had no idea about what happened at my apartment on Friday.

"Same old same old." I changed the focus. "How about you?"

Logan's famously private, closemouthed. Her longevity—and her memory—is legendary. She knows who she owes and what they owe her. She deposited her clipboard and phone on a striped wing chair, chose a coffee pod from the rack, then inserted it into the machine.

"My weekend was fine, when it finally began," she said, pushing buttons to start the brewer. "The senator and I had a late night here on Friday. The budget. As always."

The heat kicked on in the room, the ancient statehouse furnaces clanking into action, pumping a blast of hot air against my legs. I felt the heat rise in my face as well. Why was she talking about Friday night? Working late on Friday night? *Because you work in the same office,* I told myself. This is called Monday-morning chitchat. She chits, you chat. She's referring to the one thing you have in common, the process of government. *Not* that she was in that car.

"You are so devoted," I said. I opened our little fridge for milk, stalling. Hoping she'd go away. Her office is down the hall. Exactly. So what was she doing here? I sniffed the milk. *Iffy.*

I set my mug on an end table, poured some of the milk into it anyway. The necklace, hidden, was burning its golden shape into my chest. I'd be branded with tiny stars.

"We were here until, oh, might have been midnight," Logan went on. As if she and I talked about the senator's activities all the time. Which we did not. Coffee water burbled into her mug, a triumphant puff of steam announcing the cycle was complete. "Friday night. Rachel? We need to discuss that."

I could hear the sound of her spoon stirring the coffee. She had not added anything to that cup. She was simply stirring. Looking at me. Waiting for me to say something.

CHAPTER **EIGHT**

Gardiner, blazer draped over the back of her chair and the cuffs of her silk blouse unbuttoned and turned back, apparently her version of casual, clinks her full wineglass against Andrew DiPrado's, then Eli Lansberry's. "First we make an arrest, then we toast the system. And that, ladies and gentlemen, is how justice gets done."

I'm too far away down the caramel leather banquette at Alden & Harlow for Martha to clink against mine, so she wine-salutes, smiling in my direction. Nick Soderberg is absent, and no one has mentioned him. Five o'clock on a Thursday, when it's light outside and we're theoretically in work mode, seems an unsettling time to be drinking Chardonnay with your boss and colleagues in a trendy Cambridge restaurant. But Gardiner told us it's an office ritual—handcuffs, arrest, and then wine.

This place used to be a Cambridge landmark. As Casablanca, Jack's told me, it was the go-to romantic spot for Harvard students, the instant messaging that your intentions were serious. Casablanca's long gone, if seven years is long, and now, as Alden & Harlow, all pale wood, warm suede, and immersive greenery, the subterranean bistro is beloved by my law-school foodie colleagues. Those who can afford it. But Gardiner explained that since the post-arrest drinking tradition started in this space, albeit (she said "albeit") with beer, here it will continue. "Ritual is ritual," she'd proclaimed. "This is what we do."

What we do. What Gardiner and the SWAT guys did, to be more precise. I'd been on the outside, literally. Completely bummed not to be involved in the search of Jeffrey Baltrim's house and see how they handled it. Gardiner wouldn't let me go inside. Even more annoying, since Jonah refused to budge, she'd ordered me to babysit until his mother got home. Because I was a woman? Or maybe Gardiner was making sure I knew my place. If Andrew DiPrado had been there, would Gardiner have given him the same assignment? I doubt it.

I slide out of my seat, making bathroom excuses, and zigzag past tables of earnest twosomes, early drinkers, one solitary dark-suited businessman, maybe, staring into a martini glass. None of them had just participated in an arrest for murder. As I walk down a flight of industrial-concrete stairs toward the red-lacquer door marked W, I mentally reprise my morning, a high-wire act that's only beginning.

Jeff Baltrim's front door had closed with me left on the front stoop. Not a sound escaped. What were the police doing inside? How were they doing it? So frustrating to be kept on the sidelines.

"Do you have any books in there?" I'd pointed to Jonah's backpack. Might as well talk to the kid. "Maybe about dinosaurs? Or trucks?"

"Why is my uncle inside with those police? My mom says police are good. They help us."

"Do you live next door?" I asked.

"He's the *pizza* man. He's not my real uncle. We only call him that. I'm five. We get pizza all the time!" Jonah's words spilled over each other, his eyes wide with enthusiasm. "Sometimes, my mom lets me go with him, like babysitting. I don't have a dad. Because she's a nurse. In the night. Sometimes I sleep in the backseat."

I'd looked at him. Calculating. His mother was a nurse, too? I could almost hear Jack's defense. No one, he'd try to persuade a jury, would murder someone while a kid was asleep in the backseat of a pizza delivery truck. But my husband would not be able to help Jeff Baltrim. My ambition had made sure of that.

"That sounds like fun," I said. "Is it a pizza truck? Or a car?"

"It's a *car*." Jonah looked at me from under his baseball cap. *Idiot grown-up.*

"Did you go with your uncle yesterday night?" I shifted on the dusty wooden step. My black skirt would never be the same.

Jonah wrinkled his nose. "What's a yester day of the night?"

Okay, he was five. "The night before today. Did you wake up in the car today?"

I could almost see him trying to remember. Then he stood, pointing. "A butterfly!" he exclaimed. "Catch it!"

I needed him to focus. But, yeah, he's five. "Why don't we let it be free, Jonah? See how happy he is? Jonah?"

"What?" He plopped back down on the step, his eyes on the brilliant black-and-orange creature that fluttered away past a pink dogwood blooming in the yard next door.

"Did you wake up in the car today?"

"It was dark," he said. "So dark! And it wasn't even morning. And we came home. Uncle Jeff picked me up and carried me. And he smelled yucky."

Yucky, I thought. Whatever that means. Like oregano? Or death? Was this child an alibi? Or a witness for the prosecution? How would a suspect ever know who was about to be turned against them? What supposed ally was about to ruin his life?

Ben and his cadre of SWAT guys had emerged with three sealed paper bags of evidence. What they'd seized, I have no idea. Jonah's mother arrived, asking me questions I had no idea how to answer. I'd taken her name and told her—I hoped it was correct—that Gardiner would be in touch. Later I reported to Gardiner what the boy had said about accompanying his "uncle" on last night's deliveries, and the "yucky" smell.

That turned out to be a mistake.

"Doing a bit of private investigation, Ms. North?" Gardiner's voice had sounded unmistakably dismissive. "But you'll learn, I hope. Kids like that are unreliable, unpredictable, and prone to fantasy. He's maybe *five,* have you forgotten that? What's more, it would be no surprise that we'd find evidence the boy had been in the delivery car. Correct?" And that had been the end of that. She'd seemed so contemptuous I hadn't dared ask what they'd found in the search. I see why Jack hates her. But she's my boss.

Back at the banquette, Gardiner's deep into discussion with Eli and Andrew. A glossy black plate of golden fries, sprinkled with parsley flakes, has appeared on the table.

I slide in to my seat and take a sip of my white wine to paper over the moment of awkward silence. "What did I miss?"

"We were handicapping defense attorneys," Gardiner says. Using a manicured thumb and forefinger, she selects a french fry, then points it at Eli. "Correct, Mr. Lansberry? And our defendant's history."

"While you were babysitting," Eli says, "Andrew and I checked Jeff Baltrim's finances. Asset search, property search. Oregano Brothers was happy to hand over his employment application. And—"

I sneak a glance at Gardiner, who's placed her french fry on a triangular side plate and is now spooning a puddle of ketchup next to it. *Babysitting* is exactly what I'd thought at the time, but it seems unnecessarily disparaging for her to have described it that way to my colleagues.

"And?" Andrew interrupts. "Indigent city. Tough to afford a lawyer on a pizza-delivery salary. He'll get assigned someone from the murder list."

"Not Ms. North's husband, however." Gardiner pats the salt from her lips, puts the black napkin back in her lap. "Lucky for him. What you missed while you were . . . indisposed, Rachel? Today's search revealed Jeff Baltrim was once Tassie Lyle's patient at Boston Med."

"Did you know little Jonah's—?" I begin.

"That boy's mother is not involved, Rachel." Gardiner dismisses my question, rolling over it. "But it appears our suspect had been selling drugs Ms. Lyle had procured for him. Seems she'd refused to continue, and our boy was not pleased about that. Gentlemen, and Rachel, welcome to the legal profession. This one's a slam dunk for the prosecution."

BEFORE

I stared at the empty coatrack by the door of my office, at the line of empty wooden hangers. Most everyone else had gone, and some idiot had stolen my coat and scarf. Who could have possibly . . . ? But no. No one had swiped my coat. I'd left it in the coffee room, damp and soggy, before this morning's encounter with Logan Concannon. I'd been so freaked out and eager to leave the room that I'd forgotten it. No big deal, usually, but now it meant that instead of sneaking out this evening through the back hallway and down the elevator by the stairs, I'd have to retrace my steps and retrieve it from the Communications Office coffee corner.

Logan had been distracted from our "We need to discuss that," conversation, thank all that's holy, and I'd successfully dodged her all day.

"'We need to discuss that?'" I muttered. "Not a chance." Not until I could figure out what to say. At least confer with Tom. But I hadn't seen him, not all day. He probably was avoiding me on purpose, to prevent an awkward moment. I touched the necklace, nestled under my sweater, then opened my outer door and turned left into the gloomy hallway.

I'd laugh about this, I tried to convince myself, when I found out what Logan had really wanted to discuss.

If Tom—the senator—was in his private suite now, I'd be able to dash in and dash out undetected because the suite had no windows that connected to the coffee room. But the senator's front door connected to Logan Concannon's office, and therein was my dilemma.

If Logan's office door was open, she could definitely see the coffee room from her desk. And she could see *me*.

"Plus," I said out loud, then stopped as the word almost echoed in the emptiness. *Plus,* I thought, *who was there to stand up for me?* "He said, she said" was a cliché, a trope, and now, because of something I didn't do, a reality. Thomas Rafferty could say anything, *anything,* and no matter how I tried to counter it, I was the employee, the vulnerable one, the expendable one, the little guy with no power. In the final analysis, power was the only currency.

No surprise on Beacon Hill.

I pulled open the stained-glass door to the Comm room. Waited. Listened. Nothing. Logan's door was closed. The sliver of gap at the top showed only darkness, so the lights were off. Logan was gone. Score one for Rachel.

Then I remembered. I had the necklace. That was way more currency than "he said, she said."

With newfound confidence, my heart finally calming, I stepped toward my coat on the rack. Reached up a hand. My boots were there, too. And then I heard the voices.

Coming from Logan's office. *The lights are off,* my brain insisted. Yes, they were. But someone was in there.

"Rachel," a voice said. Logan's voice. "Well. I see."

I stopped, frozen, my hand midair, a few inches away from my coat. Logan had not come into the room. She was not talking *to* me. She was talking *about* me. There was not likely to be another Rachel. Was Logan on the phone? Or was someone else with her?

CHAPTER **NINE**

I swallow my gum as I click my car door locked. Huff a breath into my open palm to see if I can detect the wine. Peppermint, whew, not Chardonnay. I'm not sure drinking with the assistant district attorney is as easily rationalizable as working with her. Even though the gathering at Alden & Harlow was all perfectly professional. Maybe, I decide as I unlock the front door, I should avoid the whole topic.

"Hey," Jack calls out from the den.

I can hear the Red Sox game on TV back there. His big passion. I had hoped that as long as the game was on, Jack would be so distracted he wouldn't notice the time. Which was pushing 8:30.

"Hey you," I answer as we always do. I love that we have an always. Although he only said "Hey," I knew what he meant. On the way to Jack, I plop my briefcase on the dining room table, walk through the kitchen, then lean down to kiss him on the cheek. He's in jeans and his faded Big Papi T-shirt, his sock feet propped on the hunter-green suede ottoman in front of his favorite leather chair. "My" chair, in matching cordovan, is on the other side of a marble-topped antique table. Jack had the furniture before I moved in. A bit men's-club for me, but comfy nonetheless. Plus, it was his house before it was mine, and no reason to change the entire decor along with everything else. A plate of cheddar and crackers is beside him, and Jack's wineglass, a goblet of red, is safe on a raffia coaster. Once I get my own wine, that'll resolve my incriminating-breath situation. "What's the score?"

A cheer goes up from the TV crowd, but he clicks the sound to mute. Blinks at me. "Prosecution one, defense zero, from what I hear," he says.

"Good one," I say. I'm not taking any bait from him. And the murder-list lawyers have a buzzing email list, so as soon as one gets a tidbit or juicy case or wants to vent about a judge or prosecutor, they all pile on. But I'm unsure of what's legally appropriate between Jack and me, so I'm struggling to decide how much to say. "I'm gonna change clothes. Get rid of these shoes. Get some wine. You need anything?"

I turn to go back to the kitchen.

"Yeah," he says. "I need an explanation."

I turn back. Face him. Try to keep my expression innocently curious. "Of what?"

"What do you think?" It looks like he's doing the same expression thing. "It's almost eight thirty."

Well, yeah. I worked late. And it *was* working. And I admit that when *he* works late, he calls to let me know. I actively didn't do that. And right now, caught in my own omission, I somehow can't retrieve the explanation I'd given myself for it.

"I'm so sorry, honey." I decide to surrender. I mean, tell the truth. I walk toward him, plop down in my chair, swivel it a fraction so I can reach over and rest a peacemaking hand on his knee. "It was a crazy day."

Jack recrosses his legs, as if he's simply getting comfortable. But I worry it's to dump off my hand. He pulls out his cell phone from where it's tucked next to him on the chair, holds it up between two fingers. "Here's *my* cell phone," he says. The light from the flickering muted television plays across his glasses, the baseball game in mirror image. "Did you lose yours?"

"Oh, honey. Don't be mad, okay?" I say again. And even though I am honestly sorry and feel a little guilty, a lot guilty, I had my reasons for not telling him the entire reason I was late. I was trying to avoid making him unhappy. At which I have totally failed. "My total bad, absolutely. I lost track of time. We had a big day, which, apparently, you know."

"They don't have clocks in the DA's office?" He's holding up that phone between two fingers, now tick-tocking it back and forth.

"Hey." I put up both palms. "Objection. Listen. You want me to go stand in the corner? Take a time-out? I said I'm sorry. And I honestly am sorry, honey. I should have called. Next time I will."

"Next time?" He's still holding up the phone, but thankfully he's stopped the phony-dramatic ticking thing.

"Jack!" I can't help it, this is so unfair. I stand, hands outstretched, entreating. Blocking his view of the sixth inning. "Don't let's fight, okay? Yeah, I have a new job. You hate it. But it's only for the summer, right? So it means we have stuff to work out. But in the long run, it's gonna be worth it. It's all so we can work together. Kirkland and North. Defenders of the downtrodden, saviors of the innocent?"

"She's such a strident bitch." Jack has put down his phone. He takes a slug of wine, then picks up the remote, turns on the baseball sound again.

I stand my ground in front of him. "Agreed? Partners?"

He makes a face, rolling his eyes. "Fine. Right. Move over."

"Not until you apologize." This is pushing it, I admit, but I try to make it clear I'm joking. Kind of. I'm in the marital wrong here, but I was only trying to help. And "bitch" is unfair. Martha's tough, sure. But isn't that a good thing? She does exactly the same things Jack does. And he knows it. "So?"

"I'm sorry you screwed up," he says.

"That's my darling Jack," I say. "Touché. Give me five minutes."

By the time I'm back, in jeans and T of my own, wine in hand, barely an inning has gone by. Maybe he's forgotten about this whole being-late thing. His cheese and crackers are gone, only a few salty crumbs remaining. His wineglass is still full. Or, maybe, full again.

"Are you hungry? Should I order Chinese for us?" Top of the seventh, the timing is perfect. "Uber can deliver."

"Are *you*?" He's looking at the screen, not at me. "Hungry?"

Which I'm not, given the truffle fries and, later, the irresistible calamari, then bacon-speckled brussels sprouts, but reality is not the best answer here. "Starving," I say.

"From all your work at the office, I take it," Jack says.

This is—well, I recognize the technique. Trial Proc. 101, formally entitled Elements of Trial Procedure, teaches us how to lead unsuspecting witnesses incrementally down the path of minor admissions, one by one, and then pull the evidentiary rug out from under them. I'd fallen for this method, certainly, some years ago. But not since I started law school.

"Sweetheart? Is there something you're getting at here? Martha's only doing her job." I say it, I can't help it. Even though I don't want to fight. "Like you do. But you're being kind of nasty."

"Nasty." He repeats my word, savoring it. "Is there something you'd like to tell me, Rachel?"

The TV is a blur, the announcers' chit-chatty conversation mudded into a babbling underscore.

I stay silent. The only responses I can think of would make this situation worse.

"I called your office." Jack barely waits a beat before he goes on. "That receptionist? Leon? Told me you were at Alden & Harlow. With Gardiner. And you were . . ." He clears his throat. "'Celebrating,' I believe, was the word Leon used."

I silently curse Leon, Mr. Passive-Aggressive. But now I understand why Jack's angry. He's picturing some kind of wine-soaked BFF'ing between Gardiner and me. As if that would ever happen. "It was all of us, honey, *all* her interns. Did Leon tell you *that*? Obviously not. And celebrating? Yeah, exactly. Because of the arrest. It's a tradition."

Jack raises an eyebrow. "They celebrate? They call it that?"

"Yeah." I take a sip of wine. "So I'm told."

"After an arrest."

"Yeah," I say again. I'm irritable and confused and, mostly, feeling guilty. And, as seems to be my constant state of being these days, trying to decide whose side I'm on. If one's job is to assess the evidence, track down the bad guy, and hold him accountable before our system of justice, then yeah. That side *would* celebrate. They'd say it was another killer off the street. And that's a bad thing? Although I see how it could be.

"I know it's the other side of your personal legal equation," I say. "But the fact that there are two sides is why it works. And I'm *learning* about the other side. It's my responsibility. It's my *assignment*."

"And you're assigned to celebrate the confinement of a person who's innocent until proven guilty." Jack nods, as if this illustrates a significant paradox. "That's pitiful."

"What's your goal, here, honey?" I really want to know. "To make me feel bad? For some dumb tradition? I know you're angry with me for not letting you know where I was, and, yes, I know, I might have been hit by a bus or something, and you worried. I love you for that."

He hadn't said anything about being hit by a bus, hadn't even said he was worried, but I'll give him credit for the unstated concern. That's got to be why he called the office.

He's staring at the screen now, silently, which proves it.

"Come on, Jack." I prod his shin, gently, with one toe. "You celebrate when you get someone off who you know is guilty. When you *know* they did it. It's the same thing. From the other point of view."

"Is it?" Jack points the remote through me, snaps off the television. He stands so quickly I'm forced to take two steps backward, almost sloshing wine on my white T-shirt.

"When people get a fair shake, when some power-crazed DA can't prove their case? You better believe I'll celebrate," Jack says. "That's why we do what we do. *We* stand *up* for the little guy. But that woman is teaching you how she can push him down. Which side are you on?"

"But you *know* which."

"Rachel? Honey?" Jack punches the ball game back on and eases into his chair, crossing his legs and leaning back. He looks at the screen, not at me. "Be careful what you choose."

BEFORE

My coat is there where I left it on the Comm room rack, but I don't move to grab it. I stand, motionless, my hand poised midair. Listening as hard as I can. I remember in high school, before cell phones and texting, we had these things called truth books. We used old-fashioned spiral-on-the-top notebooks with a red line down the center of the page. Each page had a heading, like "Best Dressed" or "Most Popular" or "Weirdest" and you were supposed to fill in your votes, page by page, with a person's name. Then pass it on to the next person. The truth books, brutally vicious, were expressly forbidden, but that was part of the attraction. The cool kids would pass them around surreptitiously, between classes, trying to stay under Principal Gutierrez's radar.

What I felt now, knowing if I stayed still and silent I would hear what Logan Concannon was saying about me, was exactly what I'd felt that day a truth book got handed to me. My name would be in it, I feared, listed by someone on the page that sought the geekiest sophomore or teacher's pet. I knew I could simply hand the book off to someone else without looking inside. Or I could take it home and read each and every venomous or flattering entry, assessing and comparing and knowing, with each turn of the page, my name might show up. Biggest nerd, biggest dork. Biggest loser.

I'd stood there in the beige-brick hallway under a blue-and-gold banner for the Bethesda Barons, in my almost-right Jordache jeans and almost-right platform wedges and my completely wrong butterfly-clipped hair. Staring at the cover of the notebook I'd found tucked in the slats of my locker. Trying to decide what to do. It was two minutes before the bell. I could trash it. Or pass it on.

But I wanted to look inside. Even better, take it home. Hide in my bedroom, then open the book and, channeling my inner masochist, devour every page. Revel in the nasty words that were certain to be there about me, proof of my misfit status.

I had to see it. I needed to. As I'd mustered the courage to open it, the contraband notebook was snatched from my hands.

"I'm surprised at you, Rachel." Principal Gutierrez, in his usual knit tie and droopy suit, sallow-faced in the hallways' fluorescent glare, had never looked at me like that. Disappointed. Judgmental. "Handing around these hurtful, bullying things."

"But it's not—" I'd tried to defend myself. "Not mine. Someone gave it to me."

"I see."

His tone telegraphed that what he "saw" was that he thought I was lying.

"But you knew what it was, didn't you?" the principal went on. "And yet, you accepted it. Who gave it to you, Rachel? Who? Or was it yours to begin with?"

I'd always looked up to Mr. Gutierrez, respected him. I'd always been the best of students—prompt, reliable, diligent. But did it matter, at that moment, what the truth was? It clearly did not.

"What do *you* think?" The voice, Logan's, from the darkness in the adjacent office, brought me back from Bethesda High.

I'd learned my lesson in that locker-lined hallway. People believe what they want to believe. And information is power. Now, all those years later, I lowered my hand, left my coat behind, and took one silent step closer to Logan's door. Then another. I'd know when the phone conversation was over—I hadn't heard anyone else's voice, so I figured that's what it had to be—and by the time she got to the bye in goodbye, I'd be back at the office front door and make an innocently noisy reentrance.

"If Nina finds out, she'll go ballistic, you know that," Logan was saying. I heard what sounded like a cabinet slamming shut, or a closet door. "Not to mention the damn media."

My heart was . . . I don't even know what it was doing. Pounding didn't seem intense enough. It would be better for me, I knew it, to leave soundlessly and pretend this whole thing never happened. But problem was, it *had* happened, was *happening,* and pretending it wasn't merely delayed the inevitable. Whatever the inevitable was.

Rachel. Nina. Ballistic. Media. There was no combination of those words that could lead anywhere benign.

"Fired? That's up to you." I could hear the end-of-conversation tone in Logan's voice. She'd turned over the decision about whatever it was to someone else. And only one person had more authority than she did. "Okay, then. Fine."

CHAPTER **TEN**

I shouldn't be thinking about my own problems. I know that. But as I take my seat at the counsel table for Jeffrey Baltrim's bail hearing, I'm not savoring my first courtroom moment as an almost-lawyer. I'm wondering if my marriage will survive my summer job. Jack's "Be careful what you choose" crack last night had been so intentionally hurtful that I'd gasped after he said it, almost in physical pain. Then Jack did the last thing I'd expected. He'd started laughing.

"Kidding," he'd said. "Sweetheart, I'm *kidding.*"

Kidding again. I'd tried to be a good sport about it, even though to me it hadn't sounded one bit like kidding. But Jack, persuasively conciliatory, went on to insist he'd understood about the so-called celebration and the lateness. Even the wine. Even "my relationship" with "that manipulative" Martha Gardiner. And, as he drew me onto his lap, he admitted he'd simply been worried about me. When he hadn't heard from me, he'd feared the worst, that I was in a car accident or some disaster.

"Forgive me, honey," he'd whispered, his breath in my ear. He'd smoothed back my hair, the way he always does. I felt his chest rise and fall, so familiar and—almost—reassuring. "I know I'm not funny. I'm incredibly sorry. But if something happened to you, Rach, I'd never be happy again."

So all in all, I'd spent yesterday morning with a SWAT team, a butterfly-chasing little boy, and a murder suspect. The afternoon with a triumphant prosecutor. And the night with a darling but unpredictable husband. This morning Jack had sent me off with a sweetly promising kiss. "Knock 'em dead, kiddo," he'd said.

So, except for my emotional whiplash, I guess everything is fine. Like yesterday morning at the office, today I was the first one to arrive at Newton District Court. The court officer, a battleship in a blue uniform, had unlocked the door to courtroom A when I showed him my Harvard ID.

"One of Gardiner's new crop of interns, huh? Rachel?" He'd handed me back the laminated card, then pointed to the plastic name badge on his broad chest. "I'm Morris. Good luck to ya. You'll need it."

Everybody's kidding these days, I'd thought. But no one is funny. Maybe it's me. I pull a yellow legal pad and two pens from my briefcase, and stash the case under the table. I hope the rest of my internship is less complicated.

The Middlesex County courthouse for Newton is mid-century brick on the outside and pure movie set on the inside. Gutted and renovated a few years ago, the resulting new interior looks like someone's cost-cutting idea of intimidating. Elaborate velvet curtains, scrolled woodwork moldings, and imposing chandeliers hanging from high ceilings. The audience sits on churchlike wooden pews, designed, it looks like, to keep people uncomfortable. The place doesn't need to be inviting, I suppose, since many people who come here are hoping to leave as fast as they can. Especially the defendants.

I hear the courtroom door open.

"Good morning, ma'am," Morris is saying. "Your intern's already here. Your guy's here too, stashed in the basement. He's not a happy camper."

"They never are, Morris, they never are," Martha Gardiner says. "And he'll be even less happy when this hearing's over."

Gardiner almost smiles, almost, when she sees me at the table. The "basement" Morris referred to is two flights of stairs beneath us, the belowground holding cells. I imagine they're grim. Jeff Baltrim will be escorted into the bright lights of the courtroom by way of a glass-encased stairway, and he'll face the music sitting by his attorney at the defense-counsel table. I know Jack's gotten many a client released on bail at these hearings. But it's rare in a murder case.

"Ready for this, Ms. North? Your first bail hearing? Or not, correct? Not that there'll be bail." Gardiner, in icy green silk today, waves me to my chair, then clicks open her hard-sided leather briefcase. A shiny gold rectangle under the clasp is monogrammed with her initials. Inside it is a stack of manila folders. Gardiner selects the one on top. It has a handwritten label: *Baltrim, Jeffrey P.—Murder.*

Before I can parse what she meant by "or not," the courtroom door opens again, this time with a murmur of voices. A scrabble-haired twenty-something with a pen behind his ear enters, followed by a young woman with a chunky metal tripod over one shoulder and lugging a video camera, then an elegantly suited woman carrying a bulging tote bag. I recognize Clea Rourke, the reporter who'd mimed *You owe me* to Gardiner at the Tassie Lyle crime scene Wednesday. The tripod thuds onto the carpeted floor, then the photographer clicks her camera into place.

Gardiner gives them a quick appraising look, then shoots me a covert thumbs-up. "Coverage," she whispers. "One camera, but Clea's pool reporter. So every station will get this." She opens the file and pages through the records, tracing down each document with a forefinger.

I know what Jack would say about "coverage." Jack would say *Screw 'em. Every damn reporter buys the DA party line.* Plus, the "evidence" Gardiner will present in court is public, and the most damning parts we have, so far, will be described to the judge in the most lurid detail possible. And then reported, by people like Clea, as gospel. The defense attorney, whoever that'll be, will say only "not guilty." The Cleas will dutifully report that, too. As if anyone believes "not guilty" could possibly be true.

It's five till ten. Court stars at ten. The courtroom is almost full now. A low whisper from the audience—press and spectators and lawyers and, probably, family members of defendants to come—accentuates the solemnity and the stakes of this morning's proceedings.

Because of the way our discussion devolved last night, I didn't mention this morning's assignment to Jack. I'll tell him when I get home. Morris, now stationed at a narrow desk by the defendant's dock, is looking at his chunky watch. A red light flashes on his desk landline. He picks up the receiver.

"Here we go," Gardiner says.

Morris hangs up the phone. The light changes in the glassed-in basement stairway. The audience chatter silences. The court clerk, a messy-haired woman in a bagging dark blue suit, steps behind the desk that's positioned beneath the judge's bench and places a stack of overstuffed accordion files in front of her. I hear the click and swish of the courtroom door opening behind us again. The almost-late arrival coughs. The cough sounds familiar.

I turn to look.

Jack.

CHAPTER ELEVEN

Jack, in full business suit and the yellow paisley tie I gave him for his birthday, slides into the courtroom's front pew but doesn't sit down. He holds my eye for only a fraction of a second. Too briefly for me to gauge his demeanor, long enough for my jaw to hit the floor. Before I can telegraph my surprise, or maybe annoyance or even anger, the courtroom door creaks open once again and he turns away. Now we're both looking at the newcomer. The context is so alien it takes my brain a beat to catch up.

The woman—I struggle to retrieve her name, Linda, Lisa, something like that but weirder—glances at Jack, maybe because he's the only one standing. As he sits, Lizann, that's it, Lizann Wallace, opens the gate of the not-quite-waist-high mahogany bar between the audience and the counsel tables. She walks to the defense table, sleekly slim with severely close-cropped hair, elegant in a dark suit and silver hoop earrings. She and Gardiner almost acknowledge each other.

Wallace is about to put her black canvas briefcase on the table when she stops. I see her back straighten, and she twists her head around to look not at Gardiner, but at me. "Aren't you—?"

"Co-urt!" the clerk calls out. She stands behind her file-crowded desk, glasses hanging on a silver chain around her neck. "All rise for the Honorable Judge Daneet Harabhati. Court is now in session."

"Yeah," I answer Lizann Wallace, soundlessly. The judge, a black-robed prima ballerina with slicked-back hair, scarlet lipstick, and a puff of white scarf tucked around her neck, is mounting the steps to her bench. Lizann Wallace and I will have to catch up later. Like maybe never. I'm not quite sure what I'd say to her.

"Good morning." The judge acknowledges Wallace, then Gardiner, then me. Then she smiles toward the audience, polite, but aloof.

As Wallace quickly sits, zipping open her briefcase, I risk a glance at Gardiner to see how she's reacting to the woman who's clearly going to represent Jeff Baltrim. Lizann Wallace used to be an associate in Martha Gardiner's office. She was once a hard-nosed prosecutor. Now, apparently, she's a defense attorney. And, since she's sitting at the defense counsel table, she must be on the murder list.

I turn, almost without thinking, to confirm with Jack. *Isn't that . . . ?*

Jack, sitting now between two lawyer-looking women, is looking right at me. Like he was waiting to see if I'd make the connection. He nods and almost looks amused. Then, with one directorial swirl of a forefinger, my husband signals me to turn around and face the front.

The court clerk is standing, a file folder now open in her hands. "In the matter of *Commonwealth v. Jeffrey Paul Baltrim,*" she reads. "Now on for arraignment and bail consideration. . . ."

Lizann Wallace knows her previous employer's mind-set. She knows her history. Her tactics. Her weaknesses. Her secrets.

Gardiner also knows Wallace's. This is about to be quite the chess game.

It—justice, I suppose, or at least the courtroom proceeding—moves quickly as the clerk recites her boilerplate. Jeffrey Baltrim, still in his Oregano Brothers T-shirt, his face drawn and dark hair disheveled, takes the final steps up the glassed-in staircase. As he enters the courtroom, flanked by two uniformed tanks, I see his hands are cuffed and his running shoes have no laces. Each of Baltrim's hulking escorts has a

paw clamped on their prisoner's biceps, and their charge seems diminished, a shadow without substance, half the size I remember. As they
release him, Lizann Wallace scowls at the officers. She places a supportive hand on Baltrim's shoulder and guides her client to the chair beside
her. He hesitates, then turns to look behind him, as if he's searching the
courtroom.

Baltrim finally sits. His body, off balance, lands in the unpadded wood
chair with an audible thud. Lizann Wallace leans closer to him, maybe
whispering, her back to me and Gardiner. Baltrim peers over his lawyer's
stylish shoulder, catches me looking at him.

I'm so embarrassed—or some emotion like that—that I have to look
away. I feel terrible. Guilty. Baltrim's obviously frightened and bewildered, a stranger in a strange land. What if I were in that position?

"Defendant will rise," the clerk intones. Baltrim does, head hanging.
His lawyer gets up at the exact moment he does, standing almost
shoulder-to-shoulder, as if an invisible bond connects them. I guess it
does.

The clerk reads the complaint out loud, a chillingly brief legal pro-
nouncement that tells the world the Commonwealth of Massachusetts
thinks it has enough evidence to prove Jeffrey Paul Baltrim, with malice aforethought, did murder Tassandra Lyle in Middlesex County in
violation of Massachusetts General Law Chapter 265, Section 1.

I can't see Baltrim's face, because at this moment he's using both
hands to cover it. Wallace, with a brief touch, signals him to lower them.
Gardiner, sitting beside me, is sketching stair steps on her legal pad.

"How do you plead?" the clerk asks.

Baltrim's shoulders rise and fall. That pizza T-shirt is such an indict-
ment.

"Not guilty," he says.

"Be seated," the clerk says.

Behind her, the judge is turning pages in a black binder. "Counsel?"
The judge doesn't look up from reading as she speaks into the microphone on her desk.

Gardiner stands. Fingertips on the table, chin high. "Your Honor," she says, "I'll be brief. Tassandra Lyle was a second-shift nurse at Boston Medical Center. She'd arrived home late at night, where she lived by herself, and ordered a pizza. Mr. Baltrim was the last person to see her alive, because he delivered that pizza to her home. Upon further investigation, we found Mr. Baltrim was previously a patient of Ms. Lyle's at Boston Med and had later entered into a personal relationship with her. We will show that Mr. Baltrim coerced Ms. Lyle into procuring painkillers, opiates, from the hospital—she'd apparently thought they were for him, and against her better judgment and blinded by her affection, she agreed."

I hear Baltrim react, a strangled gasp. The judge glares at him. Wallace clamps a hand on her client's forearm.

Gardiner ignores the drama. "But eventually Ms. Lyle learned the drugs were merchandise for Mr. Baltrim's real job. He not only delivers pizza. He delivers death. Death by means of illegal drugs. When Ms. Lyle refused to participate any further, he delivered death to her as well. She was a woman deeply in love. But a woman who refused to be led further down a path of—"

"Your Honor?" Lizann Wallace stands. "There is no jury here."

Gardiner holds up a palm. She turns to Wallace and for a fraction of a second smiles at her. The defense attorney does not smile back.

"Quite so," Gardiner says. "But there soon will be. Your Honor, you have the complaint and the police reports. We ask that this defendant be held without bail."

She sits. Slashes three quick lines to create one more step. Her stairs are going up.

Lizann Wallace rises. She takes a moment, holding the room. Then, voice confident, she cites Baltrim's spotless job performance, the lease on his rented house, his nonexistent criminal record.

"He is not a danger, Your Honor," Wallace argues. "This recitation of fantasy is solely to inflame potential jurors. Ms. Gardiner has charged ahead, with her unbridled zeal and infinite power, and arrested a person who is demonstrably innocent."

"Your Honor," Gardiner begins.

"Move for *bail,* Your Honor." Wallace fails to keep the exasperation out of her voice. "It only seems prudent that we discuss—"

"Denied," the judge says.

The courtroom behind us rustles and murmurs, sixty or so people shifting in their uncomfortable seats at the same time, whispering their assessments. Are they relieved? Or disappointed? Or enraged?

As the guards take Baltrim away, I can't resist watching Gardiner. Analyzing what she might be thinking. How quickly a life is changed. How quickly freedom is lost. No matter what Lizann Wallace argued, Gardiner had only to say a few sentences, and now Jeffrey Baltrim's face will be all over the news as an accused murderer, and his days will be spent in jail. Even if he's eventually acquitted, people will wonder *What actually happened?* Friends will vanish, jobs disappear, hopes evaporate.

By the time of the actual trial, if there is one, I'll be back in law school and probably never see Jeff Baltrim again. His life intersected mine only by the randomness of the universe. If he killed his hospital girlfriend, if they were selling drugs together and she balked and he killed her—that was his decision. Martha Gardiner will accumulate the evidence to prove his guilt and send him away for good. Issue, rules, analysis, conclusion. I'll watch exactly how she does it.

"Co-urt!" the clerk says again.

The judge rises, so do we all. With one last look in our direction, her black robe disappears behind a closing door. Another triumph for justice, she must be thinking. No more dangerous murderers will have been set free to further prey on society. It must be easier for her, in a way, to keep people locked up. If she's wrong, only the defendant is harmed. "Only" the defendant.

I sneak a look toward Jack. His seat is empty. He's gone.

CHAPTER **TWELVE**

"We need to discuss this case," Martha Gardiner says as we walk side by side down the front steps of the courthouse. "How about over lunch? I saw your husband in court, by the way. What's his problem? Worried you'll screw up?"

The just-past-noontime sun blasts, the traffic on Washington Street relentlessly chaotic and impatient. Martha's aiming a key fob at her shiny gray Avalon. It's parked in a commercial-vehicles-only space, immune from ticketing by the pink DA's office placard on the dashboard. I hear the *beep* and *click* as the car doors unlock.

She's not looking at me, so she doesn't see my expression when she mentions my husband. Or lunch. As if those were things a boss typically says to an employee.

"Lunch?" I repeat. Easier than facing the Jack thing. *Was* he checking up on me? It's not even one in the afternoon. But I'm starving. And maybe Martha wants to get to know me. Whatever the purpose, lunch is a good idea.

"Martha!" A voice from behind us. "Can you wait a second?" Clea Rourke, logo microphone in hand and now wearing flat shoes, is trotting down the courtroom steps, her photographer hustling to catch up. The photographer, camera balanced on her shoulder, plants herself in front of Gardiner and aims her lens. Rourke keeps the mic down at her side. "Got time for a few questions?

"Ms. Rourke?" Gardiner clicks the car key again. "You received the news release. You heard what I said in court. I can't tell you any more than that."

I step to one side, trying to find a place on the sidewalk that's out of the camera shot and out of the cross fire. Two forty-something men, paunchy in short-sleeved shirts and wraparound sunglasses, plod down the courthouse steps, pointing to the camera. One yells, "Hey, Clea! Let's do lunch!"

I see her roll her eyes, though the men can't. She turns, with a high-wattage on-the-air-smile, and grants her fans a finger-fluttering wave. "Next time!" she says.

"Sorry about that." Rourke adjusts her fitted jacket, then speaks into her mic, her demeanor professional again.

"Got your man, apparently, Ms. Gardiner," she begins. "But here's my question. How do you know your suspect is a drug dealer?"

"That's under investigation, Ms. Rourke."

Gardiner starts to turn away, but Rourke persists, the silver Channel 3 mic logo flashing in the sunlight. "What was the cause of death?"

"Under investigation," Gardiner says.

As I listen, I'm analyzing how each of them is playing this, the tactics they use to get what they want. I also wish I knew the answers to Clea's questions.

"Come on, Martha. Give me something." Rourke has lowered her mic, and her voice has a cajoling edge. "How do you know *why* he killed her?"

Again, things I wish I knew. Baltrim certainly had the opportunity to kill her. I've learned in class that Gardiner doesn't have to prove why.

Problem is, and it's one of the things that drives Jack nuts, sometimes jurors will concoct a story, a fiction to match the prosecution's facts. And then, based on their fabrication, they'll vote to convict. When Jack first complained to me about that, I'd pretended to be outraged.

The afternoon sun is relentless. My feet are clammy in my black heels. I see a trickle of sweat roll down the photographer's cheek. Rourke and Gardiner, however, must possess their own personal air-conditioning.

"Attorney Lizann Wallace is representing Mr. Baltrim," Rourke goes on. "How do you feel about your now-adversarial situation? She once worked for you, right?"

"I have nothing more for you, Clea." Gardiner's sleek hair is perfectly in place, the square shoulders of her suit jacket unwrinkled. "Understood?"

"I understand that I'm gonna keep calling you about it, Martha. That's how we roll, right?" The reporter smiles at her, pretend-threatening, then waves the mic in my direction. "This your new intern?" She holds out her other hand toward me. "I'm Clea Rourke. Channel 3. Call me Clea. In fact, call me. Especially if there's ever anything—"

Gardiner interrupts. "Clea? This is Rachel North."

"Nice to mee—" She begins. Then she stops.

Watching her face change, I deeply wish I could read her mind. I know I'm paranoid, suspicious, gun-shy, all of the above.

I shake her hand. "Nice to see you, too, Clea." And that might even be true.

"Yeah." She draws out the word. Tucks the mic under her arm. Searches the cloudless spring sky for a brief moment as if she were trying to read what's written there, then looks back at me. "It seems like—never mind."

Exactly what is she trying to remember? I turn to Gardiner, hoping she'll extricate me. Instead, she's standing, arms crossed over her chest, as if she's waiting for an amusing punch line.

A silent message seems to travel between her and Clea. And then it's gone.

"Hey, yo. Clea? We done?" The photographer, her blue work shirt now damp and clinging, hauls the camera from her shoulder and drops it to her side like an electronic handbag.

"For now," Clea says.

Before I can worry about what that means, Martha has pivoted and headed for the car. I have to follow.

"How about Salamanca?" She opens the driver's side of the car, tosses her briefcase into the pristine backseat. "You know that restaurant? By the river. A pal owns it, and I always bring all my interns there after a win."

"You always . . . ?" Is all I can think of to say. She's apparently not worried about Clea's veiled threat. *For now.* Should *I* be?

Gardiner's already buckling herself in. "We'll get more done in an hour by ourselves than we'd ever manage at the office with those incessant interruptions."

Now she's on the phone, texting, interrupting herself. Ignoring me. *Fine.* I only work here. I open the back door, toss my briefcase into the backseat. It slips on the sleek upholstery and plops onto the floor. Lunch it is.

But I keep fretting about Clea Rourke's reaction outside the courthouse. Something in that woman's brain had obviously clicked about me. What, though? As I open the passenger-side door, I'm thinking about the lives I've touched. The harm I've done.

Like poor Jonah. His little world, backpacks and butterflies and an unfortunate "uncle," is probably ruined. By us. By me. I'm profoundly distracted by this, how the actions of one person entwine with another's, by choice or by chance, and each is forced to deal with the results. "That's life," my father would declare. "Each event is part of a bigger story, but we don't always know what it is." I never understood that, not until now.

I settle into the black leather front seat, pull the seat belt across my chest. Gardiner's still texting. The district attorney's office handles thousands of cases a year. If prosecutors sunk into existential despair over each one, none of them would get out of bed in the morning.

They move on. And I will, too. Back to law school and the rest of my life. Ten years from now, will I wonder what happened to Jeffrey Baltrim?

Trying to calculate how many lives will be forever altered after today's session, I turn, taking one last look at the courthouse facade.

There's a lone figure at the top of the courthouse steps. Wearing a khaki suit and yellow tie.

Jack.

BEFORE

It might have been the good news. It might have been that the universe, broadcasting into my kitchen by way of Clea Rourke, had come to my rescue. The red-haired anchor was using TV phrases like "Snowmageddon Tuesday" as she talked over pictures of white-out squalls in Newton and a slush-covered Mass Turnpike. Since I walked to work, traffic jams were no problem for me.

I took a bite of almost-not-stale toast, the crumbles falling into the folds of my bathrobe. I brushed them onto the tiled floor as I contemplated another reality. What if Logan Concannon hadn't even been talking about me? Eavesdropped conversations are notoriously misunderstood. We used to play drunk-telephone at the dorm, I remembered, touching the faded crest on my Georgetown coffee mug. That was the whole pitfall about eavesdropping. It was unreliable.

I'd avoided Logan since she'd told me "we need to discuss" blah-blah in the coffee room yesterday. And Tom had not contacted me, not at all. But even if they were about to fire me—because his wife was jealous of us, or somehow found out about the necklace?—I still had to go to work. They didn't know what I'd heard.

"And repeating now . . ." Clea, sitting behind a space-age blue anchor desk, continues reading the prompter. ". . . the governor says it's an 'essential-travel only' situation. All state government employees, except those who have been designated indispensable, are requested to stay home." Clea looks down at the paper, then back into the camera, twinkling like she's revealed the secret to happiness. "Snow day folks! So . . ."

I tuned her out as I padded to the front window, yanked open the curtains. I'm living in a snow globe. Outside it was fairy-tale lovely as Beacon Hill could be, especially seeing it from a cozy inside. The gas-lamp-shaped streetlights were illuminated this time of the morning and added a muted persimmon glimmer to the pristine snow. Brownstones were white, bare-branched trees were white, the cobblestoned sidewalks, white.

The snow had granted me a reprieve. I could spend the day figuring out what to do.

My landline rang.

I stood motionless, hearing the phone jangle from the kitchen, the living room, downstairs in my bedroom. "Call from . . . private number," the caller ID announced. It was never anybody real on the landline—vinyl-siding salespeople, medical alerts, robocalls, scammy fund-raisers. "Private number," the computer-voice repeated.

"No thanks," I told it.

And then my bathrobe pocket rang.

The caller ID on my cell showed a number. A number I knew. I let it ring one more time, attempting to prove I had control of the situation.

"This is Ra—" That was as far as I got.

"Rachel." Tom Rafferty finished my sentence.

"Good morning, Senator," I said, hoping my voice did not betray me. "I saw the nonessential edict. Are we—"

"Rachel?" He interrupted my attempt at normal. "We need to talk."

I flattened my hand against the wall so my knees wouldn't collapse. The world outside had come to a halt, and now my emotions stalled to an equal standstill. I could not admit I'd overheard Logan's phone call. But maybe this wasn't about that. Tom Rafferty had given me a neck-lace, after all. A Tiffany necklace. A necklace with stars. You don't fire that person.

"It's best if we do it in private," Senator Rafferty went on. "And I was hoping to discuss it in the office today. So much for that idea." I heard him chuckle, which somehow felt inappropriately intimate. Or maybe not.

"Right." I paused, waiting. Then I thought—*What the hell?* I'd ask. What can they do, fire me? "What's it about? So I can prepare?"

The worst possible scenario is haunting me now. What if Nina found out about the necklace, went ballistic, and as a result, *I* was going to get fired? *I* take the fall? For Tom Rafferty? That would be—beyond unfair.

"It's delicate," he said. "The statehouse is closed, so we can't talk there. Mind if I stop by? Maybe in an hour? It won't take long."

When I was little, and when my mom was out, my dad and I would sneak-watch the old black-and-white '50s TV show *The Twilight Zone.* I was maybe six and didn't understand it, but I was riveted because I was with my dad, and by the black-and-white, and by the scary stuff. Especially the theme music. Until the day he died, Dad and I would hum that theme music to each other when we needed to communicate that something was bizarrely inexplicable. It was all I could do to stop myself from humming it now.

I had a gold-starred necklace from my boss adorning my neck. Encircling it, possessing it. He couldn't be about to fire me. He wouldn't dare.

CHAPTER THIRTEEN

Relax, Rachel, I instruct myself. Out the wide windows of Salamanca, kayakers and rafters skim the Charles River, spending a carefree day on the water. I try to remember the last time I was carefree. I can't.

"How about over there, Sal?" Martha points to a table for four in the corner.

"It's all yours, my friend, as always. As you see." The man in the starched white chef's jacket gestures across the deserted dining room, curvy padded chairs in a mini-spectrum of watery blues and greens, each linen-clothed table centered with a spray of tiny green-edged lilies in a crystal vase. He looks at me. "We're closed until dinner on Fridays. Martha knows."

Sal pulls out a chair for Gardiner, and as she sits, he waves me to the aquamarine one across from her. She flips open her briefcase and unpacks a pile of legal pads and three-ring binders. Moving aside the pepper grinder and the lilies, she lays the paperwork out in a grid, appropriating all the empty space on the tabletop.

Sal is still hovering. "The usual?" he asks.

Martha nods. And Sal trots away.

"Alone at last," Gardiner says. "Now. Let me organize this so we can assess it." She pauses, looks at me with a smile. "And you should call me Martha."

What's she doing? This is scaring me, her cutting me out of the intern herd for an afternoon tête-á-tête. But maybe I'm paranoid. Maybe this is the best thing that's happened. I'd planned to get close to her. And now "call me Martha" is making that easy.

What the hell was Jack doing at the courthouse? He saw me with Clea. And then in Martha's car. But I was exactly where I was supposed to be. He wasn't.

Outside, the Charles River glistens in the afternoon sun. A fraternity of mallards, like aquatic entertainment, dives and splashes, then all turning at exactly the same time and at exactly the same speed, glide past us to their next stop. I wonder if these are the same ducks Jack and I see on our lake. I wonder where Jack is. If I could get one moment alone, I'd text him. My phone, nestled in my jacket pocket, is set on vibrate. But it stays silent.

"Okay. Police reports, Baltrim's record, such as it is, employment histories." Martha points to one black binder, then lays another one next to it. "Police reports, crime-scene evidence. Interviews with Lyle's hospital colleagues, Facebook-page screen grabs, a few Instagram postings." She looks at me, all business. "You do Instagram?"

"No," I say. "But I could—"

"Okay, no need, I'll put Nick on that," she says. "Moving along. Phillip Ong and CJ, the crime tech, are expediting the DNA evidence—God knows how long that'll take. Murder cases don't always proceed as quickly as we'd like, as you may be aware. Questions, Rachel?"

As I'm wondering what she means, Sal appears table-side balancing a silver tray holding two sweating ice-filled glasses. Beside them are two turkey sandwiches, cut on the diagonal, pale-green lettuce fluttering out of the edges of the whole-wheat toast.

"*Buon appetito*," Sal says. He chooses one of the glasses. "Lemonade. Ms. North, this one is yours."

"Rachel." Martha takes a sip of lemonade, puts down her glass, and looks at me. Sal has disappeared. "Listen, I didn't quite tell you the truth. I don't bring all my interns here for lunch."

"But wh—"

"I'm sorry." She puts up both palms, stopping me. "But I simply . . ."

She looks flustered. That's a new one. Though I am utterly baffled, I keep quiet.

"I see something in you, you know? A potential. But—"

"But?" Potential is good. "But" is not good.

Martha presses her fingertips to her lips, almost sighs. "Look. It's your husband."

My heart flares. "Is something wrong? About Jack?"

"I'm not handling this well," she says, shaking her head a fraction. Her sleek hair swings over one cheek, and she swipes it away. "No, no, certainly not. But you've hitched your wagon to him, haven't you, Rachel? Harvard, and his law firm, his status in the defense bar?"

"Well, no. Not really." I have to stand up for myself here. "I worked for the state senate—"

"You know I'm aware of that."

"And then got into law school on my own."

"*After* you met Jack. And married him. Funny how you met, isn't it?"

"Well, I suppose . . ." I begin.

"And come to think about it, you know what else is so odd?" She keeps talking. "I've known your husband longer than you have. Worked with him longer. Heard about more of his cases. From the inside."

"I suppose so." I look at my lemonade, bits of yellow pulp drifting downward.

Martha takes a bite of her turkey sandwich, but I'm not hungry anymore.

"Martha? What's this about?"

"I had a rough road." She leans forward, conspiratorial. "Getting where I am. And I did it—despite being a woman. I'm willing to bet you understand exactly how hard that is. As you reminded me, you worked on Beacon Hill. Wasn't there a lot of "—she rolls her eyes—"good old boys' club? Treating women like possessions or objects or stenographers? And certain women *using* men to get what they wanted? I know I sound second-wave, but good lord, Rachel, we need to get past that."

"Yeah, it was pretty bad," I venture. "But I managed."

"I guess you did," she said. "But you got out of one men's club and into another. Now your protector is Jack Kirkland. And Rachel? I assume you're planning to go into business with him. Maybe he's told you he'll make you a partner?"

I open my mouth to answer, but Martha continues, shaking her head.

"Don't be stupid, Rachel. If he takes a professional hit, if he—you know how defense attorneys are—if he gets disciplined, or even disbarred, you think you're going to get a pass?"

"What are you talking about, Martha? What do you mean, I 'know how defense attorneys are'?" I scan the room. We're entirely alone. "Is Jack in trouble?"

"Where do you think you'll wind up? If your husband's law practice, such as it is, crashes? And you were little wifey? Do you think people will give you credit for *anything* on your own? I know it sounds harsh, Rachel. But that's why I'm telling you. Straight talk. Succeeding doesn't mean using your husband to get to the top. But that's what it looks like. Like he's your meal ticket. No matter how good a lawyer you'd turn out to be."

"Martha." My voice goes a little louder than it maybe should. I lower my volume. But I can't lower my concern. "Is something going on? Is *that* why we're here?"

But she'd never be able to divulge that. Unless she can. "You're not . . . prosecuting Jack?"

"Oh! No. Don't misunderstand. Not at the moment." She touches one fingertip to her lips, then takes it away. Leans forward with a half smile. "Unless there's something you think I should know?"

"*What?*" I think about getting up, walking away. Jack was so right.

This woman is a spider. I need to escape from her web while the getting's good. "Is *that* why you—?

"Kidding, Rachel." Martha waves me off, then extracts the lettuce from her sandwich with two fingers and deposits it on the edge of her bright-blue plate. "Sort of kidding. But in all seriousness. This is about *you.* I said you had potential. That's what matters."

I blink, waiting.

"I want you to understand. To be prepared. To be your own person. Not Jack's underling or his wannabe or forever his subordinate. Listen, he came to court today to make sure you didn't embarrass him. Can there be any other reason?"

I'd been wondering that, too. "If I asked, he'd probably give me one," I had to admit.

She jabs a forefinger at me. "Exactly. Men like that always have an answer for everything. Don't they? Look. I see you as you. As *Rachel.* As a tough woman who knows how to get what she wants. Without some man always telling her what to do. I like that. Women have power, Rachel, if they work together. You and I can do that this summer. You'll be on the inside. I chose you, Rachel. Despite him, I chose *you.*"

BEFORE

"Screw it," I told the mirror. My bare feet freezing on my bedroom floor, I hurried, yanking on thick black leggings and a black turtleneck sweater and black boots. Added a scarf. Took off the scarf.

When the buzzer rang, I didn't even use the intercom to confirm who it was. When I opened the door, I saw a black turtleneck, like mine, under the senator's navy peacoat. His black knit cap was coated with snow, and a bright red plaid scarf, also snow-covered, dangled from around his neck, the fringe hanging past his waist. His laced duck boots were snowy, too. I scanned his cold-flushed face for some intent, some hint of what was to come, but there was none. The remnants of outdoors, cold, harsh, unrelenting, lingered in the air around him. His demeanor was more leading man than executioner. But he was a politician. I was not fooled by his exterior.

"Senator," I said. "What can I do for you?"

"You want to talk out here?" He smiled. "Let all the heat out? Besides . . ." He yanked off one black leather glove, reached into a jacket pocket and pulled out what looked like a stack of mail, five or six pieces. Held it out to me. "You've got mail. This was in the entryway. Neither rain nor snow, it seems."

I could hear Dad humming our *Twilight Zone* theme song. We'd also watched *Candid Camera,* which right now seemed equally appropriate. Senator Rafferty was bringing me my mail? I stepped aside, let him walk past me into my little foyer. I put the letters, random and damp, on the side table. Rafferty had stuffed his gloves into his jacket pockets, and as I watched, unbuttoned his coat and stuffed his scarf into one sleeve. Held the whole thing out to me. "Where's the best place to put this?"

"Let me hang it to dry," I said, as if acting my role in a drama or farce. Hang it to dry, ha-ha. Like me. "Have a seat." Reciting my lines, I pointed him to the living room.

Had I misunderstood? Stampeded myself into—I didn't even know what? I grabbed a hanger from the front hall closet and toted his damp outerwear into the bathroom. Hung it over the shower rod. But I did overhear Logan—*Nina, ballistic*—and I knew she'd been talking to *him,* so something was going on. *Did* poor Nina know about the necklace? And I was going to take the blame? So insanely unfair.

"So. Rachel. Getting to the point." Rafferty was seated in the center of my couch. He'd taken off his boots at the door and wore thick wool socks under his jeans. "And, as I said on the phone, I had wanted to discuss it with you at the office." He cocked his head toward outside. "But weather notwithstanding, I felt—strongly—this thing couldn't wait."

Am I supposed to know which thing? I almost said it out loud. Job?

Or necklace? Instead, I tucked my hands under my thighs. Felt my shoulders tighten.

"Laying it on the table," he said. "We're having to make some changes in the staff. Logan Concannon is no longer with our office. She's leaving for, let's characterize it at this point as 'other opportunities.'"

I blinked at him, my lines being rewritten by the second. "Oh," I said.

I thought for a beat, Rafferty waiting for my reaction. My political instincts kicked in, assessing how much Logan knew, which was a lot. I rewound the overheard phone conversation in my head, trying to re-hear it, re-parse the exact words, but it was too difficult with Rafferty right there.

"Is everything okay?"

Rafferty shrugged, flipped a palm. "You know the statehouse is a re-volving door. She had to revolve right out of it."

Had to? I swiped through my mental contacts list, trying to predict the players. See where the chess pieces might be positioned. If Rafferty were the king, then Logan, certainly, had been the queen. And was now deposed. I knew who *I'd* been in the game, and stopped myself from pursuing the pawn comparison.

"So, onward." Rafferty dusted his hands, twice, as if dismissing the entire situation. Then, plopping one hand on each of his knees, he leaned forward, looked me square in the eye. "And that means, Rachel, I'll need a new chief of staff. Acting chief of staff. You've been on my team for what, three years? You know your stuff. Everyone respects you. Your reputation is beyond reproach. I can't imagine anyone more ready for the job than you are. Or more capable."

I could hear the silence in my little living room, the splat of the un-ceasing snow, nature's insulation encasing the two of us in this urban cave. Soon, outside, the sky would grow even darker as the storm increased, the roads become even more impassable. Fifteen minutes ago I was steeled for the executioner. Now I had been offered stature and influence and power. Was the necklace the precursor to that? Or was he going to take it back and offer me the job instead? To shut me up?

"The other night . . ." I couldn't help but say. "When you gave me—"

"Oh, right. Sorry about that, Rachel," he said. "As you heard, I had to run before I could explain. But my wife—Nina? Was in the car. And when we left the statehouse, I realized I had it with me, but I couldn't let her see that box. Her birthday present, you know? We were right in your neighborhood. So. I made up the envelope thing. Just got one from my briefcase. And now I'm also here to pick it up. The box."

I touched a finger to my neck, then yanked it away. It wasn't for me. The necklace, golden stars, wasn't for me. I shouldn't even know it was a necklace.

The world inside my head went white, then black, and I could hear my own heart beating. I was an idiot, a full-fledged, freaking, devastatingly humiliated idiot. I hated this man, loathed him with every cell of my humiliated soul. Who would even *put* a person in that position?

A man who loved his wife, Rachel. And wanted to surprise her and trusted an employee with a special gift. The answer was so simple.

But you, Rachel, you are living in such a freaking dream world. I could almost hear myself criticize. *Who'd be insanely dumb enough to think it was for you?*

"I have to," I began, "go downstairs to get it." I managed somehow to smile, and turn away before he could answer. Or ask me anything.

"You're in charge, Ms. Chief of Staff," he said to my back. "I'll wait for you here. We have a lot to discuss."

He'd never know. I reassured myself, a mantra, a refrain, a prayer, as I half ran, half stumbled downstairs to my bedroom. I yanked the bubble wrap from my lowest dresser drawer, I'd kept the wrapping, sentimental idiot that I am, then replaced the golden stars in the precious turquoise box, then rewrapped the whole thing, as if pristine and untouched. My face burned, my eyes brimming with sorrow and hatred and regret and humiliation.

That man had no idea, none at all, of what he'd done. To me. Of what he'd done *to me.*

I stared at myself in my mirror. A full-length portrait of a woman scorned. The bubble-wrapped box was reflected, too, backward, exactly like this entire situation. My brain swirled, sucking me down.

At that moment, I saw the mirror reflection narrow her eyes. Then the woman in the mirror smiled at me.

He doesn't know you wore it, the woman in the mirror reminded me. *No one knows, and no one* can *know.*

I tilted my head, listening, as she explained. She tilted her head, too. "So nothing's really happened," I whispered.

I'd made a mistake. An error. But no harm done. As far as Tom knew, there was nothing amiss.

I saw the reflection smile. "You win, Rachel," she told me. And she disappeared.

"Thank you," I whispered.

"I'll let you consider my proposition, Rachel, if you need to," the senator said as I handed him the box. He didn't even look at it, just tucked it into his jacket pocket. "You'd start whenever Mother Nature allows us to return to work. And with a salary increase commensurate."

Even in the strange light, the gloom of the falling snow softening every edge, I could see the hazel flecks in his eyes, the silvery beginnings around his forehead, the tips of his ears still red. I tried to separate what was real and what was my imagination. It was Logan who'd been fired, not me. Maybe it was her own future I'd heard her talking about.

So much of how we behave depends on what we decide reality is. One wrong decision means every following decision is also wrong. Until we're trapped in a dead end of our own making.

He'd felt close enough to me to entrust me with a gift for his wife. That had to be reassuring. An example of respect and comradeship. The proof that he thought of me as an equal. He'd promoted me, after all. It was a business proposition. *I* was the one ruining it all, ruining it with my juvenile crush, when Tom, the senator, was looking for an adult business relationship. But I win now. Because he'll never know

I'd taken his wife's necklace for my own. It was better this way. Much better.

Maybe this outcome proved I knew enough, and was strong enough, to grab the brass ring when it was presented.

I loved him. But I'd make myself forget about that.

CHAPTER **FOURTEEN**

I shift into reverse, wait for a few cars to pull out of the DA's office parking lot, and contemplate Martha Gardiner's lunch-table heart-to-heart. "How I spent my summer" will be working a big murder case. And being the protégé of a top-notch prosecutor. And doing valuable personal research. *I chose you,* she'd said. She believes in me. Even though Jack's pegged her as Satan in pearls, I win. I get to learn from the best.

I wonder, as I stare out the windshield, if Jack has also some scoop on our adversary, Lizann Wallace. Maybe I can get him to tell me and use some of that info to impress Martha. Like why Lizann left the DA's office, and how she got on the murder list.

I keep my foot on the brake even though all the other cars are gone. I need to stop and consider what direction I'm going.

Might Martha not be the enemy? If she sees potential in me, *for* me, and she's up-front enough to single me out, might it make sense that she's honestly trying to warn me about—something? She'd talked about women sticking together—or whatever she said—and helping each other, and maybe she was signaling something specific. "I've known your husband longer than you have," she'd said. That was no tossed-off remark.

Is she trying to protect me from Jack? Or conscript me to harm him?

I shift into park now, the parking lot deserted and silent, only a few random cars waiting in their yellow-lined spots for owners at work in the office building behind me. Car windows open, I can hear the underscore rumbling of the highway traffic behind a barrier of spindly evergreens. I cross my arms on the steering wheel and rest my chin on my hands.

Lunch. Martha. Jack.

She and I had stayed at "lunch" far past three. Sal had brought chocolate-chip cookies, tiny ones, for dessert. Martha had checked in once with Leon, then clicked off without explanation.

"Can I be honest with you?" she'd asked.

Which frightened me, because wasn't she before? But I understood it was simply an expression. "Always," I said.

"So, Jack. Your husband. Did he—show you those crime-scene photos he kept out of the security-guard case? Blood on the walls?"

"He did," I'd been relieved to say. "He doesn't keep anything from me."

Martha smiled. "I'm sure. Did he tell you how he'd filed a formal complaint against me? With the Board of Bar Overseers?"

"A complaint? Why?"

"Ask *him*, Rachel. He as much as called me a criminal. Oh, the complaint was dismissed. But not before he'd unloaded a complete load of crap. On me."

This is thin ice, but I need to defend him. "There must have been a reason."

"A reason. Oh. Most certainly." Martha raised an eyebrow. "I knew his first wife, did he tell you *that*? Helped her find a divorce attorney. Guess he didn't approve. So he took it out on me, as well as on Caroline. But. As you say. I'm sure you knew."

Jack had told me his ex Caroline was "a nag" and "a princess." Until now I'd been happy to agree. Now it sounds Neanderthal.

"Did he tell you about little Tory Makinnis?" Martha continued. "Tory—he was six—was killed by a drunk driver. A driver who Jack had gotten acquitted a week before—after a police officer made a piddly time error on a traffic ticket. Have you asked how he feels about that? Tory's mother died soon after. Her husband says it was from grief."

"Jack doesn't control the world," I'd said. "He makes sure everyone follows the rule of law."

She'd surprised me by laughing. "The rule? Of law? Oh, my dear. Ask him about Pasco Duff. Who violated a restraining order and killed his wife with a corkscrew. Your husband convinced the jury he was insane. He's out now, by the way."

"Well, you'd have to be insane to kill someone," I'd said, wondering if that was true.

"Ask him." Martha pointed at me with a forefinger. Then shrugged. "Just so you know. You said he tells you everything. Maybe he—forgot about *those* things."

I wondered where Martha was going with this. I knew Jack hated her. I always thought it was because she's one of the few who can beat him. Maybe she hates him equally as much. Is that why we were here? So Martha could ruin his marriage by making me disloyal? That seemed— complicated. I steeled myself to ask her. She's the one who'd said she was being honest.

But then—as quickly as she'd targeted Jack, she pulled back.

"I always wanted to be on this side of the law," she'd revealed, rattling the ice cubes in her empty lemonade glass. "My father was a prosecutor. My mother was a law professor, one of the first women at Yale. So it's in my family."

"My mom was—" I began. Then stopped. Cancer's a bitch.

"I know." Martha nodded. "I'm so sorry. And you were so young. Your father was a single dad, then, after she died? Correct? That must have been a difficult childhood."

I'd skirted that, as well. "Yes, he was a lawyer, too." I told her. "Just, you know, taxes. But I first went into politics, and then . . ." No reason to go into that, either, I'd decided. Plus, it sounded like she'd back-grounded me. But makes sense she would have. I picked up another cookie instead.

"He must have taught you, then. Prosecutors have to stay vigilant." Martha stabbed her straw through the slice of lemon at the bottom of her glass. "Justice never sleeps."

"What if you're wrong, though? You charge the wrong person?"

"Then let the defense prove that to the jury," Martha said. "How of-ten do we get the 'wrong guy,' as you put it? Let me ask you, Ms. North. What's the conviction rate for our office?"

I knew that.

"Seventy percent? Or so?" I'd answered. "In thirty murders a year or so in Middlesex."

"Exactly. And do you think that's because we cheat? Or lie? Or manipulate? Or we're wrong?" She rattled her ice cubes again. "No, Rachel. It's because we work hard. We arrest the criminals. We take an oath, don't we? To be the ones who help make the world safe. It's a . . ." She took a deep breath, as if searching for words. "Powerful responsi-bility. One I take seriously."

"Does anyone ever get away with it?" Risky question. I didn't want to make her angry.

"Not if I can help it." She raised her glass as if asking for more.

Sal had appeared, silently. Not with more lemonade, but with two tiny chilled glasses filled with lemony liquid, and an ornate bottle to show us it was limoncello. "Beautiful," he said.

I wasn't sure what he was talking about, but the sun over the river was golden, and a single finger-winged hawk circled the glowing sky.

"To justice." Martha had lifted her glass. "And to us."

"Yes," I said.

Martha didn't even shift into park when she dropped me off in the DA's office parking lot a little after five. All the other spaces were empty. I opened the car door, but then, strapped in my seat belt, l turned back to her before I got out.

"Thanks for the lunch," I'd said. "And thanks for the insight. On everything."

"See you Monday," she'd said.

"Have a nice weeke—" I'd begun, but she'd already driven away.

Now I flinch as a car pulls up behind me, the driver poking me with two quick beeps of his horn. I wave across my rearview—*sorry*—shift into drive, and head toward home, brain in high gear.

Martha trusts me. Okay, that's good. Trusts me enough to make sure I know what she knows about Jack. To warn me. But there's the problem. Is that trust? Or is that her insidious way of recruiting me? Is she doing opposition research on me? Or maybe—on Jack?

Which would be hilarious. Because she has no idea I'm doing opposition research on *her*. Her confidence in me will make that even easier. Lawyers are always in battle, if they're any good. They're soldiers of the law. Whichever side they choose.

Whichever side *I* choose.

What a strange way to look at my life.

Jack's silver Audi is already in our driveway. I pull up and park beside it, and after a quick glance toward the kitchen window—is he watching me?—I touch the car's hood with a flat palm. Warm. So he hasn't been here for long. I laugh out loud at myself. It's a hot day, so my investigative techniques might not be entirely accurate.

There's nothing for him to watch, anyway. I dig for my keys and unlock the door, put my briefcase in the entryway for later.

"Hey you," I call out.

"Hey you." Jack's at the kitchen table, laptop open in front of him, cell phone in his hand.

He puts down the phone as I come toward him, and I plant a kiss on his head. He's been home long enough to change out of his court clothes and into jeans and a Red Sox T-shirt. And that reminds me. For one sweet homecoming moment, I'd forgotten the last time I'd seen him. In court.

I feel my irritation itch to the surface again.

"Anything you want to tell me?" I take two steps away, and as I say it, I can't keep the tension out of my voice. I'm picking a fight. Something I never do, except if I'm teasing or in mortal combat over the last egg roll. And that makes me even angrier. *He* picked the fight this morning in court.

"About what?" He flaps down his laptop.

"Newton District Court? Judge Harabhati's session? This morning? Ring a bell?"

"What about it?" he says. His phone pings with a text, but he ignores it. "Turned out I had to be in court anyway, so I thought I'd surprise you. I wanted to catch up with you after, but looked like you were otherwise occupied. With your new friend. Did you two have a nice day? Did you go shopping, maybe? Shoes?"

Seriously? This is exactly what Martha was talking about. Always an excuse, and then some kind of demeaning woman thing. I wish I could call him on it. But I don't want to make him angry, though I'm getting increasingly tired of being the submissive one. Martha chose *me*.

"Honey? It's a tiny bit tiresome, you know? Your attitude? It's *school,* for gosh sake. The world is not about you you you."

I turn away before he can answer. The whole thing is incredibly disturbing, and unfair, and I'm not sure what I can do to assure him that—well, assure him of what? That I'm doing this for both of us? Am I?

Maybe I'm too mad to think straight. I know I need to be careful of that.

CHAPTER **FIFTEEN**

BEFORE

Forget the speed of light. Nothing travels faster than gossip.

First this morning, one of the previously blasé statehouse security guys tipped his cap to me and even called me "ma'am," possibly for the first time in my life. A puffer-jacket-clad pack of preteens tramped past me on the 8:15 statehouse tour—and their Park Service guide made them move over to let me go by. Annabella Rigalosa, the powerful statehouse Human Resources director, saluted me with her plastic-topped Dunkin's foam cup as she hustled past me. Even though she didn't say anything out loud, she knew.

What's public knowledge moves in an instant on Beacon Hill. Secrets only take a few beats longer. Gossip is the fuel of power.

The elevator had arrived immediately, but that had to be coincidence. As the doors opened on the second floor, the corridor was empty. I turned toward my old office—then stopped. I'd have to clear it out today. Wonder who'd be taking it over? The senator—that's what I mentally call him now, even though he'd suggested I call him Tom—had instructed me to move to Logan's. The office right outside his. The gatekeeper office, the one that protected him from intruders.

I pulled open the stained-glass door, apprehensive. Politics abhors a power vacuum, so when one of us goes, someone has to take their place.

I walked more slowly than usual toward Logan's office—my office. I felt like an interloper. The statehouse was such a revolving door, like the senator said, there were probably some staff members I hadn't dealt with yet. All the chess pieces had been rearranged.

Logan's door—my door—was closed, but I could see that the light was off. I pictured her, flipping the light switch for the last time. Her lips pressed together, an armful of documents, maybe? An echoing slam of the door and a flounce down the hall. Or maybe—I stopped, trying to be compassionate. Maybe she'd been crying? Why would she be crying? Or maybe she was blissful, happy, enthusiastically off to some fabulous new job where the pay and the health insurance were better and there wasn't a job-threatening election every two years. Funny what we rely on. Funny what we'll do to change our lives.

I knocked on the door. Luckily no one was in the anteroom to laugh at my timid entrée into my new life.

No answer.

Okay, then. Here goes Rachel, the new chief of staff.

"*Acting* chief," I muttered. Apparently, there was paperwork that had to go through Director Annabella Rigalosa's Human Resources Office. Or maybe the senator was testing me.

The phone began to ring the minute I stepped across the threshold and onto the cheap beige carpet. I dropped my tote bag under the desk and, still in my coat and muffler, I picked up the receiver. My learning curve would be less a curve and more an absolute vertical.

"Rachel North," I said, sounding businesslike and confident. And as if I hadn't just arrived.

Silence.

"Hello?" I tried again. I held the receiver between my ear and shoulder, shrugging off my coat, waiting for a reply, surveying my new territory. There was nothing of Logan's left. Nothing in the bookshelves. Nothing on the chunky glass-topped wood table beneath the window. My view was one thick branch of a snow-covered tree and a hint of some statue and a sliver of what I calculated was Bowdoin Street. My desk, empty. I hung my coat over the wooden rack in the corner. Shook off my salt-stained boots, toe to heel, trying to keep my balance.

"Hel-*lo*?" As I walked in stocking feet back to my desk, I could hear someone breathing on the other end of the line and people talking in the background. Maybe a TV?

Half thinking, I pulled open the thin top desk drawer. Two unsharpened yellow pencils rattled in a narrow grooved shelf. A pad of yellow Post-its. I put the supplies on the desk. My desk.

"This is Rachel North." I tried one more time as I closed the drawer. "How can I help you?"

"Good morning," Senator Rafferty said. But not on the phone. In my doorway. Holding two Starbucks cups. He handed one across the desk to me with a gloved hand. "Milk, extra sugar," he said. "Welcome."

I hung up my desk phone, then *his* cell phone rang, and I heard laughter in the reception area, out by the coffee machine. The office was coming to life. It was unsettling to see the senator. Tom. Maybe necklace PTSD, or something. I kept trying to unremember that whole debacle. *Not* debacle.

"Thanks," I said, taking the cup. I hadn't put my shoes on yet and was happy to have my lower half hidden behind my desk. "How'd you know?"

But he was already talking on his cell. He held up his own coffee, cocked his head toward his closed office door as my desk phone rang again.

"Five minutes," he mouthed the words at me. "Sure, tomorrow," he said into his phone. "That could work."

Head spinning, I saluted him with my coffee, then put it down and picked up the ringing phone. "Rachel North," I said.

"Screw you," the voice said.

And whoever it was, definitely female, hung up.

"*Nice*," I said out loud. The call might not even have been meant for me, since disgruntled constituents were part of the deal. But I couldn't resist starting a mental list of who might have wanted to taunt me personally. Logan Concannon topped it. In fact, she was the only one on it. I'd have been angry, too, I decided. But in politics, some days you are in and some days you are out. Logan knew that. But what could she do about it?

The phone rang again, and I stared at it, apprehensive or angry, and finally grabbed it. Jammed the receiver to my cheek. "What?" I said. "Who *is* this?"

"Ah, Ms. North?" A small voice this time, a different person. "This is Danielle Zander. Dani, people call me. I'm kind of new? I've only been here a few weeks, and now I'm taking your place in Constituent Services? And wonder if I could come talk with you?"

Fabulous. Fine way to start a relationship with a new staffer, by snapping at her when I answered the phone. Danielle Zander. I wrote her name on a Post-it so I'd remember. Danielle Zander.

"Terrific." I flooded my voice with warmth. "Wonderful, Dani. Welcome. But I have to meet with the senator in a few minutes. How about at . . ." I paused. I had no idea what today's schedule would be. "Shoot me an email, and we'll set up a time today, okay? And I'll come retrieve my possessions, too. To let you get settled in."

And now it was one minute until Rafferty wanted to see me, I realized as we hung up. I dug in my tote for my shoes, took the black suede pumps out of the silky shoe bag that came with them. *What was—?* Oh. That mail the senator had delivered yesterday in the storm. I'd noticed the forgotten stack of envelopes as I was leaving this morning, grabbed it from the side table, and stashed it with my shoes. If I left the mail in the bag now, I was sure to forget about it.

I pulled it out, bills bills bills—and then something else. Even though it was bad news, I burst out laughing.

The buzz of an intercom almost made me fall off my chair. "Rach?" Tom Rafferty's voice came through the speaker on my desk. "You ready?"

I read the postcard again. SECOND REMINDER FROM THE OFFICE OF THE JURY COMMISSIONER.

NOW

"Honey? I have some bad news."

I look up from my black binders, concerned by Jack's ominous tone, and try to clear my head from the mind-numbing police jargon that reduces Tassie Lyle's murder scene to acronyms. TOD, DNA, TBD, UNK. I've been at it for hours. After reading the Sunday papers this morning, both of us resolutely ignoring our Friday-evening sparring match over my lunch with Martha, Jack took over the kitchen table with trial-prep work, so I'd commandeered the dining room.

"What? What bad news?"

"Nick Soderberg? The intern in your office?"

"Yeah? What about him? Is he okay?"

"That phone call?"

"Jack?" I stand, and a couple of police reports fall to the carpet. I haven't seen Nick since that first day at the office. According to Andrew, he's been assigned to cold cases and works in some other part of the building on those unsolved murders. I can't read Jack's expression and wonder if he's trying to figure out how to tell me something horrible about Nick. I'm increasingly aware, after being married almost six years, that Jack's bad news often has to do with his own life, not someone else's. But the words bring a chill. "*What* bad news? What happened? Who called?"

Jack puts his glasses on the top of his head, peers at me as if I've mis-understood. "Like I said. Nick Soderberg. That was him. On the phone."

I plop down in my chair, annoyed as hell. Is he *trying* to annoy me? Or is he simply annoying? Maybe it's a good thing we find this out now, before we spend every day together as law partners. Maybe, now that I'm almost a lawyer, he's realizing that he doesn't honestly see me as a partner. Maybe he doesn't think I can do it. Maybe Martha's got a point. Or maybe he's the same as he always was and it's me who's different.

In which case it might be Jack who's baffled.

"Oh, okay." I try to be pleasant, try to find common ground, try to be a partner, try not to be judgmental, try not to make him mad. "You scared me. I thought—well, I don't know. Anyway, what's up?"

"You 'have' to go to the office, Nick says. As soon as you can get there. Apparently Gardiner's calling her troops together, for whatever reason. He didn't say. And I didn't ask. None of my business." Jack puts his palms together, as if in prayer. "And forgive me, honey, but it was a while ago. I meant to tell you, but I got distracted."

If flames could explode from my head, I'm sure they would. And I don't have time to respond, either to yell at Jack or attempt to make peace. I settle for an openmouthed silence, two beats maybe, before I whirl and sprint upstairs.

I get to the office on fumes, my own fumes, and I barely remember making the drive. I'd thrown on jeans and a blazer, then slapped on makeup bit by bit at various stoplights, using the obstacles for my benefit this time. Leon greets me at the front desk with an inquisitorial look at his watch, and waves me through to the conference room. I know it's 4:00 P.M. on a Sunday. So what?

Now the corridor is empty, hallway lights off and most doors closed, but in the conference room the ceiling fluorescents are on full.

At one end of the long rectangular conference table sits Martha Gardiner, wearing a beige sweater and khakis, arms crossed over her chest. She barely glances at me as the door creaks open. Andrew DiPrado and Elijah Lansberry sit next to each other, their backs to me, legal pads in front of them. Opposite Gardiner, Nick Soderberg stands in front of an easled whiteboard, a thick black marker in one hand.

On the board, printed in black marker, is a name. *Danielle Zander.*

PART
TWO

BEFORE

CHAPTER **SIXTEEN**

JACK KIRKLAND

"Jack? Yoo-hoo. Where are you? Have you heard one thing I've said?"

Jack felt Clea's toes probe his ankle, then climb up under his pants leg. The other patrons of Gallery wouldn't notice, couldn't, since the white cloth over the restaurant's dinner table chivalrously concealed her teasing advances. He wasn't in the mood for what was apparently on her mind, not now, not even with Clea Rourke. All he cared about was that jury. The three-week murder trial had flown by some days, other times it felt like it dragged on for a lifetime. For his client, Deacon Davis, it *was* a lifetime. When this thing was over, if Jack didn't win, Deke's life would be over, too.

"And that's the hell of it," he said out loud. He swirled the cubes in his empty glass, aching for another Scotch, but it wouldn't be prudent, not on the night before the last day of testimony. *Possible* testimony. He had so much to do. Plans to make. Preparations. Homework. Being out to dinner was bordering on malpractice. But Clea had persisted. *You need to eat,* she'd coaxed, wheedled, insisted. All true, physiologically, but not in this restaurant packed with Boston's Beacon Hill big shots. A high-priced, four-star, mahogany-and-leather sanctuary in the shadow of the statehouse, Gallery was a see-and-be-seen place. Which Clea craved. And she didn't care obviously, about what *he* loved. Winning.

"Hell of *what*?" Clea sipped from her glass of red, her second.

She'd left her toes where they were, kneading his leg softly, a gentle under-the-table reminder that off-the-record could happen in more ways than one. Not that she was covering the trial—they couldn't go that far—but she knew the elements of this case. Even though she wanted to be a big-time reporter, and she was savvy enough to do it, for now she was the ratings-bait morning anchorperson. She relied on the prompter, recited whatever news they gave her to read, looked pretty, and prattled with the weather guy.

"Damn Martha Gardiner." Jack rattled his ice cubes again. Maybe the residual Macallan would melt and release some vestige of alcohol. "And that judge, too. She's a former prosecutor. Like they all are. Crap, might as well be *paid* by the DA. She's never, not freaking once, sustained one of my objections. Sure, she kept out Davis's criminal record, because she knows that'd be reversible. But Gardiner? Her blue-blood BFF—is that what you call them? Can do no wrong. And Deacon himself. He's insisting on testifying."

"He's going to testify? He has a criminal *record*?" Clea leaned forward, eyes wide, planting her elbows on the table, fingers entwined beneath her chin as if in prayer. *"Really?"*

Where was the waiter? Jack needed a check, he needed to pay, he needed to go home and figure out a way to win this thing. He remembered that old movie *The Verdict*. When some lawyer had whined "I did my best," the supposedly evil James Mason had sneered back at him. "You're not paid to do your best," Mason said. "You're paid to win." Jack always recited the line along with him. *Damn right.*

If Deacon Davis testified, swore he didn't kill Dr. Oreoso, would it help them win? Problem was, legally, Jack could not refuse to let him do it. If the client wanted to testify, the client got to testify. It was his absolute right. And if anyone ever learned Jack had twisted his arm not to, it was Jack's ass that would be in a sling. But Jack was trying to do what was best for his client. He always did.

Jack signaled, arm raised, but the waiter, a white-haired field marshal in a dinner jacket, ignored him and turned left instead. He pulled open the mahogany-and-stained-glass door Jack knew led to a plush and private party room in the back. The final notes of "Happy Birthday" and a fragment of applause escaped before the door was closed again.

"Jack?" Clea was caressing his leg again. "Please, *please* tell me. I know it's not exactly—you know, exactly fair. And the criminal-record stuff—Jack? Are you listening to me? I'll get brownie points. They'll understand that I have *sources*. This would be so *big*. For me. And Jack, he's guilty, so nothing will matter in the long run. Right?"

He hated when she did this. It was her job, he supposed. But what about *his*? Every damn thing was on the line. He tuned her out in self-defense.

"Sir? Miss Rourke? Dessert?" Their waiter strode to their table, leather-bound folder in hand, and saved Jack from a sarcastic answer. Dating a TV anchor, if "dating" was what they were doing, was a minefield. She was intelligent and she was attractive and, fine, she'd pitched some stories to her editors that made him look good. But right now, he was pretty sick of her. She could not let up. She could not let go. For one damn moment, could she not let it be about *his* life? His case? And the jury was not supposed to be watching television anyway—she should know that. They'd have to tell the judge if they did. It was too risky.

"Clee?" he said. *Please say no to dessert,* he thought. *I have to go home and work. Alone.* "I know you have to get up early."

"Yeah," she said. "Yeah. I'm working on something big now." She stopped. Twinkled at him. "Unless—are you . . . ?"

Hell no. "Yeah, no, I've got stuff to do." He turned to the waiter. "Just the check."

The door to the party room had opened again, a flash of light and a peal of laughter signaling the change. A line of partiers began to cluster out of the room, chatting and gesturing, not bothering to hide evidence of their celebration. A laughing dark-haired woman, carrying a pile of unwrapped white gift boxes, wore a silver pointy hat, the elastic snapped under her chin. A younger woman had a red ribbon draped around her neck.

Clea turned in her seat, leaned forward, squinting. "That's Senator Tom Rafferty. See? In the navy coat? Graying hair? Broad shoulders? Whoa. Someone plunked down a lot of Massachusetts taxpayer money for that birthday party. Do you see his wife? She *can't* be that little blond with the ribbon."

Clea turned back to him, questioning. When he didn't answer, she turned back. The group was now nearing their table, on their way to the front door.

"I always wanted to see her. Nina Rafferty, I mean. Wait, maybe the dark-haired woman in the birthday hat? Long wavy hair? Black coat? Right behind Rafferty, talking to him. Is that her? She *is* pretty, but I've gotta say, she doesn't look old enough."

The laughter came closer.

"Jack?" Clea leaned toward him. "What on earth is that expression on your face?"

From the moment the door opened, Jack had wished he could hide his face with his place mat or the wine list. Maybe he could duck under the table, ostensibly hunting for something, until the group went by.

Too late now. Lightning fast, his brain cataloged the possible issues and rules. He analyzed the possibilities. Came to a conclusion. He was not allowed to have any contact with her outside the courtroom.

The woman in the birthday hat, as Clea had called her, came closer. He knew exactly who she was. Juror Number Four. Rachel North. Beacon Hill staffer. The one who kept looking at her watch. He'd pegged her as a possible guilty vote, wanting to get the murder trial over with. A law-and-order hardliner. Had to be.

North paused at their table, head tilted, seeming to search for context. It took her about three seconds. "Oh," she said. She touched her silly hat. "Um."

Jack nodded. She had gray eyes, he saw.

"Rachel? You called for the car?" The man Jack knew was Senator

Tom Rafferty had caught up to her. Looked at Jack for a beat. Then at Clea. He held out a jovial hand.

"Well, well, Clea Rourke," he said. "Big fan."

Clea beamed. Jack watched her drink in the attention. Chin lifted, eyes shining. This was what she lived for. The spotlight, the glory, the access. She'd been squirreling away sources, Jack knew, always pitching herself for some investigative reporter job. Tom Rafferty would be a valuable catch.

"How was your dinner?" Clea asked, shaking his hand. "Do you have a February birthday?"

"My chief of staff does. She's—" He turned, but Rachel North had gone.

"This is Jack Kirkland," Clea said. "He's—"

"Of course. Old buddy." Rafferty nodded, interrupting. He looked at Jack's empty Scotch glass, or maybe he didn't. "Interesting."

Rafferty pulled a pair of black leather gloves from his overcoat pockets. Pointed them at Clea. "You two have a nice evening, then."

"What was that all about? Does he hate you or something?" Clea, frowning, leaned across the table, whispering as Rafferty strode away. "And I was going to give him my card, damn it."

"He doesn't hate me," Jack said. The waiter, with the check flap on a silver tray, was approaching. About time. "He's a lawyer, too. I knew him from school. Probably wonders what the hell I'm doing at Gallery, with *you,* during my murder trial."

RACHEL NORTH

Jury duty was going to kill me. When I got back from court today, I clicked on my office computer, but the glow of the screen did nothing to improve my Tuesday afternoon mood. February was gloomy and miserable. Exactly like me.

I was juggling my entire life. Doing my civic duty in court in the morning. Doing my civic duty to Senator Rafferty and the Common-wealth of Massachusetts in the afternoon. But I'd manage, like I always did, and it was all for the best. Tom—the senator—said he was proud of me. So maybe it wouldn't kill me. If the senator was happy, I could man-age anything.

Today was "motions," the judge semi-explained, so my fellow jurors and I spent most of the morning in the jury room, talking about the Red Sox and nothing. One woman, Roni Wollaskay, seemed simpatico, and even a potential campaign donor. Her husband had big money, she'd confided in me, from their furniture store. So I'd keep her close, and see where that went. It was all about Tom. Strictly professional, naturally, but my job, and my life, were always about Tom.

Plopping my tote bag under my desk, I jammed my coat on the rack, flipped off my boots, slid on my shoes, and took a deep breath. The mem-ories of last night flooded back. Those, certainly, were warm.

And I was still floating. It had been sweet of Senator Rafferty—I *had* to call him that—to throw the party for me. Only a few staffers attended, including that Dani Zander, who'd fussed over the senator like a school-girl. Nina, out of town, had sent her regrets, the senator said. Wonder if he'd given her the necklace. How she liked the golden stars. He'd pre-sented me a brass paperweight wrapped with a red ribbon, engraved with a silhouette of the statehouse. Dani had taken the ribbon and tied it around her own neck. I'd heard her giggle to Tom that now *she* was a present. Disgusting.

Now the senator's green "in office" light was off, so he was gone, though there was nothing on his schedule. "And I would know, wouldn't I?" I said out loud. He must have been grabbing lunch.

The rest of the staff seemed to be out for lunch, too.

My shoulders dropped. *Food.* I should have picked up something on the way here. For all its history and atmosphere, the statehouse had no cafeteria, only an assortment of bleak vending machines. But, hungry as I was, I refused to make another lunch out of a prefab cello-wrapped chicken sandwich and a weary apple.

"Rachel?" Dani Zander appeared in my open doorway, carrying a tablet and a white paper bag.

She'd been hired for a lower-level job, at some point, and got promoted when I did. Good for her. Last night, she'd seated herself by Tom. Or someone had. At least today she was not flaunting that stupid ribbon. I hoped she had a hangover. Serve her right.

"Sorry to bother—" she began.

"Hi, Dani. No bother. Perfect timing," I lied, forcing a smile. "What can I do for you?"

"Wasn't it so fun last night?"

I kept smiling. "*So* fun."

She took the three steps to my desk. Dressed for winter, in a black turtleneck, black tights, flat boots. Tiny black leather skirt, I couldn't help but notice. With that pixie hair, she was the blond Audrey Hepburn of Beacon Hill. Dani, smiling, offered me the white bag.

"Ham, swiss, dijon," she said. "In case you forgot to get lunch again. Whole wheat. And an iced tea. The senator told me this was your usual. My treat."

"Oh, well, no I—" I started to demur. But then, I was starving. And who was I to turn down lunch? "Fabulous," I said. I could smell the smoky ham fragrance through the bag as I accepted it, and a sharp tang of dill pickle. *The senator told her? Why were they discussing me? When?* "Next time I'll buy. Okay if I eat this now? And have a seat. Tell me how things are going."

I gestured Dani to the green damask two-person couch I'd persuaded admin to move up here from the basement storage room. It was ugly, stubby-legged, and threadbare, but it was taxpayer-thrifty and serviceable. I thought about Roni Wollaskay, the furniture juror. She'd probably have some ideas for replacing it.

"I had lunch an hour ago," Dani said. "So. I talked to Tom—"

"The senator?" I corrected her. "You mean?"

"The *senator,* sorry, this morning. He was so pleased with the party last night, and my pleasure to arrange it—while you were at jury duty.

So scary. The defendant's criminal record, you know? Deacon Davis? I saw all about that on TV this morning. But *I* know you can't talk about it."

I unwrapped the package of folded waxed paper, the thin-sliced ham spilling out of the fresh bread. "Uh-huh," I said, and licked a dab of mustard off a forefinger. Criminal record? TV? Jurors can't watch TV news. "Right. Anyway. The senator?"

"He needs to handle the water situation in Oxford." She swiped a screen on her tablet. "And they want him for a Chamber of Commerce speech, a dinner event, in Springfield. He says to tell you he wants to, it's good for the budget talks. It's an overnight, he says, tomorrow— yeah, short notice—but he says I can make the arrangements. If you agree, he says."

He says, does he? When? But then, I wasn't here half the time, so who knew what was going on. That's why I was so eager for this trial to be over. So I could regain my territory. I popped open the calendar on my computer. "Give him a meeting, half an hour, with the commissioner in Oxford. And then on to Springfield. Back whenever he decides. But let me know. What else?"

"That's it from me." She swiped a few more screens. "For now."

"You're doing okay?" I crumpled a mustardy napkin and thought about tackling the other half of the sandwich. "You were promoted right before I got snagged for jury duty, so even though I'd planned to be more available for you—"

"Sure." Dani clicked her screen to dark. Stood. "So—"

"Listen," I said, "remind me. How did you wind up here?"

"It must be in the files, Rachel. Did you lose them somehow? Should I email you another résumé?" Dani, seemingly accommodating, answered but didn't answer. "And Logan Concannon hired me. Before she, you know."

I didn't, which was also annoying. I'd asked the senator where Logan went and what happened, once, maybe twice, but he'd brushed me off. Clearly avoided the discussion, making it seem off-limits. I'd thought back to that final encounter, when Logan seemed to be baiting me about the night Rafferty brought me the . . . I felt my memories darkening my vision. It was three weeks ago, and I continued to be upset by it, even fragile. The humiliation. The narrow escape. My own raging emotions. I made myself remember my mirror-image woman and how she had calmed me. I was fine. *Fine.*

But. Logan had told me we needed to "discuss Friday night." Something like that. And then she was gone. Were those things connected?

"Yeah. I know." I smiled back at Dani, trying to look like I was telling the truth. I watched her leave the office, politely closing the door behind her, and wondered what happened to the woman who used to sit at this desk. I had to find out. Somehow.

CHAPTER **SEVENTEEN**

JACK KIRKLAND

"The jurors will think what I want them to think." Jack clicked open the two brass snaps on his briefcase, extracted two manila folders, placed them on the holding-room conference table between them. "Look. Here's your criminal record." He opened one folder, spun it so Deacon could read the printed-out black-and-white pages. Pointed with one forefinger. "Attempted robbery. Larceny under. Breaking and entering."

"But—" Deacon Davis, hollow-cheeked and swimming in a long-sleeved shirt that had fit him three weeks ago, had the look Jack had seen on so many defendants. Confused. Defeated. The perplexed demeanor of someone watching the last train pull away from the station. A train that left them in a courthouse, seated in a folding metal chair at a pitted conference table at nine on a bleak Wednesday morning. Destination possibly life in prison.

"But nothing," Jack interrupted. "You say these were screwups. Unfair. Mistakes. Miscarriages of justice. Whatever you want to call them. But there they are, buddy. And the jury will think, oh, he was a bad guy before, so it's more likely he's a bad guy now. Even when it's not true."

"But—"

"If the jury ever finds out about these convictions," Jack talked over his client, had to, "you're toast. However. If you do not give Martha

Gardiner the opportunity to open the door to your criminal history, the jury will never hear about it."

Jack assessed his client's stubborn expression, then held up both palms in pretend retreat. "You wanna do it, Deke? Testify? Your call. Gardiner's been properly notified that you might take the stand. But look . . ." Jack softened his voice, a wise coach counseling his newest player. "Don't turn that victory into a defeat because you think you can convince this jury. Let *me* do that."

"Ten minutes, sir." The conference room door had opened so quickly, the sound of the sharp knock on the wood had not quite faded. A uniformed court officer, rectangular name tag embossed SUDDETH pinned to the buttoned pocket of a too-small navy shirt, then held up ten pudgy fingers. As if to prove Suddeth knew his numbers. "Anything you need?"

"Nope. Thanks." Jack waited until the door closed again. Then waited two beats after that. Court officers were the source of all gossip, for better or worse. If Gardiner had a crew of snitches in the courthouse, this guy Suddeth might be on his way to spill Jack's strategy. Jack looked up into each corner of the room, checking for mics. Told himself he was being an idiot. Sometimes Gardiner knew things that were impossible to know.

Jack turned his attention back to his client, lowered his voice. "Juror Five likes you, the furniture-store woman. The knitting grandmother likes you. All you need is *one* of them to hold out. One 'not guilty.' One holdout."

The door opened again, this time without a knock. "Judge Saunders would like to see you," Suddeth said. "Both of you. In her chambers."

Jack stood. Tried to read Suddeth's doughy face. "Why?"

"Why?" Deacon Davis echoed.

"I just work here," the officer said.

When they arrived, Judge Saunders was in civilian clothes. Her velvet-collared black robe hung on a coat tree, arranged on a padded pink hanger. Shelves lined with green leather volumes, the Massachusetts

General Laws, covered every wall. The judge sat behind her ornate desk, wearing a purple blouse with some kind of bow at the collar, her face drawn hard in the sun piercing unforgivingly through the inch-open blinds. Jack sniffed for vodka. It was only 9:15, so maybe too early for her. He *could* almost smell his client's fear, but there was nothing he could say to comfort him. Jack was not the happiest camper himself right now.

Martha Gardiner stood, posture perfect, next to the white-and-blue Massachusetts flag. *As if posing for a damn campaign photo,* Jack thought. Her deferential associate, who'd introduced herself the first day only as "Lizann," stood a step behind her boss, carrying a stack of file folders like it was precious cargo. So Saunders had called Gardiner in first. *Women.* Wonder what the judge had told the sisterhood before Jack arrived. Wonder what they'd done as a result. Ex parte communications were outrageous. Improper. But how could Jack prove these people had even exchanged a word?

If he complained, they'd probably make it into some woman thing, like he was accusing them of forming some females-first cabal. Which they probably were, but no way to touch that hot potato.

"Good morning, all." Saunders spoke as if Gardiner hadn't been there already. "We have a situation with the jury."

RACHEL NORTH

"Anybody?" I asked the jury room in general. "Know about Momo?" Juror Anne Peretz, or Momo, she'd told them to call her, "like my grandkids do," was absent. All I got were head shakes and shrugs. I took my usual swivel chair next to Roni Wollaskay. I definitely could not afford any delays. The senator was on his way to the western part of the state, so I was relying on this afternoon to catch up. Even, I dared imagine, get ahead.

The court officers took our cell phones hostage every morning and didn't give them back until we left. All hell could be breaking loose in state government. Or in my office. I'd have no idea. "Roni? It's after nine. Strange that she's not here."

"Yeah, strange." Roni, today in pale-gray cashmere and navy suede pumps, ripped a pack of sugar into her coffee, stirred, stuck the red plastic stick into her mouth, grimaced, pulled it out dry. "But if she's not gonna be here, maybe we can all go home. Randi has some sort of nursery school crud, so she's home with the nanny. Poor baby." She took a wary sip of coffee. "Randi, I mean. Nothing more pitiful than a sick three-year-old."

"Yeah, poor baby," I said, supposing so. I always worried when someone talked about kids. Made me feel like they were curious about why *I* didn't have any, for which there was no answer other than I didn't. But I was only thirty. There was time for my life to work. "You have three children?"

"Yes, indeed," Roni said. "Rhonda, Ruthie, and Randi." She stopped. Rolled her eyes. "I know. But it was my husband's idea. His name is—" She leaned a few inches closer to me. "*Ron.* What can I tell you?"

I had to laugh, couldn't help it, and somehow that incongruous sound made me realize the magnitude of what we were doing. I'd probably never cross paths with these people otherwise, but now we were all tasked, as we said on Beacon Hill, to decide whether to send someone to prison for life. I *guessed* for life. Were any of us equipped to do that?

Roni was laughing, too, at her family's *R* names. Dabbed under her eyes with a white paper napkin. "Don't even ask me about the *dog's* name. And hey, you're an *R,* too. Maybe we're long-lost sisters."

The door to the jury room swung open.

"Did you all miss me?" Anne Peretz's voice entered before she did. She lugged a crewel-decorated knitting bag and pink leather tote, and wore a white knit cloche jammed over her gray curls. "Thank you, Grace, dear." She dismissed the court officer who'd been escorting her, then draped her coat over the last hanger in the rack as the door closed. "I'm fine now. Hello, all. Hello, Rachel."

"Are you all right?" Now we'd finally get this show on the road.

"And in all the excitement, I forgot my pills." Momo sat down, still wearing her hat. "Before they took my phone, they let me call my son to bring them here, so all's well that ends well. I hope I haven't ruined everything."

"It's not that late," I reassured her.

The jury room door opened. We all looked at court officer Kurt Suddeth, Grace O'Brien's self-important partner.

"Mrs. Wollaskay?" Suddeth stood outside the door. The randomly burned-out lightbulbs lining the narrow hallway stippled his face and his too-tight navy uniform with unnatural darkness. "I'm afraid we need to talk with you."

"Afraid? *Me?*" Roni stood, gripping my arm with her hand. "Is there an emergency? Are my kids okay?"

"Can you come with me, please?" Suddeth's request sounded more like a demand. "And please bring your belongings."

Roni went pale, it seemed to me, and let go of my arm to gather her handbag and retrieve her coat. Maybe there was something wrong with her family. She'd said little—Rhoda?—was sick.

"Rachel?" Roni's chest rose and fell, her eyes tensed with worry as she searched my face.

"It'll be okay." That's all I could think of to say, even though I had no idea. "Let me know."

As Roni turned to go, the other jurors stood as well, in solidarity or kindness or support. Her mostly empty foam coffee cup, the only thing that marked her existence, tipped over as I moved aside, leaving a tiny trickle of brown on the glossy conference table. I righted it and put a napkin on top of the spill.

Suddeth gestured Roni into the hallway, where she stood behind him, almost a head taller than the pudgy officer. I could read the fear in her eyes. The cell phone clipped to a holder on Suddeth's wide black belt vibrated, rattling so loudly against its metal clamp that I could hear it. The court officer flipped the phone up somehow and, squinting, apparently read a message. Flipped the phone back into place.

"Take your seats, ladies and gentlemen." His face betrayed no emotion, no expression, no judgment. "The court session will begin in approximately twenty minutes. Mrs. Wollaskay will likely not be rejoining you."

CHAPTER **EIGHTEEN**

JACK KIRKLAND

Sitting side by side at the defense counsel table, Jack and Deke were two of only three people in the courtroom this Thursday morning. Wednesday's session had been cut short by some judge's meeting. Making everyone but the judge unhappy.

Now the rackety heaters struggled to do their job, and the heavy blue velvet curtains, draped from frescoed ceiling to hardwood floor, fluttered out wisps of dust as the heated air pushed from behind them, trying to escape. Someone had doused their wooden table with lemon-scented wax. The place smelled like Jack's grandmother's house.

The third person in the room, court officer Kurt Suddeth, legs planted and hockey-player arms crossed over his chest, guarded the door to the hallway. In five minutes, the bailiff would undo the chains, push open the door, and let in the audience. And the press. Jack knew his client hoped to see his sister Latrelle this morning, maybe even talk to her.

Jack hadn't the heart to tell him that was unlikely, but maybe one of these days they'd get lucky with a softhearted bailiff who'd ignore the rules. Three weeks of trial had passed, with Latrelle cutting her classes at Boston College, showing up every day. The two had never been allowed a word to each other. If Deke went away for life, the chances of his seeing Latrelle again diminished with every day he stayed behind bars. Families, the free ones, simply forgot. Let go. Moved on.

The DA's table was vacant, two blocky chairs pushed all the way in, a glass pitcher of ice water and two stubby glasses waiting at one corner on a white cardboard tray. God knows where Gardiner is, Jack thought. Probably signing today's deal with the devil. Or the devil signing with her.

Deke was using a failing ballpoint to scrawl a series of interlinked circles on a yellow pad. Not tough to diagnose that psychology, Jack thought. Going around in circles. Or endless waiting. Or handcuffs. Jack pretended to be going over his notes for his closing argument, which, if all went as planned, would take place in about half an hour. But things were already not going as planned. Instead of fine-tuning his logic, Jack was trying to parse whether losing Roni Wollaskay as a juror yesterday would matter.

"Think it'll matter?" Deke's whisper echoed his thoughts in the quiet courtroom. He looked up from his circles, held Jack's eyes. "That juror? You said she was on our side. And now she's gone."

"I said I *thought* she was on our side. She *might* be. Every one of them *might* be." Jack tried to keep the frustration out of his voice. And "it's a frigging crap shoot" was not an acceptable phrase to say to a client. But it *was* the truth.

"Listen, Deke." Jack needed to make his client understand. "Give yourself a break. It won't help to worry. Let *me* worry."

"I should testify," Deke said again. "Why won't you let me?"

"It's not that I won't let you," Jack repeated. For the ten thousandth time. It would screw up his case royally if his client testified. He couldn't say that, either.

Problem was, figuring it was a done deal, Jack hadn't decently prepped for Deacon Davis to testify. Martha Gardiner had legions of lackeys to assist in the case, and Jack was fine if they chased their tails planning for testimony that was never going to happen. But strategically, there was no doubt. The best thing for the defendant was to keep quiet. "If you want to, Deke, you can. I can't stop you. I can only give you the benefit of my experience and—"

Kurt Suddeth cleared his throat, interrupting. "Gentlemen?"

Without waiting for them to respond, Suddeth clanked open the door to the courtroom, letting in a rush of hallway commotion. They both turned to look. The chatter and buzz, muted but constant, expanded to the dark walls as the spectators jockeyed for seats on the rows of wooden pews. *Clea?* What was she doing here? Her plaid-shirted photographer had barely plopped down his tripod behind the defense table when Clea pointed him to move his equipment to the right, positioned behind the DA's table. That'd be, Jack knew, to get the best shot of Deke. *Frigging Clea.* She'd said she was working on a story. He gave her a look, like *What the hell?* But she turned away.

Deke's sister Latrelle, her dark hair spilling over her turtleneck, had been the first through the door. Officer Suddeth had stepped aside, allowing her to claim a seat in the front row.

"I love you." Deke mouthed the words to her, his voice barely audible.

"You, too." Latrelle made a valiant attempt to smile as she whispered her response, then leaned forward on the wooden pew. Moved as close as she could to the waist-high bar that separated spectators from participants. Reached out a hand.

Suddeth stepped in front of her. Blocked her view of her brother. And his view of her. On purpose, had to be. Even through the officer's chunky navy-blue bulk, Jack heard the young woman gasp. He pushed his chair back. Stood. *What a jerk.*

"Come on, Suddeth," Jack said. "You're gonna be that guy?"

"Just doing my job." Suddeth, his back to the audience now, stayed put, as if facing Jack down.

"Your *job*?" Jack said. "So your job is to act like a complete—"

"Sir? You have a problem?" Suddeth interrupted, eyes narrowing, instantly combative. "If you'd like to step—"

"Court!" The bailiff called out, interrupting.

The buzz from the spectators stopped. The court clerk entered the courtroom through the back door, splitting a spread-winged decorative wooden eagle in half as she did. The eagle clicked back into place, hiding the door again, as the clerk climbed the three steps to her file-stacked desk in front of the judge's bench. The bailiff's opening announcement meant they had ten more minutes before the judge showed. Still no Gardiner.

Hell with this. Jack blew out a breath and took his seat at the table again, leaving Suddeth mid-sentence. Sweating this kind of small stuff was the least of Jack's concerns. He felt the officer's presence—and animosity—ease away. Deke had half turned back toward the spectators. He'd put one hand over his heart. Held it there. Latrelle, locking eyes, did the same thing.

Clea jabbed an elbow at her cameraman, then brazenly pointed at the pantomime of familial devotion, Latrelle and Deke's mute attempt at connection. The woman actually twirled her forefinger to make sure the photographer understood he should roll on it, capture it. *Crap.* Was everyone here only interested in how they could parlay this trial to further their own careers? Yeah. They were. They all were. Including him.

Latrelle touched four fingers to her thumb, then opened and closed them quickly several times. As if making a shadow puppet talk. She raised her eyebrows, questioning, as she kept repeating the gesture.

Will you testify? Jack knew that's what she was asking.

Clea couldn't take her eyes off the two. After what Jack had told her at Gallery about Deke wanting to take the stand, she'd probably decoded what they were "discussing." Whatever Deke answered, Clea could text out her scoop instantly. What made it worse, Jack had to admit it was partly his own fault.

But Deke didn't pantomime back. He turned to Jack instead.

"Are you sure?" he whispered. "Are you *sure* I shouldn't?"

RACHEL NORTH

I stood at the head of the conference table in the jury room, exasperated at Juror Nine, a lunk who wore a Patriots jersey every day. "I've told you, Gil. And *told* you. We're not allowed to take that into account."

Court officers Grace and Kurt—we were on a first-name basis now—had set up a blank whiteboard behind me, now balanced precariously on a flimsy metal easel. "The fact that the defendant did not testify," I went on, "cannot be held against him."

"Ever hear of the . . . which amendment is it, dear?" Juror Two, Momo Peretz, looked up from her knitting. *Miss Marple from Manhattan,* I wanted to call her. Smarter than she appeared. "Fifth," she answered her own constitutional question. "He has the right to remain silent."

"Hell with that." I was surprised to hear the teacher swear as she chimed in to the deliberations, perhaps for the first time. Delia Tibbalt's wrenny voice clashed with her language. "That man slashed that poor doctor's throat. And took her money to make it look like it was a stranger. If he hadn't, don't you think he'd want to tell us that? *I* certainly would. If he doesn't talk, he's hiding something. If you've got nothing that'll incriminate you, you talk. If you do, you don't."

I tuned out for a fraction of a second, buried in annoyance. I was used to running meetings at the statehouse, where nitpicking politicians and their pushy staffers were determined to cultivate their personal glory. This squabbling jury almost made me miss them.

"The judge has named you foreperson, Miss North," Court officer Grace O'Brien had told me earlier. "And here's what you get." She'd then presented me with four dry-erase markers, a pile of yellow legal pads, and two boxes of brand-new black Bic pens. "Any questions, buzz this thing." She'd shown me a buzzer mounted under the conference table. "Easy-peasy. Lunch at one. Out at five. No phone calls. Got it?"

"But how did . . . ? Why . . . ? Shouldn't it be . . . ?" I'd failed to finish any sentences. The last thing I'd expected—more than last, it hadn't even entered my mind—was that Judge Saunders would appoint me to lead this jury. Perhaps she saw something in me, leadership or competence, which—okay. Apparently refusing the job wasn't an option. "Never mind," I'd said. "Fine. I'll do it." And now here we were, four hours into deliberations, and Patriots-jersey guy had accelerated into full "he's guilty" mode.

Yesterday had gone by in a constant stream of people talking. The two lawyers gave their closing arguments—I was betting the reporters called them "impassioned"—and the judge gave us her instructions. Which I bet the reporters called "incredibly confusing."

Then the court clerk had carried in a little barrel on a wire stand, spun it, and the judge had spun it again, opened a flap in the side, and pulled out tokens to select the three alternate jurors. Roni Wollaskay was already permanently out of the picture. I'd hoped nothing was wrong. I'd follow up, maybe, keep in touch.

Would it be frustrating to be an alternate, after listening to the whole darn trial, not to be part of the twelve who make a decision? Personally, I'd feel off the hook. But now the stay-at-home mom and the unemployed poet and the bespectacled accountant would have to hang out in a separate room and only be called in if one of us jurors died or something. At this point, I was almost wishing I could fake my own death. I *had* to get out of here. I'd need to work all weekend.

"That he's guilty isn't the only diagnosis for why he's decided not to testify." Annette Hix had apparently decoded Delia Tibbalt's off-the-tracks train of thought. "Maybe he has a criminal record and doesn't want to be asked about it. Even though that doesn't mean he killed that poor woman, it might make us not like him."

"Well, we don't like him," Delia said. "I don't, anyway. *Does* he have a criminal record?"

"It's not about 'liking,' dear," Momo said. "It's about the law."

"Well, the law says you can't kill people."

"No one is arguing that," Annette said.

"Let's move on." I stepped in, trying to smile. According to what Danielle Zander said she'd seen on TV, this guy *did* have a criminal record, but I couldn't say anything about that. I had to herd these cats and get them to a verdict. Even though I was nervous about the office, especially now that Dani was out of town with the senator, I felt a profound responsibility. A person's life was at stake, and somehow, through the random choice of this uncaring universe, I was in charge.

CHAPTER **NINETEEN**

JACK KIRKLAND

When his cell phone rang, Jack almost couldn't place the sound. His brain struggled for equilibrium, grasping at possibilities, knowing what he was waiting for was one click away. He stared at the glass front of the sandwich machine in the courthouse vending room, at his sandwich that was properly paid for but stuck halfway down. Like his life. The news he'd get in the phone call—good or bad?—already existed, but not yet in his world. He could answer or not answer, but it didn't matter. Nothing he could do now mattered. It was only what those twelve jurors thought that mattered.

A fraction of Jack's brain continued trying to coax the jury via the power of the universe or some force of personal will. *They didn't prove his guilt. I did my job. Set him free. Let me win.*

All that before the phone began its second ring.

"Kirkland," he said. Plus, it was Friday. Jurors wanted to go home. Be done with it.

"Where are you?"

Clea.

Jack tried to tamp down his anger. Failed. He hadn't called her yesterday. Might never call her again. She'd reported that damn story about Deke's criminal record, put it all over TV. Because the world was only about Clea. The jurors had dutifully answered the judge's morning question, as they always did—no, they hadn't watched TV. But who knew what was true? And now they were deliberating, and Clea damn well knew a ringing phone was all he cared about. All that mattered.

Unless she had a good reason.

"Why?" he said. "Have you heard something?"

"About your trial?"

She was trying to piss him off. *Trying* to.

"No." He couldn't resist. Didn't even try to rein in his sarcasm. "About the existence of Santa Claus."

"Just tell me where you are," she said. "I'm in the courthouse again."

Jack's vision went dark. All he needed.

"I'm at the vending machines. And I need to keep the phone line open." He should have stopped there, he knew it, but he'd crossed the Clea bridge, in so many ways. "As you well know."

"I do," she said.

He heard her voice through the phone, but also in person. Looked up. Saw her. *Go away,* he thought.

"Clea." He clicked off his phone, kept it clutched in his hand as he tried to read her face. She was in full TV makeup, extra eyelashes, her trademark red hair—she insisted it was *auburn*—perfectly in place. But why was she here? She had to know he was furious.

Clea stood in the doorway of the vending area, the struggling lights from a soda machine flickering shadows on her face. Three grimy yellow-topped round tables, five chairs at one and none at the others, sat empty, but Jack made no move to ask her to join him. He'd get the sandwich and pace the halls, or go back and sit with Deke in the attorney-client room. What *she* was going to do, he didn't know. Or care.

"You have a minute?" She pushed back an insistent lock of hair that had fallen over one eye. "I know the timing is awful and everything, but there can't be a verdict this fast, and I . . ."

"A minute for what?" Jack banged the front of the sandwich machine, wished he could kick the thing. "You want to trash my client on TV again? Use me for information again?"

"It was correct, wasn't it? And my boss loved it." Clea paused, pressed her lips together, as if deciding whether to reveal a secret. "Anyway. Water under the bridge. Long story short. I got the job."

"The? Job?"

"In Chicago? The investigative slot? You never listen to me. The *job*." She craned her neck to look out the doorway and down the corridor. Apparently saw no one. When she turned back to him, she had her palms, as if in prayer, under her chin. "It's official. I'm on my way to the station to give them my two-weeks'. But Jack? You're the very first to know."

She opened her arms, as if to receive a congratulatory hug. Or maybe an ovation.

"That's great." An honest answer. It meant the Clea situation was solved. There was nothing he could do about her cheap-ass story. But good riddance to the storyteller.

"You *want* me to leave?" She cocked her head, like she did, looked at him with that pouty face she used when she wanted something.

Was that the phone? Jack pulled it from his pocket, checked. It wasn't. Put it back. His sandwich remained stuck. "Isn't it what you want?" Really? They were having this conversation *now*? "It's your career . . . thing. Ambition. Goal."

"There are other goals in life, Jack." Clea checked outside the doorway again, again apparently saw no one. She came closer to him, touched his arm with a pale pink fingernail. "I could stay, you know, if you want. Tell them no. For . . . personal reasons."

Jack remembered a long-ago class called Negotiation, Mediation, and Arbitration. The objective of such discussions, between parties who had opposite goals, was to end with neither side being happy. When both sides were equally disappointed, that meant the decision was fair.

It also required both sides to bargain in good faith. For Clea, there was apparently no such thing.

"Did you really get a job offer?" Jack reached into his trousers pocket for change. Fed it into the soda machine. Ran his finger down the selection numbers and letters. Wondered why life had to be so complicated.

Clea did not say a word.

D-4. Jack pushed the buttons. The Coke can clattered down the chute.

"What do you mean by that?" Clea finally asked. "'Really' get an 'offer'?"

Jack ripped open the tab top. The hiss of the release was the loudest sound in the bleak little room. No one had cleaned the mustard-colored walls, apparently, since the no-smoking ban was instituted.

"What would be the point of my telling you I *had*," she went on, "if I hadn't?"

"You tell me." Jack took a sip. He was being a jerk, he knew it, but she deserved it. She'd milked him for information. Used him. Plastered his client's criminal record all over TV.

"You complete . . . asshole," Clea said.

"Me?" Jack said. "Who knows. Maybe in Chicago you'll meet a nice news director you can sweet-talk into giving you the plum assignments. Or maybe you've already done that."

"Maybe you'll find someone who thinks you're as smart as you do," Clea said.

Jack saluted her with his Coke can.

"And you know what?" Clea's voice had thinned to a bitter whisper. "You know what? When I get famous in Chicago, you know what my life's ambition is gonna be? To come back to Boston and investigate the hell out of you."

He'd been right all along. This woman was all about getting what *she* wanted. He was better off—putting it mildly—without her.

"Be my guest," he said. "Though you already have, if you recollect, been my guest. Many times. And that might not augur well for the objectivity of your 'investigation.'"

Jack's cell phone rang.

"I've written everything down, you know," Clea said.

A noise from behind him. Then a click. And a thud.

"Oooh. Your sandwich." Clea pointed at it with one finger. "Looks awesome. And Jack? I hope your guy fries. He's guilty as hell."

Jack ignored Clea, ignored her threats, ignored the ham-and-cheese packet now taunting him from the bottom of the machine. Cared only about that ringing phone.

"Kirkland," he said.

RACHEL NORTH

I marched my jury troops down the second-floor hallway and through the open dark-paneled door into the jury box, each of us scrutinized by a dour-faced Grace. This had not been a fun morning. We'd decided to send two questions to the judge. Now everyone was being called in to hear her answers. The light in the open courtroom was softer, and the air not so full of venom and cynicism.

As foreperson, I'd been told to move from jury seat four, center front, to jury seat number one, closest to the judge. That gave me a better view of the white-faced countenance of Deacon Davis, whose life we held in our squabbling hands. If a jury could have squabbling hands. I took my seat, thinking about the four hours of bitter deliberation so far. I missed Roni Wollaskay, my only connection to sanity. With her gone, I could rely only on Momo, whose caramel-and-cream afghan was growing by the hour, our own Madame Defarge.

Behind me, Juror Nine, Patriots guy, banged his thuggy toe against the back of my chair. I closed my eyes, gritted my teeth, and refused to be baited. He'd been an outright "guilty" since the beginning of deliberations. Moments after our first round of coffee was poured, I'd vetoed his demand to simply "take a damn vote, find him guilty, and get out of here."

And now Gil reminded me, with his annoying foot, that I was only one voice. I was a "not guilty," probably, so far, as were Momo and the scientist, Larry Rosenberg. The others seemed to be leaning toward guilty. But we'd been stuck on a question none of us could answer. Davis was accused of robbing Dr. Georgina Oreoso and then killing her at an ATM. Was there testimony that Deacon Davis had an ATM card for that bank? Someone argued that was a perfect and innocent reason for him to be there, because what if he was withdrawing money?

Someone else had parried with another intriguing question. If he'd been there simply to get cash out of his account, wouldn't he have witnessed the murder? And if he had, why wasn't the real murderer on trial?

I also wondered about that broken surveillance video the bank official had testified about. Maybe Deacon Davis disabled it himself, somehow? Or someone did? Surveillance video was a slam dunk these days. If I was going to kill someone, Patriots guy for instance, I'd make sure in advance that no one could see it on tape.

Deacon Davis—murderer or not—was whispering in his lawyer's ear. The lawyer, Kirkland, looking haggard but kind of handsome, kept his arm across the back of his client's chair, nodding in response. He patted his client's back. *Good guy,* I thought. Tough job. And he'd seemed very convincing. Wonder if Kirkland knew what happened? I'd seen on TV that a lawyer wasn't supposed to let his client lie on the witness stand. Maybe that was why Davis hadn't testified.

Would money—the three hundred bucks that was stolen—be a big enough motive for murder? Or maybe it was personal? What if Davis loved Georgina Oreoso, or thought he did. And she didn't love him? Love, or unreturned love, would be enough. I could easily imagine that. If you were passionate enough. Or disappointed enough. Or hurt enough.

Martha Gardiner and her copycat associate, Lizann Wallace, today in sleek navy power suits, both sat elegantly straight-backed in their chairs, leather-bound law books and two dark red folders aligned perfectly in front of them.

We'd argued all morning in the jury room, and finally sent our questions to the judge. At noon, Kurt had brought us lunch, wrapped in the white waxed paper of the Pietro Pan Deli. The Italian sandwiches had too much salami and too many onions, and I'd wondered if that was a sneaky way to encourage us to hurry. I wished the jury room had windows we could open. Even though it had started snowing again, being cold was better than being asphyxiated by garlic.

Now, in jury seat one, I sneaked a look at my watch. One thirty. When I'd gotten back to the statehouse yesterday, Senator Rafferty had gone off on some unscheduled trip, this time to Williamstown, and I discovered Danielle Zander had gone with him. Again. In the past, he'd taken *me*. Dani would have no idea what to do or what he needed. I touched my neck. Five weeks had gone by, and I still felt the gold necklace. Its weight. Its promise. Its power. So unsettling to have a separate reality.

The judge looked up from her papers as Juror Twelve, teacher Delia Tibbalt, took her seat, followed by the alternates. For a moment the only sound was the creaking of our chairs and the rustle of the few spectators shifting in their seats. I recognized Clea Rourke in the audience, and we locked eyes briefly. Did she remember me from the other night at Gallery? She'd seemed more interested in Senator Rafferty, naturally. That had been a strange worlds-colliding moment. And odd, it crossed my mind in the silence, that Jack Kirkland, in the midst of defending an accused murderer, was having a fancy restaurant dinner with a reporter. Either he was pretty confident or pretty—what? Unconcerned? Maybe knew his client did it.

"So, ladies and gentlemen of the jury . . ." The judge's voice sounded as if she might have a cold. Like everyone in Boston did, this time of year. "You had two questions. One, whether there was evidence that Mr. Davis had an ATM card." She pursed her lips, then nodded twice as if confirming her own decisions. "For that, you will have to rely on your own collective memory."

I heard a snort from behind me, maybe Gil or Delia.

"Secondly," the judge went on, "as to your question about whether the defendant had a previous criminal record. Again, you are to only consider what is in evidence. Nothing else."

Fifteen minutes later, we were back in the jury room. In our exact same seats. And with the exact same level of sarcasm and discontent.

"Thanks for nothing, Judge," a voice from down the table said.

"Which means he *does* have a record, doesn't it? Or Kirkland would have said he doesn't. Right?" Patriots-jerseyed Gil was not about to let go of this, even though that was a leap of logic worthy of Evel Knievel. "I mean, if there's no previous record, you'd definitely say that. And they didn't. So there is."

"Agreed." Annette Hix held up one finger, signaling *count me in.*

The jury was its own creature now, no longer a group of individuals, but a force, like a flock of soaring starlings careening across the sky, following the leader's mysterious instructions. Whoever the leader was at the moment.

It struck me about juries. How this one latched on to anything that reinforced what they already believed. How, in a place like this, you're forced to consider murder in a different way. Did Deacon Davis know the surveillance cameras were broken? Did he just—snap? Rage into fury? Why? Why did any of us decide to do anything?

My colleagues, sparring and debating, were not as philosophical.

"And we know the guy doesn't have an alibi for the time. They arrested him. Why'd they do that if he didn't kill her?"

"Poor thing," Delia said.

What if Davis didn't do it? I could only vote based on the evidence that was presented. Which, certainly, was not everything the lawyers knew.

"If he didn't do it, who did? Some stranger?" Scientist Larry Rosenberg frowned. "Oreoso *knew* him."

"She knew a lot of people, for heaven's sake," Momo said.

I felt the emotional tide pulling at all of us, the undertow of a guilty verdict tugging at our ankles. "We have to go by the evidence," I said, standing in front of the blank whiteboard, black marker now in hand.

I drew a line down the middle of the board. "Let's list the pros and cons. See if we can decide. Beyond a reasonable doubt. A life is at stake here."

"And another one already taken," Gil said.

CHAPTER **TWENTY**

JACK KIRKLAND

"Are you kidding me?" Deacon Davis's anger almost levitated him out of his folding chair in the courthouse attorney-client room.

Jack knew the feeling. He'd been close to hitting the ceiling himself. Or hitting almost anything. Or anyone. He tried to decide who he'd select as his first victim—the judge, or Martha Gardiner, or the court officer, or juror Anne Peretz herself, little old lady or not. Deke dropped his head into his hands, his elbows on the table propping him up.

"She talked about me to the court officer? The knitting woman did? And now she's *excused*?" Deke's words tumbled out faster than Jack had ever heard him speak, his pale face gone red with confusion and certain fear. "Is that even fair?"

In chambers earlier this morning, the pie-faced and obstinate court officer Grace O'Brien had related an admittedly believable story. That yesterday, when Peretz had been late for deliberations and forgotten her pills, she'd "babbled"—O'Brien's word choice—to the officer something about her state of mind. She'd said she'd heard Deacon Davis had a criminal record, but that he'd changed his life and gone straight, and that she believed it. O'Brien had decided that meant Peretz had watched TV about the trial. Or had discussed deliberations with someone not on the jury. A violation of the judge's orders.

"I wrote it down, after. Exactly what she told me. That's what I gave the judge this morning," O'Brien had said.

Judge Saunders had pulled out a sorry-looking piece of paper, maybe the back of a union flyer, on which the officer, presumably, had scrawled in pencil.

Saunders offered it to Jack. Because Gardiner, no doubt, had already seen it. "Mr. Kirkland?" she said.

It had taken Jack thirty seconds, less, to read it. And about zero seconds to go into the stratosphere.

"She said she'd *heard* about a criminal record? And she'd *heard* he'd 'gone straight'?" Jack's eyes toggled between the note and the judge. His head might have exploded, except that it wouldn't have done any good. He'd scoured his brain for legal precedents, any cases where such a thing had happened before, and whether he could muster any convincing arguments that this juror's offhand remarks were meaningless when it came to the deliberations.

"'I believe he's gone straight.'" He heard the robot tone in his own voice as he read it out loud. "'I don't care what the evidence is.'" He'd paused, trying to make a battle plan. "Officer O'Brien, what did you say to encourage this?"

"Hey. No way." A spot of red appeared on each of O'Brien's cheeks. She turned to the judge, fists clenched at her sides. "You know me, Judge. I follow the rules, don't I? I didn't say a word. The woman's a talker."

"And you didn't stop her?" Jack had to turn this around.

"Mr. Kirkland?" the judge interrupted. Her tone meant *shut up*.

Martha Gardiner smoothed her perfectly pressed charcoal skirt. Didn't look at Jack, didn't look at the judge. Didn't look at Officer O'Brien, the tattle-taling rat of the courthouse, who had set in motion the certain conviction of Jack's client.

Jack paused, holding the silence. Tried another tack. "What did Mrs. Peretz herself say about this? Judge? She's told you, every day, that she hasn't watched television. Have you heard *her* side of the story?"

Based on the look the court officer shot him, Grace O'Brien probably would never speak to Jack again. Yes, his questions were calling her veracity into account. But what the hell? Anne Peretz was a not-guilty vote. Jack felt confident of that. But because she couldn't keep her mouth shut about it, they'd lost her. And maybe lost everything.

"Is it possible that Mrs. Peretz assumed talking to Officer O'Brien was not prohibited?"

The judge gave him one of those judge looks, like *defense attorneys are so pitiful*. "If you remember my instructions, Mr. Kirkland, I had clearly told the jurors not to watch television news, and to speak to no one except fellow jurors about the deliberations. Wouldn't that include Officer O'Brien?"

"How is Mrs. Peretz supposed to know that?"

"Shall we ask her?" Gardiner's interruption was the first thing she'd said.

Judge Saunders nodded at the court officer who exited via a back door. At the same time, she buzzed her damn buzzer again. The back door closed. The front door opened. Anne Peretz looked like a stray sparrow separated from her flock, but poised for battle. Shoulders square, lips thin. One of her wings began to flutter, but Jack sensed she'd get it under control.

"Thank you for coming, Mrs. Peretz." The judge, pleasant as all getout, stood as the juror entered. "Please, take a seat."

"Is everything all right?" Peretz, touching her gray hair with one hand, sat straight-backed on a chair next to the judge's desk. Jack saw her only in profile, chin up, blue-veined hands folded in the lap of her plaid skirt.

"I understand you had a chat with the court officer yesterday." The judge sat, swiveling to face her. "Grace O'Brien?"

"Oh, yes, thank you, Judge. Your Honor. I was late, and there was traffic, and I'd forgotten my pills, and I was a bit flustered. She was so lovely, allowed me to have my son bring them. So all's well that ends well. I'm fine now, thank you so much. And I won't drive myself anymore, I promise. My son will drive me. It's no problem."

"Lovely," the judge said. "What else did you say to Ms. O'Brien? If anything?"

All Jack could do was wait, so he waited.

"About what?" Peretz looked truly bewildered, her brow furrowing as if she'd tried to drag back a memory and failed.

"You tell me," Saunders said.

Jack had been a lawyer for twenty-five years, never wanted to be anything else except for a brief flirtation with surfing, a difficult goal for a kid from Cleveland. His father was a lawyer, corporate, not criminal. And his mother was a lawyer, too, an administrative law judge for the city. But Jack had grown up on *Perry Mason* reruns, and though his father scorned his legal choice, he was the first to stand and applaud at Jack's graduation. "Proud of you, son," he'd said, his bear hug maybe the first he'd given since Jack almost drowned trying to surf on Lake Erie. "Couple words of advice. Never cross a judge. Never interrupt, never disrespect. Never let him see you worry."

Jack bit back his annoyance as he remembered that now, advice from back in the days when most judges were "him." This was unfair to Mrs. Peretz. Toying with her. Jack supposed Saunders thought she was being objective.

Mrs. Peretz shook her head again, twisted a gold ring on her left hand. "I was late. I forgot my pills, I was upset," she said. "I supposed I asked if I could use the ladies' room?" She half shrugged, then readjusted the silky scarf around her neck. "But that's all."

"Did you discuss the deliberations, Mrs. Peretz? Or get outside information? Did you talk about something that wasn't in evidence?"

"With Grace? Or with the others?" The juror's silvery eyebrows went up. "Why, no. Certainly not."

"Did you say anything, for instance, about the defendant? Anything you'd heard? Seen on TV?"

"No." Peretz shook her head no, several times.

"And if she'd said you did?"

"Then she's mistaken."

"If she'd said you'd told her that nice young man could not be guilty, because you knew he'd gone straight?"

Peretz's mouth opened, but nothing came out. Jack saw her marshal her wits. She half stood, then sat down again. Her mouth a hard line. "No," she said. "I did not."

"Mrs. Peretz?" The judge laced her fingers on top of her desk. "May I ask what your pills are for?"

Jack tried not to show any reaction. This was outrageous. But if he pushed any harder, it might make it worse.

"My pills?" Peretz's voice had gone shrill, probably as anyone's would in this situation. But Jack comprehended, clearly as if some TV show had added suspenseful music as an underscore, that no matter what she said, Anne Peretz was not long for this jury.

Martha Gardiner could hardly keep the sneer off her face as she'd sauntered out of the room afterward. She was a shitty winner.

"There's nothing we can do about it." That's what Jack had to tell Deacon Davis now. Problem was, a defendant had the right to be present in hearings like that, so Jack should have brought Deke with him to chambers. Jack tried to convince himself it wouldn't have mattered, because Mrs. Peretz, her vote tainted, would have been excused no matter what. And Deke would never know Jack had cut that legal corner.

"That's the story, Deke." Jack leaned across the table, trying to look calm. "There's nothing we can do. The law says the jury must start over."

"Start *over*?" Deke shook his head. "I don't like it, Mr. Kirkland."

This time Jack told him the whole truth. "I don't like it either," he said.

RACHEL NORTH

Marcantonio Fiandaca. I wrote the new juror's name on the blank whiteboard. On Friday, we'd covered the shiny surface in my scrawly printing. On one side, listing points about the evidence of guilt: the money, the scalpel, the supposed crush Davis had on the doctor, the Skechers footprints, the lack of alibi. On the other side, the evidence of inno-cence: so few forensics. So many existing pairs of size-eleven Skechers. Broken surveillance camera. No witnesses.

I'd erased all that from the board—hadn't I?—before I left last night. Or someone had over the weekend. But now, as I turned back to my new jury, with the new guy in Momo's seat, none of that mattered.

Grace told us we were starting over. Starting *over*. My heart collapsed as the ramifications sank in. It's Monday. This would last *another* week. I'd never get back to work. Deadlines would be missed, schedules screwed, legislation delayed, constituents frustrated. The senator would get even more upset. And, icing on the cake, Danielle Zander was with him on the road again. My life was falling apart. Yes, selfish, because the trial was not about me. But it was also not my fault.

I'd listened to each of the lawyers. The imperious Martha Gardiner, the one with the power of law enforcement, and whose sworn job was to pro-tect the public. She must have had enough confidence in Deacon Davis's guilt to charge the guy. And the kinder, gentler Jack Kirkland, persuasive and eloquent, who reminded us that society protects the innocent and that we, the jury, had to do unto others as we would have them do unto us. How was I supposed to decide between them? When I believed them both?

"Welcome, Marcantonio," I lied. "And now, because Mrs. Peretz has been excused—"

"Did she say why?" The scientist, Larry, interrupted me. "The judge? Did I miss something?"

"Nope," I said. "I have no idea. But because she was excused, we have to start our deliberations from the top. Because—and I'm only re-peating what the court officer told me—if we simply *summarized* for Mr. Fiandaca—"

"Call me Marco," he said. The accountant's white shirt was buttoned to the neck, his tie up as tight as it could be. Hollow cheeks, big glasses. A turtle. "And I don't like this any more than you do. I thought you people would vote 'guilty' Friday, in fact, I made a bet with myself about it. And then we'd all go home."

"Hear, hear." Gil, in yet a different Patriots jersey, put his arms up, like, *touchdown.* "My man."

I put both *my* arms up, too, but double stop signs. Barely ten in the morning and already I was the referee. "Look, I want my real life back as much as anyone. But we have to follow the rules. If we summarize for Marco, that's not fair, because he wouldn't have been able to particâ€‘ipate along the way. We have to start over. Totally over."

Annette Hix, who wore her I'm-so-busy-and-important white doctor coat, raised her hand. As if she did not enjoy having to be called on.

"Annette?" I said.

She wheeled her swivel chair away from the table, came to the front of our little conference room, and selected a purple marker from the whiteboard tray. I was so surprised I didn't even stop her.

She drew a thick purple line down the middle of the board. At the top left, she wrote *G*. On the right, *NG*. I took a step back, waiting.

"We have to start over, they say. And so we do. But listen." She paused, and I saw every eye on her. "How are they going to know what we say or do in here? We're alone. This room is private. Probably even sound-proof. I say, let's make a de—Well, put it this way. Not a deal. A pact. An agreement. We chat, we have lunch, we come back, we vote, we decide, we go home."

Larry shook his head. "That seems backward," he said.

"This is behind. Closed. Doors." Teacher Delia Tibbalt pointed to the door as if we were her second-graders. "We can start over, sure. But we've already all said what we're going to say. This time, for Marco, we'll say it faster."

"I'm in." Jeanette the bus driver gave a thumbs-up.

"And Marco? You feel free to say whatever you want, whenever you want," Delia continued.

This was what I couldn't get past, I thought, as I watched the group nodding in agreement. You could send lawyers to law school. And judges to judge school, or whatever they had. And those people were versed in all the rules. But at the end of all the rule-following and objections and legal procedures, when the gavel banged and the door closed, when you got into a jury room, it was regular people. Flawed people. Biased people. Who may or may not agree to those rules. Who can manipulate and pressure and influence. And, depending on the power of jurors' consciences, no one would ever know.

My own conscience prodded like a stone in my shoe. *Davis might be innocent.* But I thought about the eleven others in this room who apparently disagreed with me. I thought about the work stacking up in my office. What else might be going on there in my absence. I thought about Deacon Davis, who might not have killed Dr. Georgina Oreoso, but who might have. Who might have a criminal record. Which wasn't in evidence. Who didn't even defend himself on the witness stand. Did people get away with murder? How?

"Let me say this." I returned to my chair at the head of the table, addressed the room. "If he *might not* have done it, we have to find him *not* guilty. If there's the slightest doubt. A person's future is at stake."

"Bull," Gil said. The murmur of the others underscored his derision. "People can't even decide for sure if there was a moon landing, let alone know for sure a guy killed someone."

"Poor thing," Delia said.

"There *was* a moon landing." I could not believe I had to say this. "This is different."

"Vote," Gil said.

"Vote," Annette said.

"I suppose," Larry said. "Yeah."

Whatever happened next meant I'd probably ruined my life. I'd tried, really tried, to be diligent and reasonable. Conscientious. But I could feel my patience fraying like the edges of too-taut twine. Unraveling. Irreversible. After all I'd worked for? After how far I'd come? After I finally got the perfect job and the perfect potential?

If I was trapped in this jury room another whole week, even another whole *day*, Danielle Zander would continue to take over. I'd heard the whispers every afternoon when I returned from court. Like Logan, my predecessor, I was training myself to know everything, and the undercurrent was "Dani this, Dani that, Dani, what a rock star. Dani, what a brilliant strategist." *Dani, what a witch,* I felt like saying. I knew that was petty. Normalcy would return once I was out of here.

If I stayed here, trapped, Dani might erase me. I'd vanish as completely as my predecessor Logan Concannon. Who no one had heard from, not a whisper.

Wonder what the senator's wife, Nina, thought about Dani. *Nina. Ballistic.* I remembered the words I'd overheard Logan saying. Could she have been referring to Dani? Was Nina Rafferty ballistic over Dani? Why? *Oh.*

No.

"We have to start over. And we can." I kept my demeanor oh so calm. I couldn't panic. Outwardly, at least. More and more, it felt like my career was at stake. It felt like this jury was deciding about *my* life, too. *My* future.

Part of me separated and floated away. I checked the jury room door. It was closed. I lowered my voice. "But let's get this done. Fast."

CHAPTER **TWENTY-ONE**

RACHEL NORTH

At my desk. Monday. Coffee mug half empty. Mail stacked in front of me. As I had for the last two weeks, since the trial finally, *finally* ended, I arrived here at the office hours before anyone else. Weekends, too. There was so much to do. So much to clean up. Danielle Zander wasn't in today, but I'd read all her emails and reports while I was stuck on jury duty, and when I returned, she'd continued to be her persistently helpful—and omnipresent—self.

At first, I'd tried to embrace her accompanying the senator to his political events. *Fine,* I'd thought, *let her fetch his coffee and fend off the crazies.* But now, trial weeks over, we were back to status quo. In every way. Like it was supposed to be.

Elbows on my desk, I pressed my fingertips to my eyes, trying to clear my head. And calm my brain. Dani haunted me, and I hated that. I was bigger than that. Stronger than that. I closed my mind to Danielle Zander. She could not hurt me. If I let her affect me, I would lose.

This morning, walking to the statehouse again, I'd seen a few crocus leaves peeking up along gardens' edges, timidly investigating whether it might be meteorologically safe to push all the way through. The predicted snow had fallen again overnight, though, blanketing all but a few green tips. *Go back,* I'd whispered to them. *It's only March.* Anything could happen.

Talk about "anything could happen." I stared at the letter I'd just opened. This one addressed to me. Personally. The senator got lots of mail, some of the letters on lined notebook paper with the heavy-handed printing of a (forgive me) deranged person. Those we gave to security. I was always touched by the ones on onionskin paper, written in fountain pen with perfect Palmer Method handwriting, from spindly seniors who offered a return address instead of an email. To Whom It May Concerns, ranting and demanding. Letters on yellow legal paper, page after single-minded page, from prisoners who were innocent, they swore, but no one would listen.

Secretly, I'd feared I'd get one from Deacon Davis.

That one had not arrived.

This one had. It was marked personal.

On stark white stationery, navy lettering. The letterhead said Kirkland Associates. I pictured Jack Kirkland when I looked at the signature, a strong slash of navy blue, readable and confident. It matched him. I remembered him as passionate. Authentic. Prepared. He seemed to care about his client, in a more personal way than I might have predicted. I'd admit to looking at Kirkland, from time to time, thinking about his legal skills and his quick-draw retorts to Martha Gardiner's objections. My dad always wanted me to be a lawyer, like him, but I'd resisted at every turn. Maybe my dad was right. Everyone on Beacon Hill in a position of real power was a lawyer, come to think of it. Everyone else started as a minion and stayed a minion.

Law school at age thirty? I pictured myself in a classroom or reading a textbook or cramming for tests. Studying to pass the bar exam. Could I do that?

"Dear Ms. North," the letter began.

The words blurred as I read it for the fifteenth or so time, imagining Jack Kirkland composing it, dictating it, signing it. Licking the envelope. Although he wouldn't do that personally, I guess. He was handsome—I'd thought that from the start. Maybe too old for me. Too everything for me. Exactly what I needed, to erase my crush on Tom Rafferty with a dumber crush on some older-man defense attorney. If a friend had told me she was thinking this way, clearly a father-thing, or a power-thing, I'd have sent her to a shrink. But apparently I was not my own best friend. And now I was procrastinating.

Jack Kirkland wanted to talk to me.

"Good morning," I replied to some new intern, a young woman, one of our spring crop, whose father was a muckety in the district. She waved at me, headed for the coffeepot.

"Bring you some coffee?" she asked over her shoulder.

Who brings who coffee is the ball game, I realized. The instant indication of hierarchy. Law degree or not, I ruled the roost here now. Finally.

"I'm set, thanks." I held up my mug.

Dear Ms. North, I read again.

I felt my lips purse, eyes narrow, brow furrow—all those things one did to illustrate confusion. Could Jack Kirkland do this?

The letter indicated he could. That the Massachusetts Supreme Judicial Court said so.

"We're interested in your experiences in the jury deliberations of *Commonwealth v. Deacon Davis.*" The letter got to the point after a paragraph of thanking me for my valuable service. Blah blah blah, it said, but what stood out to me, blindingly, as if it were highlighted in neon yellow, was "and determining whether extraneous influences interfered or affected those deliberations."

I frowned even harder. If I were a lawyer, I'd know all about this "extraneous influences" stuff. Did "extraneous influences" mean exactly what happened? *That I'd* . . . I let my thoughts trail off, but they returned, nastier than before. Had I been pressured—not by the others, but by myself? Had I been more interested in myself than Deacon Davis? Had I allowed myself to be "convinced"—simply so I could go back to work? Could Kirkland possibly, possibly be asking me about that? And how hideous would it be for me to admit it? I could not believe this was happening. Today of all days.

Somewhere a phone rang. Not mine. I ignored it. Could I ignore this letter, too? It said it was "optional" to meet with him.

My mind flared with questions. I'd always thought what happened in the jury room stayed in the jury room. Why else were there guards and closed doors and all those rules? The sanctity of the jury room was the whole point. And what happened in that particular jury room was something I was not comfortable discussing.

I took a sip of now-tepid coffee. Stared at the letter. My stomach *really* hurt.

"Not comfortable" wasn't going far enough. I could never tell, not anyone, not ever, especially Jack Kirkland or Deacon Davis, what I did on that jury. I would feel terrible about it forever.

I dropped my head into my hands, worrying. Deciding. Maybe if I talked to Kirkland, I could make up for it. Somehow. "Unlikely," I muttered.

But what if—what if I said no, but others said yes? What if they repeated what I'd said—"Let's get this done. Fast."? Had I said that out loud? I honestly hadn't meant it that way. What if someone else told him I did, and I'd refused to talk? Then I could be in more trouble. Maybe. Who knew what the damn rules were. I should have been a lawyer.

I drew in a deep breath. Let it out. *Come on, Rachel. Pull it together.*

"All you did was agree," I said out loud.

"Huh? Are you talking to me?" The intern, coffee now in one hand and a pink-and-white-sprinkled doughnut in the other, stopped at my desk and looked at me quizzically. Her fingernails were multicolored, I saw, spanning the rainbow.

"Oops." I tried to look like I were laughing it off. "You caught me. Nope. Just trying to win an argument with myself."

"Huh." She saluted me with the doughnut. "Good luck with that."

JACK KIRKLAND

Jack raised a hand in greeting when he saw Rachel North standing, as she'd promised, on the still-snowy steps of the Parkman Bandstand on Boston Common. Not that he made a habit of meeting people outside his office. But Ms. North had not been "comfortable" coming to his office on Friend Street, nor with talking in *her* office on Beacon Hill. He'd been surprised she called and set this up so quickly. Maybe she wanted to get it done.

She held up a gloved hand in response. Except for that one night at Gallery, he'd never seen her outside the courtroom. Now, with a knit cap pulled over all that dark hair and wearing sunglasses, he'd probably have walked right past her if she hadn't specified she'd be wearing a black coat and red plaid muffler. Since she'd refused a neutral-territory restaurant or bar, here on the Common—site of assignations, war preparations, and citizen marches since 1634—it would have to be. If he could get her to relax, maybe they could wind up at someplace more comfortable. Warmer. And with coffee.

This was all Clea's fault. Her damn TV story. Because of what Jack had confided in her at Gallery, that woman had researched Deke's life. If her story had gotten his client convicted, it might get Jack in big trouble. But, he had to admit, better he face the consequences than have a possibly innocent person rot in prison. Thing was—maybe it didn't happen that way. That's why he was here. That's why this was important.

"Ms. North," he said as he approached. "Thank you for seeing me. I know it must have been tough to clear your schedule."

She'd been leaning on the cast-iron railing of the bandstand, halfway up the step, the last of the afternoon sun giving her a glow around the edges. She stood, turning to him, and the glow vanished as she descended toward him.

"I always think about the people who walked here," she said, her gesture encompassing the park. "John Adams. Lafayette. George Washington."

"They had hangings here, too, Ms. North," Jack couldn't resist saying, although it was hardly a conversation starter. Though maybe it was.
"Deserters. Pirates. Witches. And murderers."

Her hat almost covered her raised eyebrows, and he saw her expression change.

"Sorry." He tried to walk back his grim observation. "But I like to
think the justice system has evolved since then. Which is—"

"Why you're here," she interrupted. "I get it. So I'm here, too. Call me
Rachel. I have ten minutes before I have to get back to work." She cocked
her head at the statehouse. "My boss is probably watching us out the
window right now."

"Senator Rafferty?" Jack said, turning toward the redbrick building
to their right. "For real?"

"No." The eyebrows again. "Kidding. What can I do for you?"

"Ah." This woman was making him nervous for some damn reason.
She was brusque now, and apparently distracted, fidgety, but that was
understandable. He'd instantly noticed her in the jury box, her attractive intelligence differentiating her from her random-faced colleagues.
A couple of times he'd worried she'd notice his attention, and tried to
avoid looking at her. Sometimes it worked. He hadn't convinced her of
Deke's innocence, though. "Should we walk? I'm Jack."

She walked beside him, heading toward Boylston Street. Jack saw she
was focused ahead, into the bare trees and the distance. A blue-and-gray
police car blared by, its siren insistent. Bostonians took a lot of convincing.

"Short version," he said. "You know verdicts can only be determined
using the evidence presented in court."

Rachel nodded, looking stolidly straight ahead. This was why these
things were so much easier inside. In offices. With chairs that faced each
other and doors that closed. He tried to read her, but she was making it
as difficult as possible. He wondered why she'd even shown up.

"So. The courts allow us to inquire whether a jury verdict was reached using, well, information that isn't evidence. Because that would be improper. And that could . . ." He paused, mentally confirming that it wasn't improper to tell her this. "Under certain circumstances, that could lead to a new trial."

Rachel stopped on the broad sidewalk, so he did, too. They waited until a woman in moon boots pushed a fringed stroller by them. Her fat Dalmatian, leash taut, growled at them as he went past, hackles raised, apparently deciding they were interlopers. "Dashiell! No!" the woman snapped. "Sorry," she said over her shoulder.

"You know I got *this* letter, too." Rachel slid a hand into the side pocket of her purse, pulled out a folded piece of paper and held it up to him. "It was in the envelope right under yours in the mail stack. From Martha Gardiner. She's reminding us—me—we don't have to talk to you."

Jack felt anger raise his hackles, knew how Dashiell felt. Damn Gardiner. Could she not stay out of his life? He tried to bring his blood pressure down before he answered. "Exactly," he said. "And if you remember, that's what the judge said, too, in her closing remarks." He held his hand out for the letter, but Rachel stashed it away.

"So you'll have to decide between me and Ms. Gardiner." He didn't try to hide his smile. "Guess you did that once already. In court. That verdict was a pretty clear decision."

Rachel started to walk again, perhaps not a good sign, and he caught up with her in two steps. He'd been teasing. Sort of.

"What happened to Momo Peretz?" she asked as he joined her.

"Momo?" She meant Anne Peretz, had to be, but she'd said Momo. At least she was continuing their conversation.

"Mrs. Peretz, yes. The juror. And Roni Wollaskay, too. Why'd *she* get excused, too? Is that what your letter's about?"

Now it was Jack's turn to stare straight ahead. Though it was a legal tenet never to ask a question where you didn't know the answer, this wasn't the courtroom. And he needed anything he could get.

"Are you sure you don't want some hot coffee?" he said. Maybe he could leverage Rachel's curiosity about the jurors, use that to get her into a corner booth. Get her more under control. "There's a Café Coffee," he pointed, "right on Boylston."

"To go," she said. "But you have to tell me about Momo. And Roni."

"Deal. And it'll all be in the transcript, so the information's public. Mrs. Peretz talked to a court officer about the trial, so says Grace O'Brien. Supposedly said something about—well. Anyway. That's grounds for dismissal. As for Ms. Wollaskay, she asked to be excused since her daughter was sick. And the court agreed."

They'd reached the corner of Tremont and Boylston. Rachel punched the crosswalk button. Shook her head. "Momo was a talker, that's for sure. But that's surprising. And Roni? You sure?"

"Well, yeah." Jack wondered what she was getting at. Kurt Suddeth had told the judge that Wollaskay was panicked about her sick daughter. Judge Saunders had called Wollaskay to inquire about that, and offered to excuse her. Wollaskay accepted. Jack could have objected, since judicial procedure would require him and his client to be present for that conversation, but he'd figured entitled socialite Wollaskay was a guilty vote. So good riddance.

Better if he didn't mention that. "Why do you ask?"

"Like I said. Surprising," Rachel said. "Her daughter was sick, but Roni wasn't worried. They had a nanny. Roni was happy to get out of the house. She was psyched for the trial. And the deliberations."

"To hang my guy," Jack said. Which was improper, he knew it even as the words came out. But if Rachel volunteered info, that was fine. "That's what we predicted."

"You did? Oh, no, it was the opposite," Rachel said. "She told me she didn't think he could have possibly—oh. Wait. Your letter said you're not allowed to ask me about deliberations."

He smiled, tried to look like the whole thing was loosey-goosey, no big deal, no strict rules. The light hadn't changed, so they were trapped on the curb. The more information this woman decided to offer, the better. Maybe he could keep her talking.

"True, but you can volunteer anything you like." He smiled, as if this wasn't a potentially pivotal moment. "And you can also ask me anything. I can answer if it's not confidential."

The light changed, giving him a moment to regroup as they crossed, narrowly avoiding a speeding right-turner in a blue Crown Vic, another cop car. Rachel watched it go by, putting her hands over her ears to block the siren. She'd spilled that Roni Wollaskay was an NG. A not guilty. Shit. He'd sure called that one wrong. As a result, he'd let Wollaskay go without a fight.

Rachel pushed through the coffee shop's revolving door. Took off her hat as she entered, shook out her hair, headed for an empty booth. He signaled for a server, then followed her.

Jurors often faded into a blur of forgettable faces after a trial, and there was no longer any need for Jack, or any lawyer, to remember who they were. He'd remembered Rachel, though, her random tumble of dark curls—the opposite of the coiffed Clea, he realized, and with a tenth of the makeup. He remembered her intelligent eyes and even, when the judge made a dumb joke, her genuine-looking smile. He remembered the way she'd checked her watch when it got close to lunch and recess. A juror who was hungry or impatient or both was a risky commodity. If a juror wanted the trial over, they'd agree to anything if it would expedite their departure. Had the Davis jurors reached their verdict based on something other than what was put in evidence? That's why he was here.

"Okay, then let me ask you this." Rachel slid into one side of a booth perpendicular to the window, hugging the corner. "Seems like you thought you knew how each juror would vote. How'd you peg me?"

He slid in across from her. Watched as she took off her sunglasses, eyes darting to all corners of the wide-windowed coffee shop. Another police car, siren blaring, raced by. Rachel cringed at the sound. Talk about body language. She was hiding something from him. If it was something big, he could use it to try for a new trial.

"How'd I 'peg' you? Well, the verdict was guilty," Jack said. "And it had to be unanimous, so I suppose that's moot. You were the foreperson, after all."

Did you *engineer that verdict?* Jack wanted to ask. *How?* But that was beyond the scope of the law. She looked at him, unreadable.

"So," he said. "About my letter."

CHAPTER **TWENTY-TWO**

RACHEL NORTH

I was nervous as hell in the café's too-small booth. I should have asked for my coffee to go. I fiddled with my sunglasses, something to fill up the time as I waited for the coffee I shouldn't have agreed to. And the discussion I shouldn't have agreed to. The senator didn't know where I'd gone, and it was barely four. I was relieved that Jack—it felt odd to call him that—couldn't ask me anything about the deliberations. He said he could only inquire about whether we took into account anything that wasn't evidence. Which, I could say, I hadn't.

He'd predicted I was a guilty vote anyway. Which got me off the hook. That hook, at least.

Another police car zoomed by, again in the direction of the state-house. Was that the third one? I calmed myself, spooked. Boston. Cops everywhere.

"So, yes, my letter," Jack was saying. He'd unbuttoned his coat but didn't take it off. Which meant he wasn't planning to stay long. I'd told him I had ten minutes. Eight to go.

I'd never seen Jack Kirkland this close up, funny, except for that night at Gallery, and even though I'd had three glasses of birthday champagne, I remembered him trying to hide behind his menu. He was maybe fifteen years older than I? Twenty? And certainly more personally engaging now than he was that night—but that was during the trial, so there were probably rules. There were probably rules for right now, too. I wished I knew them. Lawyers always had the advantage.

"Let me ask you," he went on. "Did anyone say anything about my client having a criminal record?"

I blinked, struggling to keep focus, wondering what he knew. Who else he'd talked to. There were eleven other people who could tell him the answer to that, so I played it straight. "I think the subject came up, but we agreed it wasn't in evidence."

"So, it was discussed. Did you see a story about it on TV?"

"Nope." Truth. Dani Zander had seen it, but she wasn't me.

Jack nodded. "Did you vote guilty because you'd heard he had a criminal record? Did anyone?"

I felt like this coffee shop was a courtroom, with me on the witness stand. But Jack Kirkland couldn't know what I *thought* when I voted guilty. No one could. I wanted this all to be over.

"No. *Does* he have a criminal record?"

"He does now," Jack said.

A barista, lavender streaks in her blond hair and wearing a black T-shirt, served our coffees along with a sheaf of brown paper napkins. She set down the white ceramic mugs, then pointed to an array of shiny aluminum pitchers and multicolored packets on a stand nearby. "Milk, sugar?" she asked. "Over there."

Jack handed her a twenty, waved away the change.

My phone vibrated against my thigh. I pulled it from the pocket of my tote bag and looked at the text ID. RAFFERTY, it read. 911.

"I have to call in," I said. My stomach lurched, I couldn't help it. Tom Rafferty's idea of an emergency ran the spectrum from potential nuclear annihilation to the loss of his yellow tie with the sailboats. But I was the one who should always be there for him. That was my job and my life. He needed me. I should have stayed at the statehouse, ready and available.

Jack raised a palm. "Take your time," he said. He leaned back in the booth, stirred his coffee, looked over my shoulder and out the window.

"It's me," I said when the senator picked up.

Another police car screamed by, siren so loud it distorted what Rafferty told me.

"What?" I said.

"What?" Jack leaned across the table, one hand reaching toward me, but not quite getting there. "Rachel? What's going on?"

I tried to listen to the senator. Tried to process. *Dead. Murdered. Dumpster.*

"Who? Who's dead?" I had to ask.

"Behind the statehouse," Rafferty said.

I pictured it as he spoke, under the weeping willow, in the cul-de-sac where no one ever went except those dealing with the daily cleanup of the statehouse. The dirty work. "*In* the dumpster? Are you okay?"

"What?" Jack persisted, his frown deepening. He was interrupting my phone conversation, which was rude as hell.

I put one hand over my non-phone ear and closed my eyes, blocking him out. This was none of his business.

"Senator Rafferty? Senator?" But Rafferty's voice had vanished, and the dull silence on the other end of the phone line taunted me. I opened my eyes and looked at the timer. We'd been talking for two minutes and fifty-three seconds. But the call had ended. Rafferty hung up. Or something happened.

"What?" Jack said. "Rachel, your face is—What happened? Are you okay? Anything I can do?"

I placed my phone on the table, faceup. I had plenty of battery. I had bars. It was nothing wrong on my end. The senator had hung up. Or something. But mid-sentence?

"It's a . . . colleague." I said. "A woman who's . . . who was . . . on the senator's staff. Danielle Zander. She's—" I stopped, regrouped, tried to convince my mouth to say the words. The lavender-haired barista appeared at the table, stopped, took one look at us, pivoted, and left.

Jack put his hand on my arm, his long fingers curling around the wrist of my coat sleeve.

"Rachel?"

"I have to go back," I said. "I . . . we . . . she . . ."

When my cell rang again, I recoiled, terrified. RAFFERTY. 911. Grabbing the phone, my elbow hit my mug of coffee, sloshed it onto the table, and a brown splash of darkness pooled on the slick red surface. It had a mind of its own, forming a thick trickle that rivered off the edge of the table and dripped onto the terra-cotta floor below. Jack took a napkin and sopped the spill away.

"Senator?" I said into the phone. "Hello?"

But it was not Tom Rafferty.

"Who?" I squinted my ears as he told me a name. "Lewis? Millin?"

Jack snatched my phone from my hand, and in an instant, hit the red dot to break the connection.

"What the hell?" The entire world was collapsing, all the rules broken. "What on earth are you doing?"

"You can call him back, say you dropped the phone," Jack said. "But Lewis Millin? Boston police homicide detective Lewis Millin?"

"Yes. Homicide." I felt my eyes widen as I tried to decode his meaning. Then I shook my head, clearing it. "Give me back my cell."

"Sure," he said. "If you want to go to jail."

"What?"

"Lewis Millin is the pit bull of detectives," Jack said. "The death star. If he wants to talk to you, that's a . . ."

I saw his chest rise and fall. His dark suit and soft red tie showed underneath his coat.

"It's a situation." He finished his sentence. "And you're lucky I'm here, I've gotta say. What'd he tell you?"

"He only got as far as saying he wanted to talk to me, Jack, and then you took my phone. And exactly how am I lucky?" I was anything but lucky. Though luckier than Danielle Zander.

My cell rang again.

"Give me that, Jack!" I said, and I knew my voice sounded strange because the people at the table across from us both turned and stared, concerned, probably wondering if they'd need to step in to avert a domestic quarrel.

"Who is she?" Jack whispered. My phone kept ringing. He held it, a hostage, apparently, until I told him. "Someone you know? Work with? Have a relationship with?"

"*Give* me that." I plucked it from his hands. I hit the button, my heart pounding. I never should have come here. I never should have left the office. But what would have happened if I'd stayed?

"Blame it on them," Jack instructed. "The dropped call."

"Hello?" I said. It was Millin.

"I worried we'd lost you, Miz North. Where'd you go?"

"Where'd *you* go?" Jack was right. I shouldn't be defensive. "I was talking to Senator Rafferty, and suddenly there was nothing. What happened?"

Jack nodded, approving. Like I needed his approval.

"Where are you right now, Miz North?" The detective's voice was cordial but unmistakably predatory. I imagined some kind of special police GPS thing, tracking my cell, pinging Boylston Street, zeroing in on Café Coffee, targeting this very table. Cops arriving, even as we talked. I twisted in the booth, looked over my shoulder to see if I was right. I wasn't.

I turned back, unsettled, watching Jack listen.

"Where am I? I'm . . ."

Jack shook his head. Made a time-out sign. Slashed his throat with one finger.

"We need to talk to you," Millin continued.

"Talk to me?" I was purposely repeating this for Jack now. Because Jack knew who Lewis Millin was. A homicide detective who wanted to talk to me. Jack had been in this position before. I hadn't. Jack reached

into his suit jacket. Pulled out a brown leather case holding a white index card and then a capped Bic pen. He pulled the cap off with his teeth
and wrote on the card.

Find out why.

"Absolutely. How can I help?" I paused as Millin answered. And then
did my repeating thing again. We were a good team. "Yes, I worked with
Danielle, but I didn't know her very—"

Jack jabbed his pen at his next printed message.

"I'm happy to do whatever I can," I read his words. "But I don't know
anything about—Oh. Her personnel file? Well, sure, but that would be
the senator's decis—I mean, sure."

Jack pen-tapped the index card so hard I was sure this detective could
hear it over the phone. I looked at it. He'd written *WHEN?*

"When?" I couldn't believe how guilty this cop made me feel, though
he'd only been polite. Danielle Zander was dead. Behind the statehouse.
I envisioned it, but my brain, protecting me I suppose, showed me only
darkness.

Poor Danielle.

"Right now," Millin said.

My hand ached from clutching the phone. And someone must have
turned down the heat in here. I drew my coat closer, shivering. I couldn't
get warm enough. I had to hold myself together. "She wasn't at work
today, I just realized."

"You 'just realized'?" Millin's voice honed to a sharper edge. "When
was the last time you saw her?"

"The last time I saw her?" I repeated for Jack, then tried to make my
brain work. My coat was suffocating me. I put the phone between my
shoulder and cheek and shrugged off one sleeve, then changed hands
and did the other side. I calculated, closing my eyes to imagine a calendar. I remembered a ham sandwich with mustard and a pickle. Almost
gagged.

"I saw her all the time," I managed to say, thinking about the day
during the trial when she'd brought me lunch. I tried to keep my stom-

ach from twisting. Tried to keep my voice steady. When *had* I last seen her? "Like, Thursday, maybe? Friday, certainly. And then she was going to an event with Senator Rafferty."

I stopped. Even to me it sounded like I was babbling. Jack's edgy concern made me nervous. With the Deacon Davis trial raw in my memory, I kept imagining myself on the witness stand. And Lewis Millin, repeating to a jury what I'd told him in the first moment of hearing that poor Danielle had been murdered. Two murders I was now involved in. One, Deacon Davis, as a result of whyever they called people to jury duty. The other the result of—well, I guess I didn't know that.

My brain raced, spiraling. Was there anything I should have known? Had I missed something? And now someone would have to write a statement for the senator. Counsel the rest of the staff. Handle the press. I looked at my watch. Four thirty. I almost stood up. I had to get out of here.

"Miz North?" Millin was saying. "We're in the senator's office. But where are *you* right now? Are you in a place where you can sit tight, stay until we get there?"

"I'll come back to the statehouse, if it's—safe?" I pictured Rafferty pacing, bitter, frantic, calculating. Grieving? Wondering where the hell I'd gone. Was Millin trying to keep me away from Beacon Hill? Did he think it was dangerous? Somehow, even with all this, the statehouse was my base. I knew it didn't make sense, but nothing did right now.

"How fast can you get here?" Millin asked.

"Ten minutes." If he wanted me to come back, that meant he didn't think there was a killer lurking in the statehouse halls. And if there were, he sure wouldn't be on the phone with me. I looked at Jack, now longing for his advice. "But I don't know—"

I stopped mid-sentence, biting the inside of my mouth. I didn't know what I didn't know. That's why they were investigating. I took a deep breath and spooled it out, trying to remember normal. And real. And how to be. *I had nothing to hide. I'd do anything in the universe to help.*

"Whatever I can do," I told him. I could handle this. This wasn't about me. They cared about poor Dani. Who'd lived a life I knew nothing about and showed up at some wrong place at the wrong time. Her killer was still out there. "This is horrible. Heartbreaking. I'll see you in my office, ten minutes."

"We'll be waiting," Millin said. And he hung up before I could.

"I'll come with you," Jack said.

"I don't need a lawyer."

"That's what they all say." Jack picked up his index card, tore it to bits, and dropped the ink-scrawled pieces into his half-full coffee cup. "Though you have an alibi."

"Huh?" I'd almost got my coat in place again, which was more than I could say for my equilibrium.

"An alibi," he repeated. "You were here with me."

I stopped in the middle of tying my belt, hands poised at my waist.

"Is that supposed to be funny somehow?"

"Who knows," he said. "But I'll come with you. As a friend. Protector. Can't hurt. Right?"

JACK KIRKLAND

They hadn't walked half a block from the coffee shop when Rachel lost it. She'd jabbed the crosswalk button and let her arm fall to her side. But when the light changed to GO, she didn't move.

"Rachel?" Jack said, taking one step onto Boylston Street. "You coming?"

He turned. And saw her face go pale. Saw her chest rise and fall. Then saw her tears begin, falling hard and furious and unhidden. He grabbed her arm, steadying her. He felt her weight against him, her shoulders shaking, and Jack smelled flowers and coffee and the chill of the coming twilight. Rachel stayed there, sobbing, her face buried in his coat, as the lighted numbers on the crosswalk sign counted down to one, then changed back to stop.

"Whoa. Sorry." She moved away in one quick motion and blinked at him, as if remembering where she was. She used both gloved hands to swipe the tears away as she tried—not very successfully—to smile. "I only . . . for a moment there, you know? It got me. Sorry. I'm okay now."

He'd wondered about her, back in the coffee shop. Wondered why she hadn't freaked out, or burst into tears, or simply leaped up and raced to the statehouse. Any of those things would have been understandable. Not helpful, certainly, but understandable. Her tears were somehow reassuring.

"It's so . . . impossible." Her eyes widened as she looked at him. The white-orange of the halogen streetlights began to emerge, changing the shadows on her face. "I'm honestly terrified to go back there. I can't imagine being in that parking lot. I've been there a million times! Now I want to . . . to go home and hide under the covers. Forever. Who do *you* think could have done such a horrible thing? Why?"

There was nothing reasonable to say. Nothing. How many times had he heard this? Even as a defense attorney. The exact question, from every family, every friend, every lover or spouse or parent of a murder victim. The answers were always a complicated amalgam of simple elements. Money, sometimes. Drugs. Love. Jealousy. Power. All of those. When the cops got closer to finding the motive, they'd be closer to finding the suspect and making an arrest. That's usually when he got involved. This time was different.

"Do you think the police think *she* was targeted? Specifically?" Rachel pulled off her gloves, then swiped under each eye with a bare forefinger. Her eyes were deeply gray, he saw, the darkest gray. "Or do they think she had the terrible misfortune to be . . ." She shook her head slowly, as she talked.

She looked at him, her face beginning to crumble again. She grabbed his arm. Held it. "This is so not me. I mean, I keep wondering if there was anything I should have done, you know? And now I'm so afraid. I know I have to go to the statehouse, and I have to think about it, but I *can't,* I can't even think about it."

They stood on the corner, silent, eye-to-eye.

"I'm so sorry," she said. And took a step into the street.

"Do you know anything that might have happened?" Following her, he had to ask, the lawyer in him. "Even . . . well, you tell me. I'm your lawyer, after all."

"It's *hor*rible." He heard the outrage or hurt or fear in her voice. "But I . . . I feel so afraid. I feel so helpless."

"You're not helpless," he said. "You have me."

CHAPTER **TWENTY-THREE**

RACHEL NORTH

A thwacking TV helicopter hovered over Beacon Hill as we passed the open wrought-iron gates at the east wing of the statehouse and walked through the statue garden toward the lower entrance. Looking up, shading my eyes from the superwattage crime-scene lights, I envisioned an insatiable photographer leaning out the chopper's curved plastic windows, zooming in, scanning, trying to locate the dumpster. The parking lot now probably looked like the photos Martha Gardiner showed us of Dr. Oreoso's ATM, wreathed in yellow police tape. Protected from intruders on the ground but not the relentless snoops in the air.

"That's where the parking lot is, right below that chopper." I pointed. "Where the lights are." On the way here, I'd filled Jack in on everything Rafferty and Millin told me. Dani Zander, the obliging newcomer. *Dumpster, body, murder.* I stopped, my stomach recoiling again. I felt such guilt. I didn't like her. But this was unbearable.

How should I deal with Jack Kirkland? So inappropriate for me to collapse *onto him*, right there on Boylston Street. He'd been sympathetic, even kind about it, but I bet he still wanted to dissect my role in the Deacon Davis jury verdict. *It won't matter,* I silently assured myself. I'd get through this, right now, and then I'd say goodbye. For now, though, I had to admit, it was comforting to be with someone who could protect me. Someone who knew the rules.

"They're shooting video for the six o'clock news," Jack said as we neared the entrance. "I know a reporter who—well, never mind. You okay?"

"She's not still in the parking lot, do you think?" It was difficult for me to say her name out loud.

"Don't worry." Jack reached out, maybe to pat me on the back, then took his hand away as if he'd crossed a line. "You can handle this. One step at a time."

I supposed so. He let me revolve through the employee entrance door first. Inside the statehouse, I predicted, the political gossip machine would be revving into high gear. Even now, pushing five in the evening, I imagined the buzz of staffers and politicos, conversation as intrusive and persistent as that helicopter. Equally on the prowl for answers.

"Did you hear? About the . . . the dumpster?" The goggle-eyed guard, pale even for him, waved us both around the metal detector. Ervin had seen me countless times, but he didn't know Jack, and I wondered where we got these guys. Ervin, recently named head of the security team, such as it was, peered over his wire-rimmed glasses and apparently realized there was a visitor with me and that he ought to appear to do his job. He jabbed an accusatory finger at Jack. "Wait. He with you?"

"He's my—he's good," I said. "I'll take responsibility. We're going up. Scary, huh?"

"Yeah." Ervin touched his radio, then peered out the revolving door. "Cops are everywhere," he said. "Press, too."

I saw what he meant as the elevator door creaked open on two. Every reporter in the world, it seemed, was gathered inside the open door of the senator's Communications Office. The *Arbella* and the *Mayflower* now sailed in front of a reception area crowded with a barricade of tripods and cameras.

"Rachel! You have a statement?" One reporter almost yelled her ques-

tion, demanding, and the others advanced toward us. We were about to
be swarmed.

"No one's talking, Rachel. No one's saying anything. Where *were*
you? Where's Rafferty?" And then they all piled on, a barrage of logoed
microphones aimed at me like the enemy's bayonets as they fired questions. At me. "Is he back in his office? Can we have a photo of the victim? Did you know her? We need a statement. Come on, Rachel."

"Shoot," I muttered toward Jack. He was media savvy, too. A cluster
like this encircled him after the Deacon Davis verdict, I saw it on the
news, and that probably wasn't the first time. The Communications Office's antique furniture was now draped with coats and mufflers, the oriental rugs dotted with open equipment cases and snaked with a tangle
of thick orange wires. These people were encamped. For the duration.

"Go on past them," Jack instructed. "Ignore them."

But they knew it wasn't my job to ignore them. I knew it, too. Here,
on *my* territory, there were rules. Times like now, I set them.

"Guys?" I held up both hands, simultaneously signaling *shut up, stay
back,* and *hang on.* "This is a very sad occasion, tragic, and we're trying
to get a handle on what's happened. You can ask me all you want—but
I don't know anything. Not anything. If you'd be patient, and let me
through, I promise I'll come back with something."

"Did you know her? Can you confirm it's Danielle Zander?"

Who the hell was telling them this stuff? My cell pinged a text. And
then another one and another one. Rafferty, for sure, or Lewis Millin
or both, but I couldn't take the time to tell them I was here. Jack had
melted into the background. The reporters hadn't taken their eyes off
me as they moved closer, not relenting for one second.

"Are the police with the senator? How well did *he* know her? Do they
think he's a suspect? Do they know when she was killed?"

"See, that's exactly what I'm trying to tell you. I have nothing for you."
I wish I knew those answers, too, I didn't say. "I'm willing to stand here
as long as you want and repeat 'I don't know what they know,' but
wouldn't it be better if you let me go and find out?"

The elevator door opened again. Two more camera lenses headed toward me, and behind them another pack of bodies carrying notebooks. The reporters hadn't budged, and every one of them was frowning. Another text pinged my phone.

"The cops won't let us into the parking lot. Or let us see anything," one TV guy complained. "It's after five. We need something for the six. Give us a break, Rachel."

There was a change in the light, somehow, and in a display of pack mentality, the reporters, row by row, all turned their backs on me and faced the opening door that was behind them. Every tripod-mounted camera swiveled in a 180. Senator Tom Rafferty, hair almost in place, yellow tie almost in place, and eyes possibly red-rimmed, stood in front of the Massachusetts flags that flanked his outer office door. A battery of still cameras whirred and flashed.

Rafferty put up both palms in a *stop* gesture that mirrored mine. Him, the reporters obeyed. The cameras all flashed again, capturing his motion.

Edging myself behind the crowd, I planned to inch closer to the front. Jack was already stationed along the wall to the senator's right, the only place there was any room. Trapped, I joined him there, wondering why I'd agreed to let him accompany me. Rafferty looked at the floor, head bowed, apparently composing himself. The reporters stayed quiet. They were about to get what they wanted.

"What's he gonna say?" Jack whispered.

I shrugged. "Who knows," I whispered back. *Thoughts and prayers,* I predicted, but that was too cynical to say out loud.

The senator looked up, scanned the room, briefly caught my eye. Scowled. But I wasn't the problem now.

"I have a statement," Rafferty began. "When you're ready?" Every camera flashed again, and videographers adjusted their tripods, jockeying for position.

When I felt someone come up behind me, I took a step closer to Jack to give whoever it was room. This was voyeurism, masquerading as news.

Everyone wanted to get closer. Capture a close-up of the grief and sorrow. Elicit a headline-worthy quote. Cash in on a murder. "A beautiful innocent harmless young woman," they'd probably call Dani. When tears came to my eyes again I blinked them away and pressed my lips together, hard, to keep my composure. The person behind me took another step closer.

"My, my." I heard the words murmured almost in my ear. I smelled— flowers?

The speaker, her notebook out and her coat over one arm, had a look on her face I couldn't read. Clearly a TV type, all makeup and Burberry scarf, her red-brown hair cut to frame her face. She looked famil—Oh. From the morning news. And Gallery. Right. When she was trying to sweet-talk the senator.

Right. She'd been sitting with Jack. "I know a reporter," he'd said a few minutes ago. Of course he did.

JACK KIRKLAND

Why did he even come to the statehouse with Rachel? To be honest, there was no good reason, and Jack knew the help-a-damsel-in-distress thing was a pathetic explanation. But a combination of strength and vulnerability drew Rachel to him. Seduced him. All the more because she kept her distance. Except when she'd fallen into his arms. She'd even smelled good.

Which was a mess, frankly, in the midst of his jury investigation. She potentially held some cards in his appeal of Deacon Davis's case. But maybe he could make things work to his advantage. Win-win. His favorite situation.

He stood next to her, by the wall, trying to become invisible. He should have realized the place would be crawling with reporters and cameras. If they recognized him, it would raise questions. But he'd cross that bridge if it presented itself. Rafferty, he saw, was like all of them— wanting a victory.

He watched the politician manipulate the silence. Focus the attention on himself. He knew how to hold a crowd's interest.

Even Rachel, he saw, could not take her eyes off her employer as he spoke. Rafferty's voice was modulated, and filled with sorrow. He'd thrown Rachel a birthday party, Jack hadn't forgotten that. At Gallery. Which was certainly unusual. Might there be something between them? More than business?

He mulled that over, and for the briefest of moments, pictured it. Imagined it. Way too specifically. He yanked himself back to reality. Fine. It was possible. But not if Rachel North had a brain. Which, in his assessment, she did. Plus, Rafferty was supposed to be happily married.

That meant Rachel was potentially available. And maybe, if he could make her feel comfortable and safe with him—and clearly, he'd already made progress—he could find out more than his court-sanctioned "boundaries" might allow. He watched her watching her boss, thinking about the relationship of power to obligation. Rachel, reliable and responsible, would do whatever her boss said.

She was vulnerable and curious. And upset. Murder would do that, especially to someone so exposed, to someone personally involved. She'd collapsed, for crap's sake. And then she'd invited him here to her safe place.

All good.

He'd melted into the background, letting Rachel do her job, be the dominant one. But eventually she'd joined him, sneaking behind the reporters, trying to be casual but clearly trying to get near him when the pressure increased and her boss was about to perform.

If *Jack* were the boss, he could convince Rachel to reveal the jury deliberations. Prove they'd been tainted. And then he'd nail Gardiner, to the freaking wall, by forcing another trial. And this time Jack would be totally prepared.

Did Deacon Davis kill Georgina Oreoso? Jack wasn't sure, not totally, but he more than suspected not. And if Deacon Davis was innocent, Jack had blown it. And would never forgive himself. But if he could prove the jury acted improperly, he could win on appeal. Justice could pre-vail. Martha Gardiner would lose. He'd do anything to make that happen.

"My, my."

He heard the words then, a sinuous whisper, encircled by a fragrance he recognized perfectly well. Recognized because he'd presented it to her, to Clea, back in the days when things were simpler. Seemed like her employers at the TV station had asked her to stay for her two final weeks. And here she was.

His stomach turned, thinking about that vending-machine encoun-ter. Her attempts to manipulate him with her new job. Her threats to investigate him. He refused to notice her. Refused to look at her.

He'd done a lot for her. Given her stories, and leads. Leaks, even, in downright circumventions of the rules.

He'd helped make her career. And then she'd done the damn story, *using* him, and assumed he wouldn't care. It would be fun, satisfying, to see her try to go it alone in Chicago. Knowing Clea, she'd find another meal ticket.

Now it was refreshing, even reassuring, to meet a woman with no ul-terior motives. Rachel wasn't asking for favors or leaks. She wasn't ask-ing for anything. He'd be happy—when was the last time he'd used that word?—to help her.

CHAPTER TWENTY-FOUR

RACHEL NORTH

The ghost of Danielle Zander haunted our office. I felt it as I opened the reception-room door. The chill and the loss and specter of a threat. Something missing. Something disturbed. A news crew had left an equipment case on the floor, the only tangible remnant of Monday's clamor. Rafferty had publicly confirmed Dani's name, which surprised me. Then he'd given the news crews "thoughts and prayers." And "personally devastated." Then, nothing more.

This morning I'd awakened to the *ping* of breaking news on my cell phone. But it was nothing about Dani, only a warning about another March snowstorm. Awake anyway, semi–crack of dawn, I'd checked all the other headlines, too. Dani was the top story again, but there wasn't much new or of substance. Mystery, murder, shocking, statehouse, dedicated detectives, cops on the case, call the tip line. No "persons of interest." No arrests. Tom's thoughts and prayers were quoted again. Danielle Zander didn't appear to have a family, at least none was mentioned.

At my desk now, I slugged down more coffee and opened my computer, forced myself to do my ordinary tasks on what could not feel like an ordinary day. The senator had me issue a warning to our office crew— don't go anywhere alone, have a buddy, get a guard to walk you to your car. Last night, staffers had again traveled en masse to the T stop. This morning I took another cab to work, but it didn't stop my jitters. No one knew what happened, so no one knew how to handle it, emotionally or physically. Who, everyone wondered, could have done such a thing? All of us were in fear. Fear for our lives.

The morning paper and TV newscasts were also full of nothing, I saw as I scrolled through my accumulated email. No motive. No suspect. No comment. I stared at the computer screen, the words and pictures blurring. The office TV volume was low, but loud enough to hear.

There's a killer out there, they were saying. Some hideous bad guy. Got to be. "And where is he now?" the TV reporter speculated, voice dramatic, scaring everyone. Police certainly weren't telling *me* anything about the investigation, and Rafferty shut down whenever I broached the subject.

"Leave it to the police," he'd muttered. "It's a nightmare."

After the reporters left Monday evening, Lewis Millin remained. Jack stayed, too. He and Millin and Rafferty, three alpha dogs circling one another. I felt the thin veneer of civilization protecting me from a snarling confrontation, but then Rafferty retreated to his office, without saying a word to me. The other two seemed to agree, silently, on a truce.

That left me as the center of attention.

"Did you know Danielle Zander?" Millin had eventually asked me. We sat in the finally empty reception area, outer door closed, inner door closed, by that time pushing eight at night. It was chilly, since after close of business, the maintenance people turned the heat way down. I'd picked up a fringed throw pillow from the damask couch, held it in my lap to keep warm.

Millin opened a spiral notebook, right out of a vintage cop novel. I'd almost expected him to lick the tip of his pencil. He wore an Irish fisherman's sweater under a tweed jacket, and even his hair was tweedy. Congenial, like someone's favorite professor. Not at all as Jack had described. No pit bull growl. No predatory menace.

When Jack pulled up a ladder-back chair beside me, the detective didn't protest. Not exactly. He focused on me instead.

"You need this lawyer guy, Miz North?" Congenial. With a dash of curious. "Tell me about that."

"I'm simply a friend." Jack's voice was equally congenial. "That a problem?"

"Not until you make it a problem," Millin said.

Still congenial. *So* congenial it began to sound unnatural. Maybe Jack was being sarcastic. Maybe to show me that was Millin's technique.

"So? Miz North. How well did you know Miz Zander?"

Huh. I knew Dani, but I didn't know anything *about* her. Beyond my own personal nosiness, her history hadn't seemed to matter. Maybe it didn't matter. Maybe it did. Maybe I should have checked further. Professor or pit bull, this guy made me feel guilty.

"Well, she worked here. She was promoted when I was. Right before I went on—" I looked at Jack.

Jack nodded. Gestured me to go ahead.

"Jury duty," I finished the sentence. "But she'd been in the office before that. Already hired."

"By who?"

"Must have been—" I stopped, then thought again about the Deacon Davis trial. The witnesses were instructed to answer the specific question asked, and not to offer anything more. "I don't know," I said.

"Do you have her résumé? Her personnel file?"

"The senator would have that." I wasn't doing a very good job at this. So far, all my answers fit in the "I don't know" category. Millin probably thought I was incompetent.

"What if he said he didn't have it?"

"Did he?" Jack said. "Tell you that?"

Millin ignored him. "Miz North? You're chief of staff. You don't have the files?"

"It doesn't work that way here," I told him. Truthfully. "The senator handles that. And Human Resources. Annabella Rigalosa is the person's name there, if you need it."

"Okay. And where were you, say, starting Saturday morning? Can you give me a quick accounting of your whereabouts?"

"What? You think she was killed Saturday?" I'd clutched my pillow like a life preserver. They couldn't suspect *me*. Why would they do that? "Why?"

I felt Jack shift in his chair, and glanced at him. Was he trying to signal me? If he was trying to surreptitiously tell me to shut up, I had blown it.

"Go ahead. Tell them." Jack nodded encouragement. "You've got nothing to hide."

I remembered Jack had asked me at the crosswalk, oh-so-casually, whether I knew anything about Danielle's death. Guess it wasn't such a casual question. He not only wondered but also needed to know, for precisely such an eventuality. *Lawyers.*

After I'd rattled off my schedule, which was easy, Millin folded his tents and flapped up his notebook with a "Let me know if you hear anything." And he left.

Did he think I was going to cough up a big piece of critical evidence? Or that some remorseful murderer was going to call me and confess?

"I wish," I said out loud now, answering myself. I took a sip of my carry-out coffee, but there was none left. Last night, Jack had offered to walk me home, and I'd agreed. What if the killer was still out there? Jack had stopped at my front door and said he'd call me to set up another meeting about the jury deliberations. Which at that point seemed like another lifetime.

For a fleeting moment then, and maybe I was wrong, I'd thought he was going to ask me for a drink. Which would have been a bizarre ending to a bizarre day.

Tuesday now. He hasn't called. Yet. Was that a good thing or a bad thing?

I instantly hated myself. Danielle Zander was dead. That was all that mattered.

JACK KIRKLAND

"Who knows about this?" Jack looked out the window of his corner office as he talked on the phone. Causeway Street was below, and then the Boston Garden arena, where nine hours from now the Celtics were playing the Knicks. Snow was beginning to fall, not the morning rush-hour blizzard those weather people had predicted, only a feathery promise. Jack was predicting the future, which, right now, was one hell of a mess. An interesting mess, but a mess.

He punched his speakerphone louder so he could pace as he listened to Tom Rafferty. Rafferty had opened this morning's conversation with "Shit. It's a cluster." From their college days together, Jack knew Rafferty didn't sweat the little stuff. "Cluster" was not little. Whatever Rafferty was calling about, certainly regarding Danielle Zander, Jack had instantly predicted must be cataclysmic. It was. Cataclysmic and impossible.

"Who the hell knows?" Rafferty's voice threatened to blow out the cheap tin and paper speaker. "I'm not answering my phone. I told the office not to, either. Shit. I'm gonna have to resign. But even though you're an asshole, you're the best defense attorney in Boston."

The press would be all over this, unstoppable. Jack had to focus. He half expected his cell phone to ring any second, and it'd be Clea, wondering what he knew and when he knew it. Wheedling again, pretending her snide "My, my" comments Monday at the Rafferty news conference were simply good-natured teasing. But intimating he'd known about this, or suspected it all along, and that's why he'd been there. Screw her.

And now Rafferty was making it about himself, instead of about dead Danielle Zander. Which, Jack supposed, was true. It *was* about Rafferty.

"Where do they have her now? At the cop shop? And she's charged? Why?"

"Yeah, at the cop shop. First-degree murder. Arraignment is today. This afternoon." Rafferty's voice seemed to catch as he spoke, whether from bluster or anger or fear, Jack couldn't tell. "Who the hell knows why."

"Seriously, Tom," and this was pivotal, "what's the motive? What's possibly the motive?"

Jack pictured the crime scene. That dumpster behind the statehouse. He stared out the window as his thoughts raced. Maybe that wasn't where the murder happened.

"Why would the victim's body be left at the statehouse? It's almost pointing to you. Or indicating an inside job. How'd she supposedly get her out there? Or *in* there? This is a hell of a narrative, Tom. They must have something. Did they tell you why they charged her? What evidence?"

Silence on the other end. Which reminded him.

"You told her not to talk, didn't you?" Jack's brain fried at the thought. All the suspects who figured they'd help their own cases by explaining. By describing to the cops, in excruciating detail, why they couldn't possibly be the guilty party. And every damn time, in doing so, cooked their own goose. "I'm on my way," Jack said.

The first rule of innocence is shut the hell up. But Rafferty knew that. He'd certainly have warned her.

Nina was, after all, his wife.

CHAPTER **TWENTY-FIVE**

RACHEL NORTH

"You think this is wise? Going this early?" I hustled to keep up with Tom, his long strides eating up the sidewalk while I navigated the cobblestones in my stupid heels. He had burst into my office, the only way to put it, five minutes before. Had my coat in one hand and a briefcase in the other. He held my coat out at me, demanding.

"Court," he said.

So here we were, on the way to Boston Municipal Court. But he was right that I should accompany him to his wife's arraignment. I had to be there, and it was a command performance for him, too, perverse as it was. He'd have to master a facial expression that combined outrage and anger and absolute certainty of Nina's innocence. And love. The press would rip him to shreds if he didn't.

We'd agreed on "no comment." Maybe that would work.

"Senator?" We hit the red light at a crosswalk. Seems like these days crosswalks were where I finally got a word in. Where people were forced to stop for thirty seconds. I talked as fast as I could. Hoping for answers. "Listen. I know you told me the police aren't telling you anything. I mean, forgive me, but are they even revealing the cause of death? Or time? Do they know? Did you get to talk to—"

The light changed, and Tom steamed ahead, not answering me. Two pedestrians headed the opposite direction flinched with recognition when they saw him. Didn't even bother to hide it. The news, electrifying, had raced over the internet and interrupted regular programming the moment it hit, right after lunch today.

WIFE OF SENATE PRESIDENT CHARGED WITH DUMPSTER MURDER, read the *Globe* website's headlines. On television, the arrest was high drama. Breathless anchorpeople, who'd never met an alliteration they didn't embrace, salivated in their chairs, exchanging knowing looks, as if this disaster were almost too delicious for words. "Beacon Hill bombshell," one said. "Senate staffer shocker." One red-and-white graphic asked IS MRS. MISTRESS MURDERER? With the obligatory question mark to shield it from being slander.

"Mistress." The word flashed neon in my brain. Danielle Zander. *Mistress*. Disgusting.

The courthouse was a white concrete modern monstrosity, all acute angles and pointy corners. It looked like someone built it from plans drawn in vanishing perspective and then thought that was how it was supposed to appear in real life.

We pushed through the heavy glass doors. Tom didn't say a word. We both showed our state senate IDs and stepped into the high-ceilinged, marble-walled lobby, gloomy in dusty low-wattage chandeliers. None of the security guards looked Tom in the eye as they gestured us through. I felt their suspicions drilling into my back as we hurried to the bank of silver art-deco elevators. One aluminum door swished open almost instantly. We stepped on—it was empty—and the doors closed us in. I'd almost convinced myself we were so early that no press would have arrived yet.

The opening door proved me wrong. A wall of bodies and cameras and microphones pressed toward us, and a din of insistent voices engulfed us, questions echoing on the white brick walls, doubling the sound, tripling the sound. We almost couldn't get out of the elevator. It crossed my mind to push the CLOSE DOOR button, escape, and sneak back into the courtroom some other way.

"Let's *do* this," I said. I lifted my chin and powered ahead, carving a path for the senator, unstoppably determined, as if I were his personal fullback.

"Is your wife a murderer, Senator?" "Why did she do it?" "Why would Nina kill Danielle Zander?" "Were you having an affair?" "Are you going to resign?"

What these people were asking, what they were demanding, what they were thinking, was outrageous. Insensitive. Demeaning. Disrespectful. And, though I hated myself for it, exactly what I wanted to know myself.

"No comment no comment, the senator has no comment," I repeated. I was a robot, a talking robot, but I felt Tom Rafferty silent and seething behind me. We made it to the tall wooden courtroom doors of room 226. I pulled one of the metal door handles. Nothing. Tried the other one. Nothing. And again. Nothing. Locked.

"No comment no comment no comment," I said as I kept trying, rattling the curved handles with one hand, knocking like crazy with the other. Tom and I were trapped here, sandwiched between the closed doors and the insistent reporters. Not a good battle strategy.

I almost fell over when one of the doors opened right onto me, and I stumbled a step backward, almost tripping on the senator, who stood close behind me. A scowling court officer, a head taller than I was and shoulders twice as broad, appeared in the doorway, clearly ready to order us away. He stopped mid-command. Closed his mouth. Regrouped.

"Get in here," he muttered, waving us through.

I went first, ducking my head, then the senator. I felt the crowd behind us surging as a group, trying to follow.

"Get back!" the officer instructed. His bulk blocked the open door, arms crossed over his chest. "Courtroom stays closed until one thirty. Rules are rules."

"Come *on*, Hector," someone whined from the back of the hallway. "If they can go in, we can go in."

"He's the president of the senate," the court officer hissed.

"Not for long!" someone called out.

JACK KIRKLAND

"Court calls *Commonwealth versus Nina Perini Rafferty.*"

The court clerk's voice, as always, betrayed not a whit of the enormity of this. The notoriety. The inescapable headlines. Jack knew they were trained to treat every case exactly the same way. Beside him, at the defense table, Nina Rafferty, straight-backed and without a hair or pearl out of place, stood as instructed. Her pale-manicured fingertips grazed the counsel table. She looked stolidly ahead.

"Jack Kirkland for the defendant, Your Honor," Jack said.

"Martha Gardiner for the Commonwealth, Your Honor," Gardiner said.

"Be seated," the clerk instructed.

Gardiner didn't deign to glance at Jack, as if to telegraph her disdain for the whole process. To the prosecutor's way of thinking, Jack figured, being charged equated to being guilty. Which meant being a defense attorney equated to being extraneous.

With a scrape of wooden chairs on marble floor, they all took their places. Up on the bench, the black-robed judge paged through a file of documents, methodically turning one page after the other, as if he were alone and without a responsibility in the world. Ralph Drybrough, short-tempered and short-fused, was not about to suck up to the senate president's wife. In fact, Jack had learned in a quick Google search, Drybrough had been appointed by one of Rafferty's political rivals, a now-retired governor who'd left this hanging judge as his legal legacy. Jack imagined the judge and Martha Gardiner as country-club dining cronies, tête-á-tête-ing over premium martinis, sharing the soufflé, lording it over the waitstaff in preparation for lording it over innocent defendants. Who knew how far those two had gone. How far Martha would go to get what she wanted. To win.

Instead of clutching Jack's arm, as some female defendants did, or moving closer to feel protected, Nina Rafferty kept a foot of inviolable personal space between them. As if the taint of the court emanated from him as well. That he wasn't her savior. That he was a necessary evil. She'd articulated it herself an hour ago in the courthouse's attorney-client room.

Jack had been there many times with his murder-list cases, often with some poor soul who professed innocence even in the face of ridiculously damning evidence. Some poor schlub who'd gotten the short straw in a drug deal or who'd gotten too greedy with the local scumbags and gang-bangers, and hotheaded or pumped full of controlled substances, got grabbed up for murder. They all had an excuse, a rationale, a reason. Some, sure, were guilty as hell. Murder-list clients often were.

But not always. Sometimes the prosecution simply couldn't prove it. But sometimes, more often than most murder-listers, Jack won. Purely won. Sometimes, because of him, a truly innocent person went home, free and safe. That's what kept him going. Not the money. The truth. The victory.

Nina Rafferty was a different story. First, she'd promised him an initial personal check for fifty thou. She hadn't wept, not even one tear. The cops picked her up at home this morning, she'd told him, arriving after her husband left for the statehouse. Tom was her one phone call. As a result, Rafferty called Jack. Within half an hour, Jack was at the cop shop, where a surly cadet with a scrawny mustache escorted Jack to Nina, sitting alone behind bars in a concrete holding cell. She wore the clothes she'd apparently been arrested in—black pants, a black sweater Jack bet was cashmere, and a pearl necklace. Black flat shoes. She also wore a frown. Her posture indicated she was attempting not to touch any of the surfaces in the room.

"These people are insane," she said. She narrowed her eyes at the cop who'd accompanied them to the cramped meeting room, not caring whether he heard her sneer. A screen panel, tiny squares of metal mesh, kept her physically separate from Jack, but her animosity had no barriers. "Get me out of this."

"I'll do my best, Nina. And push hard to get bail." Jack tried to calm the waters, waited until the officer closed them in. A heater kicked on, rattling the vents above them. Again, as always, Jack wondered if they were being watched or taped. That would be illegal, but Jack wouldn't be surprised.

"We're supposed to have total privacy here, so you can tell me whatever you like," Jack went on, pulling out a legal pad from his briefcase. "But as always, let me warn you not to say anything to anyone except me. Not anything. 'Please' and 'thank you,' if you can manage it. And you can answer 'How are you?' with 'I'm fine.' But nothing more, not a word, to anyone else you might meet."

"I'm not going to be here long enough to 'meet' anyone," Nina had pronounced. "And I can't even *imagine* talking to anyone."

"Okay, Nina. Good," Jack said. She was angry, and part of his job was to let her vent. When it was appropriate. "Your arraignment's in about an hour. We don't have much time. First. Let me ask you, did you tell the detectives anything? What did you tell them?"

Nina raised one eyebrow. "Do you think I'm an idiot?"

Jack had paused a beat before answering. Possibly, and he'd seen it happen, her reaction was bravado, borne of fear and anxiety. She was facing life in prison if convicted, and she, clearly not an idiot, knew that. Maybe this was simply her method of managing her emotions. Or maybe she was simply a self-centered bitch.

But she was *his* responsibility now.

"I know you're upset," Jack began, attempting empathy, but it only resulted in Nina rolling her eyes. "So, no, correct? You didn't say a word?"

"I asked for a lawyer," she said. "Everyone knows that's what one does."

"Good." Jack didn't bother to contradict her. "Did they tell you anything? Ask you anything? What did they seem to care about?"

Nina templed her fingers, put the point under her chin. Possibly this was one of her boardroom power moves. But none of that studied body language would be effective here. And if she *was* smart, she'd understand that.

"I'll tell you from the beginning. Won't that be more efficient?" She didn't wait for him to agree. "I answered the door. One of the men there introduced himself as Detective Odman, Odgren, something, from the Boston Police Department, homicide division. I was so—surprised. I mean, it must have been about poor Danielle, correct? And I frankly was worried they suspected Tom."

Jack nodded. "Okay. Makes sense. Then what?"

"They asked if they could come in and talk to me. I said, about what? And they said Danielle Zander. Of course, then I assumed even more strongly it was about Tom. And I wasn't about to say a word. I was polite, naturally, and said I'd prefer to call a lawyer to advise me."

She pursed her lips, as if mentally replaying the scene. "And then they asked me where I was Sunday night."

Jack nodded again. That was bull. The cops always pushed the boundaries. But the rules were clear. After a person asked for a lawyer, there could be no more questions. He made a note of that on his pad. Plus, it meant they thought the murder was Sunday night. "And you said?"

"Please. What do you take me for? I reiterated that I wanted a lawyer. I said something about having made that clear."

"And then?"

"And then the moron arrested me. It was—insane. Surreal. Read me my rights. Standing there, in my doorway! Brought out *handcuffs*, then dragged me to the car he'd parked in the damn street, so I had to walk all that way. In public. I couldn't even get a coat."

Jack pictured this, the phony politeness, the attempt to weasel information, the brazen disobedience to the rules, the orchestrated humiliation.

Nina looked at the ceiling, a checkerboard array of bright black-and-white tiles. "Jack? What is going on?" she continued, her words coming faster. "Why would they arrest me? Me? You're the lawyer, you must know. Know something."

And this was the hell of it, Jack thought. No, he didn't know why she was a suspect. Not completely. Yet again, how the legal system is stacked against the defense. Exactly the opposite of how it should be.

"At this point I only have the police report from the discovery of the body," he told her. "I know they got a nine-one-one call from the trash guy. They picked up later than usual because of the snow. Cops responded to the scene. They found Ms. Zander's body at the dumpster. No immediately apparent cause of death, like gunshot wounds or stabbing."

He heard her draw in a breath.

"Sorry," he said.

"No, no, go on." She waved aside his concern. "I need to know every-thing."

"They speculate a blow to the back of the head, 'blunt trauma,' the report says. But nothing further."

"But by now? Don't you have . . ." She shook her head, held up her hands, entreating. "*Something?* What they're going to say? What evi-dence they have?"

"Nope," Jack had to say. "That's how the system works. It . . . sucks. Sorry for the language. But we won't hear what they have until they read their statement of the case in court. We'll deal with it from there. And your bail. But before we do all that, two things. One, they're not sup-posed to ask you anything after you ask for a lawyer, but it's good they tried. We can keep that blatant misconduct in our back pocket. But, two, the better news, it gives us a clue about what they have. What they *think* they have."

"They don't have anything!" Nina's voice went up, her veneer of sar-casm and control weakening.

He put up both palms. This was the real Nina coming through, and he didn't blame her. Frankly, she didn't know the half of it. Martha Gar-diner was a freight train, every case a must-win, no matter who got flattened on the way to a guilty verdict. But Jack felt exactly the same about a *not* guilty. And here they were, again, two locomotives running head-to-head. And, Jack calculated, this damn time it was the good guy's turn to prevail.

"Listen, Nina, you need to tell me. First, how well did you know Danielle Zander? And second, where were you? And I mean—every moment. From, say, Friday night until Monday afternoon. Where?"

CHAPTER **TWENTY-SIX**

RACHEL NORTH

I'd been in court more often in the last month than I had in the entire rest of my life. I shifted on the rock-hard wooden pew in the spectator section of the courtroom, the padding of my heavy winter coat the only thing cushioning my rear. Was *every* seat in *every* courtroom designed to be uncomfortable? I remembered complaining to Roni Wollaskay about our chairs in the superior court jury box—was it only weeks ago?

Talk about uncomfortable. Senator Rafferty, his coat buttoned and a scowl darkening his face, took up twice as much room on the pew next to me as he was entitled to. No one dared to sit on the other side of him. Like at a funeral, when people gave mourners their space. Danielle Zander's actual funeral was yet to be held, put on hold for the medical examiner's investigation.

Nina Perini Rafferty sat ramrod-backed and motionless at the defense table. Today, she was the victim.

Beside her sat Jack Kirkland, pin-striped and square-shouldered, his chair turned a supportive fraction toward Nina, his arm over the back of her chair, his demeanor protective and proprietary. Like he'd been with me yesterday. And last night on my doorstep. Today, he hadn't acknowledged me at all, though he must have seen me sitting here. Did he know what evidence the prosecutors had against Tom's wife? They'd worked pretty fast, charging her after one day. I tried to imagine her killing Danielle. I imagined me sitting on her jury, deliberating whether to put the wife of my employer in prison for life for killing a young woman who worked in his office. I imagined Tom Rafferty imagining that murder and that jury. Now both of his hands were clenched into fists. Maybe he thought Nina did it.

After the news about Nina broke this morning, we got so many phone calls that it almost blew the statehouse circuits. The senator, incensed or embarrassed, closed the office and sent everyone home. But even after Nina's arrest, he ordered his staffers to travel in groups. Which meant he thought Nina *didn't* do it.

Martha Gardiner—the gang was all here—sat with her arms crossed in front of her chest. Suede pumps, hair impeccable, wearing a dark got-to-be-designer suit. She'd also angled her body toward Nina, but to mark her territory, show the defendant who was in charge. Beside her sat Lizann Wallace, the same associate-wannabe who helped her in the Deacon Davis trial. Those two hadn't acknowledged me, either.

The judge turned pages in some document, behaving as if there were nothing else in the world going on. No drama, no tension, no news cameras, no reporters, no rampant curiosity. No defendant, her future in precarious balance, waiting for the proceedings to begin. And end.

"Ms. Gardiner?" The judge moved his wire-rimmed reading glasses to the top of his balding head, then attempted a smile.

Beside me, I felt Tom let out a spool of breath. He was a lawyer. He knew what was about to happen. But this time it was about his wife. And about his career, too. Would the citizens of Massachusetts embrace a senate president whose wife was a convicted murderer? Even a suspected murderer? I knew it took months, longer even, for actual trials to get under way. After my lifelong habit of studying murder mysteries and watching crime shows on TV, I knew there'd be discovery and investigation and interviews and legal wrangling. If Jack Kirkland couldn't get Nina released on bail, then Tom would be trying to conduct senate business with his wife in state custody. I knew from real life that was not gonna fly.

Would he take a demotion, maybe? Agree to the appointment of an interim senate president, maybe agree to move all of us to a ratty dinky office in the statehouse basement, keeping his head down and profile low while the murder investigation progressed? Unlikely.

He'd have to resign.

And when he resigned, he wouldn't be my boss anymore. And I'd be as toxic as he was. No one liked to be tainted with scandal, even someone else's. If Nina was found guilty, it would make sense for me to leave town. I sneaked a look at the senator. Or stay, if that worked out.

I yanked myself back to the current reality. Martha Gardiner, her voice unsettlingly familiar, read from a police report describing the scene behind the statehouse when the then-unidentified body was found.

"Responding to a nine-one-one call," Martha told the judge, "Boston Police Officer Carmine Boteri arrived at a statehouse parking lot, wherein he discovered a white female, approximately twenty-eight to thirty years of age, lying supine on the pavement in proximity to a dumpster. The woman was fully clothed in skirt and turtleneck sweater underneath a woolen coat, and upon first examination, Officer Boteri, though he determined she was deceased, could not determine a clear-cut cause of death. Whereupon he called for an ambulance and police backup. The victim, later determined to be . . ."

She—Dani—wasn't *in* the dumpster, the way the news reporters had written it.

I envisioned the murder scene, as much as I allowed myself to do so, as Gardiner continued with investigatory details. I risked another glance at Tom, but he stared straight ahead.

"Upon closer scrutiny of the victim by the medical examiner," Gardiner was saying, "the cause of death was determined to be blunt trauma, although no weapon was found at the scene."

Why did they suspect Nina? That was all I could think about. They had to explain that. But I wasn't a lawyer, and there was no one to ask.

Certainly not Tom Rafferty, who was as much a victim as his wife. The pews behind me were silent, reporters and spectators and tragedy seekers, courthouse regulars, I guessed, all waiting for the juicy stuff. Which was vile and sordid, except that's why I was here, too.

"Soon after the murder," Gardiner went on, "we were able to confirm via a confidential interviewee that the gold necklace Ms. Zander was wearing, very distinctive, with charms of small stars . . ."

I looked at Tom. He stared ahead. Hardly breathing.

". . . was given to her by her employer, Senator Thomas Rafferty."

Gardiner paused. The air went out of the room, then rushed back in. I saw every news camera swivel. Targeting the senator. It was all I could do not to shrink back, duck down, make myself small, and stay the hell out of the shot. But that would not be loyal. I tried to look dismissive. Derisive. As if this were an obvious prosecutor trick, impugning the reputation of an upstanding citizen and public servant. My boss.

The necklace. Tom was an *idiot.* Was *everyone* crazy?

It hadn't been for his *wife.* It was for *Dani.* I felt my brain turn black and the room go dark, and—*Rachel. Stop.* Tom had no idea I'd seen the necklace that weekend he'd left it at my apartment. So . . . damn. Think think *think.*

My professional brain knew Tom needed strategy. What would we say? What would we do? Were we still no-commenting? My personal brain was frying. In*sane.* Rafferty was so damn stupid. But wait. This meant prosecutors might think that Nina Rafferty was so enraged at this beautiful young "other woman," so jealous, that she killed her. *Really?*

I pursed my lips, considering. *Nina. Ballistic.* Maybe. It depended on what evidence they thought they had. And though this was not about me, it *was,* because—But wait. *No.* Tom didn't know I knew what was in the box. No one did. No one but me.

Tom was a statue. Not a twitch of a muscle, not a throb of a vein. I felt the cameras on us, hunting for a trace of emotion, of reaction, of surprise. Or, maybe, shame. I couldn't risk conferring with him, whispering or not. It made him look too guilty. As if we were planning a defense. We needed to ice our way through this moment.

But at the defense table, Nina had openly lost it. She turned to Jack, who had already turned to face her. Her jaw dropped, her eyes widened. She leaned closer to him. I saw her mouth the words "What the hell?" At least I thought that's what she said.

I heard Gardiner draw in a deep breath. Saw her elegant shoulders rise, then fall. I bet this was theatrics, playing for time, making sure her bombshell sunk in. Letting reporters get it all down, allowing cameras to get their shot and then put her back in the spotlight.

It worked. When she cleared her throat, all eyes—and camera lenses—pivoted back to her. Nina waited. Jack waited. The judge waited. I sneaked a quick look back toward the row of journalists. They were all texting like crazy. That red-haired Clea person was there, too, the one I saw at Gallery with Jack.

"The confidential interviewee," Gardiner continued, "whose name is being redacted by the police to protect said interviewee's privacy, also revealed . . ."

She stopped again. Her associate looked up at her, nodded. I saw her in profile but couldn't read her expression. I knew my own expression must be a jumble. Half my brain was crafting news releases, and the other half crafting my new résumé. *Rafferty and Dani.* I thought about that night he came to my apartment. What if I hadn't thrown him out?

I imagined myself as a dead girl wearing a gold necklace. A necklace with stars.

Gardiner was talking again. ". . . also revealed the senator to have a history of illicit relationships with other female members of his staff. Some of whom are on the staff even now. Which, we allege, his wife, Nina Rafferty, knew full well."

This time the audience went full-out nuts. Couldn't hold back the gasp that seemed to come from all of them at once, including me and including Rafferty himself, who muttered "asshole" under his breath. The judge banged some object that wasn't a gavel, a block of wood or something. He didn't yell *order, order*, like they did on TV. But his intent was clear. When a fidgety hush fell over the courtroom, the judge waited. One beat, two.

"One more outburst," he said. "One. And you will all be removed. Then I will close this courtroom. Understood?"

Fine with me, I thought. The fewer people who heard this stuff the better. I hoped there were no more cats in the bag. Several of the reporters had raced out of the room anyway, the courtroom door banging shut behind them. I mentally shook my head. Apparently serial adultery was bigger news than murder.

Nina put her face in her hands, her elbows on the table. Jack had his arm around her shoulders again. Gardiner had the classic snarky posture of a tattletale, the kid who was proud of herself for ratting to the teacher. Or perhaps that's how prosecutors looked when they scored.

"Ms. Gardiner?" the judge said. "Continue."

"Thank you," Gardiner said.

Her voice was confident, as if she didn't care that she was ruining the lives of so many people. Though I supposed she considered it an inevitability of her job. To her, Tom Rafferty might be a sleaze, but Danielle Zander was dead. And Gardiner thought she'd nabbed the woman who killed her. Plus, the police didn't arrest people they didn't have *some* evidence about. If Nina had killed her rival out of jealousy and revenge, it would be horrible. And tragic. For everyone.

But simply because it's horrible, that doesn't mean a jury won't believe it's true.

JACK KIRKLAND

Nina was clearly shocked by the necklace thing. Jack saw two blotchy spots of red appear on her pale cheekbones. She drew in a sharp breath, and her widened eyes darted from Jack to her husband to her hands—to her wedding ring, a gold band crisscrossed with diamonds—to somewhere off in her own imaginary distance. She touched her own double-strand necklace with two trembling fingers, then dropped her hand into her lap. As if the pearls had singed her fingertips.

Rafferty must be going bullshit crazy. Jack had to resist turning around to look as Judge Drybrough banged his wooden block for order. Jack also resisted looking at Rachel North, who he knew was sitting next to her boss. He'd seen Clea, too, though he'd pretended not to. "Other female members of his staff," Gardiner had told the court. Had Rachel known about that? Or—been involved?

Now he was the one to draw a breath. Was *she* Gardiner's interviewee? Was Rachel the informant who'd revealed her boss's repeated infidelities? Jack calculated the odds, the pros and cons, the possibilities. The timing. When would she have done that? And wouldn't Tom's ruin cost Rachel her job? What if she were so principled, so ethical, that the death of a colleague overcame her loyalty? Made telling the truth her only choice?

"Jack." Nina leaned close to him. Whispering. "How can that Gardiner woman—?"

"Ms. Gardiner, continue," the judge said.

Jack put a palm on Nina's arm, felt her delicate bones under the black sweater, her thin wrist. "It's okay," he whispered.

"Your Honor, on information and belief," Gardiner was pontificating, "as a result of her continued jealousy and inability to stop her husband from his continued infidelity—including her knowledge of Ms. Zander's so-called business trips out of town with Senator Rafferty, some of which lasted for several days—we believe that on or about Sunday of this week, Nina Perini Rafferty lured the victim from the senate office where she had been working, using some pretext or pretense. After all, Ms. Zander was in the employ of Nina Rafferty's husband and would have deferred to her wishes. We have confirmed with building security that Ms. Zander was indeed working that day, as a devoted public servant—"

Jack yearned to object. This was argument, opinion, not facts in evidence. There was nothing in evidence. Still, there was nothing to be gained from making their load of bull take longer than necessary.

Gardiner had paused, a blatant ploy to lure Jack into objecting. Jack ignored the tactic, instead made what only looked like notes on his yellow pad.

"A devoted public servant," Gardiner repeated. "And, Your Honor, we believe that once the two women were in the basic area of the dumpster, on a day when the vast majority of statehouse employees are not present, and, indeed, where only an insider like Mrs. Rafferty could have known there was no video surveillance, she brutally attacked her with a rock or brick or other such blunt object, whereupon Ms. Zander fell against the heavy steel dumpster, hit her head yet again, and was soon deceased."

The courtroom buzzed again. The horror, for a fraction of a second, winning the race with the judge's wooden block.

Jack wanted to kill Gardiner. This was unnecessary. Brutal. Humiliating.

Instead of committing that crime, he wrote on his legal pad. In block printing, all caps. He turned the pad to Nina.

DO NOT WORRY.

He underlined it twice, making sure it sank in.

No matter what, he quickly scrawled underneath.

She nodded. Weary, defeated, drained.

"Nina Rafferty is charged with first-degree murder," Gardiner said, "with malice aforethought and extreme atrocity, and we request that she be held without bail until trial."

Nina gasped, covered her mouth with her hand. Her eyes filled with tears. The high-powered exec Jack had interviewed earlier this morning had vanished, replaced by a terrified middle-aged woman faced with her husband's betrayal. And life in prison. Jack kept his eyes trained on the judge.

"Mr. Kirkland? We will hear you on the request."

Jack stood, almost savoring the moment. He took a deep breath, stalling. He knew Gardiner saw dollar signs in her head, envisioned headlines about some massive bankroll-busting bail and her brilliant victory in court. Thinking Nina Rafferty would never see the sun again.

"If it please the court, Your Honor, we will not be requesting bail."

Jack paused, long enough to confirm the bafflement in Gardiner's ferrety eyes. Long enough to let the audience react. Long enough to incite the judge's block-banging again. When Nina raised her eyebrows at him, he let one finger drop to the note he'd written. Pointed to it again. *Do not worry.*

"We will not be requesting bail." He even raised his voice a little, making sure the damn TV cameras could pick it up. There were few times in a lawyer's career when they got to stomp the shit out of the prosecution. Move over, Clarence Darrow. Jack Kirkland was in the house. "Because we are asking that the court dismiss all charges against Nina Rafferty. Mrs. Rafferty has an ironclad alibi for the time of the murder."

CHAPTER **TWENTY-SEVEN**

RACHEL NORTH

Crazy crazy crazy was all I could think. Tom Rafferty and I hustled out of the courthouse as fast as we could. I wrapped my arms around myself, fighting off the biting March air that knifed through me. It was threatening snow again. The steep and narrow hill to the statehouse became a wind tunnel, the climb and the cold and the stress intensifying everything. We were headed to the bank.

The press, surrounding us, incessant, unceasing, had finally let us go. After the court officers took Nina—sobbing uncontrollably—away, that Clea Rourke person, her red hair motionless but her mouth nonstop, had led the questioning in the crowded courthouse hallway.

"Will you make the bail? How soon?" Rourke had challenged the senator to answer, pointing a stick mic at him. "What's your reaction to the judge's decision to set it so low? Is Drybrough a campaign contributor?"

We hadn't been able to snatch a moment to confer, so at this point, Rafferty was on his own. I'd step in if needed, but decided it was better to keep my mouth shut. The senator was savvy enough to steer the press to the bottom line, that Nina was free. I wondered, though, how he'd handle the "illicit relationships with other female members of his staff" part. But the big story had to be Nina's alibi. Her alibi meant someone else killed Dani Zander. Someone still out there.

Rafferty had given me his overcoat to hold, knowing it'd look better on camera for him to be in his suit jacket.

I'd tamped down my ego and stepped back. It would be bad optics for us to be in the same photo if the headlines were about those provocative "relationships" accusations.

"Let me say this, and let me make this loud and clear." Rafferty used his campaign voice, strong and authoritative. The court officer, Hector, stood, arms crossed, in front of the closed door, and seemed to be taking in Tom's every word. "I am relieved—but not surprised—at this outcome. It is impossible—let me say it again, *impossible*—that my dear wife had anything to do with this tragedy. I am grateful for the legal skill and tenacity of Jack Kirkland, one of the finest attorneys in Massachusetts, who in this chaotic time drilled to the heart of the matter and proved that this prosecution was ill-advised, ill-conceived, injudicious, and rash. In fact, I am appalled that the district attorney would allow these cruel charges based on such shabby evidence. This was a rush to judgment, pure and simple, and I am grateful that this debacle is behind us."

"Yeah, well, the judge didn't *drop* the charges, Senator." Clea Rourke jabbed her mic closer. "So are you confident he will? What will happen if the Commonwealth finds more evidence?"

"And how about what Gardiner called your illicit relationships, Senator? Was she correct?"

I couldn't tell which reporter had the guts to ask that. Part of me, frankly, wanted to hear how he'd answer. But not in this predatory arena.

"Are you going to resign?"

"When will she be released?"

It always amused me how reporters never waited for the answers to their colleagues' questions. I waited, hugging Tom's sleek vicuña coat. Darkest navy, it smelled like citrus and leather and power.

"What are you going to say to your wife about—"

I'd stepped in front of Tom then, clutching the coat. Optics be damned. "The senator is grateful for the outpouring of public support in this case," I said. "As you can imagine, his first concern is seeing his wife released. And that is what he is about to do. We ask for your patience while this matter is resolved, and that you allow the senator and his wife some privacy while they—"

"No way, Rachel," one reporter called out, trampling my attempt to wrap up the onslaught. "Kidding me? Senator, what's your reaction to the illicit-relationship charge? Are you going to resign?"

"And since the judge did not drop the charges, your wife remains charged with murder. Did your wife kill Danielle Zander?"

"Do you think the killer is at large?"

"Are *you* a suspect, Senator?"

"Hey. *Hey.* We're done here." I interrupted the barrage, stolidly kept my position in front of the senator, and handed him back his coat. "You heard the lawyer, Mr. Kirkland, say Mrs. Rafferty has an *ironclad* alibi for the time of the murder. That's why the bail is so low. We fully expect . . ." I was improvising at that point, but figured it couldn't hurt. "We fully expect the charges to be dropped. And now, if you will excuse us."

We made it to the elevator, swimming through a sea of questions. As the doors closed in front of us, Tom Rafferty, hands mashed into his coat pockets, had not said a word. From the grim look on his face, now was not the time for questions.

It was driving me crazy, though. I yearned to ask him about those "illicit relationships." I kept imagining them. Picturing them. Every explicitly lurid possibility. Tom would have to face those accusations, pretty damn soon.

We shouldered out of the wind tunnel and through the revolving doors to the lobby of the bank, its brittle gilt and marble walls so opposite from the sunshine and bluster of outdoors. Two sullen guards, motionless, observed us as we entered, barely registering the imperious but flustered man and his doting subordinate. Almost another world, glass-walled cubicles and the unseen vaults behind them. But this was the world where Rafferty could get a cashier's check, made out for the five thousand dollars, and buy his wife's freedom.

For now, at least.

If the case against Nina fell through, that meant the murderer was still on the loose. A chill rattled my entire body, and it wasn't because of the weather.

JACK KIRKLAND

The morning after the Nina arraignment, Jack walked past the uniformed guards at the statehouse. The lobby, lofty and smoky-walled, possessed an ominous stillness. As if everyone inside were holding their breath to see what would happen next.

Elevators were empty. Doors stayed closed. Somewhere down the long corridor a phone rang, then instantly fell silent. Jack's footsteps echoed, the sound bouncing off the centuries-old stone walls. This historic building had certainly weathered worse. But not recently.

Jack had the morning *Globe* tucked under his arm as he pulled open the door to the senator's Communications Office. Unnecessary to bring it, he realized, as he saw the same newspaper, folded open to the front-page headlines, on Rachel's desk. She'd already read it. He saw the yellow sticky note stuck smack in the middle, between the words SHOCKING and FREE.

Jack, wait, back five mins.—R.

The *Globe* had split the front page, overwhelmed by the journalistic tug-of-war created by yesterday's events. The once-celebrated Nina Rafferty, accused murderer of a young senate staffer, was released on bail and without even an ankle bracelet. That story, with a photo of Nina and Jack snapped over the heads of a swarming clump of reporters, got the prime upper-right placement. Her husband, once a legislative rock star, had been humiliatingly trashed in court by the assistant district attorney and accused of infidelity and adultery and general perfidy. That story, with a photo of a gesticulating Rafferty taken in the courthouse hallway, was upper left.

What a freaking mess.

Jack had to hand it to himself, though, he thought, as he stared at the photos. He'd stayed cool, asked the right questions, done his job. Did Nina kill Danielle Zander? She'd insisted she couldn't have. That wasn't his problem. He'd won. Yesterday, at least.

What the future held, no one could guess. But Nina had made good on the retainer, so he was totally on board.

He looked at his watch. Five minutes, Rachel's note said. But five minutes from when? Where was she?

Jack tossed his paper into the empty wastebasket, then paced to the wide four-paned window and perched on the wide wooden sill. He looked out over a courtyard, a blotch of snow-speckled brown grass dotted with pointy shrubs surrounding a statue of a seated woman, all wide skirt and demure dress. Mary Something, he half remembered. Right. Dyer. Mary Dyer. She'd been hanged, in 16-something. On Boston Common, exactly like he'd reminded Rachel the other day. Hanged for . . . something.

There had been a moment in court, Jack had to admit, when he'd worried. Because certainly Nina could have cooked up this alibi story, knowing that he'd never have time to check it out, but neither would Gardiner. That she'd been on "semi-sabbatical"—her description—at some inn in Maine and shut off from cell service wasn't the most slam dunk of excuses. Or the most original. But who the hell cared. If he got her out on the strength of it, that was one step closer to not guilty. Or even, he dared to hope, to dropping the charges altogether.

Yup, he had to hand it to himself. He'd stood before the court, knowing this was a roll of the damn dice, but they were the only dice he had.

"Your Honor," he'd argued, "we will be filing a notice of alibi as soon as time allows, but due to the truncated timeline of this rush to judgment, suffice it to say that Mrs. Rafferty has assured me that she was not even in the Commonwealth of Massachusetts at the time of the murder, as my colleague sets the timeline as 'on or about Sunday of this week,' nor was she in this state in the several days prior to that. As a result of the Commonwealth's ill-advised presumption and its shoddy investigation, my client has been unfairly maligned, and unjustly forced to face a charge that not only is deplorable in its subject but devastating in its scope."

And if the investigators for the imperious Gardiner hadn't been savvy enough to track down her whereabouts, then screw 'em. Although they'd have faced nothing but dead ends. Nina hadn't told them anything. And Rafferty insisted he hadn't known where she was. Some relationship. But for their purposes now, Rafferty and his wife's seemingly icy marriage served the case well. No one else but Nina, no one he knew of, had known she was off in Maine. Where in Maine, and who with? And why? *That* she wasn't saying. At this point, she didn't need to.

"Mrs. Rafferty is a pillar of the Commonwealth, Your Honor." He'd almost smiled with the power of what came next. His less-prominent clients, gangbanger murder listers, provided no such pedigrees. "She is the wife of the president of the state senate, as you are well aware. She has immeasurable ties to the community, no criminal record, is no danger whatsoever to anyone, and is no more of a flight risk than you are, Judge." Jack had risked that personal addendum, hoping it proved how confident he was. He was relieved to hear an approving murmur from the audience. And the judge's scowl did not deepen.

"The evidence against her—the so-called evidence—is weak," he'd gone on. "At best. In fact, I would argue it is nonexistent. A necklace? And a concocted motive? Your Honor, we ask that you put an end to this before the Commonwealth suffers even further public embarrassment."

He wished he'd had the nerve to look at Gardiner then. She must've been peeing her pinstripes. Served her right. Jack did have the pleasure of seeing the indecision on Drybrough's face. The judge obviously knew the shit was hitting the fan and would splat on him next. He'd wheeled his chair away from his lofty desk, as if trying to distance himself from having to make a decision. Good luck with that.

Gardiner, almost spluttering, had used the only weapons she had. Derision and sarcasm. "This is laughable," she'd said. She'd pulled out "Who's to say this is true?" and "We'll certainly investigate." She'd wound up with "This makes no difference to the evidence we have already amassed in this case," and "As a result, we strenuously object to a minimal bail and vigorously oppose Mr. Kirkland's fairy-tale motion to drop the charges."

A man and a woman, coats and briefcases, now walked into the landscape below. The couple approached the statue, then disappeared, hidden by the wide stone plinth and the seated figure of martyr Mary Dyer.

"Jack? Something going on outside? I got this for you, if you're interested."

Rachel, a paper cup of coffee in each hand, held one out to him. "Black, if I remember? So—got your text. What can I do for you?"

He stood, accepted the coffee. "Thanks. Yeah. Listen, have you ever been to that dumpster?" he asked. "Can you see it from anywhere inside the building?"

"Why?" She pulled out the swivel chair behind her desk and pointed him to a foofy little couch as she took her seat. She propped her chin on one hand and stirred her coffee with the other, the red plastic stir-stick scraping on the bottom of her white paper cup.

She looked tired, he thought. In all black. A weariness around her eyes, a sadness in her attempt to smile. Smart of her to question his motives, he had to admit. He was Nina's lawyer, after all. Rachel couldn't know if he was working on her case right now or not. If she'd known him longer, she'd know he was always working.

"Why? Because I should go see it," he said. "Can you take me there?"

She blinked once, twice. Maybe she was squeamish about seeing a murder scene close up. Or maybe she was wary of being involved at all.

Or maybe, for some reason, she didn't want to be around him. She'd agreed to see him though, answered his text this morning within ten seconds.

"The dumpster? Is *that* why you texted?" She puffed out a breath, then pointed at the folded *Globe*. "There's a thing in the paper. A diagram and everything. Can't you use that to find it, instead of me? I've gotta say, I don't want to be anywhere near that—"

"I get it," he interrupted. It was pretty inconsiderate of him, come to think of it. He'd get so focused on an investigation, a case, an innocence, that he'd forget the feelings of everyone who wasn't equally focused. His ex-wife, for instance, long gone, had not been willing to share him with his job. Caroline had called him a workaholic, as if that wasn't a good thing. But he learned from the experience with her. "And I'm sorry, you know? Should never have asked. Stupid of me. But the reason I texted? I need to talk to you in person, to find out—"

"Whether Tom Rafferty was sleeping with me?"

Rachel's interruption, her voice dusky with sarcasm, almost made him choke on his bitter coffee.

"What?"

"Did you know she—Gardiner—was going to say that? In open court?" Rachel stood so quickly that the sticky-noted newspaper slid to the floor. She didn't pick it up. "I'm sure you assumed it was me she was talking about."

"Rachel, listen." Jack put his coffee on a spindly side table. Stood. Tried to decide what to do. She probably hadn't slept last night at all. He imagined her wide-eyed, tossing and turning, haunted by public humiliation. By the whispers, the discord, the implication, the suspicion. Rafferty's office had been deserted when Jack arrived, desks empty and phones unanswered. Other staffers apparently had stayed away, shunning the very proximity, as if the senator's troubles were contagious. And maybe, because of Gardiner's insinuations, they were.

Rachel's face was crumbling now, her facade of bravado disintegrating almost into tears. It was all he could do to stop himself from reaching out to her, comforting her. He took a step closer to her, risking it. She was so vulnerable. Caught in the middle.

"Listen. Rachel." He was surprisingly concerned for her. This was not her fault. It was almost heartbreaking. As if this intelligent, successful, and—okay—gorgeous woman was yet another victim. Danielle and then Nina and now Rachel. And he could be her defender. He wanted to. He needed to. "No. I absolutely did not think she was talking about you. Martha Gardiner is an idiot. She makes shit up. Seriously. She's a train wreck. I wouldn't be surprised if—"

"Really?" Rachel whispered. She didn't move. "Then *why* would she say that? Make me look so terrible? And Jack? *Did* you think it was me? Even for a moment? Tell me, honestly."

Despite himself, he was on the hunt for answers. Motives. If Rafferty was a predator, and Nina was jealous? Or maybe Rafferty himself . . . ?

Jack yanked himself back to the moment.

"Of course I didn't think so, *don't* think so, Rachel." That was semi-true. It *had* crossed his mind, but not for long. "Martha Gardiner is a slime," he went on. "That's a legal term."

He tried a smile, seeing if he could make Rachel smile, too. He needed her to smile. He needed her to smile *at him.* And often. But it was fantasy for him to think that. Inappropriate.

"How do you know she makes stuff up?" she asked. And he'd succeeded, because she was sort of smiling. "She wins all the time, I know that. Does she cheat? Do you think she—" She stopped, raised one eyebrow. "Oh, *I* get it."

"Get what?" He didn't know where to stand now. He felt awkward, all hands and arms, and he was too close to her, but too far from her at the same time. He headed for his coffee, used it as a prop, a refuge.

"That's why you wanted to talk to me about the Deacon Davis trial. You think Gardiner cheated."

Now it was his turn to puff out a breath. That wasn't a yes-or-no question. That was a lifelong endless battle between defense and prosecution. What was cheating and what was zealous representation? What was simply more nimble use of the rules?

"No," he finally said. "But that jury's another conversation. And that's one of the reasons I texted. Our conversation about that was—interrupted."

"But what if . . ." Rachel seemed to be off in her own thoughts, and sat perched on the edge of the cluttered desk, her legs sticking out onto the oriental rug.

She wore sleek black tights. Suede shoes. A black skirt. This was not the time to be thinking about her legs. Or her neck or her hair or the way he thought she might be looking at him. He was too old for her. But was he? He was an idiot.

"What if there's like, a list?" she asked. "Would you be getting that from Gardiner? Would that be in the files?"

"Files? List?"

"Files you get on the case. Discovery, whatever they call it. And, yeah, about the women. The illicit relationships. Whatever that mysterious 'interviewee' person said. Does someone have a record of it?" Rachel put her hands over her face for a moment, then took them away. "I mean, from a Human Resources standpoint. I'm chief of staff here. I'm in charge. If there's an employment situation, I'm the one who has to handle it. You know? If Senator Rafferty—between us, I cannot even bear to imagine that level of imbecility—but if the senate president is screwing around on my watch, that's not only going to tank his career, it'll tank mine. I cannot allow that. So, Jack? For my own self-preservation? If you have access? I'd appreciate it."

Her face softened, and he saw how fragile she was, how on the edge. He didn't blame her. It was hardly business as usual, and she was at the center of it.

"Does it exist?" She put her palms together, as if praying for him to say yes.

She knew there was a killer out there. Someone who'd killed a colleague, someone from her own office. He was used to thinking about murder. He'd learned to compartmentalize and analyze, stay on the emotional outside. But Rachel? She was trying to hide her fear, he could tell.

"I'm trying to stay normal," she went on, taking a sip of coffee. "But I'm having a little difficulty with that. As you can imagine. I'm terrified. Looking over my shoulder every second."

Jack drank his coffee, too. Good old coffee, the useful stall. She knew he was stalling, and he knew she knew, but there you had it. If the case went forward, then sure, he'd be given the transcripts of the confidential informant who'd supposedly ratted out Tom Rafferty's transgressions. But if the case was nol-prossed—as he had to hope it would be—essentially dismissed and Nina no longer charged, then he'd be getting zippo. Because he'd have no reason to be given anything. That information, whatever lists there were or weren't, would languish in Danielle Zander's files. Until—if ever—they brought charges against someone else. Some cases go unsolved. Stay cold.

He explained all that to Rachel, and she seemed to understand.

"I'll wait," she said. "As long as it takes."

"Speaking of files." He'd thought of something. Not necessarily a good thing, but a valuable thing. A probative thing. "Let me ask you something."

Problem was, he couldn't figure out how to make this seem casual, mainly because it wasn't casual. He could subpoena it at some point, if it came to that, so maybe asking Rachel was a mistake. But in witness questioning, when you want to sidetrack the target from your goal, you put your focus question in the middle of a series of items, so the target is distracted. For this question, if the results were to be provided without time-consuming legalities, it was now or never.

"I'm also wondering if you could give me the senator's schedule for the past few weeks. And I also wondered"—he talked faster, to distract her from his focus on Tom Rafferty's whereabouts—"whether you'd like to have lunch with me today?"

PART
THREE

NOW

CHAPTER **TWENTY-EIGHT**

RACHEL NORTH

I hardly think about Dani Zander anymore.

The realization overwhelms me as I look at the name my fellow intern Nick Soderberg has printed on the conference room whiteboard. Danielle Zander.

I take my place at the long table, seating myself apart from the other interns, the ones who were on time for this meeting, and grateful that the general buzz is not directed at latecomer me but at Leon Colacetti, who, praise all that protects us, had just carried in a distracting tray of sugary doughnuts and a cardboard box of Dunkin's coffee.

Martha Gardiner is writing on a yellow pad and acknowledges my entrance with a fleeting smile.

"Glad you could make it," she says. "In time for refreshments. We'll take five minutes."

"I'm so sorry, Martha," I begin. "But Jack didn't tell—"

She holds up a palm. I stop.

The interns pounce on the doughnuts.

Is this what Gardiner was alluding to at Salamanca? What we'll be working on so closely? I need to decide what this means. *Danielle Zander?* From what's written on the whiteboard, they must be reopening the case. My brain stops. Reverses. Spins to another time.

Danielle Zander. I'd assumed and accepted, with all my being and understanding, that what happened that gruesome day six years ago would haunt me forever. Endlessly. Relentlessly. As well it should. That I'd always be looking over my shoulder, flinching at strangers, afraid to walk alone at night. After that day, my world had transformed. Shifted, changing color and position, like a Rubik's Cube gone mad.

Tom Rafferty had to resign. His wife, humiliated, left town for parts unknown after the charges against her were dropped. Apparently, her alibi held up. The rest of the senate office staff dispersed. It wasn't like Danielle's presence in our office—or her absence—was noticed and relived every day. None of us were in the office anymore to feel it, or to miss her. It was no longer "our" office. It was incredibly disturbing, and everyone constantly worried about what might have happened, and about the killer, who remained at large. It wasn't some crazy serial murderer, they said, since no similar crimes followed. I felt guilty, of course. Survivor guilt, I guess. And also because, truth was, I never liked Danielle.

I was steamrolled by the whole thing in another way, too, of course. "Illicit relationships" was never far from people's thoughts back then. And I felt guilty about that, too, as if they were all thinking "illicit," and then labeling me. Finding me guilty of something I didn't do. You can't be guilty of *wanting* something. That's just—life.

But I didn't leave town, as I'd considered and probably should have, but I'd definitely pulled back. Flown under most everyone's radar. Stayed inside, lost a lot of weight. A few weeks later, after Jack's approval, of course, I cut my hair and bleached it to the current streaky blond.

After Senator Rafferty resigned, though, there was hardly another whisper about his illicit relationships. The legislative powers that be, and everyone else, moved on to the next shiny-thing scandal. Little me, not specifically named in the court case, became old news, *so two years ago,* then four. Now six. And my colleagues at the law school, college kids back then, teenagers, have no idea. Not that they mention to me, anyway. I became peripheral, a bystander at a disaster, a bit player, good for one sound bite and then oblivion. Jack and I never discussed it, that black

hole of murder—I'm still feeling dramatic about it—that brought us together and binds us in silence. He thinks he won the case. I agree. And
our lives go on. Such as they are.

Because the murderer is out there. I cannot forget that. The fear haunts
me, no matter how much I try to make myself into another person with
another life.

Such as life is right now. I'm angry. *So* angry. I'd *heard* the phone ring
this afternoon, *heard* Jack answer it. And he'd "gotten distracted"? Forgot to tell me Martha called this meeting? I can't believe he passive-
aggressived me into being late. I hope Martha isn't angry. It's hard to
tell with her.

Nick begins again, after swiping powdered sugar from his lips.

I listen to his Zander cold-case update—it's still hard to fathom those
words—but Gardiner's phone buzzes. She picks up with a terse "Gardiner," and then starts listening to whoever called her.

That puts the meeting on hold again. Andrew DiPrado, in Gardiner-
worthy pressed khakis, and Eli Lansberry, who's even wearing a tie and
sport coat. *They*'d been on time, clearly, and sit next to each other on
the good-kids' side of the table. Nick Soderberg, positioned at the whiteboard and wearing a navy blazer and white T-shirt over modest jeans,
looks like J.Crew designed a campaign poster for campus president. No
one talks. I'm the outlier, the old one, the latecomer. I try to look like I
belong.

Back then, Danielle's murder case had languished. The lead detective
on the case, pit bull death star Lewis Millin, retired soon after, moved
away. Danielle had no family that anyone could find, so no agonized
mother or firebrand sister kept poor dead Danielle in the headlines.
There'd be a tiny update in the newspaper from time to time, a *Where
are they now?* kind of thing. But soon after, even the persistent Clea
Rourke had left town for some big job. She's back now, after all those
years, her hair redder and her lips weirdly puffy. I couldn't figure out if
she'd made the connection about me when we saw each other outside the
courthouse after the Jeffrey Baltrim pizza-delivery-case arraignment.

Jack finally admitted he and Clea had been "a thing," briefly, more in her head than his, he insisted. That the dinner at Gallery had been the end of it, he said, and they'd parted company amicably. Clea Rourke and Jack. Gimme a *break*.

Martha Gardiner, in disgrace, had pretended the reason she was leaving the Suffolk County DA's office back then was that she'd been offered a higher-status position in Middlesex County. Which everyone knew was a lie. Jack had ripped her case against Nina Rafferty to shreds, humiliated her and her boss, and, bottom line, Gardiner had lost. The cardinal sin. She was fired, no matter how she'd tried to gild it.

It was like a Broadway show. Where at the end of the run, the cast disperses. But at curtain close of this particular drama, the death of Danielle Zander, there was no big reveal of the bad guy.

I doodle on my yellow pad, making boxes like I always do. Perspective, I think, exactly what I need right now.

As the world forgot about Danielle, I had, too. Almost. And, ironically, if that's the proper use, I came out on top after that fiasco. Her murder is why I got married.

Jack and I first compared notes about Danielle Zander at lunch, then about the missing—he called it "vacationing"—Nina Rafferty, who'd paid him some retainer but then nothing else, figuring, correctly, the charges would be dropped.

"I'd have done anything to prove she didn't do it," Jack had told me. He'd orchestrated a booth in the back of Explorateur that day, and, ignoring the noontime bustle, we sat opposite each other on brown leather seats, drinking white wine from water glasses in case anyone noticed us. "Anything. They had a semi-case with that jealousy motive, you know, and the . . . other personal stuff. Whoever ratted Tom out, I have no idea. Or if it's even true. I was ready to go nuclear, but turned out Nina had that alibi."

"What *was* that?" I'd figured, now that the heat was off, off Nina, he might tell me.

He'd played with his BLT, rescuing an escaping shard of bacon. "Yeah, well," he finally said, "let's simply say it wasn't the greatest of all airtight alibis. But it was sufficient. Set and match."

Later, over prosecco at Spiga, we talked about the Deacon Davis jury, Jack's crusade back then. But, telling him the least amount possible, I convinced him there'd been nothing untoward in the deliberations. And there *wasn't* anything untoward, not that I knew of, or even suspected. Jack finally accepted the loss. As much as, I was to learn, as much as he ever accepted a loss. Which was never. We went on to dinner, immersed in conversation about the law and politics and power.

Then a few nights later, we had dinner without talking about any cases at all. Simply talking about us. We did the same thing at breakfast the next day. I told him about my past and my long-gone mom, even the truth-book story, I think, and about my lawyer-father, who'd usually only criticized me. Jack, rubbing my shoulders, told me I'd make a terrific lawyer. And I admit, I'd been thinking about that myself. Lawyers know the rules, and that was the only way to get ahead. Soon after, I'd resurrected my LSATs. Nailed them. Then moved in with him. Happily before my savings ran out. We'd gotten married at Boston City Hall. Hardly anyone even knew about it, and hardly anyone made a big deal. Or cared.

Life went on. I cooked. I read. I kept house. Jack supported me. He continued his relentless battles, defending hopeless cases. And winning more than his share. I made it into Harvard and through two years, vowing to spend my life defending people, protecting them, giving them a chance. Jack lost the Marcus Simmons Dorn murder case, and faced the DORN DID IT headlines. I, now signed on for the summer with Jack's sworn enemy, had investigated a murder with her my first day on the job.

And now the name Danielle Zander is front and center again. And Martha Gardiner had put it there. She must have engineered this. Made it happen. But *why?*

And I'm equally concerned about *how.*

I'm still learning the rules, but I definitely understand jurisdiction.

And I think this might be the key. If Dani Zander was killed in Suffolk County, by the dumpster in the statehouse parking lot, it's a Suffolk County case, and under the auspices of Suffolk County law enforcement. The only way Gardiner, an employee of *Middlesex* County, could get jurisdiction—I feel myself frowning, as if I'm taking a Criminal Procedure quiz.

Oh. Easy one. The crime must be prosecuted in the venue where it took place. Does Gardiner possibly think Dani's murder *didn't* happen at the dumpster? That it happened in Middlesex County?

I feel the world shift. This office might reopen the Danielle Zander murder because the murder took place *here*? That would change everything.

Gardiner's off the phone. She slides it back into her tote bag. Raises a hand, signaling Nick to go on. I tune back in to Nick's recitation of the case, facts I know all too intimately.

"A gold necklace, found clasped around the victim's neck under her turtleneck"—Nick pulls out an eight-by-ten photograph from a manila folder, magnets it with a shiny red dot to the whiteboard—"was traced to Tiffany, the one on Newbury Street. Police later found a gold clip-on earring at the scene. The earring was not Ms. Zander's. They couldn't trace it. And they held that fact back from the media."

I put two fingers to one earlobe, even though I have pierced ears. The necklace. I cannot get over that damn necklace. Even now, I can feel its weight around my neck, the gold warmed by the heat of my skin, how I'd pretended it was Tom's own touch. Even now, every cell in my body remembers, intensely, humiliatingly, the winter day when I wished I could sink into the earth. Tom Rafferty. What a total idiot.

Nick pulls something else out of the manila file.

"Police found this photo in the *Globe*." He clicks a blue-dot magnet to one corner of what looks like a photograph printed from a website, and posts it on the whiteboard. I lean forward to see better. It's Tom Rafferty, smiling in a tux, a be-gowned Nina on his arm. I remember that night, his expression and hers and the flashing cameras. I'd worn my little black, but, of course, I'm not in the photo. I don't like being in pictures. Even my statehouse profile had a faceless avatar. This particular photo of the happy couple had been in the "Names" section. The mini-headline says SENATE PRESIDENT AND WIFE ATTEND GALA FUND-RAISER.

"And wife." Wonder how she liked dealing with that, playing second fiddle. Easy to see why the cops would suspect her. Would she be dumb enough to wear earrings to kill someone, did they think? If so, was she dumb enough to lose one at the scene? Maybe they figure it was the heat of passion. Maybe they figure she didn't realize she'd lost it. And when she did, she realized she certainly couldn't go back to retrieve it.

"As you can see," Nick points out, "the earrings are clearly the same. However—"

"Mrs. Rafferty refused to confirm the one found at the murder scene was hers." Gardiner interrupts Nick's recitation of the evidence. "She refused to confirm anything, in fact, since her lawyer . . ." Martha pauses, looks at me with that knowing face she uses, then goes on. "Refused to let her speak with us. As Rachel well knows. You all remember she worked in that office, correct?"

I try to make my expression convey *Ain't life funny?* and I say nothing. And obviously Nick, Eli, and Andrew know precisely what she's talking about. There's not a confused face in the bunch. No one asks "What office?"

Will anyone ask how this case got *here,* to Middlesex, though? And why Gardiner is so interested? I change my look to attentive. Participatory. Team player. And wait.

CHAPTER **TWENTY-NINE**

MARTHA GARDINER

Martha Gardiner untied the dark red string around the accordion file, unwrapping it a bit more slowly than necessary, letting Rachel wonder what was going on. After the meeting ended, she'd asked Nick to leave the file behind, so she and Rachel could have a private chat. Rachel being late was perplexing, and if it seemed to matter, she'd ask about it. But later. Rachel now sat across from her at the conference table, silent.

Martha pulled the file open, the dark cardboard pockets expanding, wide enough to let Rachel see there were tabbed files and manila folders inside. She glanced up to see if Rachel was attempting to read them. She wouldn't dare, not at this point, but the woman was nothing if not ambitious. Hungry for information. Rachel certainly knew more than she'd revealed about the Zander murder. That husband of hers definitely did.

"Martha?" Rachel asked, her swivel chair squeaking with the abruptness of her question. "Who do you think killed poor Danielle?"

Rachel couldn't help but ask about it, Martha figured, and didn't blame her. An impossible thing, this murder. So personal. So close. But Martha wasn't totally sure of anything. That's what this summer was about.

"What do you think we think?" Martha inquired, looking eager to hear. "There's a whole list of people who might be guilty, right? A whole list of potential murderers? Ha ha, the murder list. Your husband would love that, wouldn't he? Anyway. That's why you're here. You have insight, I know it. Maybe there's something you don't realize you know. Maybe you heard something or saw something, or someone told you something back then. Even years later. Maybe we can discover it together. Is that possible?"

She saw Rachel's face darken.

"Did you . . ." The younger woman looked at the ground, then at the ceiling. Then at her, a frown creasing her forehead. "Martha? I thought you—you said at lunch you chose me to work with you because I had potential. Because of my personal skills. Not because I knew a murder victim."

Martha loved this, how people's insecurities inevitably rose to the surface. How valuable they could be. How useful. She tried to look offended.

"Oh, Rachel. Don't take everything personally. I meant exactly what I said. We can work together. That's my goal. So. As a member of the good-guy team?" Martha smiled, letting her know they were sisters and confidantes. "Is there anything, maybe now seen through the filter of your legal training—anything new that leaps to mind? Any suspicions? Any suspects?"

Rachel had picked up Nick's black marker and now rolled it between her palms. "Well? I've thought and thought about who the police suspected might have done it, and I don't know if—I don't want to speculate."

"Oh, do. Go ahead." Martha held the file in her lap. Leaned closer to Rachel, briefly, forging a connection. "And it's not speculating. It's brainstorming. Only between us. It's what partners do."

"Do you still believe it was Nina Rafferty?" Rachel pulled off the top of the marker, clicked it back on. Did it again. "I mean—I'm sorry, Martha. I know that was a defeat for you."

"Guess you know that firsthand." Martha couldn't help it, though she knew it was unworthy. She reached over, gave Rachel a quick pat on her forearm. "Sorry, Rachel. Yes, I'm a tiny bit bitter. I'm only human. But I hate to lose. And I'm sure your husband feels the same way. Does *he* think Nina did it? Have you ever asked him? You can tell me. And keep going. Who else? You said you'd thought about it. I have, too."

"I mean, who would it be?" Rachel said, her eyes widening. "Rafferty himself? I mean, that's impossible. Isn't it? Or do you suspect him? It has to be—her lover? Or some deviant stranger? But that person is out there. Do you or the police have *any* clues?"

Martha fiddled with the file strings, retying them slowly, considering Rachel's questions. She placed the fat folder on the table beside her, rested one elbow on it. She could hear the buzz of the fluorescent lights, smell the sugar from the leftover doughnuts and the harsh aroma of the coffee dregs.

Places we never expected to be, Martha thought. If Nina Rafferty had been found guilty, or if she, Martha, had won that damn case, she'd never been sitting in this cramped office. As it was, that one loss had ripped Martha's career out from under her. How could she have been so quick on the trigger, so supremely confident? How could she have let a killer go? She was older now, more experienced. Sometimes, she knew, a devastating loss was all one needed to insure a spectacular win. But it took time. And it took the correct puzzle pieces placed in the correct positions. On this bleak Sunday afternoon in a second-tier DA's office, she was sitting across from one of those pieces.

"I've never forgotten this case," Martha finally said. "Have you?"

Rachel fidgeted in her chair, winced when the wheels squeaked again. "Of course not."

"That poor young woman. She was a public servant. Trying to make the world a fairer place, a safer place. Exactly as we are. If we don't stand up for the victims, who will?"

"I know," Rachel said.

"I need you to work on this with me." Martha decided to lay it on the line. No reason to be coy. Justice had a peculiar persistence, and part of law enforcement was understanding the flow. "I can't let this go. It's my job to resolve this. That young woman's death haunts my conscience. Her *murderer* is out there. It has almost—possessed me."

"Me, too." Rachel leaned forward, clasped her hands under her chin. "But Martha, why are you looking into this now? Are you reopening the case? Did something happen? How did you get Suffolk to hand this over?"

"Yes, Nick did a fine job organizing the files from over there." *One step at a time,* Martha warned herself. She needed to be sure how trustworthy Rachel could be. How much she'd told her husband, and how much he'd told her. Or warned her. "The files were mine, after all. My case. I needed Nick to make sure everything was intact. Who knows who went through this stuff or who manhandled it. But Nick's not the one best equipped to work on the case. You are."

Rachel nodded, as if she were pondering this. Martha let her think she had a choice. Although as an intern, she didn't, in reality, have much choice at all. Martha was her boss, and Martha controlled her future. And she knew it. Rachel certainly understood this was a chess game, as all cases were. She was a particularly interesting piece of it, Martha thought. Jack, too. She kept wondering if one was the pawn. Or if they both were.

"But, and forgive me, Martha—"

"There's nothing to forgive. And I know you need to get up to speed. Of course. I'll fill you in on details when the proper time comes."

Rachel looked nervous, as if she was deciding whether to say something.

"You can ask me anything," Martha said. She slid the file into her briefcase, then looked up. Pleasant and encouraging. Whatever Rachel wanted to say, it might be helpful.

"Ethically . . ."

Martha's eyebrows went up, she could feel them. Okay, this surprised her. "Ethically what?"

"Is it ethically appropriate for me to work on this?"

"Appropriate." Martha couldn't believe this woman was taking this tack. She'd accepted this job. If she had any qualms, it would have been more *appropriate* to face them sooner.

"Well, yeah, I mean, you know. I mean, since I worked with Danielle. And all."

"Did you kill Danielle Zander?" Martha asked. "Do you know who did?"

Deer in headlights was too clichéd. Rachel clearly wasn't expecting that question, which is why Martha asked it.

"Do I *know*?" Rachel blinked, then again. "Why could you possibly think I would know? How?"

"Kidding." Martha flipped a hand. "To make a point. Since you didn't and you don't know who did—you *don't,* is that correct? Or you certainly would have mentioned that in your interview with Lewis Millin." She flattened her palms on the tabletop. Her Harvard signet ring tapped on the surface, the red stone glistening under the lights. "Which, as I know, you did not. So, in reality, you're the most valuable person we could have. You know the geography, you know the system, you know the players, you know the relationships. You know her lawyer, too, don't you? And soon enough you'll know everything in the file."

"I didn't know *her,* though, Ms.—Martha. Not well."

"Then in that way you are precisely like the rest of us. And all the more reason why it's '*appropriate.*'" Martha raised an eyebrow, to telegraph she wasn't letting Rachel off the hook. "That you should be involved."

"Okay. But." Rachel gulped. "Could I ask if Nina Rafferty is still a suspect? Since my husband—"

"Who was not your husband at the time of her arraignment years ago, correct?"

"Well, no." Rachel ducked her head, as if acknowledging the logic. "But what if, say, what if it turns out the evidence shows Nina Rafferty *is* guilty? I know we can bring charges again, if such new information is brought to light. But since Jack—"

"Forget *Jack*." Martha Gardiner stood, picked up her briefcase with the red-tied file inside. "For once. Rachel, this is about you, not him. And it's about justice for Danielle Zander. Try to remember that. It's what I'm trying to teach you. Now I'm asking *you*. If Nina Rafferty is guilty, is that a problem for *you*?"

"Of course not," Rachel said.

CHAPTER **THIRTY**

RACHEL NORTH

"Hey you. What was that all about?" Jack is sprawled in his den chair, legs across one upholstered arm, cell phone in hand, as I come in through the back door. He keeps it plugged in while he sits there, afraid to use up even a tiny percent of the battery if he doesn't have to. He stashes the phone between two fringed throw pillows. A wineglass, half full of white, is on the end table beside him. "What was so crucial that Gardiner called you in on a Sunday? And kept you this late? Pretty disrespectful, if you ask me. Which I am well aware you did not. Did someone die?"

"Hey you," I say. It was no surprise he'd asked me, simply a husband wondering why his wife was unexpectedly summoned to work. He was participating in my life, and that was appropriate.

Appropriate. The word almost made me laugh. It hadn't mattered, far as I could tell, that Jack was the one who'd made me late. Maybe he honestly did forget.

"Or did someone crack a big case?" Jack goes on, luckily for me, not waiting for me to continue. He picks up his wine, toasts me, takes a sip. What cases he's working on, or whatever, he's not saying. Since I've been working with Gardiner, Jack has decided—he told me one night just before we went to sleep—it's not fair to tell me, not fair to tempt me, because I might reveal some tactic to the enemy.

It's weird to hear the DA's office called "the enemy," but I suppose a guilty person might consider it so. Or a defense attorney.

"Funniest thing." I dump my shoulder bag under the kitchen table, unwrap the filmy scarf from around my neck, leaving the ends dangling. I pull open the fridge and stare at the contents, stalling, finalizing my tactics while choosing between water and wine. Jack has wine. "Gardiner wants to . . ."

I'd decided, on my solitary drive home, to tell him the whole truth about everything. What Gardiner assigned me to work on. Because Jack's a lawyer, not to mention my husband, which makes it double-super-confidential. He wouldn't be involved, anyway, unless Nina was under suspicion, which, right now, I could honestly say I didn't know. If Nina Rafferty is a suspect again, which Gardiner hadn't revealed—just like she hadn't revealed anything, saying we'd start planning our strategy on Monday—we'd go from there.

By the time I'd turned onto Crystal Lake Ave., I'd changed my mind. I *wasn't* going to tell Jack. Because if Nina Rafferty was a suspect, then it would only be destructive and hurtful to dangle that possibility in front of the person who was—is?—her lawyer. And to whom I couldn't possibly divulge any of our investigation. So better for me not to tell him.

I'd stopped at the red light. Outside, a candy-colored sunset streaked the sky, as if nature, encouraging our optimism, was revealing the promise of the gentle summer to come. I tapped my fingers on the steering wheel, calculating. Gardiner was right. I knew a lot about this case, and, yes, probably as much as anyone did. Who better to work on it? If I could crack the Zander case, and get Nina convicted, that would make me a rock star.

Not to Jack, however. And that would leave me in an untenable marital situation. If Martha Gardiner *does* think Nina killed Danielle

Zander, it would be my stated goal to prove my own husband was wrong. And that would never fly.

Of maybe . . . it would. Maybe it would help everyone. After all, if Nina was found guilty the case would be closed forever and all the loose ends tied up. Jack's goal was simply trying to make sure the system was fair. Everyone simply had to play by the rules.

The light turned green.

But maybe I could figure out another way to deal with it. Solve the case, get a conviction, be a legal rock star, and make my husband happy. I'll get all the case notes and lists and records. I'll do my very best, totally go for it, totally prove myself. And maybe in the end, it wouldn't be Nina who'd get convicted. Maybe no one would, the Danielle Zander murder case would stay unsolved, and I'd have just worried unnecessarily.

By the time I'd pulled up in our driveway, with motion-sensor lights spotting the last of our stalwart white tulips, I'd decided. I wasn't going to say a word. It was too preliminary. Too iffy. Too soon to make a move. I had to see what Martha Gardiner was planning. What cards she held. And then I'd play mine.

"Gardiner wants to what? Earth to Rachel? You just stopped in the middle of a sentence." Jack taps one finger to his temple. "What happened—your brain give out?"

"Funny," I say, refusing to be bullied by him. I pull out the wine, close the refrigerator door. "Sorry, honey, more like my brain's full. Of lawyer stuff. You know the feeling, right? And I was looking in here for the wine. I'll join you."

Jack digs out his phone again, starts texting or something, while I'm pouring my sauvignon blanc. I'm not gonna make a big deal of this. He works, I work, it's all in a day's.

"Nothing. Gardiner wants to assign us to teams, something like that, to learn about, I don't know, how the system works. How the office works with the staties. She mostly told stories about her big cases, you know her, and we all had to sit there and pretend to be mesmerized by how she wins all the time." I pretend to wince. "Sorry."

"I see," Jack says. Puts his phone away. "And for that she dragged you all in on Sunday?"

"'Team building' she called it. She brought coffee and doughnuts." I plop down in "my" chair on the other side of the middle table, toe off my flats, and prop my legs up on the suede ottoman. The wine is exactly what I need. "So, no big deal, right? Teams are good."

"Depends on which side you're on," Jack says.

CHAPTER THIRTY-ONE

RACHEL NORTH

Holy crap. Logan Concannon.

I'm in the backseat of a maroon Crown Vic again, same as I was a week or so ago when we approached killer pizzaman Jeffrey Baltrim's house. But this Monday morning, with one of Martha Gardiner's laconic staties behind the wheel and Martha beside him in the passenger seat, we pull up to a modest shrub-encircled Cape in the unfancy part of Brookline. Moss blooms between the flagstones that lead to a pristine front porch, and terra-cotta pots of orange and white impatiens flank the front door. We're about to go in.

Martha had only told me we were doing a re-interview of "a potential person of interest" in the Zander matter, and said she wanted me to assess what this person said without prejudice, so she wasn't going to tell me who it was. "*Better not to prepare*," she'd said. Which made no sense.

But fine, I'd thought, play your games. I'm curious, but it's simple enough to keep quiet and find out in due time. It's amazing that I get to be on the inside of this case at all, and I keep marveling at how the world works. But not so strange, really. There are only so many murders, and so many people working in the DA's office to investigate them. It's only because I went to law school that this all happened. My father would have been proud. I guess.

As we'd turned onto Sitttamore Road, I'd thought at first it was a coincidence, because I knew full well who lived here. And I even had a fleeting fantasy that we'd drive by her, out walking with her pet spider or whatever companion Gollum would have. I'd never been able to un-earth precisely what had befallen Logan Concannon, but like everything else in the world, the quest for answers eventually lost its urgency and toppled from the top of my mind, replaced by more compelling fires to extinguish. Then we pulled to the curb. Parked. And I thought—*Dumb me.* This is no coincidence. We're about to interview Logan Concannon. The chief of staff I'd replaced. The one who'd vanished from the face of the statehouse, and I'd thought, from my life. And Tom Rafferty's.

Danielle Zander had told me herself it was Logan who'd hired her, so no wonder she's "of interest."

Do they think *Logan* killed Danielle? That'd be interesting. Karmic, even. And not difficult to imagine. She'd kill anyone who got in her way. Probably wouldn't even need a weapon, just her razor-sharp words or vicious criticism. She's certainly committed political murder. In fact, in that universe, she's a serial killer. Happy to hop on to the convict-Logan bandwagon.

The whole scenario rewound, in an instant, and our history played back through my head. How we'd left it. How she'd broached the topic of that Friday night. The night Tom Rafferty came to my apartment. How, even though I never found out if it was true, I'd imagined her that same night waiting outside in that black car. How that long-ago Monday—with me wearing the necklace under my sweater!—she'd said we needed to talk. And then, before we could have that conversation, I'd heard her saying my name to someone on the phone. What a novice I'd been back then. Thirty and dumb. Well, thirty and inexperienced. Thirty and still discovering my goals. And my skills.

And then I was offered her job. And now I'm interviewing her about a murder. Today, I'm the one in charge. More than she is, at any rate.

I almost burst out laughing as I clicked open the car's back door to follow Martha Gardiner, picking my way along the patches of flagstone, trying not to slip on the dewy moss. *Dear Miss Manners,* I mentally compose a letter, *How do you handle this one?*

By the time we'd tiptoed our way to the front door, I'd retained my composure. It's been six years. Now, with my blond hair and newly acquired smart-girl glasses, I wondered how long it would take her to recognize me.

By the time we were seated in her living room, a shabby-chic mish-mash of low-slung couch, gloomily flowered Victorian wing chairs, and a glass coffee table stacked with copies of *The New Yorker,* I saw her Gollum eyes suss out my identity. She had it down pat, though, the mask of the seasoned politico. Her face betrayed not one reaction. And even knowing I knew she knew, she waited for Martha to introduce me.

"Rachel North," she says in response. "A law student." She takes a moment of silence, apparently digesting this complicated morsel. She smiles at Martha, smooths her light wool slacks, crosses her legs, and leans back in the biggest wing chair, as if she's summoned us to an audience. Her icy expression of understood knowledge, or perceived power, triggers a landslide of emotional memories for me.

"Ms. Gardiner," she says, "I hope I'm not presuming. But you are certainly aware that Ms. North—"

"Indeed." Martha, sitting on the left end of the awkward must-be-Marimekko couch, raises a palm to stop her, then sweeps her own pantomimed instruction away. "Of course, if it makes you uncomfortable for some reason, we can certainly ask Ms. North to give us the room?"

A classic Martha Gardiner question. As always, by inflection and nuance, telegraphing the way you're supposed to answer.

"Of course not," Logan says. "Have you discovered something new in the case? More than I told the investigator who interviewed me recently?"

She hasn't changed, I'm amused to see. Wiry and taut, her hair infiltrated with leaden gray, the corners of her mouth turned permanently down. And trying to keep the upper hand.

"Just following up on a few things." Martha glances at me, the signal to take out my yellow pad. I'm sitting on the other end of the couch, and it's so low it's making Logan taller than I am. It's also annoying that I have to take notes. It'll make Logan think I'm an underling, that I don't have any power. I smile, just to myself. *Wrong.*

"How did Danielle Zander come to be hired in your office?" Gardiner asks.

"As I told your investigator," Logan's voice sounds weary, or condescendingly patient, "the senator had told me privately that Ms. North here was a bit over her head. Senator Rafferty indicated I could hire someone to . . ." She pauses, as if reliving the conversation. "To make things run more smoothly. Danielle worked under my supervision, and then, of course, I left the—"

"But why Ms. Zander, in particular?" Martha interrupted. "Did you have a, say, statehouse Human Resources person who handled job applications? How did that work?"

"We do. Did. Do." Logan corrects herself. "Annabella Rigalosa. I assumed the senator somehow obtained her résumé via that channel. It seemed unimportant at the time, Ms. Gardiner. Standard."

"Rigalosa," Martha repeats, making sure I got the name. "Do you need a spelling?"

"Got it. I'm familiar with Ms. Rigalosa." I say, all calm, but inside I'm seething. Over my head? *Bull.* How dare she? And with me sitting right here? *Rachel. Stop.* I extinguish my flare of anger. She's probably making that up, probably jealous of me because Rafferty chose me, chose *me*, to replace her. So who's the one who's over her head? Not me, sister. And then, remembering what I'm supposed to be thinking about, "Is Annabella still at the statehouse?"

"How would I know?" Logan answers.

Martha shoots me a *Shut up* look. "Ms. Concannon?" Her voice is soft as a windless day. "You said you 'left' the senator's employ prior to Ms. Zander's death. Was there any animosity between you two? You and Ms. Zander?"

Logan surprises me by laughing. A full-throated head-tilted-back laugh. The sound itself unsettles the space between them. She stops herself. "I'm so sorry. That was entirely inappropriate. It's simply been so long, and Ms. Zander's death, sadly, seems like it happened so long ago. But to answer your question, Ms. Gardiner, no. Ms. Zander was a low-level staffer, one who showed considerable promise, I must say, but nonetheless was, I fear, barely a step above a fetch-and-carry. I didn't have time for animosity."

"So if Ms. Zander was not part of the equation, may I ask about Mrs. Rafferty? The senator's wife? What was your relationship with her?"

"Nina Rafferty?"

This is getting good. All questions I asked myself, so intently, six years ago. All answers I never got. All answers I need.

Martha nods. "Yes. Nina Rafferty."

Logan shifts in her chair, tucks a strand of graying hair behind one ear. She's put on earrings, apparently dressing for our visit, unless she ordinarily wears earrings around the house. Clip-ons, I see. I wonder if Martha noticed. I write that down, just in case.

Logan lets out a breath, half shrugs. "Political wives, or shall I say, spouses, are always an issue. But Nina Rafferty was no problem. Smart, self-sufficient, flexible."

"Jealous?" Martha asks. "Was she also jealous?"

I remember the telephone conversation I'd overheard. The one with me in the reception area and Logan in her office. The one I still wondered if it had been about me. The one where Logan Concannon used the words "Nina" and "ballistic."

Plus, Martha could have just as easily asked me that one. I knew full well Nina was jealous, or suspicious, and certainly observant. According to what Jack put into evidence at Nina's arraignment, Tom Rafferty had his own personal secrets. Maybe Nina did, too. Now Martha was trying to find out whether Logan Concannon had secrets as well. I could have told her that answer, too.

"Ms. Gardiner," Logan finally says. "Can you possibly tell me the point of all this? You use the word 'jealous.' No, she never told me she was jealous. She never told me anything, frankly. As a result? I am hardly the person to ask about Nina Rafferty's personal psychology. Perhaps there are others . . ." She actively doesn't look at me in her studied silence. "Others who are more, shall we say, familiar. Since the charges against Mrs. Rafferty were dropped, I assume she is not your target."

"Truth is our target." Martha's voice has gained an edge. "Were there any times that *Senator* Rafferty's behavior was in any way untoward? Specifically, to female staff members. Anyone in particular?"

I'm writing writing writing. Eager to hear what Martha wants to know about, keeping a list of it all. I remember that day at the arraignment, when Martha's "interviewee" revealed Rafferty was having "illicit relationships" with women in his office. Not a day goes by that I don't think of it, six years be damned. That kind of reputational sideswiping with public humiliation, humiliation not by name but, equally destructive, by insinuation, branded me with a permanent scarlet letter. Since Nina's case was tossed, Jack never got the files. The files with the list of the women's names.

"This is a situation that one must monitor, constantly and carefully," Logan says. "One person's 'untoward' is another's congeniality."

"I'm not as concerned with what 'one' must do, Ms. Concannon, as I am about the specifics of your time in Senator Rafferty's office. Did you get any complaints, even informal, about his behavior? Did you *suspect*—let me put it this way. We're involved in a murder investigation, so don't filter your response by what *you* might think is relevant. Let *me* make that decision."

Me, Martha says. Not us. But fine. I'm the apprentice. Am I finally about to hear the list? Certainly Danielle Zander, recipient of the gold necklace, would be on it. And certainly Nina Rafferty would be angry about that. Enough to kill her?

Logan Concannon rattles off more platitudes and stalling time fillers about sexual harassment policies and the prohibitions about "intraoffice liaisons," her actual words. but a thought hits me so hard I almost flutter a hand to my throat, like a forties-movie ingenue.

What if it turned out that Logan was the jealous one? What if Logan, faithful Logan, was, beneath her snakeskin veneer, a loyal lapdog, a devoted companion, a woman who lived the fantasy that her boss, for whom she'd slay dragons, would somehow see the light and carry her off to another life? What if Logan, graying, sinewy Logan, had been so twisted with jealousy over Danielle, the sweetly vulnerable but unmistakably attractive newcomer she had to hire, that she went off the rails and killed her? If she's capable of reputation-ruining career-ending political murder, why not the real thing?

Talk about being jealous. Logan had been suspicious enough of *me*, that's for sure. She's the one who wanted to "talk" to me that Monday morning. Maybe I should mention that encounter to Martha. I'd labeled it as snooping about my personal life. But maybe, instead of being personal about me—maybe it could be personal about *Logan.*

"Let's move on," Martha says. "Why did you leave the employ of Senator Rafferty?"

Oh, excellent. Eager to hear this.

"Does that matter?"

"Everything matters," Martha says.

Logan Concannon's eyes go hard. Her shoulders square, and her chin goes up. "You'll find out, I assume," she says. "If you don't already know. Someone reported to the police that I—*I!*—was having a relationship with my employer, Senator Rafferty."

I stare at her, my pen frozen mid-sentence. She's going there?

"Reported?" Martha's voice doesn't miss a beat. Level and even, as if Logan had said it was sunny outside. "Was it true?"

"Must we talk about this?"

"We must."

Logan's eyes widen, then she crosses her arms in front of her, her back ramrod. "No. That's beyond comprehension. But we could not allow even a whisper of such a thing. So I quit."

"You said someone 'reported' it. Do you know who reported it?"

"No."

I want to ask, *Do you suspect it might have been Nina?* But I keep quiet.

"Let's go on," Martha says. "Tell me where you were, Ms. Concannon, on the weekend preceding the murder of Danielle Zander."

"But—" Logan looks annoyed now.

"I know you've answered that." Martha's voice is placating again. "But humor me."

Logan rattles off a list of dates and events, alibis and connections and proofs. Half the time she was home alone. I sneer to myself as I write it all down. Easy-peasy to come up with a reasonable alibi, everyone knows that. And "home alone" can be effective, because how can anyone prove you weren't? It's especially a snap for a single person. Simply check the TV listings and say you were watching whatever was really on. You can even leave the TV on, in case there's a way they could check. But Martha can recross the alibi bridge with her if she needs to. Maybe Logan's annoyed because she thought the cops had already bought her alibi, and now she's worried they didn't?

But I wish Martha would get back to the jealousy question. That's where I predict she can nail her.

Martha was right. I am the perfect person to work on this.

MARTHA GARDINER

Martha stepped back from the demilune table in her hallway, tilting her head, assessing her newest arrangement. The pale-blue hyacinths and white tulips and spiny green ferns, fresh from her tiny garden, were duplicated in the ceiling-high mirror behind them, a mirror that had graced the entryway to her Beacon Hill apartment since her grandparents had owned it in the days when the Esplanade's now-iconic Hatch Shell was brand-new. Back then, though Grandpa Leggett had signed up to fight Nazis, his father's influence kept him desk-safe in Washington at the War Department.

Through her lattice of lavender-tinged windows, originals, Martha could see the early evening sun streaming through the elm trees on the green expanse of Boston Common, couples and puppies and children winding the same paths where Abigail Adams strolled, and then Lucy Stone and Margaret Fuller. Those women had made a difference, and she would, too.

She plucked a tulip from behind a stubborn green hyacinth leaf and replaced the flower front and center. The flowers were from the square of green courtyard behind her building, hardly a garden, more of a patch, the one place she felt responsibility only to nature. Sometimes, when the wind was right, she could smell the brine of the harbor, or see an optimistically wayward gull headed for the Atlantic.

The hyacinth shifted, and now a fern blocked the tulip. Using her thumb and forefinger, Martha pinched off an offending leaf. Perfect. Gardiner the gardener, her father used to joke. When he could still joke.

The graceful bay windows, her inherited Persian rugs, the polished mantle over the fireplace. The lines of silver-framed family photos. She'd lived here since she was a girl—after her college dorm years in Cambridge, of course, but after it had seemed more sensible to stay here, while her mother was sick and then her father, and then, alone, she kept the place to herself. Familiar and orderly and set in its ways. She refused to think of it as her personal metaphor.

She used her family wineglass for this evening's cabernet—who else would she use them for?—and wondered, yet again, about her choices. No pets, no friends, no hobbies except for her patch of green. Only . . . She took a deep breath and looked into her remaining wine. Only justice.

The file lay open on the supple saddle-leather couch, tempting her, yet again, to read the documents. What did she think she would find after all these years? Most people kept scrapbooks of their wins, their glory days, to reassure themselves when they failed.

Martha kept files of her losses. To *remind* her of her failures. To prod her to prevent them.

The last of the wine, and she could afford no more. If all went as

planned, there were big days coming up. And a knock on the door—
she checked her watch—in five minutes.

She moved aside the paisley throw pillows and settled herself into the
corner of the couch, toeing her pumps to the floor. She'd dropped Rachel off at the office an hour before, directing her to type up her notes
on the Logan Concannon interview. It was busywork, sure, but Rachel
had no choice. Let her complain to her damn husband, Martha thought.
How fortuitous that now Martha had access to Jack Kirkland. She smiled
with the sweetness of it. The possibilities. The power. It was better than
wine.

Opening the file of newspaper clippings, she imagined someone else
watching her doing this, an old-fashioned thing.

Why don't you just search online, they'd wonder?

The feel of the newsprint calms me, she'd have to admit. It makes
the stories real. And the facts true. She turned another page in the file,
the pinked edges of the unmounted newspaper clips thinned and frayed
from her repeated touch.

There were no clips on Logan Concannon's connection to the death
of Danielle Zander. The newspaper stories from back then showed the
snow-covered crime scene, each arriving footprint impossibly obliter-
ating whatever was buried beneath it. A nobly ravaged Tom Rafferty, all
thoughts and prayers, as if those would solve the brutal murder of his
young and seemingly unsophisticated staffer. A photo of him at a news
conference. Jack Kirkland, too, was in the shot, a slithering menace
darkening Martha's every thought.

She turned to the next clipping, to stop her focus on Jack. But it was
worse, even worse. NOT NINA—the *Globe* headline almost made her gasp,
though she'd seen it hundreds of times. And in the *Herald*—GARDINER
BLOWS IT. JACK WINS AGAIN. Martha closed her eyes with the memory.
Pride goeth, her father used to warn her. And Martha had taken the fall.
And it was Jack Kirkland's fault, his fault she was humiliated, and defeated, and fired—

Turn the page, Martha. Channel your anger. Use it to win.

A photo of Danielle Zander, there seemed to be only one. A pixie smile, those perfect teeth and innocent eyes. No family, how could that be? Where did she come from? No one seemed to know, and even Lewis Millin came up empty, with a random maybe-cousin not replying to their inquiries. Danielle would have been what, about thirty-five now? Martha had to protect her, her memory at least. Stand up for her. Avenge her.

Martha paused, thinking of her own beginnings at a too-stuffy law firm. About which women got ahead, which ones made it, and why.

Women full of their own youth and beauty and the power that comes with it. The power they *think* comes with it. The Monicas, she used to call them, before that White House intern came into a different kind of power. The wannabes, then, who used their allure to assuage the fear of aging men, men who'd passed their prime, and tried, with whatever currency they'd accumulated, to make themselves immortal. Younger women could provide the mirage for a while, until each one pushed too hard or demanded too much or threatened. It was always the interloping manipulative woman who suffered in those toxic relationships, not the equally reprehensible man.

Well, Martha corrected herself, feeling a smile come to her face again and her chest relax. Not always.

And there was the doorbell. Six thirty P.M., right on time. She'd taught her well.

CHAPTER **THIRTY-TWO**

RACHEL NORTH

I'm feeling confident and enthusiastic, free, car windows down, May breeze blowing, my hair loose—with a handle on this investigation and a vision of my future. But when I turn in to the driveway of our house, there's an unfamiliar car parked at our front door. Not in my place at the back, but near the front. Where visitors park. Jack has a guest?

My dashboard clock says it's almost six thirty, so I'm home earlier than usual. I ease beside the black two-door, a cute buzzy sports car of some kind, and manage to get into my regular place without dinging the shiny intruder. Close my car door. Stand in the driveway, hands on hips, listen to the wheating of an insistent cardinal, and stare at the house. Who's here?

Unlocking the kitchen door, I pause. Listen. Wait. Jack doesn't meet clients at home. He has a perfectly good office for that. This is personal. It has to be.

On a typical Monday, Jack would not be home yet at all. If he did come home early, he'd be in his chair, drinking his first wine and watching the news. Alone. "Hey you," he'd say when I arrived. "Hey you," I'd respond. And it would be a usual night.

But today, silence. Silence and an unfamiliar sports car.

What do I do? Sneak out, pretend I wasn't here, see how he explains it later? Or if he even mentions it?

I consider that briefly. Should I retreat and reenter later, all smiley and good-wifey and hey-you? And see what he says?

But no. I mean, why? This is my house. I live here, just as much as he does. *We* live here.

I drop my briefcase and purse on the dining room floor, aware that I'm doing it quietly. My ears are turned to parabolic, trying to hear. Is there a murmur, maybe, from the living room? The house seems alien. There's something off-kilter. Strange. I can almost physically feel the space is different.

But there's nothing to do but find out. If I tiptoe along, surreptitiously and eavesdropping the whole way, and it's only, like, the electrician, that's going to be embarrassing. Maybe it *is* a client, who somehow couldn't make it to Boston and agreed to come to our home instead. Lovely, some murderer or violent criminal is in my living room right now. Which would be better, a serial killer in the living room or another woman upstairs?

But a secret lover—ha ha—would hardly park her snazzy car in our driveway.

And I have no reason to think, not the slightest, that Jack would betray me. My brain must be going there because I spent the day steeped in Rafferty's serial infidelity. Jack's my husband, my faithful husband. Even though he knows I'm not usually home until seven.

I'll find out in the next three seconds.

"Rachel?" Jack's voice carries down the hallway. Not our "Hey you," I notice. And his voice sounds forced. Superpolite. At least they're not upstairs. Though I guess they might have raced down when they heard my car pull in.

"Yes?" His tone makes mine wary, too. In a few steps, I'm at the living room entryway. A woman is seated on our semicircular couch, and for a second I see only her back, a pale-green blouse and a mane of streaky hair. She turns. Gives me a tentative smile.

"Hi," she says. "Blast from the past, right?"

It takes me one blink. Two.

"Roni? Wollaskay?" My fellow juror from the Deacon Davis trial, six years and a million lifetimes ago. What the hell is this about? I look at Jack, questioning, but he's giving me nothing, then back at Roni. She's just the same, comfortable and affluent, silky top and gold necklace, and hardly looking six years older. I know she must be assessing the new me, now equally blond as she is. Her earrings are clip-on, too, and it takes me a beat before I realize that's irrelevant. Her necklace is irrelevant, too.

"Ah, Roni, what a surprise," I say. "How are you?"

"Great," she says. "And you? So, you're in law school now, your husband tells me. The world works in mysterious ways."

"Sure does." Time to end the small talk. "And I'm fine. Are *you* okay? Is this about Deacon Davis, somehow?" Then another thought. The more likely one. I put up both palms, realizing, and take a step back. "Or, oh. Do you need a lawyer? And that's why you called Jack? Let me get out of your way."

"Ms. Wollaskay called to chat with *you*, Rachel." Jack looks pleased with himself, or maybe I'm reading him wrong. "She—"

"I looked you up on the internet," Roni interrupts, "and you're listed, Rachel North, and so I called. Mr. Kirkland answered, though of course I didn't know it was him. When I asked for you, he asked who it was, I told him, and he asked if he could take a message, and when I said I wanted to talk with you, he invited me over. I was surprised, I have to say, but then he told me who *he* was."

"Oh, I see," I say, though that's not exactly true. Jack still has the look, and is not being at all helpful. Maybe he doesn't know why she's here. But there cannot be a reason other than the Davis trial. Jack certainly knows that. "Well, Roni, what can I do for you?"

"Great talking to you, Ms. Wollaskay," Jack says, before Roni can answer. "It's been a while."

Jack leaves, and I sit across from my guest. This whole thing is so awkward, so surprising, so unexpected, it might as well be taking place on another planet. Roni's handbag is at her feet, an elegant leather rectangle.

She picks it up as she talks. "So, yeah, I know this is strange," she says, unzipping a side pocket of the bag. She pulls out a folded white paper, dingy and frayed. "But you remember the Davis trial, of course. And can I ask—you got the letter from Jack Kirkland, after, right, back then? Like this? About wanting to talk to us jurors?" She flaps it open, holds it up.

I nod, recognizing it. Remembering what happened the day I got it. I hadn't kept mine.

"Weird that he's your husband now. Jack Kirkland, I mean. Not bad-weird, of course, I don't mean that, but—" She stops, regroups. "And you also got the letter from the prosecutor? Gardiner?"

"Yeah." It *is* weird that he's my husband now. And even weirder because Martha's my boss. Which Roni probably doesn't know, unless Jack mentioned it before I got here. The whole thing comes flooding back, my guilt, my embarrassment, my fear that someone told Gardiner or Jack what had happened in the deliberations. How I'd caved because I wanted to get back to work. But—no. That person could not have been Roni, because she'd been excused for her sick daughter. Rhoda, or Rinda, or something. "How's your daughter?" Then I laugh. "Well, she's certainly fine by now. It's been six years."

Unless she died, my conscience tells me. *Shut up,* Rachel.

But Roni's nodding and puts the letter away. "She's fine. Randi. She's nine now, going on forty-two. So, yeah, the lawyer letters. I didn't talk to either of them. I didn't even deliberate, if you remember, and I guess you do. Which is too bad for Deacon Davis, because as I said in the jury room, I thought that man was innocent." She stops, tilts her head, puffs out a breath. "Listen, first let me ask you something. What did they tell you about why I left?"

I put my fingers to my lips, trying to remember. "Ah, they said . . ." I replay that morning, I think it was morning, in the jury room. "Was his name like, Suddeth?"

"Kurt Suddeth," she says. "The court officer."

"Right," I say, pointing at her. "He came in to get you, I remember. And it was a little scary. And you seemed—surprised."

"Yes, exactly. And worried, too, and kind of terrified, like maybe something was wrong with my kids, or maybe I'd done something wrong, whatever that would be. But did you hear what happened next?"

I know I did. Somewhere. But who told me? *Oh.* Jack. Better not mention that. He's probably not supposed to be gossiping about jurors.

"Later I heard—through the grapevine, I guess—you'd asked to be excused, that you were very concerned about your sick daughter, and they agreed you should be excused."

"Right," she nods. "But that wasn't true."

"Your daughter wasn't sick?"

"No, she was. But she was fine, only a cold, and I had a nanny, all good, and I was psyched to vote not guilty. But the officer, Suddeth, told me in the hall the judge wanted to offer me the chance to be excused. I said no, it was fine. But he pushed me on it. Really pushed. Said the judge always worried when there was a juror with a sick child, because she feared if the child got worse during the deliberations and *then* the juror had to be excused, it was even more of a problem. He said that she said— Suddeth said the judge said—it was easier for me to leave now." She shrugs. "So, I did. I went home. But in fact? Turns out the judge had never said any of that."

"Really?" I feel my forehead furrow. "How do you know?"

"Getting to that. So. The judge did call me later that day, asking if Randi was okay, and I said she was. But I took it as a courtesy call. Confirming, you know?"

I'm trying to analyze if that makes sense, if that was covered in my class on trial procedure, if it's proper, if I've heard of such a thing. "But how'd you find that out? Who told you?"

"Can I get you anything?" Jack's voice comes from down the hall. Not too far down, I can gauge that. Was he listening? "Tea? Coffee?" He steps into the room, Mr. Gracious Host. "Wine?"

"Well, thank you, I almost never turn down wine," Roni says.

We agree on red, and Host Jack hustles away.

"And why are you telling *me* this?" I have to ask. "It's nice to see you and everything, and that story is perplexing, but—"

"Well, exactly. I thought we were sort of friends? You're in my R family, remember?" Roni smiles, inquiring, and I nod to reassure her. "And I thought maybe, since we'd shared this experience and seemed to be on the same page, you might have some idea about what to do. If anything. You're the only one I bonded with, I guess."

"Okay, but—"

"There's more."

Roni looks at the floor for a beat, and I do, too, because she's so intent it seems like she might be seeing something. But no.

"I guess you haven't heard? Um, Deacon Davis. Himself. Got killed. Was killed. In prison. Maybe three days ago?"

"What? How do you know?"

"TV. Some sort of riot, random, they said." Roni waves to the big screen inside the open doors of our antique armoire. "Clea Rourke, you know her, the red-haired reporter? She interviewed Latrelle Davis, remember her? The sister? And they're already clamoring to sue—someone. I forget."

"Really?" I'm trying to process all the players and all the ramifications. And how I'm somehow in the middle again.

"I can't sleep." Roni is shaking her head. "Look at the bags under my eyes. I had to talk to someone who knew something. The sister was so sad, so incredibly sad, and I can't get it out of my head."

"Yeah." He wouldn't have been in prison if we all hadn't voted guilty. That's what Roni means. He'd be alive. Except for us. *Me.*

"Then I called you, and your husband turned out to be—well, at that point it got a little more complicated. But I figured you were still you. And now, turns out you're almost a lawyer. So you might even know more."

"Okay." I draw the word out, thinking about this.

"You two catching up?" Jack arrives, carrying a silver tray with a carafe of wine and two empty glasses. Even a bowl of pretzels and a stack of cocktail napkins. All he needs is a linen cloth draped over his arm.

"Did you know Deacon Davis got killed in prison?" I should have couched it, been more careful giving such disturbing news.

"Of course I did." Jack puts down the tray. His smile disappears. "What do you think I've been on the phone about?"

"Well, how would I know?" He doesn't need to be sarcastic about it.

"Can I use your ladies' room?" Roni asks.

Jack—without another word to me—shows her the way. I stare at the wine, deep and red and impenetrable. Seeing the past and the present and the future.

This morning, I sat in a living room and talked to a person from another life—Logan Concannon. Now, tonight, I'm talking to a person from yet another life, Roni Wollaskay. My past has returned with a vengeance. And Deacon Davis is dead. Deacon Davis, who I'd only *maybe* thought was guilty but I'd voted with the others to convict because I wanted the trial to be over with so I could get back to my work and to Senator Tom Rafferty, is dead.

So this is *Tom's* fault.

It isn't. Fine. I know.

But is it Martha Gardiner's fault? If he wasn't guilty, she got him convicted, and now he's dead?

I listen to the silence, not a bird outside, not a rustle in the trees, almost able to hear my own heartbeat, my thoughts carrying me down the road of possibilities.

"Exactly what I need." Roni's back. She points to the wine, adjusts the sleeves of her luxurious blouse. "Because, listen, here's more. The rest of the story. And I've been thinking."

"I have, too." I pour wine, half a glass for each of us. Hand one to her. "You first. Tell me the rest."

Roni takes a sip, takes her seat, looks toward the entrance to the living room. Leans toward me.

"Well, thing is," she's keeping her voice low, and glances again at the doorway, seems to be wary. "*Before* I saw that on the news, I'd seen the judge at an event. Remember her? Bad hair? It was just random, a furniture-company thing, a week or so ago, and of course I mentioned she and I had met, sort of, at the Deacon Davis trial. She remembered the whole thing and, like you, asked about my daughter Randi, then laughed because it was so long ago. She said she'd remembered so clearly, because she'd worried about Randi. I said well, I was surprised to be excused. You could tell she was—I don't know, baffled by that. And then she told me that Suddeth and Martha Gardiner had told her Randi was *dying*. And that I had *insisted* on leaving."

She takes another sip. "That's just—not true."

"Did you tell her that?"

She presses her lips together, then nods her head. "Yeah, I did. I told her everything. But she, you know events like those, a million people. Someone else came up to her, and someone needed me for something, and that was the end of that. I *thought*."

"Yow," I say. "So you think you were—forced out? Somehow? And Deacon Davis was killed *after* you talked to the judge?"

"Yeah. Exactly."

We both stare at our wine. I'm thinking about how different the verdict might have been if Roni hadn't been removed from the jury. Thinking like a lawyer. Like the defense attorney I need to be. But also like a prosecutor. And about Deacon Davis being . . . dead. Because he faced a jury. And lost. Because of me?

"Roni?" I try to think of it yet another way. "Do you remember Momo Peretz? She had to leave, too. Got excused for some reason."

"I remember her, but no, I didn't know that," she says. "You never see photos of the jury, so I had no idea who was on it in the end. Why'd she get excused?"

I shake my head. "One day she was there, the next day she was gone. She was a 'not guilty,' too. Remember?"

Roni looks toward the entrance to the living room. Leans even closer toward me. "I feel so horrible," she whispers. "If they hadn't—I don't know, gotten rid of jurors like me? Deacon Davis would have been acquitted."

She reaches over, clutches my forearm. "I mean, you all voted guilty. But you didn't sentence him to death."

Her statement hangs over our silence. I can almost see Deacon Davis's face in front of me, full of reproach and blame. Blaming *me*. His beautiful sister, crying through her loss, bitter over our callous disregard for her loved one's life. Over my selfish, careless, overreaction to—

"Oh, Roni," I say, trying to stop my spiraling guilt. "It's all my fault! It *is*. I—killed him. I did. *I did*. I'm a murderer."

I feel tears come to my eyes, tears of confusion and stress and indecision, and fear and more fear. Deacon Davis—unfairly found guilty? Unfairly charged? And as a result his life was taken from him. One moment, one decision, one wrong move and our lives change and the dominoes crash. Fate steps in, unpredictable and swift. My stomach sinks, leaden with remorse. I am truly horrible.

"No, Rachel, no. Oh, no, I should never have said that." Roni moves to the couch beside me, drapes one arm across my shoulders. "I am so so *so* sorry. Please. Don't cry. Please. It's not your fault."

"But—"

"It's not," Roni insists, hugging me closer.

I feel myself wanting to hear her, to draw in her strength, to sink into the comfort of her, her warmth and her reassurance.

"Seriously, Rachel. It's not."

"You . . . you think?" I sniff, wipe my nose on the back of my hand, then, embarrassed, grab a white paper napkin.

"Definitely. This was the system working. It was the whole jury, Rach." She pulls back, then putting her hands on my shoulders, turns me to face her, like a mom instructing a child. "This. Is. Not. Your. Fault."

Is she right? Well, I suppose. I blink, thinking. My eyelashes are wet, and I swipe the tears away. I was simply one of twelve random people. Everyone else thought Davis was guilty. Did Martha Gardiner tamper with the jury? She *must* have. Or been privy to it. She manipulated that verdict, just like Jack says. And now, *I'm* the victim of it.

I press my lips together, chin up, balancing my conscience with my newest reality. There's nothing I can do to change the past. I can only manage the future.

"Here. Have more wine," Roni says. I'm so immersed in my thoughts, her voice seems far away. "It'll calm you. I am so *so* sorry to tell you."

I sit up straighter, take a sip, try to smile. Okay. I'll move on. To survive, I have to. What's more, it's cases like this that make me all the more determined to ensure that people get fair trials. This should *inspire* me. We'll be Kirkland and North. Murder-list lawyers. We'll protect people.

"Thank you, Roni," I say, giving a final sniff. "It's not you. I'd have found out anyway. But it hit me. Taking a life. I mean . . . I'm so on edge. Maybe I'm tired. But it's so awful."

"I'm so sorry, Rach. I agree. It's awful." Roni hesitates. Scratches her cheek with manicured nails. Grimaces. "But Rach? Do you—think we should tell your husband? About the jury thing? What Gardiner—or whoever—might have done?"

I swirl the last of my wine and search my brain. What might have happened behind the scenes in that trial? Telling Jack *is* a possibility. But it's not the only one.

"Maybe," I say. "But first I have another idea."

CHAPTER **THIRTY-THREE**

MARTHA GARDINER

Martha stashed her wineglass in the kitchen as the doorbell rang again. Considered selecting another one to offer her guest, then decided against it. This was a business meeting. Pure and simple.

She made it to the couch as the doorbell rang again, stepped into her shoes, closed her files, tucked the papers under the coffee table. Smoothed her hair. Pulled open the door.

"Sorry, Lizann." A wash of blush-tinged sky framed her former associate's silhouette. Lizann, with her hardscrabble background and bootstrapped law school, now looked like a successful young attorney, all briefcase and chignon. At least her fellow murder listers hadn't stolen her style along with her philosophy. Every year, the newbies were Martha's children, she thought of them that way. Her ducklings, her students, her legacy. She'd had high hopes for Lizann Wallace, maybe a partnership someday. But Lizann had disagreed with Martha's methods. Called her on it. Hard. The two had parted. Not amicably. "Come in."

"Surprised you wanted to talk here and not the office. Home-turf advantage?" Lizann's voice stayed professional, appropriate, though Martha knew her well enough to recognize some underlying nerves.

The devil you know, Martha thought.

"Simply easier." Martha escorted her to the living room, the pink light now bathing the grasscloth-papered hallway and putting a glow on the sterling picture frames and Lizann's silver earrings. She asked the question she already knew the answer to. "What can I do for you?"

"Fine, and you?" Lizann selected the wing chair, though Martha had indicated the couch.

Good for you, Martha thought, recognizing the sarcasm. Power choice, but it wouldn't matter.

"You always loved small talk." Martha perched on the arm of the couch, signaling this was not a cozy conversation. And it made her taller.

"All right then. Your way." Lizann crossed her legs, adjusted her black skirt, cleared her throat. "My client. Jeffrey Baltrim."

"Guilty," Martha said. "As hell. Next question."

Lizann tapped a black suede toe on the figured rug, once, then again, watching her own action as if counting off seconds. Those hoop earrings, Martha noted, were bigger than Martha herself cared for.

"I know you like to think my client is guilty," Lizann finally said. "But indulge me here. How do you arrive at that conclusion?"

Martha ignored the question. "You're here to inquire about a deal, I take it."

"I know you don't like to lose," Lizann said. "But you'll lose this one."

"To you?" Martha couldn't help it.

"'The devil you know' as you always say, Martha." Lizann smiled. "Before we go any further, let me ask you. I noticed in the crime-scene report that the oven was on. Why would that be?"

Martha rolled her eyes. "I know it's a wild guess, but possibly to keep the pizza hot?"

"For who?" Lizann asked. "And since two pieces were gone, and there was no pizza in Ms. Lyle's stomach, and my client is allergic to cheese, who ate them?"

Martha shrugged. Allergic to cheese? Probably a bluff.

"And the pizza place, Oregano Brothers. Did you know that closed at eleven?" Lizann went on. "But Dr. Ong estimated the time of death was around four A.M."

"Liz? Did you know that Jeffrey Baltrim had the delivery car, had a child in the car, and the child can testify? And that we found drugs from Ms. Lyle in her house? And more drugs, with the same batch number, in Baltrim's car?"

Lizann nodded. "I do know that. So he may have been a drug dealer— though I see you didn't charge him with that. But Martha? Please. Do tell me how that makes him a murderer."

"Do you want to argue this *now*?" Martha had considered all of this, certainly, and was aware the case had a few holes. But nothing she couldn't deal with. "Shall I call in some neighbors to play the jury?"

"Funny." Lizann shifted in her chair, drummed her fingers on its padded chintz arms.

Martha said nothing, since nothing Lizann was saying merited a response. This would be adjudicated in court. Jeffrey Baltrim would be found guilty, game over.

"How about manslaughter?" Lizann offered. "My client does seven years."

"The murder took place only a week or so ago." Martha shook her head, dismissive. "It's silly, as I'm sure you are well aware, to discuss this now."

Lizann tapped her toe again. Stood. "No wonder you didn't want to meet at your office," she said. "Talk about bad faith. You didn't want to meet at all."

"Always a pleasure to see you, Liz." Martha stood too, brushed down her tan slacks. Gestured to the door. "If there's nothing else?"

"What're your plans, Martha?" Lizann didn't move. "You going to disappear a witness? Get the court officers to eavesdrop on the jury?"

"That's ridiculous."

Lizann widened her eyes. "Well, you are so right, Martha. And I would have thought so too, years ago. But now . . ."

Martha took a step toward the door. She would not be intimidated by this person. Or anyone.

"Or, oh, I know." Lizann held up a forefinger. "You'll wine and dine the judge. Or have some little off-the-record discussions? Or possibly—get a few pivotal jurors dismissed? Don't forget, Martha. I've been in on those cases. I know how you operate. You're—"

"That's quite enough, Ms. Wallace." This pitiful attempt at extortion was simply the last stand of a losing battle. "If you participated in any prohibited activities, then it's your responsibility to turn yourself in. I am unaware of such a thing, certainly, but happy to facilitate your confession with the disciplinary board."

Lizann kept talking. "Or will you coerce that little boy—Jonah, remember?—into saying where he was that night, when he clearly has no idea? His mother tells me he came home just after ten. Isn't that interesting? Or, oh. Will you alter the warrant so those drugs you took—illegally, I might add—are actually listed?"

"Does it *matter* to you murder-list people? That you're letting murderers go free?" Martha planted her hands on her hips. "Because of paperwork?"

Martha knew she was going too far, letting her emotions get the better of her. But she could not let this go. "That's what makes you proud and happy? That's why you went to law school? To put guilty people like that back out on the streets to kill someone else?"

"Innocent 'til *proven* guilty, if I might remind you, Martha."

"Guilty is guilty."

"Is it?" Lizann lifted her chin, narrowing her eyes. "Imagine, if you can. What if it were someone you loved? Would you be so dismissive about the rules then? Every defendant is loved by *someone.* Just—not you."

"Jeffrey Baltrim is a killer." Martha walked to the door herself now. She'd had quite enough. "He'll face trial, he'll face a jury, and fairly and squarely. And if I do my job properly—as I always do, I might add—he'll be justly convicted and be sent to prison for life."

"Not if I can help it," Lizann said.

"You can't." Martha opened the door.

"Watch me." Lizann took one step over the threshold, then turned back. Looked Martha square in the eye. "You'll have to win this one the right way, Martha. By the rules. Not *your* rules. But the rule of law. Do you think you're capable of that? Remember, as you're plotting your clever Martha-strategies. Remember I know your secrets."

Martha didn't mean to slam the door. She paused for a moment, alone in the entryway, waiting for the quiet to return. She'd been threatened by far more powerful people. It was part of the job. And if justice was the result? That's all that mattered.

CHAPTER THIRTY-FOUR

RACHEL NORTH

I'm in the middle again. Facing past and present. Deacon Davis. And Danielle Zander. How far does Martha Gardiner go to win a case? And to protect her own reputation? Maybe, standing beside her in front of a bank of fancy elevators, I'm about to get a clue.

"Twenty-five." Martha cocks her head toward the panel of numbered buttons in this chic downtown apartment building. I push, as silently instructed. The polished aluminum doors close us in, and we ride, silent, heading up twenty-five floors.

Third floor.

How must this woman feel about Deacon Davis's death? Does she know about it? The larger question is—did she have something to do with it?

I'd deconstructed all the reasons Kurt Suddeth might have lied about Roni Wollaskay's daughter, and decided, irrevocably, that Martha herself must have been involved. I know from law school—thank goodness I'm learning the rules—that to excuse a juror that way there must have been a hearing in the judge's chambers. The judge would have to interrogate the juror, even by phone, and then hear arguments from both sides. That means both Martha and Jack must have been there. If Jack wasn't, that'd be improper. Which means Suddeth and Martha—and maybe the judge—must have lied to him.

Fifteenth floor.

But when I'd broached it last night at the dinner table, thinking Jack would be intrigued or even incensed, instead he'd been—devastated.

"Why'd Mrs. Wollaskay come over?" He'd introduced the topic, which gave me a graceful opening. "What'd you two discuss?"

"Well, Deacon Davis. It's so disturbing. I can't even—how do you live with that, honey?"

"That he was killed?" Jack tilted his chair back, teetered it on two legs. "You think that's my fault somehow?"

"Your fault? *Your* fault?" I'd been shocked by that. And I'd over-reacted. "Jack, give me a break. For once. This is not about you! *I* voted guilty! And now he's dead. And if I hadn't—"

"He *wasn't* guilty, Rachel," Jack plunked his chair back down. "Got it? End of story. Shit happens."

"He wasn't—" It took me a moment to process. Regroup. "But you never told—He didn't do it? How do you know? I mean, how could *I* have known?"

"Exactly. You couldn't. But *I* failed. Horribly. He wasn't in prison because of *you*. It was *my* fault. Because of *me*. I lost. And now he's dead."

Jack looked so solemnly mournful, eyes welling with tears. I'd never seen him this upset. And I knew it was my mistake, a little, for making it be about me.

"I'm sorry, honey," I reached out, touched his hand. "I'm so sorry. But how could the system—"

"The *system*? Listen, Rachel." He yanked his hand away, picked up his fork, jabbed it at me. "The *system* can be a death sentence. For all in-volved. Not just physically, but emotionally. I defend people because . . . my job, my motivation, my *life,* is that justice is done during the trial process. That the system, as you call it, is fair. Deacon Davis didn't kill that woman. I'm convinced of it. And yet, I couldn't convince you. Or all the others. I failed, I utterly failed. That's why I'd been pouring my life into the appeal."

No reason for that now, I'd thought. Poor Jack. "I'm so—"

"And you know what else? Now Deke's conviction gets dismissed! Mass law says so, did you learn this yet? Because there was no appeal. Remember Deke's sister Latrelle? I had to tell her that her brother was dead—but he was no longer a convicted murderer. Imagine *that* conversation."

"How awful," I said. "The justice system is—"

"The *justice* system? How about the *corrections* system? It's Dickensian. Brutality more common than you can imagine. But Rach? I can't—dwell. Sometimes doing what I have to do is impossible. You'll learn. Can we not talk about it? Please?"

Which made sense. His client was dead. And he had no idea what I suspected about that trial. "Okay," I'd said. "Sure."

Our silverware had clinked against our white plates. A minute passed. Two.

No. I had to pursue it. I could *help* him. "But Jack? One thing, okay? D'you remember the hearing when they excused Roni? In the judge's chambers?"

"A hearing?" Jack sighed, then grimaced as if he were trying to recall. "Not really. Why?"

"Do you remember that the court officer told Judge Saunders that Roni's daughter was possibly going to die?"

"Yeah, no," Jack shook his head, then he examined every roll in the wicker bread basket, chose one. "Long time ago," he said. "And you know? None of it matters. End of story. Like I said." Then he'd almost twinkled at me. "And if I remembered anything about jurors, it would have been about you, right?"

"But Jack, see, it *might* matter," I persisted, ignoring his surprisingly flirty tone. "Roni said—"

"Rach? How was your day otherwise?" At that point, Jack had resolutely changed the subject. "What're you and your Martha working on in the lion's den?"

I'd almost choked on my rice pilaf, imagining me telling him about the interview with Logan Concannon, including Martha's speculations about the philandering Tom Rafferty and the jealous Nina. Who, it seemed to me, was once again in Martha's gunsights. And who, no doubt, would once again be Jack's client. Which meant I could not talk about it.

"Ah, paperwork," I said. "Boring intern stuff. I hardly see Eli and Nick and Andrew. Who knows what my fellow baby lawyers are working on. But let me ask you, making sure I'm clear on the rules. The factor that determines which county's DA's office will investigate is where the crime was committed, is that correct? That's the only thing?"

"*Bzzzt.*" Jack made a noise like a wrong-answer buzzer. "Better study up before the bar exam, sweetheart. First, *allegedly* committed. Even though you're playing prosecutor this summer, it's allegedly."

"Allegedly." This is what we talked about at the dinner table. Death and murder. "But there was a crime, for gosh sake."

"Is this about something specific?"

I'd kept forgetting how smart he was. But this had been bugging me, and when I brought it up to Martha, she waved me off. I'd looked it up, but the law is complicated.

"No, no," I said, "I'm only trying to understand. This is why I'm lucky to be married to a fancy successful lawyer. So. Could the investigation of a crime change jurisdiction? Why would that be?"

"Can of worms," Jack said. "Mass General Laws, chapter two-seven-seven, section sixty. Says, essentially, prosecution of a crime shall take place in the county in which the crime occurred."

"Show-off," I'd said. "Any exceptions, though?"

Jack had put on his recitation-of-legal-facts expression. "Murder on the high seas, or close to a geographical boundary, or if it's not clear where the crime was committed. Or, for instance, if you poisoned me at the dinner table here in Middlesex County and drove me to Suffolk

County, where I then died. Then you could be prosecuted in either county." He forked up a bit of chicken and rice, examined it. "You didn't do that, though, did you, sweetheart? Poison me with this chicken? At least it's delicious, thank you. Did Martha put you up to it? Give you instructions? Promise to get you acquitted?"

We'd gone on that way, spousal banter—*No, I didn't poison you and won't unless you keep leaving your towels on the floor*—and soon we were deep into scraping and stashing the dishes, and then Netflix.

But I was still chewing over my question. Did Martha Gardiner convince someone—the DA or a judge or grand jury or someone, I wasn't exactly clear on how it would work—that she thought the murder of Danielle Zander took place in Middlesex County and *not* at the statehouse, which was in Suffolk County? And convinced whoever that her body was *moved* to the statehouse from Middlesex?

Whoa. Nina lived in Middlesex. As did Tom Rafferty. As did Logan Concannon. As did Jack, not that it mattered. And, in fact, as do I, although not back then. But as a result of my dear husband's legal knowledge, I got a better idea of what was under way. What Martha Gardiner must suspect about Dani's murderer.

Now I glance at my boss who's all bespoke dove-gray suit and silk scarf, stolidly watching the lighted green numbers on the elevator count higher and higher. I'm tempted to float the jurisdiction question to her, oh-so-casually. And maybe also ask her about why Roni Wollaskay was excused. But now's not the time. I can wait.

The elevator dings to signal we've arrived. It also means I'm about to cross another threshold. As we approach apartment 2505, walking down the plush wall-to-wall, past the glowing lily-shaped sconces and brass-plated numbers, my heart is racing. I scold myself. *So silly.* But I smooth my hair and then the shoulder of my linen blazer and swipe my tongue across my teeth to make sure there's no lipstick.

Martha knocks, one elegant fist rapping the white-lacquered door. It opens.

MARTHA GARDINER

Martha had stepped aside after she knocked. Put Rachel front and center. Old cop trick, learned in her own intern days. But just out of curiosity, she wanted to see Tom Rafferty's face when he saw Rachel North. The poor man flinched, his neck flushing red, though she had to give him credit for a quick recovery. Martha wasn't surprised. Photos and videos of Rachel from six years ago, of the person Tom Rafferty knew and promoted, might have been of an entirely different person. The Rachel North *she'd* seen for the first time on the Deacon Davis jury, then sitting in the courtroom cozying up to Rafferty, was dark-haired, with a mass of wild curls, and fresh-faced, a voluptuous cat. That barely jibed with this new Rachel—blond, thin, and brittle around the edges.

"Rachel," he said now. "Martha."

"Senator." Rachel's voice did not falter.

"Tom," Martha said. She'd tried to read Rachel's expression, too, but couldn't manage the choreography. "Thank you for making the time."

In reality, Tom had no choice, of course, and he knew it as well as she did. But it never hurt to be polite. Even to a predator. Or a power-drunk pol. But he knew what this was about. The murder of a young aide. The possible guilt of his own wife. His own precarious position.

They followed Rafferty out of the corridor into the austere apartment, Martha briefing Tom on Rachel's internship along the way. It hardly looked as if someone lived in the cookie-cutter living room—magazines stacked edge to edge on a glass coffee table, tawny suede throw pillows lining a creamy tweed couch, a fake orchid curving against the bare walls, the flower's blood-purple center the only color in the white-walled rectangle. On the bookshelves, the faded leather-bound spines stood perfectly aligned. Unseen air conditioners hummed, a pulsing undercurrent to this drama's stage setting.

"Please. Both of you." Tom gestured them toward the living room. "What can I do for you, Martha?"

Tom had changed over the years, too, Martha noted. He'd gained weight. And lost hair. But he remained the basic Tom Rafferty, knit shirt and boat shoes, insistently power-casual.

"As I mentioned on the phone," Martha began. "It's about Danielle Zander. May we sit?"

"Cut to the chase, shall we?" Rafferty remained standing. "Do I need a lawyer?"

"Let's sit, why don't we, Senator?" Martha understood his nerves. This was a tightrope. "Always pleased if you'd like to call a lawyer, of course. We'll wait. But at this point we're only gathering information. As I said. Take a seat. Rachel?"

Martha signaled her not only to sit, but to take out her yellow pad. Rachel had to obey, and accept her place. That she was an observer, a stenographer. With no personal stakes in this session other than getting experience.

"I'm at Harvard Law now," Rachel explained, as she retrieved her pad and stashed her leather bag beside the couch. "I'll graduate next year."

Martha almost smiled. Tactics, even now. Telegraphing to her former boss that their positions had changed, their power structure. Fine. Rachel was learning about being a lawyer, and that meant learning even more about manipulation. That things weren't always what they first appeared.

Time to put Rafferty through his paces.

"Senator?" She took the formal approach. He'd sat in a cordovan leather wing chair, surrounded by saddle leather, its curved arms studded with brass decorations. She took the chair opposite.

"First. Did Danielle Zander ever come to your home in Cambridge?" Martha asked. "Was your wife with you in Middlesex County at the time?"

"Of course not," Rafferty answered.

"Are you getting this, Rachel? Cambridge? Middlesex?"

"Yes." Rachel looked up from her pad, an expression of understanding on her face.

Good. "Tom? Did you know Danielle Zander before she came to work in your office?"

"No."

"Her family?"

"No."

"And where were you on that Saturday night? The weekend of her murder?"

Martha glanced at Rachel, who was frowning as she wrote.

"At home, of course."

"And your wife?"

"This is already on the record, Martha." Tom leaned back in his chair, crossed his arms over his chest. "And at the hearing, didn't you tell the court the murder was on Sunday?"

Good, Martha thought. Perfect. Exactly why she'd said that.

"And you well understand the boundaries of spousal privilege, Senator, just to clarify," she continued. "Speaking of what's on the record. If either of you *chose* to testify against the other, you understand you could do that."

Martha could hear the sound of Rachel's pen scratching on the pad. Was she grasping Martha's point? Nina could rat out her husband. Even trade his freedom for hers. Or the other way around—he could rat Nina out. That a husband and wife had leverage, for better or for worse. Till death did them part.

"Martha? Have you lost your mind?" Tom had crossed one leg over the other, and one boat-shoed foot was twitching. "Why are you reopening the case now?"

"Because Danielle Zander is still dead." Martha kept her voice icier than the air-conditioning. "And we haven't convicted her killer."

She paused. They all paused. Martha wished she could read Rachel's thoughts, know how she felt about this man Martha more than suspected she'd once pursued. Not that Tom wasn't equally culpable. Maybe more so. He should have known better. She almost laughed out loud with her fleeting moment of naïveté. When was the last time someone like Tom knew better?

"We have your interview notes, Senator, such as they were, from the initial investigation."

"Where you attempted to railroad not only my wife's life, but *my* life, trashing my reputation and career."

Martha let him take the jab. Then went on. "But there were a few things we didn't cover back then."

"Like what?"

"I was interested, for instance," she continued, "in the information the police gave me about your so-called illicit relationships with certain members of your staff."

"Bullshit."

Martha saw Rachel look up from her pad. Tom did not acknowledge her.

"I don't know where the hell you got that." Tom's foot jiggled as if possessed. "Or who the hell people you're talking about. And while we're at it, who the hell this 'interviewee' you 'quoted' at the hearing was. Listen, I'm a lawyer, too, Martha. Don't float this spousal privilege junk at me. And if you all were using some phony informant, or—"

"Did you and your wife have a loving relationship?" Martha asked.

Rachel turned a page, the paper crackling as she flapped the pad back onto her lap.

"None of your business. And I'm about to be finished with this improper—"

"You gave Danielle Zander that gold necklace." Martha ignored his bluster, put her question in the form of a statement.

Silence.

"Your wife's earring was found at the scene."

Silence.

CHAPTER **THIRTY-FIVE**

RACHEL NORTH

"Did you give any jewelry or gifts to any other of your female staffers?"

Martha, poised on the edge of Tom's wing chair, is now asking another thing I'd sure like to know. *Staffers,* plural, she's saying. There were only so many female staffers. I've thought about them, cataloged them in my head, making lists of them, over and over, trying to figure it out. Even though it was long ago, every face is photograph-clear. I also wonder how long Tom's going to put up with this before he calls his lawyer. And I almost burst out laughing, as it crosses my mind that he might call my husband, Jack.

But there's only silence.

I hate taking these damn notes, and I hate the subservience, but it does let me decide when I want to look at Tom. And when I don't. It's been . . . so long. A lifetime. Or two. He's older, and the sun's done him no favors. A drinking nose, my father once called it. That paunch. I bet Dani Zander would not be so attracted to him now. *An unworthy thought, Rachel.* Which I tamp down with all the others. I wonder how his wife feels about him these days.

And I wonder, too, what he thinks of me, the new me, no longer that workaholic, dutiful staffer, the reliable dependable Rachel, who came in early and stayed late and was good enough for everything—except him. I changed my entire life, my entire future, my entire self, all because of Tom. But I'm fine now. Better now. Much better.

"The interviewee reported that you were having liaisons with current staffers," Martha persists. "Back then. Was that true? And if so, did your wife know about it?"

"Why don't you ask *her*?"

I flinch, for a moment, thinking Tom is referring to *me*, wondering why doesn't Martha ask me. Does she think *I* slept with him? Slept my way to the top? I stifle a gasp, and luckily, too, because he's going on, and he didn't mean me.

"Why don't you ask Nina?"

"Good idea," Martha says. "Where is she?"

Tom shakes his head. "No idea."

"I see." Martha clearly doesn't believe him.

"If there's nothing else?" Tom stands.

"There is, indeed." Martha makes no move. "I asked you about Saturday, but now I'd like to hear where you were the entire weekend of the murder. And Tom? You might want to sit. I'm going to need to hear that hour by hour."

I do, too, I think. I need it hour by hour. And Tom hadn't answered the illicit-relationships question. Why doesn't Martha push him on that? I need her to understand I'm not . . . that kind of a person. She sees potential in me, she told me that. I cannot let her picture a manipulating opportunist who sleeps her way to power. She'd never trust me, or respect me, or protect me, if she thought I had done that.

Tom stays standing. Forces Martha to look up at him. "I told your investigators six damn years ago."

"Tell me again."

"Here's what I'll tell you." Tom backs up, positions himself behind his chair, an upholstered barricade. Gestures toward the doorway with a stabbing forefinger. "We're done. I want a lawyer."

"Good for you." Martha leans back against a throw pillow, the pale fringe sticking out behind her gray suit jacket. "But as even Rachel here knows, you're not in custody. Did you hear any Miranda rights, Rachel?"

I don't enjoy being used as a prop for her sarcasm, but I have no choice. "No," I say.

"So, Tom?" Martha goes on, her voice hardening. "If you insist you're finished talking to me, I'll not force you to continue. But as you well know, it may inure to your favor if you tell us the truth. You can have no doubt that once you're on the stand, I'll elicit from you that you refused to answer my questions."

"On the *stand*? What imaginary world do you inhabit? Ms. North, do you know anything about a trial?"

"No," I say again.

"And we're done," Tom says. He stalks to the front door. Opens it. "Right now."

Martha and I are in the hallway, the sound of the slammed door echoing in the long empty corridor.

"Oh," Martha says. "Oh, no."

"What? Are you okay?"

"I left my briefcase inside." She looks at the carpet, then at the apartment door. "And it'll be awkward for me to retrieve it. Could you get it for me, please? I'll meet you in the lobby."

She turns on her heel and glances at me over her shoulder as she strides away. "Don't be long. We need to get back."

Staring at Tom's front door, I count to five. Slowly. Silently. Terrified. Listening. The elevator arrives, and departs, with Martha inside.

I lift my hand to knock. But the door swings open before I make a sound.

"Clever," Tom says.

Clever? I am, but what's he talking about?

"Martha left her briefcase," I say, using her first name so he knows we're equals. "Sorry to bother you."

Tom blocks my exit through the still-open doorway. "I *meant*, do you think this is clever? Barging in here with that woman. Trying to ruin my life, after all this time. Gloating over me."

I shake my head, almost sad. He never understood. I take a deep breath. Martha is waiting for me in the lobby. I don't have long.

"*I'm* not trying to ruin your life, Tom. You ruined it, quite on your own, didn't you?"

Tom's about to dismiss me. I know that imperious look. Better yank him into reality, fast.

"Did you do it?" I hear the strange tone in my voice, and try to tamp down the menace. "Did you kill Danielle?"

"What?" Tom does a credible startle.

Most people would have instantly believed he was sincere.

"I-I never—" He's actually sputtering. "Of all the in*sane*—"

"Good." I nod, approving. "Say that. Keep saying that. No one's accused you yet, have they? Whatever your alibi to the police was, it worked. I've read the transcripts. I know everything. And I completely know what's true. So. Keep saying that."

"I am not 'saying that.'" He shakes his head as if he's trying to think of what to do next. "Ms. North, I most certainly would never . . ." He narrows his eyes again, laser-focused. "Is there something I should know?"

Probably, but that's hardly my goal.

"Maybe the police think you did it *with* Nina. Both of you. And was that why you were so stressed at the arraignment? I mean, not only was your wife's future in the balance, yours was, too. And mine. All of ours."

I can almost hear the seconds ticking by. Envision Martha in the lobby, looking at her watch, eyeing the elevator, becoming more and more aggravated. How long can it take to retrieve a briefcase? But if I can get Tom to implicate himself, confess to his—whatever—with Danielle, or change his original story somehow so he's caught in a lie, my life and career are set. I'll win.

"*With?* Nina? No. That's craziness. Besides, Nina had nothing to do with this. You know that. She wasn't prosecuted, they dropped the charges. They know she didn't—"

"That alibi of hers, where did that come from? You? Very convenient."

"Not from me! Nina was away. We were having—this is none of your business, I have to say, Rachel. I'm surprised."

Surprised. And now I'm "Rachel." So very Tom.

"The necklace, remember?" I set Martha's briefcase on the carpet.

Tom turns and in one motion closes the door behind him. Stands in front of it, a body-language barricade. He always takes up all the room. "Rachel, you need to tell me. If you ever cared about—Is this why Gardiner's questioning me? Are you trying to threaten me? Or warn me? Why would she—or you—possibly think I—"

"Poor Danielle. You gave her that necklace."

"I did not. I did *not*."

And there's the lie. I had the necklace. For an entire weekend. Thinking it was mine. But he doesn't know I knew what it was. We're on equal ground now.

"You did." I point to him, chin high, reveling in my secret knowledge. "The jewelry store has indisputable records. You bought it. You went to Tiffany, and you bought it."

"For Nina." He spits the name. "But the necklace was stolen. From my desk."

"Uh-*huh*." I nod, scornful. "Tom? That is such—forgive me—total preposterous bullshit. Did you report it to the insurance company? Or the credit card company?" See if he has such a fast answer to *that* one.

"I was going to."

I widen my eyes, the light dawning.

"So you could say Danielle took it? And that's what you'd tell Nina? You are *such* a selfish, self-centered—I cannot believe I *ever*—" I draw in a breath. *Stop, Rachel. Not now.* "And you—Oh. I see. *That's* what you're afraid of. That they'll think you confronted her about it. In the parking lot. And you didn't mean to push her, maybe."

"Rachel, what the hell is this about? Is this you talking? Or is this Gardiner?" Tom swoops open the front door. The length of the hall, the part I can see, is empty.

"Out," he says.

I stand my ground, the seconds ticking away. I'll tell Martha I had to use the bathroom.

"Here's the thing, *Senator*." I step farther into the apartment. Farther into his life. Farther into his soul. I trusted him—but he tricked me, deceived me, ruined me. Look who I am now. "Martha's reopening the case. Why do you think that is?"

"I have no idea! That's what I'm asking you. I know you, Rachel."

"And *I* know she's after you. Maybe even you and Nina. If she's the guilty one, why not help them find her? Because Martha Gardiner is relentless, she's—"

"That's ludicrous. Are you wearing a wire?"

"You had nothing, a flimsy alibi. They know that. And Martha is on the hunt, believe me. But that 'interviewee'—whoever that informant was—laid your sleazy cards on the courtroom table. After Gardiner's statement at the arraignment? Your career was over. You were hounded from the senate. Your wife left you. You had nowhere to turn. Better than prison, though. Because what if you got away with murder?"

"You should go, Rachel."

I don't budge. Now that I've gone this far. "Whose apartment is this, anyway? Yours?"

"It's a friend's."

"Nice," I say. "But what're you going to do when Martha Gardiner lowers the legal boom on you? Or Nina? You going to call Jack? My *husband*? And remember, you're the bigger fish. When Martha Gardiner gets enough ammunition to prove it—if she hasn't already—how are you going to prove you didn't do it?"

"Are you wearing a wire? Rachel? I mean it."

"Of course not." I pat my chest, pretend to fiddle with a blouse button. "Want me to prove it?"

"I *didn't kill her*," Tom says, eyeing me. "That's . . . beyond any comprehension."

"You're a liar," I say. "You know why?"

I picture Gardiner, down in the marble-walled lobby, texting or pacing or fuming. Or leaving. I have to go. "You know *why*?"

"Rachel." Tom takes a step toward me.

I step away. I have the power now. "Here's why. I opened that box, Tom." I feel my heart racing again, and this time I don't try to stop it. I try to keep up with it. It's time for me to say this, after all these years. Now, or never. And it's now.

"That Tiffany box. Oh, right, you're shocked. Please. You gave *me* that necklace, Tom. And then you took it back! You took it *back*! Like *I* wasn't good enough for you. But when you told me it was for your wife . . ." I take a deep breath, remembering. Confessing. "I even—can you believe it?—admired you. Decided you were a faithful husband. Decided I was silly, and you were a professional, and it was so, *so* embarrassing, and I was so glad you had no idea. . . ."

"No, Rachel, oh, I am so sorry."

Tom reaches out a hand, but I push it away.

"I *never* thought you'd open—" he begins.

"Of course you didn't. Because little Rachel, little pitiful Rachel, wasn't *good* enough for a necklace. Or for you. You *used* me. And, hmm. Let's think about that." I tap one forefinger to my cheek. Tap tap tap. "You told me it was for your wife. Which I'd have to reveal, if Martha asks, because that's what you told me. So. Either you were lying about it being for your wife, which makes you an immoral, unethical sleaze who thinks the women in his office are not only his subordinates but his personal harem—"

"Rachel!"

"Or—" I'm enjoying this now. "It truly *was* for your wife. In which case, how did it wind up on Danielle? Are you going to try out your "she stole it" story? Turn a poor murder victim into a thief? Lovely. But, Tom? Why, oh, why was your wife's earring at the murder scene?"

I touch my neck, caressing, as if the necklace were there. He's transfixed, I can tell. *Got you, you bastard.* "The necklace I had for one brief shining moment? Only the two of us know about that."

He grabs my arm with one hand, holds it, tight. "Not. One. Word." Puts his face close to mine. "Hear me, Rachel? Not one word."

"Oh, now you want me to help you? Now I'm good enough?" I whisper back. *I've won, I've won, I've finally won.* "So interesting, Tom. And here's why. Because, now? Now, I have the power. Right? Now *you're* the potential victim. And you're gonna wonder, every moment, what I'm going to do."

CHAPTER **THIRTY-SIX**

RACHEL NORTH

I'd told Jack I had to work late, which is essentially true. And although I *was* working on the Zander case, my other investigation had to stay under the radar. For now.

Roni Wollaskay is driving. I'm in the front seat of her buzzy little car, eating a granola bar. We're on our way to see Momo Peretz. To find out if Martha Gardiner, my new boss, tampered with the Deacon Davis jury.

Sure, Deacon Davis is dead. But jury tampering is a crime. A big, bad, embarrassing, career-ruining crime. If it's true, Jack would be thrilled to know about Martha's shocking transgression. Roni and I are on the way to dig up the past.

Speaking of the past, I think, as Roni maneuvers us through Kenmore Square traffic. When I'd finally gotten downstairs from seeing Tom, *Tom*, my skin was tingling. My heart out of control. And my brain on fire.

Our statie chauffeur had been waiting outside to take us back to the office, and Martha changed tactics, joining me in the backseat. She'd angled herself toward me as we drove, almost effusive, reciting tidbits of the interview and assessing Tom's answers.

"Did you believe Tom was telling the truth?" she'd asked. "About whether Ms. Zander came to his house? Did you know about that? Whether she did? Did he have a relationship with her?"

"I don't know," I said, trying to focus. "They were out of town together. A lot. Like you said in Nina's arraignment, remember?"

"Listen, did you think Tom's wife suspected anything untoward? Especially on those trips? Or, say, did Logan Concannon? Do you think she's telling everything she knows?"

I had to laugh. "Never," I said. "Logan's, like, the keeper of the secrets."

"Agreed," Martha had said. "But we're making progress. So perfect to be working with you on this. Now, how about the . . ."

As she'd continued questioning me, there were times I felt like I was on the witness stand, the way she asked about the office, the security, even the trash collection. What Jack might or might not have told me. But that kind of grilling is a lawyer thing. Jack does it to me, too. I've learned not to take it personally. Plus Martha'd said it was perfect that we were working together. I agreed.

And now, even more perfect, because this afternoon she'd brought me to Tom. Face-to-face. I heard that voice, felt his breath on me. But no longer as pitiful, subservient Rachel. I had the power. It filled me with joy and hope and transformation. With justice. It was all worth it.

As we'd pulled into the office parking lot, Martha tapped her forefingers together. "So. What did Tom tell you when you went back for the briefcase?"

My eyes widened with a possibility. "Martha? Did you do that on purpose?"

She smiled, dismissing that. "Of course not. But I must admit, I was intrigued at leaving you two alone. You were there for a while. Did he try to pump you?"

"No," I said. "He didn't. It only took longer because I used his bathroom."

"Oh." Martha nodded. "That makes sense. But I knew you two had a history."

"He was my boss." All I need to say. "A long time ago."

"You're blushing," she said. Then jabbed me with an elbow. "Kidding. Come on. Let's go in."

She'd opened the glass front door and walked into the office ahead of me. As we entered, I saw Leon was not at the reception desk, and most office lights were off.

"Might as well close up for the day," she said. "Big day tomorrow. Thanks so much for today. It was helpful to have you there."

"Big day?" I'd said. "Why? And listen, could I just ask about the Baltrim case? How are we doing with that? Who's working on that? I haven't been able to eat pizza since, I must say." I tried for a little camaraderie.

"Under way," Martha said. "It's a process. I met with Lizann Wallace. Remember her? She's a murder-lister now. But Baltrim's a slam dunk. No bail, no worries. And that little boy, Jonah? He's fine, I checked on him. So forget about that. It's Danielle Zander we need to focus on. It's time for that case to be solved. Closed. Once and for all. So we can all rest easy, including Danielle. See you tomorrow, okay?"

But by that time, we were down the hall and she was in her office and her door had closed her away. But we'd bonded, that was for sure. Martha had taken me under her elegant wing. Woman power. Sure, whatever works.

And Martha's a good teacher. I'm using her techniques right now. In the car with Roni.

"Momo's a piece of work," I say, brushing a few granola crumbs from my black skirt onto the floor of her little car. "'Momo,' you know? All that knitting, all that granny personality? That was her misdirection. She'd look up, nail someone with perfect logic, then go back to her angora."

Roni accelerates around a rattling landscape truck, rakes and shovels lashed to its side. "She's no dummy."

"Neither are you," I say. Neither am I. "Listen. We know Deacon Davis is dead. But even so. Someone obviously lied to the judge about your daughter."

"Yup." Roni keeps her eyes on the road.

"And you were excused—or whatever—*before* the deliberations even started. So why would that be?"

"Well?" she says, when we finally stop for the red light. "What if someone was getting rid of the jurors they thought would vote not guilty? And decided to start with me? *Before* the deliberations even began, which is less obvious."

"Whoa," I say. As if I'd never thought of that. "You think Momo got excused for a bogus reason, too? Maybe to get some other juror *in* to the deliberations? That could only be done by . . ." Martha Gardiner, I don't say.

"Parking place. Awesome." Roni slams to a stop and pulls up behind a departing SUV. "Momo was a not guilty. She said so all the time. Like I did. Three-fifty-nine," she points to an apartment building. "There. Looks like Manderley. Before the fire."

We buzz Momo's bell. The prewar elevator's accordion doors, zigzag brass, close Roni and me in, and then the tiny car creaks us up to the third floor. Momo's wearing a white shirt over khaki slacks, black flats with bows. She's more spindly now than she was, and barely five feet tall.

"We have to stop meeting like this," she says, gesturing us inside.

There are no handshakes, no hugs. We're not old pals, or long-lost colleagues. We barely know each other. We have only one thing in common. The search for justice.

Roni and I both say no to white wine, and sitting on Momo's flowered couch I wonder if life is just a series of living rooms and secrets, and those of us who are on the hunt for answers must visit one after another like a scavenger hunt, one clue to the next. This room, white curtains open to a pink-blooming magnolia and crowded with silver-framed photos of smiling faces, families, maybe, arm in arm, on beaches and snow-covered mountains, hardly seems the place for us to consider some sinister plot.

Roni uses one forefinger to trace the curved mahogany-looking arm of a yellow gingham armchair as she sits down. "Such a good piece. Where'd you have it reupholstered?"

She laughs, at herself, it seems. "Sorry. It's furniture. I can't help it."

"This one's nice, too," I say, sitting on cobalt blue.

"We can talk about chairs later, dears." Momo scoops up her knitting, depositing it on the pale gray carpet, then takes its place on another chair. "But you two have me so curious."

Roni explains, in broad strokes, that Deacon Davis was killed in a prison "altercation," the papers called it, which Momo knew, and the deal about her sick daughter. Which Momo didn't know. Mid-story, Momo picks up her knitting, frowning over it as she listens.

"She wasn't sick?" Her needles keep moving.

"Not that sick." Roni looks at me as if to confirm, but this is her story to tell.

"And you didn't ask to be excused. Didn't ask that Officer Suddeth, or the judge."

"Nope."

Momo stops, holding the needles scarf-width apart. "Wouldn't there have to be a, some kind of a hearing on that?" She smiles, her parchment face softening. "My dear departed husband was a lawyer, did I mention that? I put that man through law school. Helped him study for the bar. We lived on canned tuna, and—" She stops herself. "*Was* there a hearing? With those court officers? Rachel? Does your husband remember?"

So much for doddering old Momo.

"The look on your face!" Roni laughs again. "I *told* her, Rach. Who you were married to. And that you're in law school now as well."

I laugh too. Aren't we all one happy sisterhood.

"That explains it," I say. "But no, Jack doesn't remember a hearing. On the other hand, he also doesn't remember that there wasn't a hearing. Apparently, he didn't think it was a big deal."

"But *you* do. Think it's a big deal. You both do," Momo says.

I look at Roni so she'll keep the floor.

"Well, we just wondered, I guess, how you came to be excused."

Momo tells the story, exactly as I remember it, about forgetting her pills, and the son driving her to the courthouse, and being late for deliberations.

"Did they have a hearing about *you*, Momo?" I ask.

She nods, several times, as if retrieving a memory, or reliving something. "The Grace person, remember her?"

"The other court officer," I say.

"Yes. She brought me in to the judge's chambers. Your husband was there, dear, and the district attorney. In front of everyone, Grace said I talked to her about Deacon Davis being not guilty. She told the judge I'd said something to *her*, Grace, like—" She pauses, raising her eyebrows like she's reciting bad dialogue. "'He has a criminal record, but now I know he's gone straight.'"

"Oh," I say. "Did you hear that on TV?"

"Because you can't do that," Roni says. "The judge instructed us—"

"But I didn't." Momo's voice hardens, no more silly granny. "I know the rules. I never said that. Ever. And I never watched television."

"You *did* think he was not guilty though, didn't you?" I purse my lips, remembering. "You said so."

"Well, we jurors were *supposed* to be talking about the trial, dear. I certainly never said anything like that to Grace. But when she said so, and that I'd been late because of my pills, the judge got all—excuse my language—pissy. She asked me, in that voice"—Momo makes a prune face—"'What are those pills *for*?'"

She gets her own face back. "Like I was senile."

"Wow." I lean forward, elbows on knees. "Listen, what did Martha Gardiner say? Did she believe you? Or Grace?"

"I was excused from the jury, wasn't I?" Momo smooths the knitting across her lap, the multicolored stripes bright against her khaki slacks. "And I remember that day, so well, because I was almost in tears. Since then, I'd often considered writing to that poor man. But he's dead now, and it's all—so tragic. I feel as if I'm the one who's guilty."

"Oh, Momo, no. You can't know your vote would have changed the outcome," Roni says, trying to reassure her.

Momo shakes her head. "I never would have voted guilty."

"I wouldn't have, either." Roni turns to me.

I take a deep breath, blow it out. And tell the flat solid truth. Some of it. "I've felt bad about it ever since."

But it all sinks in for a moment, how one person's actions can torpedo someone's life, or save it. Sometimes deliberately, sometimes simply because it's easier. Or more expedient. I'm wishing we had said yes to the wine.

"Momo?" I break our silence. I have to ask two questions. "First. In that hearing. Did my—did Jack Kirkland do or say anything? Defend you, or argue, or object?"

"Not a word." She sighs, looks apologetic. "Maybe he did, but before I got there?"

"Maybe." I stand by my man. "What did Deacon Davis say?"

The knitting needles stop again. "Say? Well, nothing. He wasn't there."

Bingo. Roni, a non-lawyer, has no idea why it's important, but for Jack to attend a hearing about a questionable juror, during the deliberations, and not bring his client is improper. Possibly grounds for a new trial on the basis that Jack gave what's called "ineffective assistance." If anyone found out, that'd be disastrous for him. Why would Jack let that happen?

"What do we do now?" Roni asks. We're on the way home, and she turns at me as we stop at the light on Beacon Street. "It's squirrely. That Momo and I were *both* excused. For iffy reasons."

"Coincidence?"

"No way." Roni shifts into first, then second, punctuating her verdict after the light turns green. "Something's going on."

I stay quiet, letting her stew about it.

"Yeah." Roni shifts into third for the Storrow Drive straightaway toward Newton. "Does it even matter, though? Since Deacon Davis is dead."

"It might," I lie. Because jury tampering is a big fat crime, dead criminal or not, and my holier-than-thou boss Martha Gardiner has got to be involved. "Let me think. Do some digging. I'm on the inside now, you know? Of both sides."

I smile and turn to her. Life is strange. "Keep this to yourself for now, okay?"

"There's nothing to tell," Roni says. "We don't really know anything."

"True," I lie again. I have a lot of practice now.

The Charles River flies by on my right, dotted with white-bannered sailboats on twilight cruises, the tender-leafed weeping willows on its historic banks fluttering in the May breeze.

My brain is going faster than Roni's little car, and we're now getting every green light as we head toward Crystal Lake and home.

A good omen. It has to be.

CHAPTER **THIRTY-SEVEN**

RACHEL NORTH

"Sweetheart?" I slide one finger along Jack's bare arm, the white cotton blanket over us barely heavy enough to notice. Our bedroom windows are open, the soft night air coming through the open shutters and the screens Jack showed me he'd installed tonight after he got home. Nothing else to do while he waited for me to get there, he'd semi-complained. He hadn't even asked where I'd been. Which gave me time to decide how to introduce my new idea. My lifesaving idea. "Are you awake?"

"Hmm." He turns over, putting his back to me, but reaches around and draws me into the curve of him.

I breathe in his citrus shampoo and the minty toothpaste, feel the shape of the muscles in his back. Six years we've slept like this.

"Seriously." I have to persist or I might lose my nerve. Maybe it would be easier to let this all go, see what happens, not try to mold the world into the shape I prefer. But I can't do that. "Can you keep your eyes open a minute more? Honey?"

He flops over, his eyes closed but facing me now. He scoots one hand under his pillow, rearranging. "I'm all yours," he mutters. "Completely awake. What?"

"I had a thought," I begin. I should have practiced this, maybe. It has to sound spontaneous. "You know Martha Gardiner?"

"Is this some sort of quiz?" Jack's eyes are still closed, his voice a mumble. "Or a trick question?"

"Sorry." I touch his shoulder, let my fingers trail down his arm. "I'm just, you know, nervous."

One eye struggles open. "About what?"

"So you know Roni and I talked. About Deacon—"

"Deacon Davis, got it." Jack's eyes are closed again, and he takes in a deep breath. I can feel his mind slipping away from me, but for some reason this seems like the right time.

"And remember Momo Peretz? The juror who got—"

Jack surprises me. Extricates himself from me. In an instant, he's sitting up, his back leaning against three plumped pillows, eyes open now. "Rachel? What's this about? Why did you wait until one in the morning to discuss whatever this is?"

Good. He's awake. I sit up, too, and turn myself toward him, pulling the ice-blue sheet up to my neck.

"Because I didn't know," I begin, "whether even to float this. But I think—you're right about Martha Gardiner. She cheats."

"Cheats? She's a royal pain, that's for sure, which is why I can't believe you're working there, but—"

"Did you know there was a hearing on Roni Wollaskay? When she was dismissed? Did you know she never requested to be excused? Never said her daughter was deathly ill, or anything remotely like that?"

"She didn't?"

"Nope. Martha was there when the judge called her to chambers, and the other officer, too, the man. But they never told you about that, did they?"

Jack looks concerned, so I know I'm on the right track.

"And Momo Peretz. Same thing. When they accused her of talking to Grace O'Brien about Davis's criminal record? That's where I was this evening, talking to Momo. She insists she never talked to Grace about that. And did you know she was a total 'not guilty'?"

More concerned look from Jack. "She didn't say that to the judge, Rach."

Not the point, but it is the point. "Exactly. I think Martha's in cahoots with maybe the court officers to get rid of jurors they think will vote to acquit. How they know, I have no idea. Maybe they listen. Somehow. Maybe Martha gets them, or someone, to interfere with witnesses, too."

Jack is silent, so I know I have him intrigued. He hates Martha, so I know he's open to believe the worst.

"Listen. Remember the throat-slash killer, Marcus Simmons Dorn? In that apartment building. The West—"

"Moreland. Westmoreland. Yeah."

"Remember you were so upset because there was a missing witness? That someone didn't show up to testify? Or couldn't? You said"—I think I'd remembered this correctly—"he was an alibi witness?"

Yeah. He yawns, but nods yes. He's interested, I can tell.

"What specifically happened to that person?"

"He was detained." Jack runs his hands over his face. "Deported. I think some feds, ICE, came to his house, took him away."

"Is it possible Gardiner could have engineered that somehow? Sicced ICE on your witness? To get rid of him and clinch the case. So she could win. No matter how she did it."

Silence.

"She only wants to win, Jack. And she doesn't care how she does it."

"You shouldn't be talking to me about this, Rachel."

"Huh?"

"You have to report it to the Board of Bar Overseers if you're genuinely concerned. End of story."

"Like you reported her? That's hardly the end of the story." I see the surprise on his face. "Might have been the beginning of it, in fact."

"What?" Jack shakes his head. I can feel him remembering. "Well, she deserved it. But—she told you that?"

"Oh, yeah. She—" I need to push harder. I take a deep breath, clutch the sheet and go for it. "Listen. Let me talk one more minute, and if there's something else I should do, I will, but you're my only hope here. I've been pretending to be this *lawyer,* all these months, but all this makes me realize I'm just a naïve—so listen. Remember the pizza guy? Baltrim? Gardiner totally made me lie about being lost to get him to identify himself. She even made me trick a little kid to confirm the ID. I mean, I'm only a law student, but I know enough rules to know what's"—I remember Roni's word—"squirrely. Over the line. Unfair."

"That's not my case, Rachel."

"All the more reason for me to tell you! It's *mine!*" I've raised my voice a notch, so I bring it down. "And by participating, aren't I potentially in trouble, too? We take one step over the line, a line that seems okay at the time, then we take another step and another, and at some point we're way into the weeds and entangled, and my career is over before it even begins."

Jack brushes a strand of hair from my face, and I close my eyes at his touch. "You might be making too much of this, Rach. All lawyers—well, there are shortcuts and concessions and things we all do for the greater good. For expedience. Marcus Dorn was a sick puppy, Rach. Vanishing witness or not, he was toast. And yeah, I hate to lose, but—sometimes they're guilty."

He leans over, kisses my cheek, his touch a whisper. "And I'll deny I said any of that, of course."

I twist away, crossing my arms in front of me, undeterred.

"No. Listen, Jack. Listen. You were right, you were completely right. She's predatory. And I get so upset when I think now that I didn't listen to you in the first place. I wanted to learn the ropes so we could work together. But these aren't the ropes I want to learn. Jack? Look what she did to Nina Rafferty. Humiliated her and her husband, and didn't even check out that flimsy alibi. If you hadn't been such a brilliant lawyer, she might have . . ."

To let him think, I take a swig of water from the bottle on my night-stand. I can't tell whether Jack's with me yet. Our bedroom is illumi-nated by streaks of light coming through the white shutters, slashes of streetlights banding the ceiling and striping the wall. The shutter slats rattle after each impatient puff of breeze. Jack's hair is nighttime straw, his chest bare, the white blanket only up to his waist.

"Honey?" He's staring straight ahead, his back against the headboard. "It's the middle of the night. Is there something you're trying to tell me?"

"We interviewed Tom Rafferty today," I say. "And yesterday Logan Concannon."

"What?" Jack's turned to me now, full on. "Why?"

"Is it okay if I tell you?" I gather our blanket up around me. This is risky territory, personally, professionally, and in every other way. But the wheels are in motion, and if I don't guide them, I'll be crushed under their inevitable path.

"Is it *okay*? Rachel? You woke me up, talked for fifteen solid minutes, it's after one in the morning, and now you've decided to ask permission?" Jack scratches his forehead, then waves one hand in an arc above our heads. "We're in the bubble. This is off the lawyer record, off the professional record, off all the records. This is you and me, husband and wife. As confidential as anything can be."

"You sure?"

"Rachel."

That's his enough-is-enough tone. Good.

"Martha's reopening the Danielle Zander case." I pause, letting that megaton bombshell crash into our suburban bedroom.

"What? The Danielle—but that was—six years ago. And it's . . ."

I stay quiet, watching Jack's mind assess and calculate, can almost see the cogs and gears churning through case law and precedent, through issue, rule, analysis, conclusion.

"It's not in her jurisdiction," Jack pronounces, coming to the critical realization. "Which means—shit, Rachel, is this what you were asking me about? With poisoned chicken and all?"

"You got me," I pretend to confess.

"Clever," he says. "Who's she looking at for it?"

"She hasn't told me."

Jack's perplexed, I can tell. Join the club. "Is there a grand jury? She can't open the case without *some* theory of the case."

"Which is why I'm concerned." I nod, encouraging this line of thought. "What if she's like, so obsessed with the loss . . ."

I bite my lower lip, thinking. I hadn't thought of it until this very second. "Listen. Would there be a way she could do this under the radar? Under the guise of reopening the case, but in reality, for herself? Like Javert in *Les Misérables*? And she's using me like bait?"

"Bait?"

"Yeah." An intriguing thought, and believable. "To keep those people, Tom and Logan and whoever, unsettled or frightened, and see if she can get someone to say something to maybe incriminate Nina? Or even Tom?"

"Using you."

"Yeah. Because she can't stand to lose. Especially to you. And she knows because I'm such a goody two-shoes, I'm never going to tell you. You were right. This is why she chose me. To get back at you."

I let that settle, just for a beat. Then go on.

"But what if it's not only this case? I mean, she's ruthless. Take the whole Deacon Davis thing. Momo and Roni. And he was killed *after* Roni told the judge what happened!"

I let that settle, too.

"But Martha doesn't know I know about that. And *you'd* never have known if not for me. And what if *she* 'disappeared' your slasher witness? And what if she's trying to railroad Jeffrey Baltrim? What if she has a whole list of murder cases, and she's—I don't know. Making sure she wins, no matter how. She was so freaked out over your victory at the Nina Rafferty arraignment, who knows what she might do to win? She *could* indict Nina in Middlesex now, couldn't she? If Dani was killed there?"

"Is *that* what she's planning? To indict Nina again?" He's wide awake now, wrenches the twist top off his water bottle, frowns at it. "Son of a—What does she have on her? Is there new evidence?"

"I don't know," I honestly say. "But it's exactly as you said, Jack. She asks me about you *all* the time. Milks me for information about you. And she told me a whole bunch of stuff about you—things she hoped would upset me. You were so right. This summer isn't about me. It's about *you*. We have to stop her."

"Stop Martha Gardiner."

"Yes." I nod, agreeing with myself. "She's obsessed. I'm all about justice, and I know you are, too. She wants to nail someone for Dani's death, and that's admirable. But she's over the edge. Nuts. Dangerous. She's obsessed with *you*, Jack, not true justice. Obsessed with Nina, and with her own defeat. She can't deal with it."

"You think she's after Nina? Rach? You *have* to tell me."

"She's like—you're her white whale," I tell him. All true. "She hates you. What if she decides to put Nina—or even Tom, or both of them, or an innocent person?—away simply to torment you? But it's too much for me. I can't do it alone. *We* have to get her off that case. And, even better, off the job. Think how much better *our* lives will be, too. Kirkland and North."

The next morning, I smile, remembering, as I carry my coffee in an aluminum travel mug. Usually I brew my Double Black Diamond myself, but this morning Jack presented it to me, along with a blueberry muffin he'd wrapped in plastic and a surprisingly lingering kiss. No scrawly dismissive notes on yellow pads. No disdainful silence. No earlier-than-me departures. It felt like it did before, sexy and entangled, like when we were first married. My newly admitted suspicions and animosity toward Martha Gardiner seem to have rekindled our relationship.

Today my goal is to see if I can get her to let me in closer. There are things I need to know. For me, for Tom, for Jack. But mostly for me. Martha says she wants to work with me, that she sees something in me. Let's see what I can get her to tell me.

The enemy of my enemy, and all that.

CHAPTER THIRTY-EIGHT

MARTHA GARDINER

"It's only June. It's too soon to be excited about the Red Sox." Martha Gardiner had shut down this afternoon's driver in mid-chat. She needed to marshal her thoughts. She buckled herself into the front seat, to convey to Rachel that yesterday's backseat side-by-side was not the norm.

Rachel had started to feel comfortable with her, that was good. If Rachel was a pipeline to Jack, that's exactly what Martha had hoped. She watched the woman stride across the parking lot, noticing how Rachel had chosen her clothes—black skirt, black jacket—to mimic Martha's own. Almost a team uniform. Perfect. Time to harness Rachel's goodwill. Tap in to her curiosity. See what she could discover.

"Where're we off to?" Rachel tossed her briefcase into the backseat, then slid in beside it, juggling a coffee mug and her cell phone.

"Hi, Rachel," Martha said. "I see you have your afternoon coffee—good. Thanks for doing all that filing this morning, much appreciated. We're efforting another interview, but it's unconfirmed. In the interest of efficiency"—Martha glanced over into the backseat, making sure Rachel was listening—"and optimism, we're headed there as if it'll happen. I'll let you know when we know. So. This is Officer McGann, by the way."

"Shawn," he said, adjusting the rearview.

"Hi," Rachel said. "Great."

"So, Rachel." Martha began her experiment as Shawn pulled their black Charger into the street. "What questions do you have for me? While we drive?"

Rachel coughed, then coughed again, holding her hand over her mouth. Holding her coffee mug away from her.

"You okay?" Martha asked, turning to check. "Want us to stop?"

"No, no," Rachel's voice was a choking whisper. "Went down the wrong way. The coffee."

"That'll happen. Put your coffee in the cup holder." Martha could almost picture the inside of Rachel's brain, first surprised at Martha's sudden openness, and then trying to come up with a question that didn't make her sound incompetent or needy or too ambitious. Choking on her surprise, not her coffee, Martha diagnosed.

They drove in silence, headed toward the outskirts of Boston, the crazy-quilt neighborhood called Brighton. Martha waited, letting Rachel recover, allowing her own mind a moment to evaluate the trimmed gardens rolling by outside her window.

Homes with front lawns and driveways. And families. Everything Martha would never have. Had chosen *not* to have. Was she wrong?

A woman in a white visor and turquoise tunic clipped plump red peonies and laid them across a wide wicker garden basket. Had she, or any of her neighbors, faced a loss, a death, a withering injustice? Martha knew, so often, what lay behind innocent-looking closed doors. The regret and the sorrow. The framed photos of now-lifeless faces, the ones whose murders were never truly resolved. Like Danielle Zander's. The killers who Jack Kirkland and his comrades managed to extricate from the jaws of truth. Her blood ran cold with it. That's why Martha did what she did. Had to.

Rachel cleared her throat. Martha focused herself back into the present.

"Tell me about unsolved cases," Rachel finally said. She held up her cell phone. "I did some research on cold cases, and it says there are lots of them, like two hundred thousand. And one study said there's a one-in-three chance that the police will never identify the killer."

Martha saw Shawn roll his eyes. She longed to do the same thing but didn't want Rachel to feel hesitant about asking questions.

"Oh, sure." Martha could see Rachel's reaction in the rearview. Another plus of having her in the back. "Technically, a person can get away with murder. Sure. We—we're not happy with that. But numbers are numbers. And remember, that one in three you point to encompasses the cases that aren't quickly solved. The difficult ones, the complicated ones, the outliers. It doesn't mean the perpetrator is smart. More like, lucky. As in the Danielle Zander case."

"True," Rachel says. "But what makes you open a cold case? How do they usually get solved?"

"In general?" Martha should teach Rachel that to get specific answers, lawyers had to ask specific questions. But it'd be instructive, and possibly revealing, to nail down precisely what Rachel was interested in. And especially what she already knew. Some of it might have come from Rachel's potential pipeline of a husband. What he'd learned in confidential conversations with the first suspect in the case. Or, perhaps, what Rachel herself knew about Nina Rafferty. Or Tom Rafferty. Or a few other people.

Martha was counting on Rachel not being able to keep track of it all. She twisted her body toward the backseat again, looking her intern in the eye. "Or are you asking about Danielle Zander?"

"Well, either. In general, or Dani's case in particular." Rachel coughed again, looking embarrassed. "I mean, is there DNA? Don't you have to be a criminal or a soldier or a government hotshot to be in the DNA database? How do you find someone who's not in the database? Or can you? If the bad guy's DNA isn't there, there's nothing to compare the crime scene DNA to. Except if you have those ancestry things, I suppose."

Martha almost laughed. Questions were so often also answers. A window on someone's thoughts or fears or plans. Or inexperience. Or an insight about who really wanted to know. Like, perhaps, the questioner's husband.

"Sure, DNA's a pitfall," Martha said. "Did Jack ask about that? Your husband certainly knows that even in those ancestry files, a relative's DNA must be there in the first place. In reality . . ." She tilted her head, deciding exactly how to put this. "Cold cases often rely more on the emergence of new witnesses."

Martha turned to look again, couldn't resist.

Rachel's eyes had widened. "Is there a new witness in Danielle's case?"

"Good specific question." Martha nodded her approval. "Does Jack know of anyone? Speaking of which, have you been back to that dumpster? What can you see from there?"

Rachel closed her eyes, maybe envisioning it. Opened them. "Apartments, I guess. Statehouse windows. It was snowy then, I think. It was a long time ago." She shook her head. Looked out her window for a beat. "No one liked to go back there. I certainly didn't."

"I'm not surprised you felt that way," Martha said. "Anyone would, after such a tragedy. Were there surveillance cameras? Did Nina Rafferty tell Jack about them?"

"They were broken," Rachel said. "You mentioned that in the hearing."

"Tom Rafferty knew that?"

Silence.

"Rachel?"

"Yes. He'd written a dear-colleague letter about it, calling for his fellow legislators to appropriate money to get it fixed. He was angry that the surveillance was so unreliable. It was a big deal to him."

"So he knew," Martha said again, confirming. "Did Nina? Did Jack say anything about that?"

"I don't remember him saying anything, no." Rachel looked down, fiddled with her cell phone.

As if she wanted to call someone. Martha bet she knew who.

"But Martha, now it's my turn to ask *you*." Rachel first pointed to herself, then Martha. "You're investigating. And you're Middlesex, and that means the murder must have taken place in Middlesex. So—"

"Very good, Rachel," Martha nodded her approval. "I see you know your jurisdictional stuff. That was a little test. Which you passed."

Rachel cleared her throat again. Martha's cell phone pinged a text. She read it. *Good*.

"We're a go, Shawn," Martha said.

"Gotcha, Ms. Gardiner."

"Rachel?" Martha pointed ahead of them, "Our destination is two blocks from here. So—you can have one more question." She turned to look over the seat back again. "Go."

"Um." Rachel looked at the phone in her hand again. "Do you think the killer is someone Dani knew? Because no one else has gotten killed like that since then."

"Possibly." Martha nodded, as if considering. "You set with your yellow pad?"

Shawn had steered them into an almost-legal parking spot in front of a yellow vinyl house. A cottage, Martha thought, with an intensely manicured lawn and regimented red tulips.

"It's someone from your old office," Martha said. "Ready?"

CHAPTER **THIRTY-NINE**

RACHEL NORTH

It crossed my mind, as we turned down the narrow Brighton street, that Danielle Zander was somehow still alive. And that's who we were about to see. It almost brought tears to my eyes, that impossible possibility. I imagined, in the flash of a second, how different my life would be if that were true. Tom and Nina still married, maybe. Tom a powerful state leader. Dani, who knows what?

And Jack, would we have bonded? He'd been with me that afternoon when I'd gotten the word that they'd found Dani. Watched my reaction, caught me when I probably almost fainted. He'd supported me and reassured me, even stood up for me when Lewis Millin—I'll never forget that name—tried to interrogate me.

If Tom Rafferty hadn't seen Jack with me in the Communications Office at his news conference, he might not have hired him to represent Nina, and who knows what might have happened to her? It was Jack's skill—and Martha Gardiner's arrogant decision not to check out Nina's alibi—that got her off. A lesser defense attorney might have capitulated, figuring an attack on the prosecutor's credibility might make it worse. Nina might have been held without bail. Who knows what a jury might have decided.

If Jack and I'd simply gone out for coffee that afternoon, and he'd tried to get me to talk about the Deacon Davis jury, and if I'd stayed on my ten-minutes-tops schedule, our relationship would have stopped after that brief and chilly encounter.

But that's not what happened, and Dani's dead, and her murder is unsolved.

Tom's essentially ruined. Nina's off somewhere.

I'm married to Jack, and almost a lawyer myself.

And Martha Gardiner is still the bad guy.

"Someone from your old office," she'd promised. My mental Rolodex spins as we walk toward the sweet little yellow house, name after name, but no one comes to mind. Though this house clearly belongs to a woman—frilly front curtains. All those tulips. A wreath of white-painted pinecones on the white front door. *Nina,* maybe? My heart twists. My brain rushes down that path, then skids to a halt. It was pretty enough, but she wouldn't be in a tiny place like this.

Who? There's no one and everyone. The statehouse is an employment way station, employees election-bound and nomadic, dozens of war-rened offices and fluctuating interns and serial rivals.

And now Martha is lifting the brass knocker, a shiny pineapple.

I stand two steps behind her, on the wood front porch, the leaves of a spindly potted fern in a terra-cotta pot tickling the backs of my bare legs. A dog, a yappy one, barks at the top of its lungs. I hear a voice from inside, a woman.

"Don't mind Henry David," a woman's voice says. A voice I've heard before, for sure, but the opening door blocks her face. I take a step back, needing to see but trying not to be obvious about it. She bends down, scooping up the button-eyed dog, her face hidden. My statehouse job ended six years ago. People change. "I never should have named him after Thoreau," she says, "because he's hardly . . ."

And she keeps talking, but I have no idea what she's saying as she shakes Martha's hand with the one that's not encircling the squirmy dog. It's Annabella Rigalosa. Grayer now, heavier makeup, tighter messy bun and brighter red fingernails. She was the statehouse Human Resources director, and I am—possibly—screwed.

I meet Annabella's eyes, waiting a beat to see if she recognizes me. There's no widened eyes, no smile of welcome, but also no pursed lips of disapproval. Or apprehension. I'm also baffled by Martha's game. She'd been so chatty and receptive in the car, but she kept this from me.

She clearly knows Annabella and I are acquainted. The unanswered question is does she know *how*. What do I do if Martha is about to find out?

But maybe that's me being paranoid. Annabella works—worked?—at the statehouse. As did I. As did Danielle Zander. Martha knows *they* knew each other, because Logan Concannon told us yesterday that Danielle's name came from the applicants in Annabella's Human Resources office. Time for me to pull out my yellow pad and be an observer. Another living room, another minefield.

"You know Rachel North," Martha is saying, pleasant in her non-introduction.

"I do," she says, nodding at me. No emotion, no judgment. "I thought that was you."

"Long time," I say. "I'm at Harvard Law School now. Working at the DA's office."

"Indeed."

Martha and Annabella begin with weather small talk. Our hostess pours tea, a white ceramic pot and thin white cups, almost translucent. If she had tea and sugar cookies prepared, she knew we were coming. And she didn't greet us with questions—*Who are you? And what's all this about?* Plus, a guilty person doesn't make tea for the prosecutor. Do they? Annabella's home is like a pristine dollhouse, perfect and miniature. Henry David, another miniature, curls up at her feet, his—I suppose—eyes bulging and protective. I'm worried he'll growl at me. Dogs don't like me, which has always been embarrassing.

"Are you still at the statehouse?" What's Martha going to do, fire me for asking a question? I'm an intern.

"Yes," she says. "Plus ça change."

She must have stayed home from work today. Must have wanted to talk to Martha here, not in her office. I accept the tea, balancing as I sit on her couch. Another couch. The amber tea is lemony, pungent and strong.

"Cookie?" she says. "And there are napkins."

Martha, perched in a flowered side chair, rifles through her briefcase, ignoring me.

What's this about? I can't decide what to do until I know. I take a napkin and then a mini-cookie, but I couldn't possibly eat it.

"So. As we discussed," Martha begins, in medias res. As if I'm not here and they're simply continuing a conversation they began another time. Which, clearly, they did. "As the HR person for the statehouse, you're involved with employment, including hiring—"

"And firing." Annabella says. "For more than ten years."

"I see. And you also handle employee complaints, perceived unfair firing, or vacation disputes, employee interaction, complaints about working conditions? Things of that nature?"

"The statehouse is a petri dish." Annabella breaks an already tiny cookie in half and places both halves on a lacy square napkin. "A hothouse. Things grow. And sometimes fester. Someone has to oversee it all. Make sure the ecosystem is not toxic. Part of my job is that people tell me things. I look—'unthreatening'? I suppose is the word."

"Hiring and firing," Martha repeats. Checks to see if I'm taking notes, which, obedient me, I am. "Harassment claims."

"The people who come to the statehouse to work are self-selectedly competitive." Annabella almost talks over her. "It's always about winning and losing. That's politics. That's the game on Beacon Hill. It's high pressure. The power structure is precarious. People can be toppled by words. It's my job to make sure those weapons—words as well as actions—are used appropriately."

"That's my job, too," Martha says.

Of course, I'm invisible. She didn't say "our" job.

"You investigate harassment claims."

Annabella nods. I see her face change. Under all that makeup, she's maybe mid-fifties, chic, petite, self-assured. But something is going on here.

"Tell me about that, Ms. Rigalosa. Specifically in regard to Senator Tom Rafferty."

My stupid felt-tip pen chooses this moment to run out of ink. My notes are faint as shadows, like disappearing ink.

"My pen." I hold it up, as if they can tell it's dry simply by looking. I flip open my briefcase, scramble on the bottom for a new one. "I'm so sorry."

"You'll catch up." Martha doesn't look at me. "As I was saying, Ms. Rigalosa. About Senator Rafferty."

"No." Her voice goes so tough that the lemony tea and cookies seem incongruous. "As *I* was saying."

I jam the plastic cover onto the end of my replacement pen and look back and forth between the two, pen poised, wondering what "no" means. No, she's never had a complaint about Tom Rafferty? I know *that's* not true. Not that I'm gonna say anything. Is that what she means by "no"?

If so, I know she's lying, and I'll have to figure out how to deal with that. But I have to see where Martha is going with this.

"No, you've never heard complaints about him? Not from anyone?"

"That's not what I said," the woman replies. The dog opens its poppy eyes, maybe reacting to the harsh tone of her voice.

"So—you *did*." Martha pushes her. "Have complaints against Senator Rafferty."

"That's not what I said."

"I see. Let me ask you this. Did you have any complaints about anyone else in Senator Rafferty's office? Or—*from* anyone in Senator Rafferty's office? Not necessarily about the senator himself?"

If this is the chase, Martha is cutting to it, fast. I try to keep the surprise from my expression, and look down at the pad.

"Ms. Gardiner," Annabella's voice is honey again, "as I have told you. I am a Human Resources professional. Not a gossip, not a source of information, not a disseminator of chitchat or fantasy or human frailty. The code of conduct for my profession might as well be that of a medical doctor—first do no harm. Yes, my job is to encourage people to trust me. And part of that is to make sure those who come to me understand, with their fullest hearts, that I will never inappropriately reveal what they divulged to me." She stands, smiling, adjusts her skirt. The dog scrambles to his feet, plasters himself to his mistress's leg, rumbles a tiny growl. "If those are the types of questions you plan to pursue in your investigation of Thomas Rafferty, this is a waste of all of our time."

She raises her eyebrows, almost challenging. She catches my eye, a tiny fraction of a second, but long enough that we connect. I wonder what she's trying to tell me.

Martha stays seated. Takes a sip of tea. Her phone buzzes, and she taps it off.

"Please sit down, Ms. Rigalosa," she says. "And why are you calling it an investigation of Thomas Rafferty?"

A beat of silence. And then—and this time I'm sure my surprise is evident, I can't help it—Annabella sits, her back rigid and shoulders square. Now I see her clip-on earrings. She couldn't have known what I was thinking, but she reaches up and touches the one on her left ear.

She says nothing.

"I understand your reluctance." Martha crumples a tiny napkin, places it on an end table. "But as I am sure you're aware, in Massachusetts there is no shield for your profession. You are not a medical doctor or a psychologist or even a licensed social worker. You are merely—and I say this with all due respect—the person who is tasked with handling personnel issues in a public office. I am a representative of the justice system. That—perhaps I need to remind you—is not an even playing field. But it is a fair one."

Martha stops, maybe assessing. If Annabella could growl like her dog does, she'd be doing it, too. Martha just dissed her, taunted her, and essentially threatened her.

"And here's what I did not tell you on the phone yesterday morning." Martha's using her predatory tone. I've heard it in court. Jack uses the same tactics. When, after leading the witness step-by-step, question-by-question, he finally has his quarry in reach. About to pounce. "We're investigating the death of Danielle Zander."

Even Annabella's experienced poker face disintegrates at this. She leans forward, places her teacup onto the coffee table in front of her. The room is so quiet, I can hear the china cup rattle in its gold-rimmed saucer. "Thank goodness. But why?"

"If you are willing to help us, here and now, I'd be grateful. And, let me add, it would be easier. If you're not?" Martha clears her throat, whether of necessity or to increase the dramatic tension, I have no idea.

"Then we'll call you to testify," she continues. "In a grand jury. In a courtroom. Wherever we need. If you refuse to answer . . . well. I'm sure I don't need to advise you that before a judge? Your otherwise commendable ethics will hold no sway."

Silence. This is a tug-of-war with no rope, a battle of resolve and will. But Martha knows the rules. And I'm sure her adversary—is she an adversary?—does too.

Martha lets out a breath, then smooths the air in front of her, palms down, maybe trying to soften the moment. "I know I sound harsh, Ms. Rigalosa. And I know no one likes lawyers."

Annabella gives half a shrug, agreeing, but seemingly reluctant to fully accept Martha's self-deprecating olive branch.

"Right," Martha goes on. Her phone buzzes again, and again she taps it off. "And that's what Rachel here is learning, too."

I flinch at the sound of my name. I've felt so invisible, even I almost forgot I was here.

"They won't teach her that at Harvard, but the cultural animosity— lawyer jokes and instant derision—is what we all accept as part of our lives. We have difficult jobs, difficult realities, difficult conversations. Difficult decisions. But that's why the system works, doesn't it? Because. Exactly as in your job at the statehouse, someone has to make sure the ecosystem, as you put it, is not toxic. And we do that by the rule of law."

Annabella nods.

"So." Martha wears a different expression now. Victory. "I don't en-joy threatening you with jail for contempt. I'm merely stating a difficult reality. And that unpleasantness can easily be avoided. Let's start again. Have you had harassment complaints about Tom Rafferty? In connec-tion with whom? From whom? I have to believe *you* are the informant who reported his indiscretions to the police. If you told *them*, you can tell *me*."

Martha's phone buzzes again. This time when she ignores it, the buzz-ing seems to get louder as Annabella's silence continues.

The phone stops.

Annabella stands. The dog stands. They're both statues, motionless. Ice, or stone.

"See you in court," she finally says.

This time Martha stands, too.

She picks up her briefcase, snaps it closed. Pockets her phone. Sig-nals at me with a cock of her head, as if I'm a dog, too.

"I see." Martha brushes past me as she strides to the front door, leav-ing two women and a dog behind her. I see her pull out her cell again as she opens the door. "Rachel?" she says. And she's gone.

I put my pad away, and Annabella comes closer. Stands so close to me that I'm startled, but I hold my ground.

She leans in, one manicured hand briefly touching the shoulder of my linen blazer.

"I won't tell," she whispers. "Not unless I have to."

CHAPTER **FORTY**

RACHEL NORTH

Martha is already in the front seat as I open the back door to the cruiser. She's on her cell, head down, one ear covered with the black phone, the other ear covered with her hand, as if to block out the extraneous noise.

Fine. She can talk, the statie can drive us back to the office, and I can finally eat the rest of my blueberry muffin. And think. Figure out what to do. About what Annabelle said, and a whole lot of other stuff.

I pull out my own phone. Martha's mumbling into hers as the car backs up and swerves out of our parking space. With a little more speed than I might have expected, but then Martha always has an agenda. Which she eventually tells me.

No message from Tom. What could he have meant yesterday at the apartment, when he'd said "Not one word?" Doesn't he need to explain that? Or am I supposed to make the next move? I'd already looked up the records on which "friend" of his owned that immaculately impersonal apartment. But it's a real estate trust, so no public way to discover identities of the people involved. Unless I risk using some DA clout to pursue it.

No message from Jack, either. I need to fill him in on today's interview, let him know what Martha's up to. See if there's anything manipulative or unethical about her current tactics. And why is she investigating *Tom*? Annabella picked up on that, too.

What if the whole Danielle investigation is a cover-up for something else? Maybe that's why Tom asked Martha if he needed a lawyer.

That'd be legally questionable, Martha pretending to be asking about one thing when she's really asking about another. I'll see what Jack thinks. Maybe that gives us more ammunition.

I also need to see if Jack has contacted the Board of Bar Overseers or someone who can take Martha out. Jack was right from day one. She's using me. It makes my skin crawl, how I almost fell for it. All that coddling and praise. She's duplicitous. Predatory.

It's comical. Here I was thinking I was the spy, when in reality, Martha's spying on *me*. Because of Jack. She hates him, hates that she lost the Nina Rafferty case, and probably hates me, too. Lucky I figured it out. Now I can fight back.

And I wonder how the powers that be will react to her milking me for information. I'm supposed to be learning from her. I guess I am.

I've learned she's a menace, and we have to stop her. It's almost empowering that she's making me part of her investigation of Danielle Zander's murder, when in truth, I'm investigating *Martha*. Guilt is a complicated thing. Maybe Jack and I can make things right. Help the world see it's Martha who's the guilty one.

Half my muffin is left, so I peel back the wrapping and break off some cakey sections, making sure not to dribble crumbs on the statie's black upholstery. Which makes me think of Roni. And Momo. They're waiting, too, to hear what I find out. Were we all manipulated? Was justice manipulated? All because Martha Gardiner needed to win a case? If Deacon Davis didn't kill that woman, that's beyond horrifying.

And I keep thinking about my fellow interns, Eli and Nick and Andrew. What are they working on while I'm out here with Gardiner? Maybe the pizza-guy case? They were all in the conference room that Sunday when Nick made his whiteboard presentation about Danielle Zander. But they've not been involved since.

I'd seen all three of them around the office. "Whatcha working on?" I'd asked, honestly curious. "Document search," Andrew had reported. "Busywork," Eli had said.

"Danielle Zander?" I'd pushed, gently, asking each one separately. "Working on that at all?" Maybe they knew more about Martha's theory of the case than I did. Which was almost nothing. But Nick had rolled his eyes and pretended to shoot himself in the head with a forefinger. "Bor-ing," he'd said. "I live for five o'clock."

Clearly Martha was doing something different with me. Why?

I look out the window. Today's driver is taking side streets, to avoid the notorious traffic, I suppose. Martha's still on the phone. I can't see her face, and I can't hear her. Plus, annoyingly, the statie is listening to NPR.

Crumbling the muffin-wrapper plastic into a tiny ball, I worry it between my fingers.

I wish I could remember that Sunday meeting in Martha's conference room more clearly. What precisely was said about Danielle Zander? I was so flummoxed that my brain wasn't running on all cylinders, and now that's a problem. Some train has left the station, and I'm on it, but why?

Well, why is because of Jack. And my connection to him.

This morning, though, the train arrived at Annabella Rigalosa. That's another dilemma.

Back in my statehouse days, I'd called her, talked to her several times. Including after that nasty phone call my first day on the job. When an anonymous caller says, "Screw you," it was my responsibility to report it. I'd told her I was sure it was Logan.

What if she's done it before, to someone else? That's what I'd said. If something bad happened, I'd said, and I hadn't put it on the record, no one would believe me. I'd contemplated a mental list of other caller possibilities, but no one bore me as much animosity back then than Logan Concannon. I'd taken her job.

But before that, before everything, I'd also mentioned to Annabella— just coffee room chitchat—that I'd thought I'd seen Tom and Logan, looking cozy, pulling out of the statehouse parking lot together a few times. Late night. It was completely true, I thought I had.

Annabella could investigate on her own, I'd assured her back then. I would step out of the picture.

I stare at the floor of the backseat, at a paper clip, a broken pencil, a few escaped muffin crumbs.

My theory was that Annabella had told Logan someone had reported their late-night "coziness"—I think that's how I'd put it, I never said "affair"—with Tom. If Annabella had pursued it, interviewing other people, the controversy would've spread through the statehouse in a blue minute. No one could unhear it. Or unbelieve it. No one would care what was true. That's how the statehouse worked. I imagine Logan offered to quit if Annabella would drop it. Logan, promised confidentiality for her own transgressions, had fallen on her sword to protect her boss.

Annabella had kept my secrets, too, as well she should. Still, it would not be pretty to see her go up against Gardiner in court. Could I let her go to jail for contempt to protect me? It was such a long time ago. We both thought, I venture to imagine, that part of our lives was over.

But why did Martha care? All that had nothing to do with Danielle Zander's murder.

"Shawn? Now," Martha says to the statie. I look up, startled out of my woolgathering. She's pointing at the dashboard.

"Okay," the statie says. I see Shawn lower one hand and flip a metal toggle switch attached under the dashboard clock. A siren sputters, then revs into a keening wail. I'm thrown back against the seat as he accelerates, screaming through a stop sign and then a red light, careening around a corner. I lean forward, straining my seat belt, one hand clutching the back of the front seat.

"Martha?" She can't think I'll simply sit back and wait to see what this is about. I raise my voice over the siren. "What's going on?"

"Nina Rafferty," she says.

CHAPTER **FORTY-ONE**

RACHEL NORTH

"Stay in the car, you two," Martha says. "Shawn, five minutes."

We've pulled up at the back-door entrance of the DA's office, not at some yellow-tape festooned crime scene. I'd imagined, instantly playing out a whole dramatic scenario, that Nina Rafferty was dead. Although that still might be true. Maybe Martha's here to pick up paperwork or something. Maybe a warrant for Tom's arrest.

If I had known, would I have warned him?

Shawn shifts into park, turns off the siren, and leaves the motor running. I'd taken off my seat belt in preparation for going inside with Martha, but now I've been told to stay. Good dog, Rachel.

"What's up?" I ask Shawn, after Martha's door slams behind her.

"Your guess is as good as mine," he says into the rearview mirror.

Doubtful, I want to say. Because I have no guesses. What couldn't Martha do by phone or text? Why do I have to stay in the car? Shawn's only the driver, so no biggie. Waiting is what state troopers are paid to do. But I'm almost Martha's equal.

I frown, watching out my window. Martha jabs a code onto a back-door keypad, disappears inside. I make a futile attempt to see through the frosted glass door. But there's only the softened reflection of our car, black, shiny, generally the carrier of bad news. I reassure myself. I'm on the inside now.

This rear parking lot is surrounded on three sides by a grassy field, clogged with parched weeds and occasional purple wildflowers, unkempt, uncared for, forgotten. My phone buzzes in my tote bag, and I leap to retrieve it. Maybe Martha needs me.

It's Jack.

"Hey you." I wonder if he's calling to tell me what happened with the Board of Bar Overseers. But he wouldn't have contacted them without clearing it with me. We're a team again.

"Listen, I don't have long. Have you gotten any phone calls this morning?" He's not saying, "Hey you" back, and he's not sounding affectionate anymore. Maybe someone's with him. Listening. Monitoring.

"From who?"

"So you did, get a call," he says. "From who?"

"No, no. I didn't." I was only fast-forwarding him to get to the point. "Who's going to call me?"

"Rachel?" His voice is softer now, so soft I have to squint my ears to hear him. I bend down, thinking I can muffle out the parking-lot sounds. But Shawn has turned the AC on full blast, so all I get is a cold face. I sit up again.

"Yeah?"

I hear him sigh on the other end of the line. Martha's been gone several minutes now, and when she comes back I don't want to be chitchatting with Jack. But no sign of her yet. Shawn is changing the stations on the radio, turning the dial, so I hear jagged shards of voices and music, not enough to recognize, but enough to be annoying.

"Don't answer any calls," he says. "Especially ones that come through as 'private caller.'"

"What? And did you say *do* answer? Or *don't*?" I think he said *don't* answer the call, but Shawn has shifted into drive and revved the engine. I look up, no sign of Martha. It's certainly been five minutes.

"Rachel. Listen. Don't. Do not. It might be, um, Clea Rourke. She's—

on a mission. To punish me. She's . . ." I know Jack, can almost picture him, trying to choose exactly the right words. He's such a stickler. "She was pissed when we broke up, and apparently she still wants to ruin me. She's *vowed* to. If people do that these days. Vow."

"Jack?"

"Honey. Just don't answer the phone."

"Jack?" I have to interrupt. Maybe I can help him. "I bet Roni and Momo went to her, told her that you didn't bring Deacon Davis to those stupid hearings. And Clea had interviewed the sister on TV. So listen—go on the offense. You call Clea. Tell her *you're* not the problem."

I remember where I am and who might be listening, so I lean over again, face to knees, and whisper as softly as I can. Fast as I can. "Tell *her* about you-know-who and the jury. Tell her the court officers were feeding her info about Momo and Roni. Tell her about the ICE guys, too, how they snatched your pivotal slasher witness. Tell her what you 'heard' about the intimidation of Jeff Baltrim. Clea Rourke only wants the best story. Get her off your back. Sic her on . . ." I pause. Shawn is sitting up straighter. Listening to me? "You-know-who. Remember? Like I've been telling you. We have to stop her."

The back door opens. You-know-who is returning.

"Where are you?" I whisper. "I've gotta go."

"Do not say anything to anyone about anything," Jack says. "Promise me. Not anyone. Not anything. Not until I get out there."

"Get out there—*where*?" I say.

But Jack has hung up. And my passenger-side door has opened.

Martha.

I hang up.

"Hi," I say, looking up at her. She's taken off her sunglasses, but I cannot read her expression. "What's up?"

Shawn shifts into park.

The office back door opens again.

Jack?

Jack stops. He's framed in the doorway.

"Jack?" I say out loud.

In the otherwise empty parking lot, Martha Gardiner stands between us.

I look left to right, trying to figure out what's going on. On either side of us, the glaring sun intensifies the purple wildflowers. Then the parking lot's yellow stripes, sharp-edged on hot black asphalt. Past that, Jack is a motionless silhouette. A butterfly, white and ordinary, escapes from the meadow and dances over us, and for a second, I think about the black-and-gold one that little Jonah and I saw that morning. The one I urged him not to capture. Shawn clicks off the ignition, and I feel the car settle under me, then die. Time seems to stop.

"Rachel," Martha says. "Get out of the car, please."

PART
FOUR

EARLIER THAT DAY

CHAPTER **FORTY-TWO**

MARTHA GARDINER

"You'll stay here," Martha Gardiner told them. Andrew DiPrado and Eli Lansberry sat in the backseat of the tan four-door sedan, a lidded cardboard evidence box of files balanced between them. Nick Soderberg was beside her in the front seat. Martha hadn't chosen this summer's interns at random. Andrew was an ROTC MP, Eli a criminal research prodigy, and Nick—with his mother on the Suffolk County DA's staff—her eyes and ears.

She'd kept Rachel back at the office this morning, doing busywork filing. This was no place for her. Not this time. "This may take a while," she told her guys. "You wanted to be here, fine, but you can't come in. You okay with that?"

She didn't wait for an answer. Of course they were okay.

The white-painted house across the suburban street—front bay window curtains drawn, porch empty, driveway with mailbox at the end, mown grass and a strip of pink peonies and geraniums at curbside—looked serene. Their Chevy was unmarked, though it wouldn't fool anyone with half a brain. But their target might not be looking. Not that it would matter.

Most people had already left for work this time of the morning, or for school. The entire neighborhood seemed quiet. Empty. Good thing. Better this way.

Lieutenant Oscar Saldono was driving the state police white Crown Vic that would soon arrive and park behind them. Oz would do backup for Martha. Or Martha for him. Another car was on the way.

Martha twisted off the ignition. Powered down her car window. Almost time. She turned to face her team, one arm draped over the steering wheel.

"You've handled this matter like pros," she said. "It's complicated. And unusual. But you did it. Bravo." She'd always believed in offering praise where praise was due—especially to interns. It conveyed a message to young people about how leadership worked. How the prosecution worked. With a mission. A goal. A search—no matter how disturbing— for justice. Evidence was evidence. The law was the law. The law doesn't care who you are or who you know. And especially not what you want.

"It's fair that you're part of this now," Martha went on. "Be patient a little longer. You'll see how your hard work, your teamwork, is about to pay off."

"Is anyone home?" Nick looked at the front door. They all did. "Should we make a call?"

Martha saw the calculation in his expression. The analysis. Exactly like his mother, who was waiting for word across town. This was the end—she hoped—of six shitty years. Of the case that got away. Almost. She lost this case once. She wasn't about to lose it again.

"Well, how would you assess the situation?" Martha didn't take her eyes off the house as she asked the three of them, but she put a smile in her voice. "A car is in the driveway. The newspaper—good thing some people never change—is also in the driveway."

The three didn't respond. They knew when to keep quiet. And they'd worked hard on this case. She'd taught them well. That's one reason this had been successful. So far.

"What's more, a no-knock warrant means?" she continued.

"If no one is there, we can go in," Eli said. "However we have to do it."

"Correct. However we have to do it." Martha nodded, confirming. She often wondered what would happen to each summer's crop of wannabes after they left. Her ducklings. Some would wind up on her side. Others, lured by the potential four-figure hourly rates and mahogany desks, would opt for the soul-crushing indentureship of a big firm. Others, "true believers" they'd call themselves, would descend into the double-talking legal underworld of the defense bar, congregating in moth-eaten walk-ups, foraging for clients, grateful when they became experienced enough at working the system to be appointed to the murder list, an opportunity to try to defend the dregs of society.

True believers. She'd once tried out the phrase on a murder-list lawyer. "What is it you believe in?" she'd asked. "Setting criminals free? That's not what the law is about."

But whoever it was had walked away. "We'll find the bad guys, and convict them, in spite of you!" Martha had actually called it out after the guy. Embarrassing, maybe, but it mattered. Someone had to stand up for the victims, offer justice to mourners left behind. Martha would do whatever she could to even the score.

Jack Kirkland was an exception. He believed as much in his justice as Martha believed in hers. Now, though, he had a choice. He could either remain as part of the problem, or realize he'd be better off as part of the solution.

A car engine rumbled behind them. A glance in the rearview confirmed Oz Saldono had pulled up at the curb, the trooper's front bumper a foot from their rear. The vehicles would get no closer to the house. If there were trouble, Martha didn't want them stuck in the driveway. Even though it'd trap their target inside.

Oz appeared outside her door. "We a go?" His eyes stayed on the house across the street. "Think we're expected?"

"You never know." Martha Gardiner hadn't seen a movement from inside, but that didn't mean anything. "Maybe."

"That's why I have this." Oz patted his weapon, holstered now, at his side.

"And that's why I have this." Martha, patting the papers in her jacket pocket, could not resist the gibe.

She did not slam the car door on the way out. Nodded at the three left behind. Andrew, eager for the collar, gave a thumbs-up, then stopped, looking embarrassed. They all fell silent. Watching.

In fifteen seconds, Martha and the trooper were on the front porch. Oz took a position behind her at five o'clock, an unnecessary precaution, but like everything they did, it had a purpose. Serving a search warrant, nothing was predictable.

Martha heard the doorbell echo down the hall. Exchanged an affirmative nod with Oz, who'd also heard the footsteps approaching. No need to say anything. Only two people lived here. They knew where the other one was.

She took out the warrant. Unfolded it. Three pages. The morning sun, slanting through some kind of trellised vine, spackled stripes on the white paper. Those pages meant that after all those years, Danielle Zander was about to be Martha's case again. And hers to win.

The door opened. Halfway.

Martha watched Jack Kirkland's face go pale, his eyes narrow, his mind working. He took in Oz, then Martha herself, then Oz again, and then the papers in Martha's hand.

"Martha?" Kirkland's hand stayed on the doorknob, the door not quite open. He was dressed for work, apparently, shirt and tie, suit jacket open. "What's wrong? Is Rachel okay?"

"Jack Kirkland?" Martha had wondered how he'd deal with this. Was it out of the clear blue, a devastating gut punch? Or was he expecting it? Dreading it? Already prepared to fight it? No matter now. These wheels were in motion. "Your wife is fine. But we have a warrant to search the premises, and we will provide you a copy if you so desire."

Martha held out the folded warrant, offering it to him as protocol required. Kirkland's reaction would be a key. Would he ask why? Or simply take the thing?

"What's this about?" He snatched the papers from her hand, flapped the pages open, and read them, his eyes skimming down the pages. "You're sure Rachel is . . ."

His voice trailed off as he read the warrant. Martha knew precisely what Jack was reading. In an abundance of caution, she'd typed it herself. And gotten her pal Judge Saunders to sign it.

There is cause to believe that on the premises there is now concealed property described herein, to wit, notes from Thomas A. Rafferty, as well and including letters, emails, diaries, photographs, and possessions, including jewelry, connected with him or referring to him and others on his staff or related to him during his term in office as the senate president, clothing, computer data, thumb drives, telephone, cell phones, answering machine results, files, or any other personal effects of Rachel Minifee North and/or Jack Morgan Kirkland that could be used as evidence in a criminal prosecution regarding the death of Danielle Zander.

"*My* possessions?" Kirkland took a step forward, away from the door and out onto the porch.

"You gonna let us in, sir?" Oz had stepped up behind Gardiner, now standing shoulder-to-shoulder with her as he inquired, effectively blocking Jack's exit.

But Martha had the next move.

"So that's a surprise?" she asked. "Our interest in you? But our interest in Rachel is not?"

"Bullshit," Kirkland said. "Where is she?"

"We can talk all you want," she replied. "But inside. While Lieutenant Saldono is executing."

"Bull." But Kirkland, scowling, stepped back, allowing the two into the dim hallway of the house.

Martha took in hardwood floors, a modest chandelier, a carpeted stairway going up, silver-framed photographs lining one wall. Kirkland had entered the living room, where he sat, radiating anger, on a brown leather armchair.

She stood in the entryway, facing a photo-covered baby grand, as Kirkland's eyes followed the statie tramp up the stairway and go out of sight.

"Martha? What the hell are you thinking?" Kirkland had pulled his cell phone from his suit jacket pocket. "I'm calling her."

"Put that away," she said. Kirkland put it on the coffee table instead. He's screwing with me, Martha thought. But if Rachel called *him*, she'd see the caller ID. So all good.

"Martha. Tell me. Does Rachel know about this?"

"About what?" As always, Martha had to admit, Kirkland had asked the pivotal question. She was surprised Jack was talking at all. Most lawyers would have shut the hell up. "About the warrant? Or about the murder of Danielle Zander?"

"Bull." Kirkland shook his head.

Both lawyers looked up at the same time. Upstairs, a door had slammed. Then neither spoke as the noise from above continued, footsteps, drawers opening, and closet doors. Eli Lansberry had pulled the home's layout for her from the town assessor's records—three bedrooms upstairs, a bath, a hallway. Downstairs, it was living room, dining room, kitchen, den, and another bathroom. Only two residents. This wouldn't take long, Martha predicted. Unless it did.

Kirkland had steepled his palms, silently tapping one forefinger against the other. Head down, he stared at his own fingertips. Muffled footsteps moved across the ceiling above them. Kirkland's shoulders rose and fell. He took a long breath, then looked Martha straight in the eye. "Is she in on this?"

Martha needed to keep him talking. Even slippery Jack Kirkland could make a mistake, especially juggling a fraught situation like this. Now was the time to play husband and wife against each other.

"'In' on what? On helping me get this warrant? Or in on the murder? What—are you afraid she's throwing you under the bus? And waiting back at the office to take you into custody? Rachel North, accusing her own husband of murder. Is that what you mean? Is she right?"

Martha read the apparent confusion on Kirkland's face and needed to decide whether he was genuinely angry. Or genuinely complicit.

According to Detective Lewis Millin's notes, Kirkland and Rachel had been together when the body was found. Very convenient.

And gotten married soon after. Again. Convenient.

Whatever Kirkland knew, he could not be compelled to tell. Convenient.

CHAPTER **FORTY-THREE**

JACK KIRKLAND

Jack had almost lost it on his own front porch, gut-punched with worry that Rachel was dead or in the hospital, something so unthinkable it had to be said in person.

He was almost right. The unthinkable part was true. Martha Gardiner thought they—he and Rachel—had something to do with Danielle Zander's murder.

That woman had been obsessed with this case since I beat her ass, Jack thought. But he'd never imagined she'd sink to such depths. Standing in his living room, offering this load of bull. She was delusional. Possibly insane. Definitely dangerous.

He leaned back in his chair, crossed arms over his chest. Tried to pretend he was amused about this, not enraged. Rage could come later. Now he needed information. This whole thing was spurious. A tactic. Starting with that warrant.

He could tell it was bogus the moment he read it. No sane judge would have signed such a generic piece of crap. Unless Gardiner had Saunders in her pocket, which, of course, she might. Was this another corner she'd cut? Another rule she'd manipulated? Gardiner was arrogant, had always been, but she'd plummeted over the edge.

"How'd you even get this case, Gardiner?" That'd bothered him ever since Rachel divulged she was working on it. "You think Danielle Zander was killed in *Middlesex*? In your new jurisdiction? And then, let's see. You think Rachel and I toted her, maybe in my car, to the statehouse parking lot and dumped her body there? When, why, how? And while we're at it. How do you think I knew Rachel back then—that we'd hooked up while she was on my jury?"

"You two got married at City Hall?" Gardiner pointed toward the framed photos on the piano. She crossed in front of him. Picked one up.

Jack held himself back, had to, from leaping up and snatching it from her hand.

"Happy couple," she said. "How much younger is she than you are?"

"What?"

"Ever wonder—why she picked you?"

"Picked?" Jack tried to ignore his impulse to pick up the fireplace poker and bash the hell out of the woman. "Give me a break, Gardiner. This is beneath you. Even you."

Gardiner put the photo back on the piano. Something thudded on the floor upstairs. Then again. Jack imagined their mattresses flipped over, landing on the crazy white rugs Rachel chose. A door slammed. What the hell were they looking for? Or was Gardiner, relishing her power, simply screwing with him?

"Where is she, anyway?" Jack imagined the worst. In a cell or custody. But if she'd been arrested, she would have called him. Rachel knew the rules.

"Like I said. Rachel's fine." Gardiner returned to her spot in the entryway, glanced upstairs, then glanced at her watch. Recrossed her arms as if to demonstrate she was in charge. "You can be in touch with her soon."

"Let me ask you . . ." Jack stood, mimicking her crossed arms and her supercilious attitude. "While we wait for your thug upstairs to finish whatever goose chase he's on, let me get your take on something. It's about the Marcus Dorn case."

"Your pillar of the community? Your security-guard slasher?"

"Be that as it may. Off the record, tell me what happened to my disappearing witness. Remember? The one the feds suddenly 'detained'? Out of the clear frigging blue?"

A shadow passed over Gardiner's face. "Why should I?"

"Yeah, well." Jack sat on the arm of the chair. Supercasual. "You might be hearing from my people about it. Working on the appeal. You know?"

Jack waited a beat, then walked to the bay window, yanked open the curtains. Saw the cruiser and the unmarked Chevy. He waved at whoever was out there waiting for Gardiner's exit. Another car was paused at the stop sign. He turned back to Gardiner, who was leaning against the wall, watching him. "And while we're at it. Deacon Davis?"

"Another in your loss column, Jack, if I remember correctly."

"Back then," Jack went on, ignoring her sarcasm, "your court-officer lackeys told you about the two 'not guilty' jurors, didn't they? And you got them excused. But hey—did you know they're all getting together again? To nail you and your cronies? They're getting ready to drop a dime to Clea Rourke—did you know that?"

Gardiner's face changed. "Clea Rourke?"

She was worried. Good. Time to push.

"What other inside information have your courthouse rats divulged?" Jack returned to his perch on the arm of the leather chair, refusing to sit on the couch like a suspect. Or stand like a combatant. "Did Deacon Davis somehow figure out he'd been railroaded? And then—before he could contact me—he got killed in prison. Pretty damn odd. You know, his sister's convinced *you* made it happen." Jack shook his head. "Yeah, wacky. But the sister's talking to Clea, too. And you know our Clea. Murder for hire, with you bankrolling it? That's a big damn headline."

Gardiner pressed her lips together. Jack could tell she was considering. If she's smart, Jack thought, she won't react.

"What'll that do to your career, Martha? Everyone knows you're gunning to be the next AG. Jury tampering, witness tampering, and murder?" Jack pushed even harder. Until he calculated his next move, he needed to keep this playing field level. Sure, this was all Gardiner's obsession. Her revenge. But she had power, and knew how to use it. She could ruin his life. And Rachel's. He would not let that happen. "And what do you think the bar overseers will say about that?"

More sounds from upstairs. The warrant was open on the coffee table, an instrument of prosecutorial power.

"They'll laugh," Gardiner said, waving him off. "They know as well as you do that court officers always talk. Am I supposed to tell them to keep quiet? I'm sure *you've* never gotten information from them." She raised a dismissive eyebrow. "Besides. Your clients were guilty as sin."

"You threw those cases, Gardiner." Jack leaned forward, stabbed a forefinger at her. "You engineered those jurors' dismissals with the help of a complicit judge. The same one who signed this ridiculous warrant."

"You're watching too much TV, Jack."

"Possibly. Possibly." He tried to not smile. His accusations were pretty much right out of Rachel's imagination, but from Martha's reaction, they might not be far off the mark. Plus, Deacon Davis. This was for *him*, too. "But when Clea Rourke gets her teeth into a story, well. You know those TV types."

Gardiner gestured toward the wedding photo. "Jack? I know a different story your Clea—oh, yes, I know about you and her—might be interested in." She walked toward it, touched the silver frame with one finger. "What if your beloved Rachel has forgotten about her vow of 'for better, for worse'? And has decided to do what's better—for her?"

"What?"

"Just throwing this out to you. She came to work this morning as usual. But have you heard from her? No? So, say we confronted her with our evidence. Say we offered her a deal. She gives you up for the murder—or else we take *her* in. She's no dummy, Jack. You or her? You know her better than I do. What do you think she'd do?"

That was Gardiner's fantasy. Her attempt to distract him from her own transgressions. To take the heat off herself and put it back on him.

They were playing courtroom in his living room. Prosecution and defense. But here they didn't have to play by any rules.

"What *evidence*?" he asked.

Her phone rang, a nasty trill.

"Yes?" She held up a palm, turned away from him.

Jack stared at the wedding photo. Gardiner was right, it had been Rachel who—he supposed, thinking about it now—had pushed to get married. But wasn't that what women did? She hadn't even bought a new dress for the occasion, though he'd urged her to. "It's not about a dress," she'd told him one night when she wasn't wearing anything at all. "It's about you and me, together forever no matter what."

Now Gardiner was suggesting Rachel sent her here. To rat him out? Or frame him? Did Martha think Rachel killed Danielle Zander?

The first to talk is the first to walk, that was a law school cliché. Which by now in Rachel's classes, she'd heard more than once.

But if the other person in the equation knew nothing about the crime, it was not about the first to talk. It was about the first to lie.

CHAPTER **FORTY-FOUR**

MARTHA GARDINER

Martha clicked off her phone, her eyes on Jack and her mind on tactics. Reinforcements were on the way.

But right now? Negotiations.

Jack had gone on the attack. Instantly. Like defense attorneys always did. Questioning, pushing, demanding answers. He was almost certainly bluffing. But about which parts?

Now Jack glared at her, waiting. She listened for Oz, who was still upstairs. Today was a fishing expedition, she knew it. Judge Saunders, always helpful and especially so after a sip or two from her "water" glass, had given Martha some leeway on the required specificity of the warrant. But if Kirkland was tarring Saunders with jury conspiracy, that judge's signature on the warrant might taint this whole operation. Martha was not about to lose this case a second time.

Kirkland had forced her hand. So let the negotiations begin. Martha looked at her watch. Almost time.

"Okay, listen, Jack." She'd move to first names, change the dynamic. "Give me that warrant."

Jack looked at her, suspicious. Handed it over. She could feel his anger.

Mustering her inner calm, she sat on the couch, opposite Jack's chair.

She set her phone on the glass-topped coffee table. Pulled a fountain pen from her jacket pocket. Unfolded the warrant. Crossed out Jack's name. Initialed the change, *MLG*. Capped the pen and handed the warrant back.

"What the hell is this?" Jack looked appropriately confused. "You can't do that, as you well know."

"Yeah. I can. Look. We know you didn't do it. And I've got to believe that you—even you—would not be complicit in a murder. You might defend a killer, but you wouldn't stay married to one. There's a difference."

She picked up her cell phone again, clicked to the photo section. Handed the phone to Jack.

"Hit play on this," Martha instructed. "The audio is low, but that won't matter."

The room was silent for a beat or two, muffled sounds coming from her phone. She knew what Jack was seeing, but it would take him a moment to grasp it. She saw him look bewildered, hold the phone closer, push a button on the phone, watch again.

"The Deacon Davis jury?" he finally said. "How'd you get video of that? Someone took cell phone video of the *jury*? There's not supposed to be—"

Here's where it got dicey. Dicier.

"Let's not go into that now, okay?" Martha needed to move on. "But sometimes reporters shoot surreptitious video of jurors, since their colleagues outside the courtroom have to try to follow them when the trial's over. It's sleazy—what else is new?—but it never gets on TV. It's a simple way to identify them. So. I had an acquaintance covering that trial . . ."

"Clea Rourke," Jack said. He kept looking at the cell phone.

"And when I needed video of Rachel from back then to show a few potential witnesses—because she looks so different now—I asked that reporter if there was one of this jury. There was. She knows where her bread is buttered. She gave it to me."

Silence again.

"My father always taught me you should never look at a picture only once," Martha went on. "That later, the second time or the third time, you'd see something that hadn't mattered before. And you know what? I did. And look. Zoom in to a close-up. Rachel's wearing them. The clip-on earrings."

"Are you freaking kidding me? So are probably dozens of other women." Jack rolled his eyes as he handed the phone back. "Like Deacon Davis's ubiquitous Skechers."

"Not like the Skechers, Jack. Rafferty gave Rachel those earrings. After some birthday dinner he hosted for her. Before she murdered Danielle." Martha tucked her phone back into her pocket. Checked her watch. "And they're exactly like his wife Nina's. He confirmed that. Said they were 'meaningless.' Men. Rachel must have pierced her ears *after* the murder. We couldn't find a salon that did it—one of my interns canvassed for days, but apparently those establishments close up shop pretty quickly. Who knows, maybe she did it herself."

"No. No way. You got your guy upstairs looking for a matching *earring*? From six years ago? If she dropped an earring at the murder scene she wouldn't be dumb enough to save the matching—Wait. The murder scene. So you *do* think the murder scene was in Suffolk? At the statehouse?"

"Of course." Martha was delighted to let him understand how silly it was to believe anything different. "What d'you think, that Rachel North killed Ms. Zander elsewhere, maybe in Harvard Yard? And then managed to get her body to the snowy statehouse parking lot? Hardly likely."

"But how are *you* investigating? The jurisdiction—"

"Well, turns out, it's because she's married to *you*. And you live in Middlesex. If you were in on it, or even if you knew about it later and helped her cover it up?" Martha paused, letting Jack think it through. "Then that's a crime too, isn't it? The Suffolk DA and I made a deal. I'll investigate, I'll prepare the case, she'll prosecute. You and Rachel both, or just her, or just you. I don't think it's you, I must say, unless you wear earrings."

"That's nuts." Jack stood, pointed upstairs. "Get out of here, Gardiner. And take your lackey, too. You're gonna make a case based on an *earring*? Try it. I dare you. Not a chance."

"Point taken, counselor." Martha, almost smiling, stayed seated. "Say we forget about the earrings. Keep it between us. We don't want that reporter to lose her job, right? Well, you might, I suppose. But here's another blast from the past. Remember Lewis Millin?"

"Where's this going, Martha? That has-been cop left town, retired early, probably got run out on a rail after he blew the Nina alibi. So much for the pit bull detective."

"I'd be upset, too, if I were you, Jack," Martha could read the suspicion on Jack's face, the wary disbelief. It never got easier to explain how a loved one was guilty of a crime. Husbands could never believe wives would betray them or lie to them or manipulate them or use them. She looked at her watch again, then stood. "Hang on," she said.

She walked to the front door as the doorbell rang, and opened it before it stopped.

"Who the hell—?" Jack was on his feet as Martha stood next to the new arrival.

"Lewis Millin, you remember him." Martha gestured to the gray-haired man standing next to her. She hadn't seen him in years, his shoulders now rounder, his arms tanned, in a navy-blue knit polo shirt, with a ballpoint pen and spiral notebook at the ready in the front pocket. Duck shoes. "Came down from Maine for this. Turns out he kept all his notes. Cold cases, you know. Sometimes you've simply got to look at everything again."

"Hello, Jack," Millin said. "Sorry about this. You were always a stand-up guy."

"Lew and I never stopped working on this, Jack," Martha said as she closed the door. "And I could not believe Rachel accepted the internship in my office. Volunteered, did you know that? Pretty damn auda-cious. It almost—but not quite—made me wonder if I was wrong."

She paused. "But I'm not. Can't believe you let her do it."

"Rachel did not kill Danielle Zander," Jack insisted, shaking his head.

"Yeah," Millin said. "She did."

CHAPTER **FORTY-FIVE**

JACK KIRKLAND

The three stood in his entryway. A tense, silent triangle. Jack whirled, took a seat, *in* the armchair this time. Planted both feet wide apart on the floor, opened his arms.

"Give me all you got," he challenged. "I mean it. Take a seat. Bring it on. And call your thug down from up there, Gardiner. This whole thing is bogus. Bogus as your illegal warrant. But we'll deal with that after I hear your so-called evidence."

Millin perched himself in the center of the couch. He scratched one ear like his life depended on it. Then took out his spiral notebook and flapped it open, talking as he turned the pages.

"She had an alibi, back then. Rachel North? That she was home, alone, watching TV. Or else working at the statehouse, which was not suspicious. I mean, she worked there."

"Which, in retrospect, was pretty damn convenient," Gardiner said. She'd stayed in the entryway, a solo Greek chorus.

"That's absurd," Jack said. "Truth is not convenient. It's simply true."

"To continue." Millin flipped a page. "The TV show she supposedly was watching was actually on. No way for us to prove she wasn't home. No calls, no texts. She had a pattern of working weekends. She had no history of violence, no problems in the office. There was no DNA—she wasn't in the database anyway. She didn't seem to have a motive."

"Exactly," Jack said.

"In fact," Millin went on, "back then, she seemed like a good guy. On the right side of this. Rachel North wasn't on our radar."

"So what the hell put her there?" Jack leaned forward. This was the crux of it. The future legal—and personal—battleground.

"Jack?" Martha took a few steps toward him, high-signing Millin that she was taking point. "In fact, *you* did. Though not on purpose."

"What?"

Martha shrugged. "By choosing her for the Deacon Davis jury. Which gave Rachel's suspicions of her beloved Senator Rafferty's relationship with Danielle Zander time to fester. She couldn't stand it, thinking of them, together—that's what I imagine. And she turned out to be correct about their affair. But she couldn't let it go. Had to punish him. By punishing her rival. It was Rachel North who was the jealous one, not Nina Rafferty."

Jack was silent, for a fraction of a second. *No.* Rachel was not that kind of a girl. An old-fashioned phrase, and she'd hate that he'd put it that way, but still. No.

"How the hell do you know that?" Jack challenged her, his tone dismissive. "Did Rachel confide in you, in some half-assed sorority-sister confessional? Did you get her to spill the beans without letting her know she was a target? None of that's admissible, Gardiner. And you know it."

"May I go on?"

Jack rolled his eyes at Martha. "Cannot wait to hear this."

"Because the person who ratted out Tom Rafferty? The confidential interviewee, the informant who ruined Tom Rafferty's career? And Logan Concannon's? And who knows who else who got in her way? The one who provided us with the salacious motive to convict Nina Rafferty? And who now, every day, tries to get us to convict someone else?"

"No." Jack's head turned from side to side again. His brain stumbled, faltered, failed him.

"Yes." Millin flipped his notebook closed.

"Yes." Gardiner repeated. "Your wife."

RACHEL NORTH

NOW

I hate this, I honestly do, and I'm sick of being told what to do by everybody else.

"Rachel North, you have the right to remain silent," that statie Oz instructs me as I get out of the car. The punishing June sun is belting down on me, my flat shoes threatening to melt into the asphalt. "If you cannot afford an attorney, one will be provided for you."

Like I don't know that.

"Don't say anything, Rachel." Jack's talking over him, my husband's hand grasping my arm.

Like I don't know what's best for myself. I'm almost a lawyer, for God's sake. I feel like wrenching out of Jack's clutches, but his clutches are exactly what I need.

"What's going on, Jack?" My eyes are welling with tears as I look at him, and it's honestly true that I don't know.

Me and Jack. And Martha.

My mentor, my colleague, my good buddy Martha Gardiner, the one who *promised* she saw potential in me, completes the parking lot triangle of people telling me what to do.

"Tell us, Rachel. Tell us what happened." Martha opens her arms to me, and her voice is saccharine and poison. "You can't hide this any longer. Let's go inside. And you can tell us the truth."

Like I can't make my own decisions about what's true.

Oz hovers at my side like some muscle-bound nanny as we troop through the back door and down the hall. A studiedly uninterested Leon passes us, going the other way. He doesn't even flinch. So he knew, too.

Does everyone know what's going on but me?

I'm ready to explain, perfectly, whatever it is. I simply need to know what it is.

Ten minutes later, I do.

Jack had demanded to be here after Martha revealed her "findings" at our house. Our house! He'd demanded, wisdom aside, to represent me. He'd promised he wouldn't warn me to keep quiet, but he'd called anyway. Because he cares about me. And needs to protect me.

They think I killed Danielle Zander.

That I lured her out to the parking lot. That I pushed her, hard, against a dumpster. And when she fell, I made sure she was dead. That I dragged her between two big green garbage containers and waited for the Sunday night snowfall to cover her. That I knew the surveillance camera was down, the statehouse was closed for a snow day, and the trash collection wasn't until Monday night. Because I was jealous of Dani and Tom Rafferty.

Far as I'm concerned, they can concoct all the outrageous stories they want. They have no proof. None. At all. Because there *is* none. I'll handle this, and I'll walk out of here, and Jack and I, partners, will sue them for everything they've got.

Jack has his arm over the back of my metal chair. We're sitting across the conference table from Martha, who's opened that red accordion file folder she'd never let me see. Based on the drivel evidence she's attempting to foist on us, I should have swiped it.

I sit, silent, taking it in. I know not to say a word, but I mentally respond to every one of Martha's idiotic pieces of "evidence."

That I reported Logan's "screw you" call to Annabella? So what? That's statehouse protocol. And screw Annabella for telling. That's supposed to be confidential. I could nail her for that, I bet. And hey, I win, because Martha revealed Logan *admitted* she did it. Which is probably illegal, some kind of sexual harassment. I could nail her, too.

Martha's saying it's proof of my jealousy that I made up a story about Logan and Tom Rafferty's late-night parking-lot encounters and told it to Annabella. Made *up*? Who's to say I didn't see them? Everyone worked late.

They should focus on the real bad guys. Annabella and Logan, for two. And *Tom*. And Nina. One of those is a far more likely suspect for Danielle's murder. Or, as I've always hoped, they could charge both of the entitled Raffertys. Poetic justice.

Martha's back is to the door. Behind her, seated in a row of plastic swivel chairs, Nick and Andrew and Eli, acting like they don't know me. They all have yellow pads, and are taking notes like obedient do-bees. That statie's posted outside the door.

"Do you have more?" Jack's been taking notes, too, though he's not as outraged as I might have expected. We need to talk. I need to make sure he knows how to handle this.

"We do," Martha says, "We do have more. But don't you want to—confer with your client? Tell her whatever you decide to tell her? I'm happy to give you two whatever time you need."

Damn right, I think.

"We do." Jack turns his yellow pad facedown. Places his pen on top of it. Waits.

Martha and her minions stand. The three good interns let her open the door, then troop out after her.

I wait until I hear the door click closed.

"Can you believe this?" I turn to Jack, eyes wide. "What do you think, honey?"

"I think they're prosecutors, Rach," he says. "And they're convinced they have a case."

"But we have a *plan*! Martha Gardiner's a sleaze, a cheater. We have all that proof! She thought she had a case against your slasher-killer, too. Until you were too good and she had to disappear that witness."

"Rachel."

"Jack. Don't interrupt me. Seriously. Listen. She knew she was losing the Deacon Davis case, so she got rid of those jurors. With the help of the judge, too, had to be. All we have to do is drop a big freaking dime. Several dimes. Or flat-out tell her we're going to spill the beans. Rat her out. Her credibility will be zero. We know how to play this game. It's worked out so well that I took this job. Wasn't I right? I've learned so much from both of you."

"Rachel." Jack was shaking his head. Like I'm wrong? I'm totally not wrong.

"Jack, no, I'm right. Remember? You told me it was a bad idea, working here, but I truly thought I could learn the other side of the law. But she'd cheated on you—oh, that sounds funny—and I knew I had to report her. *We* had to. Because it wasn't fair to you! Or poor poor Deacon Davis."

"Rachel."

"What?" I hate that tone. It's like he thinks I'm an idiot.

"Rach? You think it's random that you wound up in Martha Gardiner's office?"

"I don't want to argue with you, honey," I say. "You know we never argue. But wait. Martha said—you could decide what to tell me about what you talked about his morning. What's 'this morning'?"

A sharp rap on the door. I look up, frowning. They're not supposed to interrupt us until we say it's time.

"Jack? What happened this morning?"

"Come in," Jack says.

CHAPTER **FORTY-SIX**

MARTHA GARDINER

"One more thing." Martha kept one hand on the conference room doorjamb. Kept her body in the hall. In the room, but not in the room.

"We were *talking*," Rachel said. "Are you supposed to interrupt?"

"Rachel?" Jack shot his wife a look. Martha tried to read his face. She felt sorry for him. Yes, they were adversaries, but they played fair, or equally fair. No one was perfect. And winning was the goal for both of them. Only one side could prevail, though. That was the accepted and indelible reality. Signing on to the law was signing up for war.

Martha almost laughed at herself for the unexpected sentimentality.

"One more thing," Martha repeated. "Rachel, do you remember that day in the car? When you oh-so-casually asked me about cold cases? Like you thought I had no idea what you were really asking about?"

"Don't say anything, Rachel," Jack said.

"You asked me, What's the reason most cold cases are solved? And what did I say?"

Rachel opened her mouth as if to answer, but Jack clamped a restraining hand on her forearm.

"I remember," Martha said. "I told you—it's if a new witness emerges."

Martha turned, with a certain lift in her heart, and opened the door wider. It was dramatic, she knew, and she might have handled it less sensationally. But life was dramatic. The law was dramatic. It revealed the truth.

"I'm sure you all know Nina Rafferty," she said.

Martha could tell Rachel didn't know where to look. At Jack or Martha or Nina. But Nina stood framed in the doorway, elegantly cool, hair slicked back and wearing a reserved dress, sleeveless and so charcoal it was almost black, so fashionably effortless it almost didn't exist. No earrings, no jewelry. Not even a wedding ring.

The senator's ex-wife stood motionless. Martha had advised her not to sit down, but to stand there, let them see her, and then observe what happened. She was a brave woman, with cards of her own to play and a game of her own to lose. She'd already lost personally, that was for sure. But Martha herself, believing what Rachel North had told Annabella Rigalosa, had—with only the most honorable of intentions—almost ruined this woman's life. And that's what made Nina Perini Rafferty brave. That even at such a cost, and even in service of a one-time adversary, she'd come forward to find justice.

Martha might have been furious over what Nina told her. But it meant she'd made a mistake with Nina. Martha had admitted it to her, and then apologized.

"Ms. Perini?" Martha used Nina's now-preferred surname.

"What's this all about?" Jack stood, as of course he would. And faced his former client. The one he'd saved from prison. "Nina?"

"Nina?" Martha turned to the woman, giving her the cue to begin. Nina had legal problems of her own. And Martha could never condone what Nina had decided six years ago. But four weeks ago, Nina had called her. And justice delayed, Martha had decided, was justice nonetheless.

"I saw you, Rachel," she said. "I saw you in the parking lot."

"Saw what?" Jack said. "When?"

Of course it was only Nina's word now, Martha thought. But she needed to see what would happen as a result.

"I lied to you, Jack, about where I was." Nina's voice was sorrowful.

Contrite. "But the alibi was good enough, wasn't it? And you believed me. And for that I thank you."

"What?" Rachel rose from her chair, standing, looking at Nina eye-to-eye. Twenty years separated them, and a lifetime of decisions.

"Rachel? I hated her, too, frankly. Danielle." Nina pressed her palms together and touched them to her lips. Took a deep breath. "It's embarrassing, and I feel so—guilty. But—I didn't care that you killed her. She deserved it. She tried to steal my husband. Does it sound old-fashioned to say it? Though he and I had long parted over his statehouse flings. Danielle Zander wasn't Tom's first, Rachel. As I'm sure you know."

"He gave her a gold necklace!" Rachel pointed at Nina, her face flushing, her eyes wide. "A Tiffany necklace. An *expensive* necklace. And he told me it was for *you*! How do you feel about *that*? He lied to you, every single day. *Cheated* on you."

Nina put up two palms, stopping her. "There's nothing you can say to upset me anymore, Rachel. I'm sorry he hurt you. And I'm sorry he drove you to this. But he ruins everything he touches. I managed to leave him, though at that time he was so self-absorbed he didn't know it. You, on the other hand, didn't. Leave."

"Are you kidding me, Nina?" Jack stood now, too. Almost pushed his wife behind him as he widened his arms, entreating. "You perjured yourself? Why didn't you tell the truth?"

Martha had never seen his face like that, fierce in anger. And sorrow. In court—who knows how many times?—Jack Kirkland weathered whatever surprises ambushed him. This time was different.

"I'm so sorry, Jack." Nina shook her head, pressed her lips together. "But I couldn't. If I had said where I was? Who I was with? It would have ruined his life, too. And I loved him too much to do that. But I wasn't in Maine, I was in a townhouse on Beacon Hill. A townhouse that overlooked the parking lot. Not to mention that you were my lawyer, the best in Boston, and the person I saw was—Well."

"That's *cra*—" Rachel began, but Jack shushed her again.

"If my hearing had gone the other way, I would have told you," Nina said. "He—and, no, I'll never tell you who it was—had given me permission to go ahead. But if all went as we hoped, he promised to stick to our story. He'd alibi me in Maine, say we'd happened by chance to be at the same place. And as long as the case stayed cold—I wanted to protect him. I could leave Tom. Let the scandal be *his* scandal, and not mine. He deserved it. *I* deserved it."

"Go on," Martha encouraged her. It had been obstruction of justice as well as perjury, and Nina knew the sword that was hanging over her.

"But a few weeks ago, Ms. Gardiner's interns came to see me, to interview me. They said Ms. Gardiner had seen some video and was reopening the case and talking to everyone involved. They told me that you, Rachel, had tried to ruin Tom. Poison people against him. And they asked me if there was anything I hadn't said back then—anything I knew about Tom and Danielle. But it wasn't only what Danielle did that I knew about. It was what *you* did."

CHAPTER **FORTY-SEVEN**

MARTHA GARDINER

Martha handed Jack the envelope. Friday afternoon at Salamanca, deserted and empty. The Charles River, uncaring and having witnessed endless human dramas unfold, flowed outside the vast picture window. Sal had left them alone with iced tea and turkey sandwiches. She watched Jack open the envelope, take out the piece of paper inside. He'd agreed to talk to her here, where no one would witness the two adversaries conferring.

"It's blank, Martha!" He waved the paper at her, frowning. "Is this a goddamned joke?"

Jack Kirkland was angry with her, and rightly so. He'd demanded the return on the warrant, the list of what they'd discovered in the search of his home. Of course there was nothing. Martha never expected there would be. But she had to make sure.

"Rachel's not dumb," Martha said. "You think she'd keep an incriminating earring? Or an incriminating anything?"

Jack shrugged, worried a straw around his iced tea. "The whole thing is—"

"We did find a stash of, I guess, memorabilia. From Rachel's statehouse days. But we can't make a murder case out of a bunch of newspaper clippings and photos of Tom Rafferty."

Martha let that linger, hoping Jack would realize that Rachel latched on to whatever power figure she thought would help her. She'd tried it with Rafferty, and then Jack, and then Martha herself, signing on to the prosecution side without so much as a whisper of loyalty.

"We shouldn't be talking," Jack said.

"We're not," Martha assured him. "But we have the same goal, don't we? That the system works. That there's justice? And we all do that the best way we can."

"I can't envision it." Jack shook his head. "My mind won't accept it. It cannot be true. There's got to be another explanation."

"Nina *saw* her. And Jack? Rachel asked me herself, when she felt confident enough to discuss the investigation of the murder she herself committed—"

"Allegedly."

"Sure. But Jack? Rachel had the nerve to ask me who I thought was the killer. I'd suspected her from the beginning, but back then we had nothing. No way to prove it. And then—she went to law school."

"My idea," Jack said. "We were gonna be partners."

"*Was* it your idea?" Martha paused a beat, to let Jack consider that. "Because here's the thing. The whole thing. As prosecutor—God forgive me for this, but you'd get it on discovery anyway. . . ."

Outside, a duck flapped in the Charles, and both turned to watch the iridescent mallard and then the dusky female slash off into the sky.

"I took Rachel with me on a few so-called interviews. Did she tell you? But they were all shams, set up in advance with the interviewees' knowledge and preparation. The other interns helped with that. But we needed to see how she would respond. To see what she'd do and say. And every time, we got a bingo. When Logan Concannon told about her betrayal by a coworker, Rachel acted as if she'd never heard such a thing. She also feigned surprise that Annabella Rigalosa had received complaints about Tom Rafferty. Completely phony, because she's the one who complained. But Tom Rafferty himself was the clincher."

Jack was poking a straw into his iced tea. But Martha could tell he was listening.

"After our interview, I engineered a way for her to be with Rafferty alone. And she intimated to Rafferty that he was in my sights."

Jack held up both hands, making a time-out signal. "Wait. How do you know if you weren't there?"

"We had that apartment wired, with hidden cameras and mics. It's one of our safe houses. We own it in a trust. And your wife? She essentially threatened Rafferty, suggested we suspected him, and then offered to give him inside information on the progress of the murder investigation. Offered to protect him. He's moved up to Maine now, joined some law firm. But he'll come back to testify if we need him to. Want to see that video, though? Happy to show you."

"Bull. You got video of nothing." Jack sat up straighter. "Maybe Rachel was trying to *help* you. Maybe she was doing her *job*."

"Good try, Jack. But there's more. Logan Concannon knew all about Ms. North's crush on Rafferty. Annabella Rigalosa, too. Your Rachel is the one who tried to convince her to think it was *Logan* who'd been having the affair. By the way, she ruined Logan's life with that lie. Logan sacrificed her career to protect her boss from an ugly inquiry. Rachel was not as noble. And then there's Clea Rourke's jury video."

"Clea *Rourke*? Knows about this?"

Martha nodded. "Yeah. And I know about you and her."

"From her?"

Martha ducked her head, acknowledging. "You're not her favorite."

"She threatened me, once, when I . . . well, never mind. But she made good on her threat, that's the damn truth of it. She's ruined my life. And it was that video that did it."

"Reporters," Martha said.

"Yeah."

Martha waited. Both of their sandwiches were untouched, the edges of the thin-sliced rye beginning to curl.

Jack moved his plate aside, leaned across the table. "Did you disappear my slasher witness? In the Marcus Dorn case?"

"I have no idea what you're talking about," Martha said.

"Rachel thinks you're railroading Jeffrey Baltrim. 'Pizza guy' she calls him."

"Lizann Wallace has his case. She knows the ropes." She lifted her glass. "May the better lawyer win."

"And you clearly screwed me on the Deacon Davis trial. The jurors. That was cheap."

"I wouldn't use that word, so much, as I took advantage of a reality. Jack? Don't we all do that? And you had ethical problems of your own there, if I remember. I heard through the—shall we say, grapevine—that you tried to talk your client out of testifying."

She shook her head, as if considering a tragedy. "Sadly, your client will never know how you failed to stand up for him in those hearings."

There was nothing he could say, and they both knew it.

"What do we do about Momo Peretz and Roni Wollaskay?" Jack rattled his ice cubes, staring into his glass. "And the fact that Deacon Davis was killed *after* the judge knew Roni Wollaskay was sniffing around?"

Martha took a deep breath and looked into the far distance, as if seeing the future.

"We'll tell them it all turned out to be on the up-and-up. That everything is fine. That there was nothing improper about them being excused from the jury, and it was all fair. And that Deacon Davis's death was a coincidence. Which I promise you, it was. They'll buy it. That's how they want to believe the system works. I'm not a murderer. Which is more than I can say for your wife."

"I'm going to represent Rachel myself," Jack said. "If it comes to that. Look. It was winter. Let's see—coat, hat, scarf, gloves. And you plan to rely on eyewitness ID from someone a couple of stories up in an apartment building? Nina Rafferty perjured herself at her arraignment. She's a liar. Who's to say she's telling the truth now?"

Martha blinked. Waited for him to realize that defending Rachel was a poor decision.

He kept silent.

"You love her, don't you, Jack?" She reached across the table, put her hand on the arm of his suit jacket, left it for a fraction of a second. "That must be impossible."

"What am I supposed to do, Martha?" He looked at her, steely-eyed. "Abandon her?"

Now it was her turn to be silent. How would she feel, she wondered, if she had to choose between love and the law? Between love and justice? She'd never faced that.

"You're a good lawyer, Jack. Although I'll deny I said that. And the evidence against her is—well, between us, it's—well, never mind." She picked up her linen napkin, smoothed it on the table, folded it, then folded it again. She paused, one beat, two, and then went on.

"But if you get Rachel acquitted, how is that different than helping someone get away with murder?"

"It's not—"

"And Jack? I know you love her. And I'm sorry. But say you get her off—then what are you going to do?"

EPILOGUE

RACHEL NORTH

So it's fine. Totally fine. Jack will get me acquitted.

Issue, rule, analysis, conclusion.

The issue is murder. And now I know the rules. I turn to my cell's cinder-block wall. Ignore the metal bars to my right. Ignore my paper flip-flops. My turn now. I'll take over this case.

And then the faces appear. Emerge from the cinder block, as I *will* them to, one by one. The jury, *my* jury now, faces me. There's Roni. And Momo, wrenny Delia Tibbalt and Larry the scientist and even Patriots guy Gil. I stand so tall, lift my chin so high, I'm a ballerina. A virtuoso. A maestro. Every eye is on me. As it should be. I smooth back my hair, adjust my orange jumpsuit, and, standing with elegant Martha-like posture, I open my arms, entreating.

"Call CJ Malinoff," I say. CJ, the crime-scene tech. The one who'd also processed Tassie Lyle's house. He appears, sitting on the witness stand. His eyes are on me, too.

"You tested the victim, Ms. Zander, for foreign DNA?"

He nods. "Yes."

"Was there any that matched Rachel North?" I ask.

"No, ma'am," he says.

Never ask a question you don't know the answer to—I'd learned that my first year of law school. I knew there was no DNA—I'd been careful. It was winter. Hats, gloves, mufflers, boots.

Next witness. Ervin, the goggle-eyed statehouse security chief. He shuffles to the stand.

"Was there surveillance video of the parking lot?" I ask him. "Back then?"

"No, miss," he says, adjusting his glasses. "It'd been broken for weeks. In fact, Senator Rafferty had written a letter to our office about it. We didn't have the money to fix it."

Another answer I already knew. Senators don't write their own dear-colleague letters. I'd composed that one from Tom myself.

The medical examiner appears, wearing his white lab coat and his stethoscope, as I'd requested, to give him credibility. My jury will believe him.

"What was the time, of death, Dr. Ong?" I ask him.

"Difficult to estimate," he says. "Ms. Zander was covered with snow."

I knew that, too. And thanks to the hot oven in the pizza-guy case, I knew intense or unusual temperature complicated the TOD determination.

And eyewitnesses? Ha. There were no witnesses. Not that had any credibility. I lick my lips. The dank gray walls are shimmering now, waiting to see who I need.

"Call Nina Rafferty," I say. She appears from the cinder block, ephemeral, looking pallid and fragile and terrified. And so very *very* old. Poor thing.

"Mrs. Rafferty." I try to sound respectful. She cannot meet my eyes, even now. "Is it not true that you told this very court"—I gesture toward the judge and jury as I've seen Jack do—"that you were out of town the weekend of the murder? And now, Mrs. *Rafferty,* you're telling us that's *not* true?"

Nina has no answer, of course, because she's a lying perjuring shrew.

"Why should anyone believe you *now*?" I'm so good at this. "And isn't it possible you're now covering up for your *own* crime?"

"Objection!" Martha Gardiner leaps to her feet at the prosecution table, and I see her stumble in her snooty heels. *She's* old, too.

"Overruled," the judge declares.

I hear the audience buzz with disdain for her. And approval for me.

"Do you know the penalty for perjury, Mrs. Rafferty?" I push even harder. She deserves it.

The jury gasps. The judge bangs her gavel. Jack looks at me, so proud. Martha scowls. We are winning. *I* am winning.

And now. My final witness. Even my own eyes widen as she insinuates herself through the cinder-block door. All attitude, nose in the air, and an unnecessary swing in her too-wide hips. This is *my* life at stake, and *she's* hogging the spotlight. As always. I hope she's finally afraid of me.

"Miss Zander," I say, infinitely polite. She looks at me under those eyelashes. "Isn't it true that I only asked you to take a walk?"

"*After* you saw the necklace," she begins. It's around her neck, even now, the tiny stars catching the light. Magnifying them. She touches one, as if it were lucky. But no. She doesn't get any more luck. "You were my boss, remember? I had to do what you told me."

Damn right. "And what do *you* remember, Miss Zander, about what you said to me?"

"It was snowing," she says. "I probably said I was cold."

"Isn't it true . . ." I put my nose in the air exactly as she did. I can match her, tactic for tactic. Disdain for disdain. "Isn't it true that you revealed your sordid affair with the senator? Isn't it true that you told me, in so many words, that you were trying to convince him to leave his wife? For *you*?"

"And isn't it true," she sneers back at me, scornful, like in the parking lot, "That *you* lost it? *Lost* it? And pushed me against the dumpster? What did I ever do to you?"

"Do? To me?" My voice gets louder, like it isn't even mine, my astonishment crashing against the low ceiling and shattering to the concrete floor. "You—"

"You were never good enough, Rachel, not for anything. Not ever. And certainly—" Dani looks at me, I see it, with pity. Pity! "And certainly not enough for him."

"I never pushed you," I had to say it. Make it true. "You *fell*. If you hadn't been pushing me and pushing me and pushing me, it never would have happened. It's all *your* fault. Yours!"

I say it again. Louder, and louder. "Yours! Yours!"

"*Shut up!*" A voice, shouting, echoes from down the hall.

I'm not sure what happened—but her face fades, like a predatory Cheshire cat, then vanishes. I'm left alone again. No more Danielle. Not ever. Not ever.

I erase her, purge her ruinous venom. The jury has watched her, listened to her, and they hate her, too. I can tell.

I draw a breath in the dank and airless silence. As if the universe is waiting for me.

Collecting myself, separating myself, my fingertips tingle and my ears ring and the buzz of the lights gets so loud, then even louder, and then there's only stillness. Complete and perfect silence.

And then, in my closing argument, I tell the waiting cinder-block jury my truth.

"It was *her* fault," I say, my voice confident and assured. "You heard it, did you not? You heard that woman's thieving manipulative behavior. Trying to steal Tom from me. Trying to ruin my life. He'd lied. Lied! He'd given *her* that necklace. *Her*. He's a liar. She's a thief. She stole my *life*. They both did. But I only—truly—I only meant to warn her. She fell. She did. She *fell*."

I pause, my jurors nodding in sympathetic agreement. Gil, and Delia, and Roni.

"Reasonable doubt, ladies and gentlemen," I remind them. "But here, you can have no doubt at all. You can only come to one conclusion. The right thing happened. *Justice*. And isn't that why we're all here?"

Momo puts her hands together in prayer, beaming her approval. I smile at her, my soul mate.

Then, closing my eyes in gratitude, and hearing the sound of my own heartbeat, I bask in my courtroom victory. The jury vanishes, *poof,* then reappears. They are smiling. At me. Every one of them.

"Not guilty," the judge pronounces. "You are free to go."

"Thank you," I say. "Thank you all."

I turn to Clea Rourke, who's holding her microphone toward me, eager for my response. "Why didn't you help her?" Clea asks. "How were you sure she was dead? You simply—left her? Didn't even call for help?"

She's gotten fat, and her lips are even fatter. I don't need to answer her repulsive questions. The verdict is final.

"I'm an innocent woman," I tell her, "and the jury agrees. Now I plan to devote my life to helping other unfairly accused people get the justice they deserve. It's my *destiny.*"

I smile, victorious, as I watch her struggle to decide how to respond to my eloquence. Then I seize the opportunity to take control.

"And Clea?" I feel my expression change. My smile vanishes. "Stay the *fuck* away from my husband."

"Shut *up!*" The strident voice yells at me again, the order racketing down the cell-block corridor. "Stop yelling! You're freaking *nuts!*"

Enraged, I whirl to confront whoever is tormenting me now—but see only bars and darkness and gloom and nothing.

I plop down on the thin ticking-stripe mattress, one dingy layer of simulated comfort placed on the metal bed-bench bolted to the wall. Plant my feet on the concrete.

"I am not nuts," I whisper. "They can't prove anything. Not. One. Thing."

So why can't Jack get them to set bail? He promised he's doing his best. I know he'll deal with Martha, conniving, manipulative loser Martha. These things take time.

I look through the double-thick window, the mesh wire, thick, unbreakable glass. Through this almost-opaque opening, it's always gray outside, no matter what the weather. Sunny day or snowstorm, all the same. I've been here since June and now it's November. And the snow will come again.

Like the day Dani wore the damn necklace.

I touch my neck, remembering how it felt for those three perfect days.

When that woman came in wearing it? *My* necklace? I can remember it, so clearly, it almost makes my head explode. She'd come in flaunting that thing, and when I'd asked her where she got it, she lied. Lied! And said it was a gift from her father. Her father's *dead*. Did she think I hadn't checked her files?

I'll give you a gift, I'd thought.

"Let's take a walk in the snow," I'd said. I stand in my cell again, acting out the moment. "I know it's crazy," I'd told Dani, "but it's so beautiful. There are lovely places around the statehouse I'd adore to show you," I'd said. "Let's play a little girlfriend hooky—it's Sunday after all."

And she—stupid girl—had gone along with it. She was right about one thing. I was her boss. How could she say no?

I only meant to talk to her. Tell her what's what. Put her in her place. I'd even thought about firing her. I had the power, didn't I? All of what happened was her fault. Not *mine*.

I'd considered taking the necklace, after. It would have taken one tiny second. One brief touch. I could have done it. And no one could have known, of course, because no one knew she had it. Only Tom. And *he* would not have mentioned it.

I laugh out loud at that, laugh and laugh, my bitterness clattering on the gray walls and escaping through the bars.

"What's so damn funny?" The guard's voice again. "You *want* me to come shut you up? You *want* it?"

It's fine. It's fine. I can stand it. Until Jack rescues me.

And I can even do some good.

We're all women here, and many of us, like me, have been accused of crimes we did not commit. Or that they can't prove. Or where the victim deserved it. That should be a defense, right there.

And the perfect thing is that now I can do what I always wanted to do.

These poor women, so devalued and so misunderstood. I'm almost a lawyer now. I can help them. I can advise them. They're without friends or support or money, the ones who only killed a cheating boyfriend or a manipulative spouse, or who had a bad day because the world isn't fair. But we women need to support each other, like Martha says. Help each other. That's why I'm so valuable.

It's like I'm their personal attorney. Their *special* attorney. After all, I learned from the best. I know all the secrets.

I'm the only one on their murder list.

I win.

ACKNOWLEDGMENTS

Unending gratitude to:

Kristin Sevick, my brilliant, hilarious, and gracious editor. You are endlessly wise, and infinitely patient, and thank you for the fabulous ideas. The remarkable team at Forge Books: the incomparable Linda Quinton, the indefatigable Alexis Saarela, and copy editor Kate Davis, who saved me at least twice from career-ending errors. And thank you, Daniela Medina, what a cool and sinister cover! Bess Cozby and Lili Feinberg, you're the best. Brian Heller, my constant champion. The inspirational Tom Doherty. And my dear darling Laura Pennock. Eileen Lawrence and Lucille Rettino—you are life-changing. What a terrifically smart and unfailingly supportive team. I am so thrilled to be part of it. Thank you.

Lisa Gallagher, my stellar and incredible agent. You changed my life and continue to do so every day. I am so honored to work with you.

Dana Isaacson, you astonish me. Your editing skill—and care and commitment and friendship—shines on every page.

The artistry and savvy of Madeira James, Mary-Liz Murray, Nina Zagorscak, Charlie Anctil, Mary Zanor, and Nicolette Roger.

Sue Grafton, always. Mary Higgins Clark, ditto. Mary Kubica, Lynne

Constantine, B. A. Paris, Lisa Unger. Erin Mitchell. Sasha Quinton. Barbara Peters, Joanne Sinchuk, and Robin Agnew.

My incredible blog sisters at Jungle Red Writers: Julia Spencer-Fleming, Hallie Ephron, Roberta Isleib/Lucy Burdette, Jenn McKinlay, Ingrid Thoft, Deborah Crombie, and Rhys Bowen. And my Career Authors posse, captained by the brilliant Glenn Miller.

My dear friends Mary Schwager, Laura DiSilverio, Elisabeth Elo, and Paula Munier. And my treasured sister Nancy Landman.

The Nevis-based legal team of Jonathan Shapiro, Marjorie Suisman, Roger Geller, Liza Lunt, and Tony Doniger. Thank you for taking your fees in Killer Bees at Sunshine's.

Jonathan is my darling husband, of course. Thank you for answering the legal question of the day—every day.

Do you see your name in this book? Some very generous souls allowed their names to be used in return for an auction donation to charity. To retain the magic, I will let you find yourselves.

Sharp-eyed readers will notice I have tweaked Massachusetts geography a bit. It's only to protect the innocent. And I adore it when people read the acknowledgments.

Keep in touch, okay?

www.hankphillippiryan.com
www.jungleredwriters.com
www.careerauthors.com

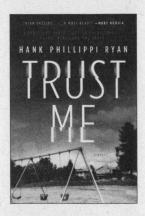